ON SOUNDINGS

a novel by

Irv C. Rogers

PARK PLACE
PUBLICATIONS

Cover illustration by Gordon Grant

First trade paperback edition August 2016
Designed by Patricia Hamilton
Manufactured in the United States of America

Published by
Park Place Publications
Pacific Grove, California
www.parkplacepublications.com

ISBN: 978-1-943887-27-9

Printed in U.S.A.

BOOKS BY IRV C. ROGERS

Motoo Eetee—Shipwrecked at the Edge of the World

Tales of Monterey . . . and More

On Soundings

Dedication

To our "squeakers" from Nick to Benjamin

Chapter One

Water! Water! Water! Aye ... water! My gums, my tongue, my flesh were taking up my mouthful. I could feel it seeping in to replenish my body. I stood knee-deep in the stream, naked as a savage, and with head back let it ease down my throat. Slowly... slowly... so slowly ... what relief! What pleasure! Even with its puckery taste steeped from the sodden leaves of the forest, I swore it was more delicious than any water I had ever swallowed. I dipped my cupped hands into the current once more, raised them to my lips, and spilled in the restoring fluid. With open palms held to my nose, I breathed a moist air, the fragrance of life. Ah, it was luscious! Yes... ah, yes. I would have given my whole share of the voyage for a drink of it yesterday. If my sixty-fifth lay of thousands of prime seal skins and hundreds of barrels of oil could have bought a mere gill of the sweet drink, I would have done it in a trice ... without the least thought.

After days sitting in the dugout, the intense burning and swelling knot in my throat had driven me to consider a single drink ... a timid sip from the sea ... just enough to wet my mouth. Several times in every hour I had opened my eyes and watched the heaving, dipping waves and wondered if their salt water could staunch the fire in my gullet. In the hottest part of the day, the sun was no longer that warmer of the morning chill but an inescapable, uncaring eye that stared while I scooped up a handful of sea water, held it near my lips, and wavered between the urge to live and the craving for release from that never-ending torture of thirst.

What I had suffered then in the canoe brought back the memory of old, bearded Zeph always smoking his pipe on the dock at Stonington. For most of the day he sat watching the loading and unloading of ships, but if there were a soul about who could not evade him with some frail excuse he would recite how, when adrift off the Western Isles, he had fought the temptation to drink from the sea.

"We were on the *Hannibal* not more than two year after Mr. Madison's war," he would begin with the same sentence that never varied by a single word. "I was in the larboard quarter boat and we went miles from the ship after a whale. It was late and when we didn't see no spout for a while we give up and rowed back for the ship, for hours it bein' the deadest calm. We never made it and lost the *Hannibal* in the night. Our water was gone in four days. Oh, I warned my younger mates not to drink the sea water, but would they listen to Zeph? Nooo, nooo, nooo, they drank it and they went all mad raving about seeing the *Hannibal* coming back for us. I saw they was crazy dreamin'. They died one by one." At that point Zeph would lean back, take a puff from his pipe, and pause for what he considered a great dramatic effect. Then with his right hand placed on his chest, he boasted, "I wouldn't drink ... and I was the only one alive when they found us."

The man endured the same thirst as the others; yet he had resisted the temptation to drink seawater. Remembering Zeph's story I swore not to give over, not to expire, but to hold onto life as he had to the very last minute. My will held for the moment. I let the water in my hand drain through my fingers. The dreadful thirst returned in a short while even stronger and became unbearable. I imagined the salt water easing the pain for an hour or at least a few minutes and readied myself to suck it up with my split lips.

Only my discovery of a straggling white line low on the eastern horizon stopped me from making that error. I spied small crests on it when the canoe lifted with the next swell; and on rise after rise its milk-whiteness remained. After staring stupidly at each brief glimpse, I recognized it was not fog, not a low bank of clouds, not a fancy of my fuddled mind; but snow on the mountains of New Zealand ... the middle island ... *Tovy Poenamoo*! Aye, snow it was! So it certainly had to be that island. I was convinced it was, and searched its extent fading into the sea haze far to the north and south. The moment I realized it was *Tovy Poenamoo* I glimpsed when on the crests, my time on earth suddenly multiplied in my mind from hours to days, and hopefully to many years. Each time the canoe rose with the wave, the bit of white reappeared and kept my heart racing. That horizon meant there would be more images of life to witness ... multitudes! ... yes great, grand multitudes of them: green fields, sea coasts, trees, broad rivers, smiling friends at home, and the eager, innocent faces of children. I was not to perish in pain and madness having lived only my twenty-two years and then denied any more delicious sights of the earth. I would not become a shriveled, discolored corpse in the narrow hull, a mere fleck drifting in the immense Southern Ocean rising and dropping with the swells. No sea birds would squawk and duel each other over dried flesh to be pecked from my bones. It might be a year or more, but I was determined to walk the roads of Connecticut again and greet Father and my old friends.

It had been far easier to bear the next hours of thirst while I pictured in my mind the snow on that long range of mountains melting into rills, pouring over cliffs as it did down in Dusky Sound. Each minute hundreds of barrels of water spilled over falls there, dashed on rocks, and merged into brawly streams. That was all I could think of then, of how I would gulp it down, dash it on my face, and revel in its coolness and abundance. Water, sweet water, the thing I desperately needed was flowing from the mountains to the sea and was now within my reach.

The little stream cascaded over rocks near me, splashed into shaded pools, and prattled sounds refreshing as the water itself. Its tea-tinge here was lighter than in the loops of water meandering on the flat ground at the coast.

I held my hands in the runnel and felt the cool liquid pass between my fingers. How infernally proud a man may become to suppose all things in the world could be bent to his use and all would carry forward as he wished. The water flowing past my hands and bare legs was a wealth beyond all imaginings. Yesterday, it had come down to a few mouthfuls of it or my last failing breath.

What would the people think of me if I appeared on one of the roads about home that very instant? My sun-bleached hair hung in tangled strings still damp from my tumbling in the surf. I swept it back with wet fingers and smoothed my auburn beard. No one would recognize me though I had lived at Stonington Boro for the whole of my life. Not one, no not one, would suspect I was Thomas, son of the shoemaker. By mere sight I was now a savage, a wild man, or at best a recluse who had lost all reason and cast off his clothes. Dressed in my rude animal skins I would be an apparition there, an ogre who might drive everyone behind doors, one given a dreadful name by mothers to frighten children into obedience. My reflection in a still pond revealed the hood of my jacket failed to protect all of my face. In the days sailing from the island of the wreck, my nose burned and peeled; and my lips had swelled and split.

There were some events in my life that had ended well, but this was a dreadful, damned, lamentable finish to a profitable cruise. In one night it had suddenly gone awry. By my stout resolve I had survived the wreck of the *Dove* and lived through the mischief of men and nature. Of we four who scrambled ashore, only I remained. Only I escaped the great volcano blasts and fires which had destroyed our little island. A miracle, it had to be a miracle that I was still alive.

The barque was already a year past due; I must surely be lamented now as lost. It could be another year or possibly 1824 before I might reach home and see Father. All was up to fortune and what ships I might fall in with to the north.

My guts were stodged, bloated; I could not take another swallow of water. Yet, I still felt thirsty and craved to gulp more. It might help to walk some.

For assurance that the waves had not carried my canoe back into the surf, I had to leave this stream and its lush margins and return to the shingle beach. My path was along the edge of the purling water. A few times it was stepping from rock to rock to the opposite bank to find a way around a tangle of ferns and vines. At the verge of the thick greenery where the stream splayed from the forest onto open ground, I saw no signs of savages. The morning sun had cleared the crests of the mountains, and its rays slanted over the coast, sharpening the contrast between the creamy white of breaking waves and the dense blue of the sea beyond.

The thump and rumble of the surf was the background to the soughing of wind in the trees and its rustle in the thickets. A small, green bird alighted on a branch a fathom away and studied me with its right eye, then its left eye. With curiosity abated it remained perched and plinked high, sweet notes over the sounds of wind and sea. How glorious it was to stand there, breathe the clear sea air, and hear those reassuring sounds of life.

To the north and south of the stream, the land was slightly higher, molded into hills quilted with trees and bush farther inland. Between those raised portions of the coast, the stream, partially hidden in a grass-covered flat, flowed from one curve into its reverse in a meandering toward the sea. At the shore a low bar of sand had dammed the flow into a slough. Driftwood had been cast onto the bar in a long windrow twenty yards inland. No animal, even one of cat size, moved on the open ground, though a tall, white bird stood on stilt legs at the edge of the water. A reward for its stolid pose, one without a twitch or blink, might be a frog or fish before another hour passed. Above the surf a few gulls dived, swooped up, and shifted wing and tail to balance on new rises of the wind.

Morning was advancing. I scanned the slopes, especially where they met the lower ground. Most likely there were people there but no signs of any around the edges of the flat, or dark figures slipping through the ferns. They might search from such places to find me if they knew I was on this coast. On the far side of the island, in the Queen Charlotte inlet, Captain Furneaux had lost an entire boat's crew to the New Zealand Indians, who had butchered and cooked them. That well-known fact kept me crouching low within the cover of the bushes as I made for the shore. An entire village might be nigh on the other side of the higher land to the north or south, or such savages could be concealed in the underwood. There was no lack of spinneys in which they might hide, and at any instant a dozen of them, bearing fearsome, tattooed faces, might leap out and charge at me screaming and swinging their clubs to smash my skull.

I edged ahead, weak-legged and shaking, scanning the bushes to the right and left for anything that I might chew and swallow. No berries, no nuts were on the branches I pulled aside and searched. A patch of leaves growing close to the earth would be the very thing, aye, potatoes. Yes, they would be a great find. A pound or two of them cooked or raw, yes even raw, would be very welcome just then for I would gnaw them, grind them with my teeth, and suck the juices, anything to fill my empty gut. Fern roots could be parched and eaten, but which ones would serve? Clams, crabs, and crawfish might be found on the shore; and birds' eggs could be eaten if freshly laid. There surely was food on such a lush coast. I had only to find it.

Ahead were a dozen clumps of flax plants seven to eight feet tall. In each clump two or three black stalks extended above the tips of the long, sword-like leaves. Several stems bearing a line of red blossoms angled up and out along each thick stalk.

I forgot any danger of being seen, stumbled over fallen limbs, and waded in ankle-deep water to reach a plant. I thrust my hand between the leaves and pulled the first stalk down. I plucked a flower, peeled back its petals, and sucked up the large drop of nectar it held. Ah, it was intensely sweet, perhaps made so by my hunger. I pinched all the blossoms from the stalks of the first clump and went to the next one. The older, nearly spent ones had little nectar, yet I tried them all. Bright orange pollen covered my fingertips, and my mustache and lips were probably dusted the same color. The nectar had an immediate effect; at least, I felt more strength in my arms and they stopped shaking. The nectar helped but was not wholly satisfying; I needed better grub and much of it if I were to sail on to Cook's Strait.

I had not the least idea where I had met the coast of *Tovy Poenamoo*, but when the sun set it was opposite the mountains, tinting the snow on them to orange and reddish hues. Cook's Strait must then lie to the north, for in the few days I was at sea the wind and current could not have carried me beyond it. I could see travel up the coast ashore would be nearly impossible through the thick growth of ferns and vines. In an hour a distance could be sailed toward the Strait which might take a day or two to travel through the forest. There were surely rivers to swim and cliffs to scale before I could reach that goal by land. Indians were on the other side of the island and to the south, so odds were high that some were on this coast, though it appeared wild and empty. My only choice was to repair the canoe and sail north. That was certain.

At the shore my worn skin clothing, all that I owned on my side of the world, was spread to dry on the grass. They had served well, tied in the end of my long line and cast astern as a drogue, or so I thought.

The canoe, overset in landing, still rested on the shingle. It had taken weeks to burn, scrape, and hack out the heart of that log. With the addition of the spar, the hollowed bole became the outrigger, the life saver that had carried me perhaps two hundred miles from the island of the wreck. The tide was on the ebb, yet waves still thrust up the beach, struck the broad side of the inverted hull, then divided and swirled around its ends to meet again in gyres and foam on its landward side. On their retreat they washed the pebbles, hissing and gnarling, down slope.

It would be easy to turn the hull over on the beach and replace the broken mast and parted stay. The air was warming. It would be comfortable with the sun beaming down on my back while I worked with the skins, the needle, and the twine.

That must be done soon, but the search for something to eat was more pressing. All things must be done in their particular order. The canoe would remain safely tied to the rock where waves could not draw it away to sea.

I stood in need of flesh, good solid food. If the birds did not fly at my approach, they could be taken from their nests with any eggs fresh enough to eat. They must be found soon, or I would lack the strength to climb the rocks and search. An ebbing tide would give me the chance to discover cockles or clams of some sort out on the bar, and enough of them, small though they might be, could make a true meal.

Stout, clever men armed with clubs were certainly on the coast, perhaps now only a cable's length away, and if they discovered any footprint or other mark of mine, they would make sport of hunting me down. With troops of them searching every bush, there was small chance of escape. Yet I had to go into the surf to find food or grow too weak to find a shelter or build one. Being ashore was not the answer to all my problems.

Hunger lessened my fear of walking out on the bar, and I hoped the line of driftwood might hide me from some parts of the island. The effect of the nectar and the prospect of solid grub doubled my pace toward the surf.

After food, shelter was another concern for it might rain in the next few days, and to be wet, even in the lee of a large rock or crouched in thick brush, was misery. Palms scattered in the forest to the north and south offered fronds for a good thatch, and the long leaves of the flax, split into narrow strips and twisted, were tough enough to serve as cords. With those items I could build a rude hovel if a cave or an overhanging rock were not to be found.

My only choice was to repair the canoe quickly and sail for Cook's Strait, landing only at night or when short of water. There had been high swells but no storms in the last week. Such tolerable weather could not last, thus a start had to be made soon to take advantage of it. If I were timid and waited a mite too long, a gale or a boisterous wind might drive me onto a lee shore. With luck I could keep a half mile off the coast and fall in with some sealers or whalers farther north. Yet it may be that such men no longer lived or fished about the Strait, or that the tales told of them were false. Fortune alone would decide my fate, then.

Sea birds were rising from the shore with coarse calls and flapping their way west in long, angled lines toward their feeding places for the day. Like them, I was searching for a good meal.

Each few minutes I scanned the forest edges and the low ground for any sign of Indians.

I arrived at the bar. In two turns up and down the beach in waist deep water, my toes touched a few stones but nothing else. The search, plus a pause for each collapsed wave as it rolled past, took a half an hour and left me chilled, fatigued, and disappointed not having found even an empty shell.

With no success there, I swept the water from my body and started off toward the rocky point at the north end of the bar hoping to discover sea ears, crabs, or the like. Waves washing in and out had cut a shallow channel in the beach sand next to the rocks. There my eye caught the pearly glint of a shell fragment, a mere flake, yet it showed to be part of a mussel when it was turned over and over by the edge of another wave flowing in. There was my food! More bits of shell, along with tatters of rockweed, washed in. Yes, food for certain. I picked a way up and across the low, crannied rocks and found scattered fragments of mussel shells lying about. No fleshy parts clung to them, only dried, sinewy curls. They looked to be weeks or even months old. Had animals of some sort taken them from the rocks? Had they been gathered and broken open by cannibals?

It was only a few steps from rock to rock to the wet outliers. A wave heaved shoreward, dashed at the point, and for a second or two blanketed it with froth. With all energy spent it sucked and gurgled away through the crevices. I thought I saw mussels under the draining water. The next wave surged in and its greater haul back revealed the lips of mussel shells. What a relief! There was time for a rest while the ebbing of the tide put my meal within reach. I eased into a slot between the warmed stones and drew my knees up against my body. The less time I was visible meant less chance of being discovered, and in the crevice while waiting for slack water I was least chilled by the breeze.

From that moment it was another beginning. There were days, perhaps a week, yet to travel and then what ... rescue or greater dangers in Cook's Strait?

The hard, unyielding rock at my side and back was a reminder of the sweet life left in the body. I had my fill of water. Food was only three fathoms away. What strange turns of fortune had left me alive?

In an hour the tide appeared to be at its lowest. Rest and the warmth of the sun had increased my strength, and I stepped out on slippery rocks to reach mussels exposed by the retreat of a wave. From several places, I pulled three dozen from their anchoring threads, some to eat, some to steam in a cooking hole if I managed to make fire. The size of the mussels was puzzling though, being smaller than the fat, seven and eight inch ones I had seen in other places. Had the Indians taken the larger ones on this part of the coast? There were gaps in the mats of them clinging to the rocks, perhaps where some had never grown or had been torn loose by storms. I hid again in my space between the rocks with my prizes. It would be hours or the next day before I might build a fire and dress a meal, for a shelter of some kind must be found or made first. I set to cracking the shells open with a stone. Water and juices ran down my beard and onto my chest as I scraped the animal out of its broken shell with my teeth. They tasted well enough even uncooked … indeed, hunger was the best pickle. Most likely I would suffer looseness from eating them. A bellyful of water would make it even worse, yet I had no choice but to bear it. I flung the emptied shells out into the surf where they would not betray me.

What might these Indians do if I were discovered and taken? Would I be killed or made a slave? If they did take me and keep me alive, might I escape to a trader or whaler if it did call in the Strait? If not bound or injured, I could swim to a ship, yet if its crew spied me swimming near their vessel, might they take me for a savage and drive me away, even shoot me?

The murders of Captain Furneaux's boat crew had been on my mind since landing. The tale of the attack had been told aboard our barque several times, but it was of little concern to us when we called down at Cape South Island, since it had happened fifty years before in the days of Captain Cook. Now I was closer to Queen Charlotte Sound where the killings had taken place, and it was said these cannibals were much fiercer in the north. Another tale repeated among sealers was the massacre of the crew of the *Boyd*, a far more worrisome one since it had occurred only a few years past. There was no choice in my course to be taken. There was a better chance to find traders or whalers in the Strait than in the south and it was also far nearer.

While standing on and off the coast during the night, I could have tied off the canoe's steering oar and dozed, but there was a danger I might not wake before being caught in the surf. Once ashore the cold wind and my wet clothes had allowed only short naps.

No figure of a man, woman, or child showed when I peeked over the rocks to the north and south. A search of the shaded openings between the trees and bushes on the rising ground around the flat revealed nothing that was not natural to the earth, not one thing fashioned by man. With the unclouded sun full on me I could lie there and doze off. So with a small feeling of safety, I rolled back against the warmed stone of my cranny. Within a minute a soft, desired sleep muffled the crack and rumble of the surf.

Then I was in a dream, sailing from the island of the wreck. Instead of having the fair weather, my catamaran was being driven over the swells in a gale. Gusts of wind tore at the sail. The bindings that held the boomkins to the spar and hull were working loose. It had been my greatest worry that the canoe might break apart. "Why must I sail it all again?" I shouted to the wind. Then in a trice, somehow I was on the deck of a ship. Every sail of her plan—mains, topsails, t'galants, t'galant royals, even the stunsails—had been sheeted home. The huge spreads of fabric were belied out by a breeze, yet the ship barely moved. "Heave away," a voice called out. From forward came the splash of the dipsea lead as it hit the water. The ship was taking soundings! Moments later the call came from starboard: "Watch! Ho, watch!" Another long pause, then another call. "Watch! Ho, watch!" Only the sound of the wind for seconds. Then a man shouted from the mizzen chains, "Bottom! By the deep, ninety!" Then after the second heave he called, "By the deep eighty!" The vessel might be off Yankeeland ... with less than a hundred fathoms below her keel. Was home there beyond the jib boom mere hours away? Then I was being lifted from the deck. Shrouds, sails, and masts fell away, fading from my sight.

The crash of the surf on the rocks and its sucking haul back through crevices grew from a whisper to full volume. Drops of water splashed on my leg and I opened my eyes. I had had a refreshing rest. The sun, now partially screened by high clouds, was past the zenith.

The thought of the trip I must make to find a whale ship or a trader returned. With no Indians to trade with and perhaps no whales to dart and boil, it might be years before any vessel was drawn by curiosity to the coast. Remaining there was not a choice for me. New Zealanders who lived to the north or south or in the mountains would come upon me sooner or later. There was no end to the tales of their ferocity told aboard ships.

Coast, sea, and sky were a pleasing prospect nudging away my dreadful thoughts of savages.

Food and rest had left me stronger, ready to begin the trip north. It was time to pull the canoe farther up the beach. The extra mussels might stay there until I returned with a sack. Two hands could not hold a quarter of them.

I raised my head just high enough to peek over the rock, but no figures walked across the low ground or along the bar. That, though, was no assurance the coast about was unpeopled. There might be savages living where they could not view the beach, and missed seeing me in the surf. I went back to the bar and started south, walking along the windrow of tree trunks, broken limbs, and roots. Days and weeks of rolling in the surf had abraded the bark on the boles and snapped their branches, leaving only stubs. Weathering by rain and the salt-charged wind had turned them gray, almost silver. Plenty of long sticks were in that jumble fit to build a sort of shelter or just a sloping roof, so there was no need to hack at sapling trees with my rude ax.

At the shingle beach, the waves were again touching the hull and drifting the broken rigging in and out. I waded in, lifted the spar of the outrigger, and was surprised by how little effort was needed to swing it over my head and right the hull. With the water bailed out, the canoe floated free, and I easily towed it higher up the beach and levered it beyond the reach of the waves. I fitted the broken mast, stay, shrouds, and sail inside the hull, and untied my tool sack from the after boomkin.

My clothes, spread on the rocks, were still damp even after hours in the sun, yet I had to wear them in the hope the warmth of my body would dry them before dark. If not it would be a chill, uncomfortable night. The touch of the damp leather gave me a shiver when I pulled them on. Then I set off to explore the coast to the north and south to the distance of a quarter mile, thinking it was better to discover the savages first and find their number and how they might be avoided.

Before each step forward, I searched the greenery right and left and then in the middle distance and beyond for plots once cleared for crops. In America, whole swaths of trees were cut away to clear for the plow, but here I did not see a bit of earth five yards square that might have yielded a crop of potatoes and then left fallow. I paced slowly around the trees and bushes, scanning for any limb that had been twisted aside or any twig snapped by a hand. There might have been footprints, but leaves, fronds, and rain had fallen and there was not a hint of one. I advanced, watching the ground for any plant that might have been trampled; then looked up to search the hills. There were few openings between the bushes and ferns that may have been paths where savages once passed through. It seemed a wilderness never once touched by man.

In the small portion of the coast I searched, there was neither a sign of the cannibals nor were there any overhanging rocks or a cave to be used as shelter. A site for a lean-to had to be found where it would be well hidden. There was plenty of cover where one might be built in the few hours of light left. Thick bushes would screen it from most of the wind, and perhaps even conceal a fire from any wandering Indians.

In late afternoon I gathered long sticks from the driftwood piles and hacked leaves from the flax plants to bind the parts of the shelter together. Palm fronds were fibrous and after they were partially cut, or, more accurately, chewed by the ax, I wrenched them off. By sunset I had a roof on a canted framework supported between two trees. Its thatch of palm fronds tied on with strips of twisted flax leaves looked haphazard, as if someone had tossed them onto a pile, yet they looked to be passably rainproof. My bed was four full armloads of ferns spread on the earth. Even with them under the body it would be a cold night.

With my empty tool sack, I fetched the extra mussels from the rocky point; then returned to the shelter and had a dozen of them for supper. The next day I would try for birds' eggs and with luck, some might be newly laid and provide a better meal.

The last bit of twilight came down through the bushes and trees, leaving only the faintest illumination. Overhead a narrow patch of sky, gemmy with bright stars, showed along the stump ends of the fronds at the ragged edge of the shelter. Each night at sea, there had been the stars turning slowly above all night. Here, the weaker ones first and later the bolder ones dimmed away by an overcast or clouds carried in over the coast. Inside and outside the shelter became a complete darkness, as if I were in the far depths of a cave.

At sea, I had been reduced to a mere fleck by the expanse of the sea rising and falling around an unbroken horizon.

How comforting it would be if another were here, a mate or a friend, a familiar voice to be heard near at hand in the darkness. Even a dog, a small dog curled up on the fronds, would serve for a companion.

Like Zeph, I might tell a tale at the Boro upon returning, yet how could my words ever give listeners the feel of being cold and wretched on a cannibal coast?

There had not been one sign of another human; yet cannibals might arrive from north or south and discover me in the next day or two. I touched my ax, my sole weapon, lying on the ferns where it would be instantly at hand. What a conceit! They would not come at me one at a time but by dozens, all screaming to be the first to halve my skull with a sharpened stone club.

There was nothing to do but lie in the blackness and mull the repair of the canoe, the voyage up the coast, or what I might do if savages appeared. After tossing on the fronds a while, I managed to doze off, but the mussels did not sit well in the stomach and my guts gurgled, bringing me out of short naps. The thump and rumble of the surf was constant, and cats' paws of wind stirred through the taller trees. Those sounds could be dismissed, but later a scratching in the litter of leaves brought me up on one elbow to listen with all muscles tensed and my heart pounding. Was it a savage creeping up on me? I listened intently for several minutes. I heard nothing more. What was I thinking? Am I such a little ninny to be frightened by a few noises in the bushes? It was most likely a small animal, a rat or a mouse stirring about. I relaxed on the makeshift bed once more.

It grew colder. I pulled the hood close about my head, crossed my arms, and held my hands in my armpits. Knees drawn up kept me slightly warmer but not my bare lower legs and feet. Sleep came only as short dozing between long spans of chilly wakefulness.

At the first light I searched for the birds' nests, but none of the eggs I found were fit to eat. The ones I broke open were too far gone, and I was not so desperate to eat the half-feathered and bulbous-eyed creatures. Perhaps it was too late in the season for that particular bird. There were many hatched and growing chicks, though. I killed four of the fattest, downy ones, plucked and drew them, and tried nibbling the raw flesh, but thought it better to wait until they were cooked. The mussels and nectar had lessened my hunger a little.

With bare hands I scooped out a pit in the sandy soil for an earth oven and filled it with driftwood and stones. Next to it I made my pile of fine twigs and dry, crumbled leaves, ready to feed a glowing ember made with bow and drill. An hour later the juices of the chicks impaled on sticks over the fire dripped fat, which flamed on the burning wood and sizzled on the heating stones. Though not needed, it was a sound that raised my appetite. The chicks' taste was tolerable when they were well roasted.

The fire waned, and it was time to place the mussels, bundled in ferns, on the remaining coals and the heated stones. Over all I spread a thick layer fronds and then one of earth. In the late afternoon, I opened the cooking pit and found the mussels well steamed.

"Ah, such a meal for a famished man," I said aloud. The sound of my voice startled me. I had no reason to speak a word for over two weeks, and the only sounds I heard in that time were the wind and the sea, the coarse calls of gulls and the sweet ones of land birds.

Having eaten well and slept some better, I went to the shore the next morning to sit cross-legged on the beach and sew up the tears in the sail.

A bright sun had cleared the mountains. The surf breaking on the bar and the blue sky drove away fears of cannibals. If such fair weather held, I thought, I might reach Cook's Strait in one or two days of sailing; but in the afternoon clouds approached from seaward, graying away the blues and greens of the swells. Waves driven higher by a gusting wind dashed the rocks and covered them for a second with mats of foam. Slaty hazes of rain blurred the horizon. To the north, tall waves broke onto the bar, each strike felt as much as heard, then rebounded in geysers of foam.

If that storm with its high swells and driving wind had come upon me days before, I doubted the canoe would have held together. Repair would have been impossible if its bindings had parted. Without water and unable to sail, I would not have survived.

A scattering of drops began falling from the clouds driving in overhead. I trotted back to the lean-to just as heavier rain began spatting on the crude thatch of palm fronds. I could do nothing but lie on my bed of ferns, listen to the wind tearing at the trees, and watch water drip from the shiny leaves of the bushes.

Chapter Two

The rain stopped during the night and tatters of clouds drifted toward the mountains in the morning, allowing me warm sun while I repaired the mast and backstay. In the forenoon of the next day the canoe was finished and ready to be levered into the water. Six roasted sea birds dangled by their feet from the backstay, and my crude water butts were full and hitched to the boomkins. Most important of all, I felt recovered enough in strength to continue on to the Strait. All that was needed was a less boisterous sea, but scattered clouds continued to move in, hinting of another nearing storm. I watched the peaking waves tip, collapse, and sweep in. Could I get through them to the unbroken swells beyond, or should I wait for better weather? I opted to wait one more day.

Mid stride on my way to the shore the next morning, I spotted a rectangular shape about the length of the hand and half its width imbedded in the earth before me. I knelt on one knee and ran a finger across its black surface. It was a stone, but the visible side was not a natural break. It was far too smooth; obviously it had been ground against another stone. I worked my thumb and a finger around it, pulled it free, and brushed off the bits of earth. It was neatly fashioned, an inch thick, and shaped into a blade at one end. A half inch of that edge and some of one corner had broken off. When hafted to a handle it must have served as an adze and not an ax, as it had a slight curve to it, but what tedious labor it must have been to cut with. Down at The Bluff, at least five hundred miles away, the Indians always put aside their stone blades whenever a steel one could be gotten, and they worked for weeks or met any price in fish, pigs, or potatoes that were asked for them.

That tool was the veriest sign that they had visited the shore and perhaps might return soon to fish and hunt. The broken mussel shells on the rocks surely had been their doing. It was far too dangerous to remain on this coast searching about for food every day. New Zealanders might appear from anywhere to discover the canoe, footprints, and cuts made on the flax plants and palms. They would instantly set about searching and most likely find me. Then what would be my fate?

There could be no holding back. The waves hadn't lowered, yet since they hadn't risen, it was a good time to leave. I stripped off my clothes and tied them next to the chicks on the backstay. I levered the vessel into the surf and towed it along the shore to the center of the bar. If the canoe were overset again, there was less chance it would be smashed on the rocks at either end. Cannibals ashore and perils out at sea were my choices. Swells continually rose up, and if one broke on the canoe it would be smashed. I guided the vessel out until I was chest deep in the frothing remains of each wave. The next dashed in and lifted the hull. As it passed I heaved myself up over the side. The following one met the canoe at an angle and swung it beam to the surf. I jumped out and held onto the hull as it drifted back to where there was enough purchase underfoot to aid turning the hull seaward again. I had to try many times if I were to see home again. The second attempt was no better and had the same result. If my vessel veered close to a breaking wave, it would be overturned and the mast snapped again. After two more tries I rolled into the hull and, with rapid work with the paddle, kept the bow toward the breakers to meet them before or after they broke. Even then water spilled in as the canoe cut through each. The hull tipped up at a steep angle and then dropped as the waves slipped from beneath it. By pulling hard, I drove the canoe beyond the breaking waves and into the swells.

The full press of a larger sail would have driven my hull faster, but the small, dependable one worked well and gave no trouble. I put my paddle aside, dipped out water sloshing fore and aft, and dressed. It was a relief to be moving again, and it set my heart pounding as I quartered the swells and drove north toward Cook's Strait.

There was a bit of rock weed washing fore and aft in the last skim of water in the hull. I tossed it forward at the bow and counted the seconds required for the length of the hull to pass it. An estimate of the canoe's speed of three to four miles each hour was a good one if any current running down the coast were not subtracted. A day's and night's run could be as much as seventy or eighty miles if the wind held abeam or aft.

How much of the coast was yet needed to travel was out of my reckoning, for the Strait might be a hundred fifty or two hundred miles distant or perhaps beyond the next headland.

The wind was on the quarter and the bindings of the canoe proved taut. At three quarters of a mile from shore, lifted by the swells and dropped into the hollows, there would be fewer fears to plague me. Danger from the Indians was not threatening each moment. Nighttime, though I disliked it, should be no worse.

The first hours sailing were along a low coast of hills covered with trees, palms, and tangles of bushes. Farther back, the mountains rose to great heights; all was in shades of dark green as if it were the renewed earth after the deluge. I kept returning my eyes to that shore, yet not a single hut, cleared field, or the least sign of men showed on it. The Indians I had seen in the far south had their neatly planted fields of potatoes near their houses and close to the sea, but here they might have built their villages back from the shore, hidden them from view behind a low hill or rise, or masked them behind a stand of trees. At the distance I was from the land they would be difficult to see. Farther back were the massive bluffs where savages would never have chosen to live. Seeing no cleared land eased my mind.

If the wind became fresh and the swells higher, a landing might be safe where the coast was not rocky. Fortunately the wind held all day from abaft the beam, keeping my speed constant, which meant I was thirty to forty miles nearer the Strait when the sun touched its edge to the horizon. I thought it would be better to keep to sea all night, as the canoe was traveling well. Any attempt to go ashore in the dark was folly, for it might be an ironbound coast where I might be drowned. Even if I survived, the canoe would be a total ruin, leaving me stranded, helpless where the Indians might find me.

It was possible that by the first morning light tomorrow, the way into the Strait could be in sight with the sails of a whaler or a trader's ship on the horizon. Aye, relief was possibly only a day or two away. Then there will be good grub to eat, though I would settle for salt meat and hard biscuit. I did not forget clean, dry togs to wear, and that too kept my spirits high, higher than the day we rowed away from the last seal rookery and sheeted our topsails home.

Some patchy clouds were still drifting overhead. It was my hope they wouldn't cover the stars altogether. Those points of light would be an assurance I was heading north and not out to sea where I would be lost, or toward the shore where darkness would hide any danger. Mountains on the starboard, even partially hidden under low clouds, were a guide in the daylight, but at night there would not be the least sign of them. Stars would be sorely needed then. To run in close and use the white of the surf and its rumbling as a guide was too much of a danger. In the darkness I might be misled by a small point or isle lying out from the coast; then be trapped before I could retreat from the breaking waves. There was also a chance of striking some rocks awash offshore.

It was a long, tedious night, though a few stars to the north were visible now and again granting me a rough course toward the Strait.

A rosy, welcome glow came at last over the crests of the mountains, and the sun made a heartening peep through a tear in the clouds.

Thus far, there were still no signs of New Zealanders ashore. No brief glim of a campfire had shown during the entire night, but empty as this coast appeared, the stone adz was a sure sign they visited at times.

A few short beaches of sand appeared, possible landing places between the rocky portions of the coast. I debated trying for them, but decided not to risk it as long as the wind held and the swells grew no higher. Coming ashore even in a well-manned whaleboat had its perils on an unknown coast. In the canoe, with only one small paddle to steer and drive it, passage through the surf was dangerous. The landing on the shingle beach had been the only one I made in the canoe, and I had been forced to leap clear and swim for the shore. With all going well and with a steady wind on the larboard quarter, there was no need to take the chance. For each hour the canoe sailed, I was miles nearer the Strait, which might be just beyond a great bulge of the coast ahead.

At mid-morning the horizon began to darken in the southwest.

More clouds drifted in from that quarter and spread against the mountains. By midday they had covered a last hopeful patch of blue. The dimming light degraded the coast to a murky strip. Wind began to whip about in flaws, this way and that, swinging the boom back and forth. Then it blew from the north, forcing me to make boards on and off shore. It was looking very squally. The wind freshened more and left me no choice but to head east and land before the surf rose any higher. I turned to go with the waves and drive on a beam reach. It made little difference that rain drops pelted down, since the sea dashing against the hull had wet me through. That rain and the surf mist reduced all the details of the coast to dark smudges.

Perhaps I had traveled another forty or fifty miles up the coast in the night, yet I had to admit that it was a guess, possibly one too favorable. With a current making south it might be half that. Foolishly I had kept on sailing when a landing had been possible much sooner. What was a hundred miles closer to the Strait if I drowned here? Now a landing would have to be made through high surf and onto a shore that might be all rocks.

Waves tossed the canoe back and forth, and gave a twisting motion to the spar and boomkins. The bindings that bound them together I feared were weakening. They had held well while riding on long, reaching swells far out at sea. Maybe it was the confused mix of waves here that caused them to work. Nothing could be done about that; I was too busy keeping the craft heading inshore. The increasing wind opened gaps at the seams and at the hanks of the sail. Letting the sheet out some eased the strain. All had gone so well until that last shift of the wind to the north; now I must pass through the breakers and hope there was a sand beach there to land on before my outrigger broke apart.

Damn! Damn! What a sheep's head. Impatience was ever my fault. I could have made it to shore miles back before the wind rose, where some rock-free shores offered safer landings. To continue on had been a poor gamble, a witless thing.

The rain was easing. Despite the mist and spray of the breakers, some details of the shore began to take shape. Each wave peaked and cast forward into a confused, roiling surf. Sand or rock there? For a minute the rain nearly stopped and the greenery, a quarter mile away, separated into trees. Behind them was a palisade of logs … then barely showing above it, hut roofs. Ach! Indians ashore there! Several dark figures began running back and forth on the beach. Will they be fierce enemies to strangers? For the last hours I had doubted there were any New Zealanders between my landing place and Cook's Strait. Here they were just where I must land. Damn! The sea and wind were delivering me up to these Indians. I will have to run in through high surf and onto a shore filled with murderous savages.

A gust of wind slammed into the sail from aft, snapping the backstay. Its frayed end flew past my head. Mast, boom, sail, cooked birds, and shrouds all landed in a heap across the bow and the forward boomkin. Damn and blast all! That would sink any man's spirit. It was a wan hope that I could set up the mast and re-tie the stay while standing in the hull pitching one way and another. No, it was impossible. I could only hope to paddle through the breaking waves and reach the shore without drowning. I drew the mast and sail back across both boomkins and tied them to keep the mess from dragging in the water. Swells running some crossways nudged the bow off course, and I pulled with the paddle to counter each one. Water spilled over the sides, and bailing it took time from paddling.

On the coast a dozen savages were sliding a canoe toward the surf. It was daft of them to take such an unneeded risk. A half minute later I was lifted on a swell and saw their canoe had made it through the breakers. My progress without the sail was barely noticeable, and I could do no more than to keep the bow aimed for the surf. Even if I still had the mast and sail intact and was running downwind, there could be no escape from those men. Their canoe was moving twice as fast as mine ever had. More people were spilling from the palisade onto the beach to watch, and there was no doubt I was to become their prisoner and then their victim. When their canoe came nearer I could see seven men in it. Six of them leaned forward in unison and plunged their paddles into the sea and pulled their hull ahead. The seventh man, in the stern, was continually bailing with a scoop. The powerful arms of the paddlers, with their strokes timed to their voices, drove their prow through the waves directly for me. I saw each savage had his hair twisted up into a knot on the top of his head. All wore cloaks or some manner of capes on their backs. They looked much like the men down around The Bluff. Those living in the villages there had been quite friendly and eager to trade their potatoes when they had them, but these men with deep, chanting voices were unnerving. I glanced up at them each time I emptied the bailer over the side. They slowed their paddling and neared the larboard side of my little craft. Their canoe had been made from a single log, but it was twice the length of mine and had a wale fixed on each gunwale to raise it a foot, making it more seaworthy.

Like most Indians in these islands their faces were tattooed, and the markings were not merely stains in the skin but fine grooves cut into the flesh. Two or three blue-black lines started from point of the chin, skirted the corners of the mouth, and ended at the sides of the nostrils. More lines ran from the inside ends of the eyebrows and arched up and out across the forehead to the temples. Some men had large swirls on each cheek and smaller ones on the sides of their noses, with those designs covering a good portion of their faces their expressions appeared fiercer. Their dark eyes scanned me and my craft for most of a minute while the two canoes heaved up and fell with the swells. Those men at The Bluff and on Cape South Island had not been half as threatening as these men glowering at me. The rain resumed and pelted down as we stared at each other.

My only weapon, the ax, was tied securely in the tool bag. It would be foolish to bring it out, for it would be taken as a challenge and bring a deadly response. I could only wait to see what their intent was.

There was not the least favor in their faces. A spasm gripped my I stomach as if a round shot had dropped into it. The older sealers had told of men taken when on shore and even seized from boats to be knocked on the head and thrown into cooking pits. I recalled the fate of the *Boyd's* crew again and feared my life was shoaling. A shiver ran through my body. What a frightful thing to suffer now ... to pass through so much peril ... and die so miserably. No one would ever know my fate, and my gnawed bones might lie scattered like rubbish on that shore, never to be gathered together and buried. Then the sad end of one sealer would never be known along the coasts of Long Island Sound.

The men began to chatter to each other, perhaps wondering where I had come from. Since they had seen no ship out at sea, perhaps they guessed I had dropped from the sky, canoe and all. I knew that with my beard and in my wild state I would not be taken for any of the traders or whalers from Van Diemen's Land. Might they see me as some evil spirit come to do harm and instantly cleave my skull?

One man in the middle of the canoe had a wide scar on the left side of his head which reached from the temple back to an inch past the hole where his left ear should have been. No hair grew on the lighter skin of the old wound. The blow that caused it must have been a powerful one, for there was an indentation in the skull at the middle of the scar. Such a deep wound would have killed most men or left them simpletons had they lived. His scowl made him more menacing than the others. It slipped into an arrogant sneer. One man pointed at my canoe and spat at it. Another man reached for the cooked birds floating in the sea with his paddle and flipped them back and forth.

The one with the scar shouted something and motioned for me to get into their canoe. I took that as evidence he was in command. There was no choice: go or perhaps be killed on the spot. I crouched, balancing myself, and then stepped across the gap between the two hulls. At that moment the lift of the swell carried them apart and my foot slipped off its mark. My left hand caught the gunwale of their canoe as I plunged into the cold water. I came back up to the surface and the Indian seized my hair with a powerful grip. With that hand he lifted me, aiding my crawl into their canoe. I squatted in the hull, coughing up water and returning stares of the New Zealanders who leaned one way or another to look me over.

The man behind me laid hold of my hide jacket and rudely yanked it back and forth three times as if trying to rip it from my back. I turned to face what I feared was the swing of a club, but he lunged forward with his eyes fully open and his tongue curled downward out of his gaping mouth, making a face as grotesque as the carvings of their demons. "EEEYAAAAAH," he screamed a foot from my nose, sending a hot, fishy breath at me. The man's eyes rolled up until the pupils were nearly hidden; and the blank white orbs turned his tattooed face into a ghastly sight. Don't show fear! Don't show fear! I was chanting to myself again and again. Look stern, look determined. That's what the old hands on the sealing islands had advised. It was these Indians' habit to test a stranger to see what sort of man he was. I wanted to leap out of the canoe, but in the water and empty handed I could not strike a blow in my defense. They in turn could slash at my skull with their sharp-edged bludgeons. I was panting with fright; but knew I must not to show it, else they would count me a coward fit only to be a slave or eaten. The man with the scar shouted another order, and the crew swept their paddles in the sea, driving the canoe in a circle around my dugout and then toward the shore. Chanting and pulling in strong, quick strokes, the crew drove the canoe through the swells. Water splashed over the sides and kept the one man bailing. We touched the shore on a spreading wave, and the paddlers leaped into the water. From a cluster of people standing on the sand, four men came forward into the waves to help push the canoe up the beach.

A quick hop from the hull, and then I waded out of the foaming surf to return the stares of the women, the naked children, and the gray-haired oldsters wrapped in capes. A few of the women had tattoos, but only small ones confined to their lips and chins. Suddenly they all began to chatter. Two miserable-looking dogs edged toward me, cautiously sniffed at my legs, and then, not liking my scent, backed away whining. One of the young men with arms and chest daubed with a red pigment approached me. That coloring must have been mixed with fish oil, for he smelled like a basket of mackerel. His right hand moved up menacingly toward my throat. I leaned back, holding my arms up to protect myself, but the he darted his hand past my guard and yanked some hair from my beard.

"Ach. Damn it," I cried, jumping a step back.

The Indian held the auburn hairs close to his face and studied them. Two others crowded in next to inspect the sample and relay their opinions to the rest of those on the beach. Another Indian, talking rapidly, pushed towards me, and expecting another pull at my beard, I stepped back and bumped against two others standing behind me to block any retreat. They pressed their faces close to mine, peering into my eyes and ears. One man gripped my beard and forced my head from side to side. The others pointed at my skin clothing and every item of my bedraggled figure and jabbered away. I looked for some indication of my fate, but their intent, amiable or devilish, was hidden in expressions distorted by the black scrolls and curves of their tattoos. A boy of about twelve years age with some smears of red paint on his face and shoulders dashed forward and swung at me with a stick. It was a glancing blow, yet caused my arm to smart. The one with the old head wound shouted at the boy, grabbed the stick from him, and then pointed to the palisade, ordering him inside.

In my mind I dubbed that fierce-looking man Scarhead, and seeing how all obeyed him I expected he must be a sachem or priest of some sort. In his right hand he held a short paddle-like club of black stone which had been ground to a thin edge sharp enough to split any skull from forehead to chin

He faced me and spoke while his left hand traced a path from the mountains in the east, across the sky overhead to the horizon where the sun would set.

What did all that talk mean? How could I understand a word of it? Was it a count of how many days or full moons before I was to be killed? It was useless to resist or dash away, for I was not yet fit as these men who could easily overtake me and slay me with their clubs. Two of them pointed to the opening in the enclosure and shoved me roughly toward it. The crowd to the right and left and behind me walked along, herding me into the palisade. Inside, several houses of different sizes were backed up to the log walls and faced a central yard. Two miniature houses like ones intended for a large dog or some other pet were each built on top of a post ten or twelve-feet high. I had seen one like them at the strait in the south. I looked to each side to see all I could, but whenever my pace slowed the men grunted some words and prodded me forward like an ox.

Several more dogs approached, and once getting my scent wandered away to nose some bones scattered on the ground for some overlooked nibble of dried flesh. Any of those bones, I suspected, might be the cast-off remains of some unfortunate sealer.

They pushed me toward one of the houses. The gable end of its roof and its side walls extended several feet beyond the front wall, creating an open porch. They forced me to my knees at the foot of the recessed wall and pointed to an opening in it a mere yard square. They needed no words to order me inside; the stern looks on their tattooed faces sufficed. With no other choice, I had to crawl inside. Without windows in its walls, the only light admitted to the single room was through the one small entrance. In the gloom overhead I could make out the ridgepole nine or ten feet above the earth at the front end. From there it sloped down, allowing only a yard and a half between it and the floor at the opposite end. Inside, I was out of the rain and wind, but it was meager comfort.

Two men settled on the ground outside of the entrance to keep watch. One of them looked in at me and gave a menacing shake of his club and two growled words. I sat on the earth floor shivering from cold and also from the fear that I might be killed in the next few hours or days. There had been wild tales told in the fo'c'sle of men kept as prisoners in some islands and fattened for weeks until needed for a cannibal feast.

My eyes became accustomed to the darkness and I crawled over to the wall made of riven slabs of wood set endwise into the earth with each edge lapped over the next piece. I attempted to work my fingers between them and pull them apart, but they would not yield. They were lodged too deeply into the soil and could not be moved the least bit. Even if my guards fell asleep, they would awaken if I kicked at the wall. Digging a piece of the wood out was not possible, for the earth was packed hard and I had nothing to dig with except my bare hands. They would be bloodied before one slab was even loosened. If the men happened to look in and see me scratching away, they might club my brains out merely for the attempt to escape. I crawled to the low end of the house and put my shoulder against the roof and tried to lift a portion of it. It creaked a little with my heaving. One of the guards came halfway in and shouted something at me, letting me know he had heard the noise. My try at raising the sooted battens and thatch had only made them yield the width of a finger. The cords that bound the parts together were knotted where I could not reach them, and I had no blade to cut with. All my slivers of volcano glass and the ax were out there in the canoe beyond the surf. Rudely built though it was, there was no escape from my prison while being watched, and any noise made would alarm the guards. I could only hope I was not to be slain and could find some opportunity to escape. I would try, even in this land filled with these savages, if it were night.

I lay on the earth in my wet skins intending to sleep, but after a half hour I felt many needle pricks in my skin. Inside my clothes, fleas were exploring my body, and once they found a favorable spot, they bit.

I had not dozed off for a minute during the entire night whilst coming up the coast, yet my sleep was fitful. After awaking from each short nap, I could only think of what my fate would be amongst these savages. It had been a monstrous mistake to continue along the coast when the storm threatened. If I had come ashore sooner and waited out the thick weather, I might have made the Strait. Impatience … impatience again.

As many had said, there was no predicting the storms and the sea about *Tovy Poenamoo*. It was a contrary place.

Yet, even if I had gotten into the Strait, I might have been spied there and taken prisoner. Any attempt at crossing the mountains meant more days of travel and more time in which to be discovered. The odds had been much against making the Strait by any route. It would have been a foolish dream to fetch the Bay of Islands far to the north, something wholly beyond my reach. The only hope at present was the mercy of Scarhead, if he had any. He looked treacherous enough for a dozen villains.

I fell asleep and awakened several times. On my last arousal I noticed the first rays of the sun on the hardened earth of the yard outside. Another man joined the two who were on guard, and disputed with them for a few minutes. The new guard peered in and motioned for me to come out. I crawled through the opening and had risen to my feet when an old woman handed me a small basket woven of green flax leaves. In it were a few pieces of fish, cooked but cold. Ha! At least they weren't intending to fatten me for slaughter with this first meal. I grabbed it and moved to the end of a log to sit and eat. The dogs approached in their begging poses and simpered when I shoved them away, allowing them not the least crumb. Children ran calling to each other and then clustered around to stare with dark, oily eyes and chatter about my clothes, hair, and beard again. It was the same here as in the southern parts at The Bluff where white men were considered peculiar beings … pale goblins.

Scarhead approached a few minutes later and spoke a few words to me. They must know I can't understand; why did they try? He stopped talking and walked toward the opening in the palisade. Another man slapped the basket from my hands and motioned for me to follow. Three more guards, armed with carved staffs decorated with feathers, fell into line behind me.

We exited the gate and turned north along a line of low trees. It felt better to be marching in the open air than shivering in the flea-cursed interior of the house. Fifty yards up the beach we turned inland and followed a stream along its shingly bank.

I considered a try at an escape, yet I saw no opportunity for any of the five Indians could be upon me in a trice. Lying on the cold earth through the night had stiffened my legs, and I was doubtful I could outrun my guards. Each side of the track we were following was heavily wooded, and any openings between the trees were filled with thickets of fern. We traveled all day through the forest at a fast pace, almost a trot. I hoped we would stop at some village for something to eat, for the New Zealanders had brought only their weapons along. Not one of them carried a basket or net bag of food. Something was needed in my stomach for the mite of fish I had did not stay me. Hunger had already made my arms and legs shaky and weak, and whenever my pace slowed the least, the man following jabbed me in the back with the end of his staff.

In the evening, there was a glimpse of a lake between the trees, one reflecting the last glow of the sky. Once out on its shore I saw it spread miles to the east, too far for a lake. It had to be an expanse of ocean, and the only place where there was a passage that far to the east was near the Strait. It had to be. Yes, it must be near Cook's Strait or the very Strait itself; my goal was reached but as a prisoner.

We squished through the mud along a low coast for a half mile; then ahead the gables of several houses showed above a palisade. Dogs began howling and their noise and number increased at our approach. A figure was nearing us on the path and calling out. Scarhead slowed his stride and answered the greeting.

We had no rest in our steady pace over the flat ground, and I was glad to pause while the men talked. Once their gam was over, we started forward again and entered the palisade a few minutes later. Inside the enclosure two women were feeding limbs to a small fire and stirring it up to increase the light. At each prodding, the flames licked higher and sent sparks rolling upward. A few minutes later it was bright enough to reveal several house fronts and a crowd of people.

The new tribe, babbling without pause, rushed forward to examine me and, like the others before, poke and pick at my clothes and rudely pull my hair. One very old man, with a leering, toothless face grotesque in the firelight, lifted my skin jacket and scratched a fingernail across my stomach to find if its paleness was natural or paint. A woman standing beside him reached forward and poked her finger into my navel and giggled. I pushed her hand aside and was relieved when Scarhead stepped forward and chased them all off.

The long day's hike over hills and ridges had given me a raging appetite, but since no meal was offered, I pointed to my mouth and mimed chewing. Scarhead snapped out two sharp words which could only be a refusal.

Again I was forced to crawl into one of the houses and, with two guards stationed at its doorway, held secure as the night before. There was no meal intended for me, and no bed but the ground covered with a few fern fronds to sleep on. My stomach growled for the first hour, a reminder of my hunger.

In the morning I was allowed to go outside, and there a few paces in front of the house an old woman with lips tattooed blue and a deeply wrinkled face approached and handed me a small basket half-filled with whitish lumps. They appeared to be potatoes, but one bite told me they were some kind of turnip. Whatever they were, it was food and tasted better than the meal of cold fish given me the previous morning. I ate them quickly and took the basket back to the ancient who had given it to me. She ignored my dumb show of pointing to the bowl and then to my mouth, so there weren't any more turnips or anything else to be had. Then remembering some few words I had learned in the south, I pointed to the basket and asked, "*Kai?*" Her eyes, clouded by age, looked blankly from beneath her mop of gray hair. "*Kai, kai,*" I insisted. She bit her lower lip, and simply walked away. Apparently it was a different language here. This village was several hundreds of miles from The Bluff, and the word there for food was not understood here. My mime, though, could not be mistaken: my want was plain. Her refusal meant there was only a short allowance for me. Damn.

Permission to walk about was allowed, a betterment of my condition, yet any idea could come into their savage heads at any time. Many were watching me: women, children, and especially the men who were sitting about on the ground with only their topknots, their foreheads, and their eyes showing above the edges of the capes or blankets wrapped about their bodies. All those about appeared to be waiting for something to occur. Everyone sat or wandered around inside and outside of the palisade. Of them all only three women were doing anything with a purpose. Did they always spend the day in that fashion, in idleness? Perhaps they had many slaves distant somewhere who raised and gathered their food.

If I were allowed to walk about, I would go out to see what was on the water, perhaps a ship passing through or one anchored there. I started for the narrow opening in the wall, but immediately one of the men rose to his feet and stepped over in front of me to block my way. The man made a short turn of his head to one side and back. It was a move instantly understood: I was not to go out.

The dingy white blanket the man had wrapped about his body was a good woolen one, one like those traded to the Indians in the south. That was a sure sign ships called somewhere about, a clue that there might be some means to escape.

Chapter Three

A few minutes later there were noises and chatter on the other side of the palisade, and all the children and dogs rushed out the gate to the beach. Scarhead then entered with his men. He spoke a few words to me and led me out to the shore where a canoe was held ready in the small waves.

Now in full daylight I could see the village was on a large bay many miles across, and it opened into another, far larger expanse of water farther east. Certainly all that sea out there was Cook's Strait. I had doubted there would be a ship offshore or one sailing on the horizon, yet I was disappointed when I saw none.

One of the men motioned to me into the canoe, and once aboard the crew drove it swiftly with their paddles on a course south, skirting the coast. As a passenger and with no paddle in hand, I felt like a prize animal being carried about to be shown to another mob of spectators. Perhaps I appeared so strange they would spare my life and keep me as an attraction, an oddity to be shown as freaks are at home.

We passed groups of houses on the shore, and beyond them inland there were neatly planted fields, the first ones I had seen. A dense tangle of vines, ferns, and trees covered the West Coast, but here at the north end of the island, it was cleared and well-peopled. Though savages, they had abundant gardens that gave the land a civilized look, agreeable, peaceful.

The paddlers in the canoe never slackened their pace or chattering. There was not one word with which I could ask a question about our destination. *Kai, moana, ika, wahine, wai,* and *waka,* I remembered those words and their meanings but no others, not having been near the people in the south long enough to learn more.

In the late afternoon, two days later, we arrived at one more group of stockaded houses set back a short distance from the shore. Scarhead got out and went directly within the wall of logs. The greeting I received on that beach was the same as in the other villages: a close examination of my face, hair, and beard while a dozen scruffy dogs dodged about and whined, adding to the confusion. The animals soon overcame their fear and leaned forward to sample my scent.

I craved to know what these Indians were thinking. Did they find my appearance so novel, the light skin, beard, and odd clothes; that they might keep me alive?

With one hand an old woman slipped loose the bowknot of the drawstring that held my trousers up, and with the other pulled the waistband open and looked in to see what was there. I yanked the trousers from her grip, and stepping back, stumbled over several children behind me. I landed flat on my back and lay there while they all giggled and danced about me.

By the time I got to my feet and retied the drawstring, Scarhead had returned with a gray-haired man wearing a long, feathered cloak. If judged by his dress and the deference given him, it was certain he was another sachem or priest of even greater importance. Instead of wrapping his hair into one topknot as all the others preferred, he had gathered his into two, with one on either side of his head. A tall wooden comb was stuck into each wad of hair and the two together greatly resembled horns. Aye, horns, I thought. Old Scratch for certain. He looked like the devil and I dubbed him so. A line of white whiskers on his chin added to the picture of an evil spirit. A stone pendant about the length of a forefinger and polished to a translucent green dangled from one ear where its weight swinging on its cord had pulled the hole in the wrinkled lobe into a slit an inch long. A two inch shark's tooth hung from his other ear. The face had a full complement of scrolls and arched lines carved into the flesh and stained blue-black. His stare, fierce and gallying, could well make younger, stronger men obey. Sharp wits appeared behind those eyes, and perhaps he was a man who might have use for a goblin and keep him alive. I had heard tales on the sealing islands, possibly true, about men who were kept with the tribes to help in their trade with the ships, but that was not a thing I wanted to do. Yet I would gladly do it to avoid the earth oven. Scratch's glowering face was unnerving, and I held my muscles taut, trying not to shake or show the least fright while my heart thumped and my stomach felt weighted.

Scratch stalked about very close, looking into my eyes and ears. He poked at my lips and grimaced, meaning he wanted to see inside a goblin's mouth. The sachem peered in when I opened my jaw. Was he counting my teeth like a buyer inspecting a plow horse for sale? I hoped the man was considering the age and condition of a new slave, and that idea lessened my dread, since if I were to be slain, my teeth would be of no interest.

At the front of a house I was allowed to sit with these Indians and eat a meal. The fare was a repetition of my last one, a few potatoes but with a little fish added. I welcomed food of any kind and ate every speck of it. At sunset I was led back to another of the houses.

One of the Indians sent a boy off on an errand, and he returned in less than a minute with several lengths of plaited cord. One man seized my hands and forced the wrists together. Another man took one of the cords, made several wraps around them, and knotted the ends securely. How could I prevent it? Any resistance I made might have been stopped with a club strike to my skull.

They pulled me along, and I could only hop forward on my knees and bound hands through the low door of the house. A line was tied to my wrists and then to a stout corner post. Another tether was hitched around my ankles and its end taken diagonally to the opposite corner, drawing me out at length across the earthen floor like a ship moored in a river channel. I rolled over and faced the doorway as the men crawled out. The last one turned and gave me a final look and, assured that all was secure, left. This was something new and strange. Why the bindings? They hadn't been used before. Getting loose was my first thought, but stretched between the two corners I could not bring my wrists to my mouth and gnaw at the cords. Wrenching my hands and feet to get them loose merely caused the bindings to chafe my skin.

The square of the door opening and vague shapes next to the walls were all that was visible. An hour later clouds must have covered the sky, for there was only the faintest light on the ground outside and all blackness inside my prison.

Was I being traded to this new sachem? If I was, Old Scratch must have a great concern I might escape.

The holes worn in the knees and elbows of my clothing let cool night air reach my body, and the trousers, still damp from wading ashore, lay cold against my calves. With the cords holding me stretched out on the bare earth, I was unable to curl up and save any of my body's warmth.

I could think only of what Scarhead and Old Scratch intended for me the next day; unease returned in my stomach and barred sleep. The New Zealanders had prodded and shoved me about, yet had shown no want to kill me, though that idea might come upon them at any moment.

Several dogs howled for a few minutes, breaking the quiet of the night; then gave up trying to arouse anyone with their alarms or complaints. It was quiet for a long time, perhaps an hour or so, then an owl puffed out its paired notes at intervals. I finally managed a series of naps, but the sense of desolation in the wakeful times between them was making the night endless for me.

I had to piss and called out, "Hello! Hello anyone!" I called again, three times, four times, but there was no answer. The pressure became unbearable and since no one was coming to untie me, I let the hot fluid out. Then, despite the bites of fleas, wet trousers, and the cold ground beneath me, I dozed off for longer naps.

Morning's first light revealed the walls and the roof above, and bit by bit the room's contents; fishing nets, coils of plaited rope, paddles, and baskets became more defined. A cracked looking glass hung by a cord from one of the crosspieces of the wall and returned two disjointed images. Below the glass were a dirty, wadded blanket and a rusty oil lamp. These Indians must have traded with the New Holland ships, or from where had they gotten those items … from other tribes farther away who have met with the traders? If ships had called here about, they might return and give me the only means of escape.

The warmth of the sun was quite welcome until it reached the zenith, and then the hovel heated and became stuffy, increasing the odors of old fish and my piss that hung in the air. No waft moved in or out of the small opening that entire day. I perspired freely, and by the light from the door I saw vapor rising from the damp hide of my trousers. Flies buzzed in and out of the opening and around the room. Small ones, mere black specks, landed on my wrists and ankles and bit continually. Rolling from side to side kept the pests moving.

The children returned to look in many times. My mouth was dry and sticky. "*Wai, wai,*" I begged them, but they ignored the plea. Well blast them all! I could cook in this damn hovel and die from thirst for all they cared. Perhaps I was not such a great oddity but just one more of the goblins who came into the Strait now and then, one more to be dismembered and cast into the earth oven. What was my life; what was any life worth, to these people?

My two guards arrived and unhitched me and led me out to the privy, but it was far too late. My trousers were wet and smelled.

A boy of about six arrived and handed me a small basket and a halved gourd. I seized the gourd, nearly full of water, and gulped it down, not stopping until the contents were gone. The basket held an entire fish; and it was good, better than anything I had eaten in the last few weeks. I was sorry there was not more of it. "Is there more fish … *ika?* Would you have more of that? *Kai, kai?*" I asked the boy and shook the empty basket, but the child seized it and turned it over to let me know that was all there was and walked away.

Many eyes followed me for the remainder of the day while I wandered about inside the palings. It was a relief to bend arms and legs and walk about after all movement had been restricted at night.

The women sat and wove long flax leaves into baskets and mats or scraped the length of them to extract the silky fibers. The men simply sat and talked. At the far end of the enclosure, a half dozen children grasped ropes hitched to the top of a tall pole, swung around it singing songs, and let go, landing at a run.

Just before sundown I was taken back inside and bound once again. Children, mostly naked and all with wet or muddied feet, returned, peeked in at the doorway, and giggled. With my bindings on again their attention made me feel less human, more like a strange animal caged in a menagerie. What did those children think as they looked in at me? Did they consider me some monster fished from the sea to be sacrificed to appease some leering, ferocious god? They lost interest after several minutes and went off chattering to each other, their curiosity satisfied for the moment.

How long was I going to be kept bound to the framework in the house? Days? A week? What horrible things might they do to me? If meant to be a slave, they would not have bound me but put me to work the instant I arrived. If not to be a slave, what else might be my fate? Beheaded? … My body dismembered, wrapped in leaves, and lodged in the oven? A shiver ran through my entire body.

I rolled from side to side and again regretted my foolish choice to sail on when the signs of the weather were against it. It was going to be another night of short naps if I did not cease recalling the past few days. I had to put those events aside. How was I to escape other than by swimming to a ship in the bay, one I might not reach before I was killed? To steal a canoe and paddle father north where whale ships might call was not possible, for there were too many of these sharp-eyed people. Even free of my bindings and outside the enclosure, it would be a most hopeless attempt.

It was growing colder. I wished to draw the wadded blanket over me for the night, but even if I could roll far enough to reach it with my teeth, there was no way I could spread it.

The light in the room suddenly dimmed. I turned my head and saw the figure of a girl crouched in the small doorway, holding a rolled mat in her hands. Her face was in dark shadow, but her hair and shoulders were crested with light. For half a minute she knelt there, watching me. She wore the usual skirt of flax decorated with small bands of black. Finally she entered and sat beside me where I could see her face. Her jet eyes scanned me intently, almost fiercely. She had a thin line tattooed along the edge of her upper lip, and two wide, vertical lines an inch apart began from her lower lip and reached to the tip of her chin where they ended in hook shapes. Between those two were two shorter marks with less of a curve at their ends. Her head was haloed with black hair. I guessed her age to be about sixteen or seventeen.

I drew my face across my sleeve to wipe any dirt from it.

She placed the mat of woven flax leaves on the ground; then turned to me and slowly ran one finger down across my forehead and the length of my nose. Next she grasped my hair and rubbed it between fingers and thumb. I expected it was a novel thing for these people to see such a color of hair, for the sun had bleached much of it to a wheaten hue during the last year. The girl grabbed my beard and pulled my head slowly to the left and right to view each side of my face. Then she untied the mat and rolled it out, quickly snatching up a small object that had been inside. She clenched it in her right hand, and her other hand grasped my whiskers again. Her curiosity I saw was natural, but her next move shot panic through me. From the corner of my eye I saw her right hand flick a razor open. I wrenched my beard free and rolled as far away as possible. She got up, put one leg over my body, and saddled herself on my stomach to hold me in place. In rolling away from the girl, the bit of slack in the lines holding me fore and aft was taken up. With her weight pressing on me and with my hands and feet held by the taut bindings, I could only squirm. The girl gripped my beard once more with her left hand, and then, whispering a few Indian words into my ear, she twisted my head, pressing my right cheek against my shoulder. I craved to scream but froze with fear. None of my wiggling would dislodge her. I was good as dead! There was no one out there to call to for mercy, not one who cared that I was being murdered! They must all be outside waiting to hear the screams of my wretched end! She had been sent in to slash my throat, to bleed me, to slaughter me like a swine while I lay there bound and helpless. The keen blade gripped in her right hand was moving toward my head. I strained and twisted to shield my neck with my left shoulder, but her hold on my beard gave her good purchase to hold it exposed. Every muscle of my body stiffened; my heart hammered, nearly bursting my chest. That blade was about to slice into my exposed throat ... hot blood would gush over my body ... it was the moment of my death ... but out of the corner of my left eye I saw the bright, honed edge slow before it touched my skin.

Chapter Four

She drew the blade gently across my cheek, shaving my whiskers. I stopped struggling. Reprieved for the moment, I relaxed a bit, but I knew she might still slay me. It was a puzzle. Why was she removing my beard? Did they want a clean-shaven head to be smoked and hung as a prize in one of their houses? I felt the blade sting my skin, though my sweat had softened my whiskers and the girl worked with care. Each time it happened I winced, thinking she had changed her mind and was about to slash my throat. She wiped drops of blood from my face with her left hand and then gave it a light slap. She smiled, admiring her finished work, and yet a remnant of fear kept the blood pounding in my ears and my breathing quick and shallow. I stared up at her. Even with the tattoo on her chin she would be a fair lass in any man's country. Fair or not, any minute she might sever my head from my body with that thin blade. She leaned her smooth, brown face down until her dark eyes looked directly into mine. Our noses pressed together and her hair tickled my face. Then she sat up and allowed her mouth another smile. It had been only a few years since she was a child, and in my mind I begged she had not yet reached the age of guile. At least I wanted to believe in that artless look, one implying there was no wish to harm me. The warmth of her body straddling mine and the cast of her gaze gave me fragments of hope. Perhaps I was not to be murdered after all.

The girl then dismounted, spread the mat alongside me, and tugged at my shoulder to indicate I should roll onto it. I turned over and found it was better than lying directly on the earth. Ah. It meant there was some small concern for my comfort.

But why had she removed my beard ... was it to tattoo dark lines and swirls on a clean face ... to decorate their prize before it was cut from my body? It was a puzzle to me until I noticed her gathering up the shaven hair. When we called at

Rio de Janeiro, some of the crew said there were old black women there who would conjure curses or love spells if given enough silver and some fragment, a hair or nail, from the subject's body. By the look the girl then gave me, I didn't expect she intended the least injury.

As she was crouching at the door to leave, I asked, "The blanket, can you cover me?" I jerked my head toward the wad of fabric near the wall.

She showed no understanding of what I meant.

"The blanket," I repeated and raised my chin in its direction.

The girl glanced at me and then at the collection of things against the wall. She pointed to the looking glass and gave me a questioning look. I closed my eyes and shook my head. She was touching the lantern when I looked again.

"No, no, below that," I said, nodding to indicate something lower and keeping my eyes focused on the blanket. She followed my gaze and then understood what I wanted. "*Te parankiti*," the girl said and pulled the dirty, torn thing out. With unexpected care she spread it out and tucked it close around my body. Minutes before, the girl might have beheaded me, but now to the contrary she had covered me neatly. It was a great relief … for the moment.

Were my whiskers meant to make a love charm? Surely not that. She was a *wahine maoree*, and down in Foveaux's Strait and The Bluff we of the ships were those other beings. Yet women were sent to the ships after arrangements were made and goods were sent to the fathers or brothers. That was the expected exchange in ports far to the south, but I had arrived in the village dressed in dirty skins and without one thing they valued.

At the doorway just before she crawled out she turned and spoke a few words I had no hope of understanding.

Sleep was again short naps between spans of wakefulness when there was only the black interior of the house and the faint square of light from the doorway to look at and the calls of night a bird and the howl of a dog to hear. The blanket kept me warmer and lengthened my portions of sleep. Still it proved a weary a night. Any shift of the body was limited by the bindings, and a pull against them awakened me.

Clouds must have cleared during the night, for in the morning bright sunshine was visible through the doorway. I felt a mite better as the sun rose higher and the interior of the house began to warm. By rolling to one side and back again I worked the old blanket off when it was no longer needed. The ropes had chafed my wrists, and one ankle showed blood where the fetters had rubbed it raw.

Sounds outside continued the same throughout the morning. Children shouted and squealed and dogs added their whines at intervals. A pig or two grunted and snorted somewhere nearby. Later there came a tapping as if on wood that went on for a half minute, paused, and then resumed for another half minute. It continued like that for hours, but I could not guess what caused it.

It became hotter. I managed naps, but the little black flies continued to annoy and waken me. What little sleep I managed only left me feeling groggy and dull-witted, hardly making up for long hours awake at night.

My clothes were damp. Much water had sweated out of my body, leaving my tongue stuck to my teeth.

There was a slight rustle at the door. The lighted outline of the girl was there, crouched in the opening again, a sight I welcomed. "Wai," I croaked, "wai." She watched me for a few seconds and left. Minutes later she returned with a gourd of water and cradled my head in one hand while she held the gourd to my lips.

"*Wai, wai.* Ah yes, *wai,*" I gasped and drank every drop. "Thank you. Many thanks. Ah. I was about to die of thirst."

She said nothing, but there was a pleased smile on her face when I spoke my words. The girl turned about and slipped out the door on hands and knees.

In the late afternoon two men came in again to unhitch my ropes and take me out. It was an opportunity to gasp breaths of the cooler air outside and look around the palisade again.

Every man, woman, and child within the palisade instantly noticed my shaven face. With my beard gone it was a new attraction, and once more they clustered around and drew their fingers across my cheeks until my two guards shooed them off and led me away to the latrine.

Outside of the palisade, barely visible through the opening, two men with adzes were hewing on a canoe. That was the source of the constant tapping. It had been placed there after I had been tied off in my prison.

No ship's sail yet appeared on the horizon of the bay. At least none was visible through the slim gateway or the slits between the palings. I had hoped a vessel was anchored offshore in the portion of the bay screened from me, and if one were there and I freed myself, I might swim to it. Escape would have to be at night when only my head would show among the waves. Such might be the reason for them keeping me well-bound during the night. In daylight with so many people about, I could not slip away unnoticed. Even if I managed to do it by some hoax or diversion, the crowd there, once alarmed, could spread about and hunt me down in a few minutes.

My two guards gave me a meal, and in the early evening herded me into my prison and retied my wrists and ankles to the posts.

A few minutes after they left the girl crawled in, spread the blanket over my body, and sat eying me. She crawled out a few minutes later. What was the reason for her unexpected care? Was it just curiosity? Perhaps. If aboard a ship, any attention given me would be to divert my eyes while another savage made off with some gear or clothing, but I owned nothing but the ragged skins that barely covered my body, a dirty, smelly lot of no use to anyone. What they prized above all were muskets, tobacco, and tools; and they knew the men of the ships had a store of those wonderful things on board and treasures of them far away in Port Jackson. Yet I had not arrived with any muskets, hoop iron, tobacco, blankets, or naught else they valued. Perhaps she thought there was some magic I could perform. In their eyes the goblins had many kinds of magic. Perhaps she had seen how we put our talk as many little marks on thin white leaves and send them across the sea. Then by magic the marks could be made to speak the same words again. Perhaps she imagined I had some other clever art, but the one thing I could not do was break free. If mere plaits held me powerless, that alone should prove to her I had no magic. For certain I would not be bound and left alone if Old Scratch thought I had any such ability to escape. I gave up those thoughts and squirmed around on the mat, hoping to crush or at least annoy the dozens of fleas which, in addition to the flies, were biting.

Shortly after daylight there were many loud voices approaching outside, plus the howling of dogs somewhere out on the beach. The girl brought in a gourd of water but quickly left after I finished my drink. Children and women were again gathered at the door taking turns peering in; for some reason they had renewed interest in their goblin. The two men who always took me out to the privy pushed them aside, entered, and unhitched my "cables." That was a good name for them, I having been moored like the French Fleet in the Nile and all the while hoping it would not end in an equal disaster. It was early for me to be released from my bindings, so there was something strange in the wind. Once outside the house, I stroked my fingers alternately over each wrist made raw by the cords and the bites of the flies.

The sun had not cleared the mountains to the east, yet it promised a fine day. I looked about to see what was the cause of all the commotion, trusting they had not decided to make a sacrifice of me this morning. A circle of Indians watched me and were continually talking. My girl was peeping over the shoulders of those in the front rank with only her eyes and the upper half of her face showing amid the others. At least there was one out of the entire village who had some concern for me.

A few minutes later Old Scratch threaded his way into the palisade. He was carrying a musket and fingering the lock mechanism. Men followed at each side and pressed close to see the weapon. One even reached out to touch it, but Old Scratch snapped out a word and the man instantly drew his hand back.

Four men dressed in the white ducks and the dark blue jackets of sailors entered several yards behind the crowd of New Zealanders. I stared at their every detail as they approached. One of them was wearing a tarpaulin hat, two had on straws of the same shape, and another wore a very old tricorne, now a shabby black with a trace of gold edging. Of the four, three were white men and the forth, the one who wore the tricorne, was a New Zealander with long hair that reached to his shoulders. The Indians must have traded for the hat or filched it from one of the early visiting ships and treasured it since.

My heart thumped several heavy beats. They walked freely with no bonds on their wrists and came forward watching me, talking casually as they pleased. It was puzzling. The men's trousers were clean and unworn, and their jackets and blouses were in good repair. All four were hale and well fed. One of the men who wore a short beard was smoking a new clay pipe. Where had they come from? What was to happen? Those four men in the familiar sailor's dress did not look to be prisoners as they came toward me. They might have heard some wild man had been captured and came from their ship to see if such a rumor were true. I waited fixed to the spot as they neared. The man in the lead stood a head taller than the others, and he was not only taller but also a thick-shouldered, powerful man. A smile spread across his broad, freshly shaven face. He came up to me and held out a big, callused hand.

"D'ye speaks English?" he asked in a deep, gravelly voice.

The other three men gathered closely around eying me and taking note of my rude suit of worn, dirty, skins.

I took the hand offered and stuttered, "Ye … yes. Yes."

"So! I'm Monk Monkhouse. I heads the Two Brothers," he announced and turned to introduce his companions. "This here fellow with the thrummy chin is Knobby John Shea. He steers." He pointed to another man and continued, "And there's little Peter Peck, only nine and a half stone but pulls a good after-oar. This Indian here, *Ruru*, is our mid-ship oar. He's got a long handle that means he's one who fights whales; but we just call him *Ruru*. That's a kind of a night bird around here."

Ruru's upper lids barely touched the colored portion of his eyes. The wide-open look gave him the appearance of someone pleasantly surprised or one curious of everything he saw. The ancient bit of finery, the tricorne, sitting atop his abundant hair gave him a comical look. With a studied motion he swept the tricorne off his head and gave me a short bow. With no hat I could not respond, only nod and check an urge to smile.

"Our tub oarsman is Bryan," the big man added. "When we go out, you can see him down there watching our boat."

I fitted together all I was seeing and hearing, and blurted out, "Tub oarsmen! You're whalers!"

"Aye, and God damned good ones," little Peck boasted. "The Two Brothers is the best boat in the Strait. Took more whales than three boats from a ship that was whaling over in Cloudy Bay last season."

"Your ship is here, close by?"

"Hah! We have no ship," Monk replied. "We whale from shore, and all on our own account. Every shilling we make goes in our pockets."

"Only a boat! You have only a boat? Is there no whale ship about?"

"None will call before May. The season here is May to about the end of September. We won't see more than two or three ships even then. So!" Then Monk asked, "Now who you be?"

I stared at the men. They were a strange lot from little Peter Peck to the great bulk of the headsman. They were all clean-shaven except for Knobby, who sported the fringe of whiskers on the edge of his lower jaw. That man drew on his pipe and waited for my answer to Monk's question. *Ruru's* stare prompted me to give an account of myself.

"Oh … Thomas … I'm Thomas Wightman. I belong to Stonington, close by New London."

"Ah, do you now," Monkhouse replied. "Now Peck here's a Yankee from New York. You two can have a gam on the way back. These people say you were found over on the west coast. What brought you to be there?"

"I was skinning seals and boiling sea elephants."

Monk shook his big head and said, "Not many seals left about that coast now. A few stray old wigs perhaps. We hear the breed has been about done for on that coast."

"No, no, we were on islands far to the south. We looked in at all the rookeries and then found an island not discovered before. It was covered with seals and we filled our ship. We were making for Canton when we raised another island and struck upon a rock there. Only four of us got ashore. We had not a rag between us and made our clothes from skins." I held out my arm to show them the skin sleeve.

"That was near the coast over there?" Knobby asked.

"No, rising two hundred mile or so out," I said, pointing to what I thought was due west or about.

Knobby looked in that direction and murmured, "Never heard tell of any island 'twixt here and Van Diemen's."

"Well, it's not there anymore, or at least not much of it. It burst apart, exploded. Went up all in smoke and ashes and hot rocks. I scarce got away."

"Arrah now. So that was what we saw," Knobby said. "We wondered what made such a dark cloud here for days."

Monk asked, "These people say you came onto the coast over there in a canoe?"

"Aye, one like a proa, a catamaran. I burned out a log for the hull and fixed booms and a spar to it. I'm the only one left after a year. Now what's to happen to me? I fear these Indians mean to kill me."

Monkhouse threw his head back and broke out in guffaws, "HA, HA, HA, have no more fear, lad. HA, HA, HA. We bought you. There, you see the nob there with the two knots on his head, he wanted five shooting sticks and fifty pounds of dust for you, but he agreed to let you go for one stick and five pounds of the dust because he's a relative of mine by my wife *Karee*."

"Shooting sticks ... dust? What are those? I asked.

"Muskets and powder," Knobby explained. "We call them such between us so they won't know what we're talking about.

"I call that one Old Scratch," I said.

Knobby nodded and agreed, "Well he does look like he could be a sort of devil with those two bunches of hair and combs on his head. Aye, he sometimes thinks in a devil's way. So we call him Ol' Harry, Clootie, or Old Nick ourselves, but Ol' Scratch sounds as good ... we'll call him that now; it's all the same. He'll be out settlin' scores with someone next month. Even had we not ransomed you, he would have kept you for a *mokai* and took you in tow around for all the other Indians to gape at. That sandy pate of yours fascinates them."

"A *mokai?*" I asked.

Knobby held his pipe by the bowl and took a puff from it and then replied, "Oh, it's something like being a dog with an extra leg or a curious, odd sort of a bird. You get fed but you can't leave. No, for sure he'd never let you get away."

Monk added, "That one there with the old cut on his head brought you over from Murderer's Bay to trade you to Scratch for something. Or maybe he gave you for a gift. He is a big nob on the West Coast there about Rocks Point."

"Yes, the one with the scar. A nob?" I asked.

"Aye, a chief. One of the *arikis*."

"Where are we? Is this Cook's Strait here?" I asked.

"No, this right here is Blind Bay. The Strait's yonder, farther out there." He pointed northeast, and swept his arm to due east and explained, "Over there. Runs north and south. Now, Queen Charlotte, where Cap'n Cook was, is over beyond those mountains you see there. To make it back to our place we have to sail up north along this side of the bay. Then it's up between the islands into Admiralty Bay, then halfway out to Cape Stephens. We take our fish between there and north of Point Jackson."

I pointed to my bloodied ankles and held out my wrists. "They kept me tied in one of the houses hand and foot for days and let the flies feed on me. A girl came in one day with a razor. I thought she was going to take my head off with it, but she just shaved my beard."

"So!" Monk snapped. "Scratch wanted to keep you for ransom for sure. Surely didn't want you gittin' away. Now he's got the musket and dust we give for you, he's most happy."

Women and children had been crowding closer, chattering as we were talking.

Ruru turned from one to the other, trying to listen to them all. A grin was constantly on his face as they asked him questions. The demand for answers appeared to give him an importance he enjoyed.

Ruru looked at me. "*Kuri*, you meka froma *kuri* ?" he inquired, pointing to my skin clothes and then to one of the dogs.

"No," I replied with a shake of the head.

"Dena, *kake?*" he asked, indicating something swimming with a wiggling hand.

Ruru took my blank expression as a no.

"Ah, *manu?*" he ventured. Then pointing to the sky, aped the flapping of wings with both hands.

I could only shrug my shoulders at the question, being unable to tell him what sort of animal it was if I didn't know myself. "It looks like a small bear but has the fur of a hare and a pouch of an opossum. There were some on our island," I explained.

Ruru was totally baffled by such a long description and shook his head.

Peck chuckled, "No animal like that about here. Never heard of such a creature on this island. Even if there was one, he might not have seen it."

"Well, not a dog, but something like a dog. So then *kuri*." I said to *Ruru*. Happy to get an answer he could at last understand, he turned to the crowd and pronounced, "*Kuri, kuri.*"

Some of the people looked quizzically at him and then at me, unsure that they had gotten the proper answer.

One of Scratch's men crowded forward and spoke to *Ruru*. *Ruru* held his left hand up for the attention of the whalers. He pointed to me, then to the girl now standing in the front row and said, smiling, "*Wahine* wanta man wita *uru*,...,*one-tea*. The whalers all burst out howling. Monk did not laugh, but looked at the girl, nodded, and slyly smiled.

The laughter ebbed. Peck punched my shoulder with his fist and chuckled, "You got someone here that fancies you. Likes your sandy hair. What d'ye say lads? Tom might git her for two grunters and couple hundred weight o' spuds."

Monk kept his even smile and did not join the other whalers in a round of chuckling.

Peck gave me a knowing wink and crowed, "Hoo, hoo, you might see more o' her if you stay in the Strait for the season. That nob'l be lookin' for more dust and another shooting stick. For sure Monk could make a good bargain for that titter."

Their laughs died away and I asked, "A titter?"

"It's not what you're thinking, lad, it's not her dairy," Peck said. "It's our name for them girls by the way they laugh. You know, a titter, hee, hee, hee, like that."

"She was the one who scraped off my beard. Ach, it's been a plaguey bad cruise for me and I want to get home. I mean to sign on a whaler when they arrive here."

"That won't be till later after the season starts," Peck said. "But you'll do better if you come oiling with us. If it's a ship near full, they'll not want anyone. On a clean ship or one with some months to go, the captain will expect you're in a bad way out here and will offer you a long lay, one no better than a steward's. Then you'll have to buy your slops and tobacco from them. They'll cheat you fore and aft and athwart the beam like always. So much for insurance and the medicine chest. So much for leakage and interest. When you get back to Nantucket or Boston and they settle up, you'll still owe them money. You'll never work off a dead horse. No, no, be your own man, fish with us in the Two Brothers. No salt meat and biscuit and the scurvy for us here on the coast. We eat spuds and greens and grunters. We make our hams and bacon. Here you can have your titter to cook, wash, keep your house neat, and be cozy with you at night."

Monk turned to me and said, "We must make it up through the Gut and into the next bay before the tide turns. Then another two hours if the wind is right and we'll be home before dark. We're out there on the Strait. Our station, try kettles, sheers, boat ways, and all are in a cove."

"And our *wahines* and squeakers and whares," Knobby John added.

"Whares? Squeakers?" I asked.

Knobby pointed to each of the buildings in turn and explained, "Out here that's a *whare* … that's a *whare* … and that's a *whare*. It's their name for a house."

"Yes, I recall now," I said, remembering the word used at The Bluff. Then I asked, "Squeakers?"

"The babies, the kids. We don't live like monks out there," Peck replied with roguish smile and slapped me on the shoulder.

"So! Come boys," Monk ordered. "It's a long pull up the coast if the wind dies or draws ahead." He led us out through the narrow gate with all the men, women, and children following in a parade to the beach. I looked back twice over my shoulder, wondering if I were truly free or if they were going to rush forward and take me prisoner again.

A whaleboat was pulled inshore with its mast stepped but with its sail lowered. A man of about fifty years of age sat on its gunwale, serving as a sentry. On our approach he struggled to his feet and hobbled out of the water to meet us. His face was engraved with dark lines and whorls like a New Zealander, but he was dressed as the other whalers in white ducks and a blue-black monkey jacket. His hair, showing a bit beneath the brim of his straw hat, was gray. The tattooed face didn't fit with his pale blue eyes. It was a strange sight; for sure he was not one of the Indians.

"Ah, Bry, this here is Thomas. D'ye thinks he was worth the musket and the powder?" Monkhouse asked.

The man's marked face broke into a smile and he replied, "Oh, surely. Tip us your daddle." He put forward his right hand. The man's grip was like Monk's: rough and almost crushing. "Thomas is it, and where do you belong to?"

"Stonington," I answered.

"And where that be?"

"In America. Between Boston and New York."

"Ah, so 'tis. They calls me Breaker Bryan here. I come from Yorkshire and other places not so pleasant. We're most glad we could ransom you and you're most welcome to our mob."

"Come along. Get ready to sail," Monk ordered. "We must get through the Gut before the turn of the tide or we'll not reach the station 'fore dark."

The whaleboat's hull was buttercup yellow except for the first three feet of the bow, which was painted light blue. Two stars were painted on the blue portion, one of them above and slightly to the side of the other, and from their angle off plumb I guessed they were meant to be the Gemini. A neat, narrow band of the same blue extended the length of the gunwale. The boat's name, Two Brothers, was in neat, black lettering on its stern. All the harpoons had been taken out, but two killing lances were still stowed. A water breaker and a tapered provision cask were aft under the short decking. There was no tub of whale line and in its place were a few wool blankets.

"Thomas, you pull the bow oar there, two-side," the headsman ordered. "I expect you have rowed a whaleboat, you being a sealer."

"Oh, many a mile, many a mile, with landings every day," I said, waded out, and took my seat on the thwart. We set off rowing. Monk stood in the stern with the handle of the long steering oar gripped in one hand and, with the other, waved to those on the beach. At a quarter mile from the shore the wind freshened and he called out, "All apeak." We levered our oar blades out of the water and slipped the handles into their cleats.

"Hoist sail," the headsman ordered. It filled out in a good breeze. "No need to fag it all the way back. With this wind while we can make six or seven knots."

Monk kept the boat a quarter-mile offing from the coast.

Tufts of bright white clouds edged across the blue sky, promising a pleasant sail along a shore indented with little coves. In some of them the heavy growth of trees and bush nearly touched the sea. In other places there were narrow strips of sand beach.

Peck, sitting aft, turned and asked me, "You were driven from your island? You had to leave?"

"It was leave or else be crushed or burned to death by the volcano."

"And the others?"

"All killed in one way or the other."

"Ah, but you made it here," Knobby said.

"By much luck and labor," I replied.

"Well, Tom," Knobby added, "you made it here dressed in your skins. Ha! That's a rum thing. Tom in his skins! Tom arrives here in his skins. Ha, Ha, Ha. Is that his name now, Tom Skins?" Knobby asked the others, "What do you say lads? He will be our Tom Skins?"

Peck held out an arm toward me with his palm spread wide and announced, "Aye, from this hour forth you will be Tom Skins."

"Wait now. Wait. Wait. Wait. We must do it all proper," Knobby corrected him and reached over the side and dipped his right hand into the sea. He leaned over his thwart to me and drew a wet cross on my forehead with his forefinger. "In the name of Monk's father, my son, and Bry's crazy ghost I baptize thee ... Tom Skins!" The other men laughed at the fit of my new title.

At midday Monk ordered, "Grub, Peter."

Peck pulled the cask from under the aft decking and worked the lid off. He reached over the thwarts, passing out boiled potatoes and meat still on the bone to us.

I seized my piece of the meat from Peck and tore at it with my teeth. Ah! Was meat ever so good, so tasty, so satisfying? When I looked up, the others were holding their food in their hands and staring at me.

"Hungry, lad?" Monk inquired with a smile.

"For sure. Those Indians stinted my food."

"Only Lenten fare for you, eh?" Knobby asked.

"Aye, and while sailing to the coast here I lost my food when a wave overset my canoe. I was so weak I doubted I'd live through the surf. When I got ashore, I found only mussels and bird chicks to eat."

Monk nodded and said, "Well, you're with us now, lad, and safe. Eat all you please. That there's good pig meat. We raise it aplenty at our station."

I munched the potatoes and alternately gnawed the meat from a bone. After finishing one mouthful, I said, "How many nights I dreamed of a feast like this. I could eat until I burst."

"Oh don't do that, Tom Skins," Knobby advised, "we need a good hand. We're short one for the next season and have no men at all for the other boat, only Bry's two boys to row about after us."

"They're good lads," Bryan boasted. "They will grow to the business in a few years. And their mother's a fine woman. I could ask for no better. I'd not be alive if it was not for her."

"There, Bry, tell Tom Skins how you came to be here," Peck urged. "It's a good yarn."

Bryan shook his head in refusal.

"Come now," Knobby insisted, "why should Tom Skins care that you're a transport?"

Byran murmured a bit and finally spoke, "Well, you'll soon learn it all, Tom. It's no secret here that I'm a lag, but now don't think I lived on the cross. And I was never a breaker. No, I did not choose my company well. Someone did me a mischief when they swore they saw me drinking with some frame-breakers. I didn't know they were such. I was tried with the others, taken to the hulks, and then sent Bayside for seven. I was in Van Diemen's. Food was filched there. Being anywhere near where the food was taken meant I was surely guilty. So I was flogged and ironed. That wasn't enough for them but they must flog me again lest I even think of stealing more.

"Once I got my ticket of leave, another lag and me slipped aboard a whaler, the *Peter and Paul*. They were glad enough to discover us on it and give us the wink, they having lost some men by desertion. We fished off Cape Saunders and Solander's for some weeks and then came up from there to the far side of the Strait.

"*Eeka-na-Mowee* they call the island on that side. Sometimes you can see the great mountain on it. The captain sent us ashore for wood and no sooner had we set about gathering it, but they rowed off and left us. We were lags and no longer worth feeding after the ship was filled. We were left there on that cannibal shore, and all our labor on board the ship was lost to the profit of the owners.

"What could we do? In a day's time the Indians took us. My mate was marched off somewheres and I never saw him more. They stripped me of my clothes and asked about everything in my pockets. Now, I had an iron pin out of a small, single block and they pointed to it and to an old musket they had. I couldn't understand their blather, but I figured out what they wanted. Their musket wouldn't fire and they thought that pin was a part of a gun. Well, I learned a trick or two in my day. I put the pin between the thumb and finger of my left hand just so. Now, if I swept my right hand over and grabbed at it like this, you'd swear 'twas in that hand, but it would be in my left because I'd dropped it there while you was watching my right hand. Ho! I was magic then! Ho! I had no more fear of them killing me. I cleaned their old musket, picked out the touch hole, and reset the flint so it would make good sparks. I had *mana* then. Yes, I had respect, power. Oh, I was a fine fellow after that.

"But things, places were *tapu*, forbidden to be handled or used. I had to be careful what I touched and where I stepped. I couldn't walk near a potato patch; sit where I liked, or drink water from a certain part of the stream. *Tapu* here, *tapu* there. Oh, it was worrisome. It near drove me crazy until a woman there called *Kotuku* began watching over me. She was a relation of a chief, a *rangatira*, and kept me out of trouble, warning me not to do the things that were *tapu*. After two months, I asked for *Kotuku*, and they made her over to me for my wife. I never thought I'd find the like of such a woman anywhere.

"Then they expected I could conjure up some cures to relieve their fevers and such. I knew naught about herbs and simples. To bide my time I merely picked some leaves from here and there and put them in water and made a cold tea. I waved my hands over it and mumbled some foolish talk like 'Ring around the Rosy' or 'Ride a-cock horse to Banbury Cross' and gave it to the sick to drink. Well, some got better and some not. If one died, I blamed it on a bad spirit, or some *tapu* I said they confessed to me they had broken. They always remembered the ones that lived and forgot the ones that died. I became a wizard not because of what I did but for what they thought I did. Then they started this tattooing, the *moko* on my face. I saw it was all part of the game of being a wizard and such. After I had been there about four, five years, *Kotuku* heard it that a *tohunga*, he's a seer or a preacher-like fellow, was spreading it about that I could do *mataku*. Now, that's the black arts, cursing and the evil eye. If anything was to happen to the nobs, if they got to ailing or lost a fight, he'd say that I had caused it." Then Bryan put his right forefinger to the side of his throat and drew it across slowly. "I knew trouble was afoot and getting closer, so I bolted one night with my *Kotuku* and her boys for the Strait. They were close on us when we reached the coast, and I thought for sure that I'd be taken. Then I remembered the wreck of a little schooner near where we were. I found it and with wood from her hull I built a big fire. They never burn wood that's been part of a canoe or *whare*. Oh, that's very *tapu*. Well, the schooner had been coppered and the flames went up all bright green and blue. Ha! They never saw that before. I stood in front of it and sang and waved my arms. I could see them hang an arse in the bushes. No one came close after that. They were all afraid I'd maybe point a finger, put a spell on them to make them lame or ill or even die. We came across the Strait in a canoe one night that promised fair but got terrible windy as we neared this side. Oh, I feared sinking and we was bailing all the while."

Peck gave his head a shake and said, "That's always a good one, Bry. I like to hear how you fooled 'em all. I'll lay they're still afraid of you."

Knobby turned around, pointed ahead, and explained, "Tom Skins, we go between that island there, *Rangitoto*, and the one on the other side. That's Admiralty Bay beyond. Then we go out of it and we're in the Strait. We just turn the point and we're home. Oh, you'll like it there, Tom Skins."

The others nodded and muttered their firm approval.

Knobby continued, "Peck and me heard about Monk being out there three years ago. We were in *The Bruce* of Hobart. It was a cursed ship and we had nothing but Jonah's luck on our cruise. We saw there was much work to do but no money to be made by it. We owed more than we would ever earn, so we took this boat here we're in and came across to join with him."

After midday we entered a long, narrow passage between steep hills. A small portion of the next bay was visible through it, plus a few islands, little shapes slightly darker than the horizon.

The land closing in on each side brought the wind ahead.

"Down sail," Monk ordered and we went back to pulling.

Our oar blades dipped into the sea, swept aft swirling its surface, and lifted, out flashing in the sunlight on their return for the next stroke. The vessel, trailing a slim wake, glided on the water. On the nearer shore wavelets washed up and back on narrow strips of unmarked, yellow sand.

Everything appeared sunnier and brighter than out on the other coast where I had landed. The growth on the hillsides was a lighter, friendlier green. Was it because of a brighter sun, or was it because the prospects of my life were now far better? I was among good mates; no longer fearful of being slain in the next hour or day. Whale ships will arrive in a few months and I will sign on one and be bound for some port in America. I felt almost secure as if I were on soundings off home. What a change there was in my condition since I had awakened. All was going well. May it keep so.

The hills were closing in.

"It's the Gut boys," the headsman called out.

Chapter Five

I leaned forward for my next stroke and turned to see we were approaching the narrowest point, only two cable lengths from shore to shore, a good enough passage except for rocks strewn like monstrous teeth protruding a foot or two above the water. Oddly the sea on our side was higher than that beyond the rocks, and the water poured through, swirling in ominous eddies. Off to our larboard it was all confused waves and gyres that might draw a man down into the depths. A boat caught in that portion of the pass would be spun about, smashed, or capsized. Monk steered close to the starboard bank where there was an opening fifty or sixty fathoms clear of danger.

"Give way, lads, give way," Monk shouted, working the steering oar. "Give way, lads, give way. Can't wait for slack water."

The Two Brothers was caught in a flow rushing like a millrace into the next bay; the current and the pull of our oars shot us past wooded slopes. In seconds we were through. The headsman pulled on his oar to bring the boat back on course after it turned in an eddy.

"What causes that?" I asked.

"Tide. It comes through from Blind Bay back there to this one, Admiralty Bay, and then goes back the other way at the turning. You can't make it through against that flow. At slack water it's quiet for a while, but not for long."

"I wouldn't want to take even a small sloop through there."

"Ha, no chance for one a'tall unless you're with the tide and the wind is steady aft. They were never to be depended on the times I've been through here.

"There, Tom Skins," Monk said, pointing to the steep, northwest shore blocking a quarter of the sky. "That there island is about twenty mile long all the way out to Cape Stephens." He steered the Two Brothers away from it, and when out of the lee of its mountains, the sail filled and drove the boat northeast and into a larger expanse of water for about two hours.

"There, Tom Skins," Knobby said, "that there's Cook's Strait. You can see across to the other side. That's *Eeka-na-Mowee*. We're nearly home."

The other shore of the Strait was only a dark blue line of mountains to the east.

Monk pulled his oar, turning the boat around in that direction. For a mile or two the wind held on the quarter. I shifted on my thwart and looked forward. We were nearing a point of land on our starboard and beyond it there was another headland with a tall pole set up on it. The Two Brothers veered, entering between the two heads, allowing a full view of a cove.

Patches of trees had been cleared away from the flatter ground and four small houses had been built along the shore. Lines were strung between some remaining trees and draped with drying wash. The walls of another house, not yet roofed, were north of the others near the bank of a little stream that emptied into the cove. Between two of the houses a heavy post had been set upright in the earth and a platform built on its upper end about ten feet above the ground. Something was stored on it and showed as a hump under a tarpaulin cover. A much larger house, older and of far sturdier build, was sited farther from the cove and higher up on a slope of a hill.

Beyond the last house to the south, a field had been recently cleared of bushes and trees; and vagrant columns of white and gray smoke rose from piles of cuttings which had not dried sufficiently to burn well. A start had already been made to fence it. The cove with its houses and garden plots was a snug, comfortable retreat.

North of the unfinished house on the shoreline, tall spars had been set up on their ends in the water and their tops brought together and lashed tightly to form a set of sheers. A platform was attached from one leg to the other to make a stage like those on whale ships where men stood to cut the blubber from the whale.

Knobby saw me studying the shore ahead and said, "Aye, that's where we peel our fish with those sheers and a windlass we made ourselves."

The water of the cove, tinted green inshore and shading to blue farther out, was touched by the breeze and reflected the sheers, clouds, houses, and hillside as rippling patches of various colors.

To the left of the sheers were two try kettles fitted into rude rock masonry. A good stone's throw beyond the kettles, lines of palings had been driven into the earth, forming a fence around a square about twenty yards on a side. A soft mass within it was a foot higher than the palings. A few cask heads showed through gaps in the fence, and it was my guess they were full of oil and kept damp under a mat of grass or rockweed to prevent leakage. At the right side of the sheers were two boat ways, one with a boat on it and one empty. A canoe was also drawn up on the beach.

Six New Zealand women in loose-fitting dresses were walking down a path toward the shore. All except one carried a baby or led a naked little toddler.

The Two Brothers sailed into the lee of the western point, and losing some of the wind slowed almost to a stop. "Down oars. Head all," the headsman ordered. Each oar blade bit into the water in unison. The stem of the boat led a wide chevron across the surface of the cove, and in a few minutes the Two Brothers was closing with the beach. At ten yards from the shore, Monk called out, "Heave up," leaving the vessel to glide the remainder of the way to the beach. The bow touched. We unshipped our oars and hopped out to wade ashore.

Two Indian boys, one of about twelve and one about thirteen, dressed in outsized trousers and button-less shirts, the castoff dress of some tar, pulled the boat toward the end of the empty ways. Each of the ways had been cleverly built with rollers in its bottom to carry the keel of the whaleboat and posts driven into the beach along each side to guide the hull and keep it upright.

It was apparently a well-set routine with the boys to handle the Two Brothers, and they chattered away as they unstepped the mast and rolled the sail around it. With a tackle the two easily drew the boat from the water.

Between each task performed, they talked and eyed me; I guessed they were making comments about my strange clothes and long hair.

To protect the boat from the sun and rain, the boys drew a cover of painted canvas over it. Its identical mate, named the Two Sisters, on the other ways was under the same kind of awning. Its bow was also painted blue and had two stars painted on it, but they leaned at an angle opposite those on the Two Brothers.

At one side of the sheers there was a heavy spar mounted across short posts sunk into the earth

"Ah, this is your windlass?" I asked Knobby.

"Aye," he replied, "we take the fall from a treble block up there at the head, reeve it through the leading block at the bottom of that leg, and then bring it out to here."

"And the windlass can hoist the blubber?"

"With ease," Knobby explained. "Push a strap from the block through the blubber and toggle it and the fish rolls over and over as we hoist and cut. We can lift near a ton at a time with four men on the bars. But we don't have enough hands and our wives and the boys have to turn it while we cut in. Sometimes we hire some of the Indians when they're about."

The sand of the beach behind the sheers was soaked with old oil, and it had packed well, making it a fair surface to work on. Several sections of a whale's spine were sitting about. My nose picked up the rank odor of the place, though I could see that there had been no blubber cut and rendered recently.

"Ahoy, there," Monk called and motioned for me to come and meet the women who had now arrived. I approached and Monk announced to the women, "This here is Tom Skins. You always know he's ahead of you by the old skins covering his arse. Yessir."

Bryan was holding his arm around a woman about his own age. Her lips were outlined, and her chin was tattooed with curled lines similar to those on the girl at Blind Bay. "Tom, this is my wife *Kotuku*," Bryan said. Her calm, poised face eased into a smile; and then she put a hand on each of my shoulders, drew me close, and pressed her nose to mine. "Those are her two lads, *Wehe* and *Tokee*," Bryan explained, pointing to the boys knotting the last of the ties that held the cover on the Two Brothers. He turned to another woman standing next to *Kotuku*. "And this is Amelia, Peter Peck's wife," Bryan said, presenting her to me. She was much younger than the others, hardly more than a girl, yet had a baby in her arms. She gave my dirty hide garments an uneasy, doubting look; but leaned close to greet me in the same manner as *Kotuku*.

Ruru then brought his wife forward, attired like all the women in a loose dress that reached below mid shin. She had a naked child by the hand and held another one, a mere baby, against her breast with her other arm. "*Aihe*," *Ruru* announced. I was prepared this time and touched my nose to hers. The movement woke the baby and it began to cry, but *Aihe* nuzzled it and rocked it in her arms.

"This is my Sarah," Knobby explained, and led her a few steps forward. She was the most substantial one of the all the women, with a girth half again that of her husband, and sported a double chin. "She can't speak her name proper," Knobby explained, "so we call her Harah because that's the way she says it."

Like *Aihe*, Sarah held a baby in her arms and had a toddler by the hand. She leaned her head forward for the greeting.

"Hello, Harah," I said.

The women were certainly a fruitful lot, each carrying a baby, leading a child, or doing both. Some of the children were quite fair and had light brown hair. There was a tap on my shoulder and I turned to see Monk standing between two women. "And these are my wives," he said with a big smile. Both were a head and a half shorter than he was and each had a toddler by the hand. He put an arm around the one on his right. "This is *Karee*," he said. Then he wrapped his left arm around the other and added, "And this is *Maree*." He squeezed their smiling faces to his big chest. "Ha! Ha! Ha!" he bellowed. "I'm a big man and I need a lot of wifin'. You need some of that too, lad, you being too long without quim." Monk released *Karee* and *Maree* and sent them forward to greet me.

"Well, Tom Skins, we go up to my place now," the headsman said. "We will get some new togs put on your back. You look like a sheared sheep and a damned dirty, greasy one at that."

He started up a path leading the women and men in a single file past the house that was half built. Knobby pulled me aside to allow the others to pass and then explained, "This will be our new *whare* for storing our staves, gear, and the bone when we have it. All that lumber is up in our places now. With our squeakers born these last years we need more room. Now, we keep our oil back on the other side of the try works; there where you see those barrels under that mat of *raupo*. We sold all but a mite of our oil and bone for good prices at the end of the season."

A few yards farther on we hopped across a small stream on rocks placed a long stride apart, then came to a garden tightly fenced all around with saplings driven into the earth and their top ends bound with split flax leaves to a horizontal rail. Inside the enclosure there were turnips, onions, and greens growing lushly. Knobby stopped and boasted, "There, you see how we live here. We also got pigs on the point and they root the fern out there on the other side of that fence. We corn or smoke their flesh. There's fish aplenty in the cove and out between the islands at times, and we hang some in Monk's chimney with the pig meat. You'll not see any like it if you fag it on a ship. It's always tack and salt horse on them with a few potatoes, maybe rice. Aye, naught but slavery on a whaler. That's why Peck and me deserted and came over to help Monk build this place. Stay and go whale fishing with us, Tom. You could have no better life anywhere."

I shook my head as we started up the path and said, "I have a need to go home. I have been away too long."

"Oh, you might go home," Knobby said, following a pace after me, "but I'd lay half my year's share you'll be back. There's a feelin' you get being out here, Tom, like nowhere else in the world. You're working only for yourself. No man gittin' rich from all your labor like a leech and then cheatin' you at every turn. You have your own house, woman, and squeakers. Plenty o' tobacco and a damn good booze-up now and then to make life worth the effort. Yes, sir."

I stopped by the post that held the platform on its top and pointed up at it.

"A *whata*," Knobby explained. "You've seen one before over in Blind Bay, but with a little house on top."

"Yes, but what are they for?"

"Our dry beans, peas, pumpkins, and such is kept up there, Tom. Rats can't git to them." He pointed to a notched spar lying on the ground and explained, "We lean that up there, take our grub up or bring it down, and then take the log away. Rats might get up the post, but they can't hang on the underside of that deck and reach its edge. We keep our spuds and turnips in a hole over there dug back into the bank."

Farther on we reached another fenced garden which had peas, cabbages and more onions growing in it.

"Yes, damned rats," Knobby swore and leaned over to inspect the vegetables. "Always rats. That's why we need to have all the cats around and make snares."

"I don't see any marks of the rats," I said. "Your snares and cats must serve well."

"They do mostly. But there are times when there's rats about. We hope to get some Indian corn to raise here. It keeps well; and if we could buy a small mill the women could make a sort of johnnycake. I'd like that."

A half-enclosed structure like a summer house was a few yards farther up the trail from the garden. Firewood was stacked neatly under the eaves of the thatch, forming two low walls facing each other. On a third side a fireplace had been built of laid-up stones mortared with clay. Knobby nodded toward it and mumbled, "Aye, the cookhouse there."

Kotuku and *Maree* were under its roof, and both looked up from their work and smiled at us as we passed on our way up the slope.

Monk had led everyone else up to the building on the slope. It was solidly built of timbers with nogging between them that looked to be clay daub applied over wattled sticks and dried hard. The wedge of space between the level of the floor and the angle of the hill was closed off all around in the same fashion. The roof and side walls at the opposite end from the hill extended over half of a porch deck. To reach the porch level there was a notched log with one end resting on the earth and the top end leaning against the edge of the deck. It was much like the one lying by the *whata* but larger in girth, allowing wider steps to be cut into its upper side. There was no rail or line provided for the hand to grip at either side, thus making the stepped log a precarious way to get up. Only one person at a time could ascend or descend. It would have been better to clear the path farther up the slope to the point where the floor of the house met the hill and put a doorway there or even go to the back where the opposite gable faced the slope. The only way to reach the porch deck and the house was by the stepped log. I made a wobbly climb up and saw the gable of the building had barge boards fitted to it as on the Indian houses. It was not the two boards' first use for rust stains, generous coats of paint, and holes drilled into their wood were evidence both pieces had been strakes on the side of a ship and had likely washed ashore from a wreck.

A stout wooden bracket was nailed to the post at the side of the door above head height, and from it hung a ship's bell with a fancy, braided lanyard tied to its clapper. Someone had polished its bronze body, and even the clapper had a high shine.

Below the bell an old, grizzled hound was asleep next to the wall. The animal, awakened by voices, looked up but without the cocked head and quizzical interest of a young dog. He rose to his feet with painful effort and wandered over to sniff my legs. The hound's ears were limp and ragged, and several old battle scars decorated his head. I reached down and patted the creature and he closed his eyes in enjoyment of the attention.

"That's Bonaparte, Boney we call him," Knobby remarked. "Damned, worthless beast. He used to chase pigs, but he's too old to do much now but eat and get under your feet. He can get up the steps, but can't get down by himself and stays up here most of the time. We have to kick his shit over the side."

"Tom Skins! Knobby!" Monk shouted from the inside. "Come in here! Bring your arses to anchor."

The interior of the building was a long, undivided room. On the right side, attached to the south wall, were two tiers of three bunks. Each bunk, built like those on board a ship, had its curtain which could be drawn along a cord. Casks and kegs were lined along the opposite wall; and stacked neatly atop them were boxes, chests, rolls of cloth, new blankets, and clean, folded laundry. Above those stored items was an opening cut into the wall. Frames covered with old, patched sailcloth were fitted in grooves at the right and left and could be slid in to close the opening. A table nine or ten feet in length, possibly fitted together from the same source of lumber as the barge boards, occupied the center of the room. One third of the end wall backed up to the hill was filled with a large fireplace constructed of layers of flat stones and clay. The chimney above it was of clay plastered over a wooden framework.

The remains of a fire glowed under a goashore placed just inside the opening. Some additional cooking was being done there; and *Kotuku's* boy, *Wehe*, was kneeling, feeding small wood to the coals to encourage larger flames.

Luscious aromas drifted from the steaming kettle and ignited my hunger. In just moments I would have a meal, a great meal, an unmatchable one with tastes I had not known in three years.

Kotuku, *Tokee*, and *Maree* carried in another goashore and a smaller kettle from the cookhouse. Sarah and *Aihe*, with their babies saddled on a hip and held with one hand, paced back and forth, setting the table with pewter plates and steaming bowls of food.

Lined along each side of the table were three sections of a whale's backbone serving for seats. Monk settled his big body onto one of the bones and motioned for me to take another on the opposite side. Knobby sat on my right. "Here, have some pig meat and fish," he said and piled big servings of them on my plate. Peck on my left, not to be outdone, filled the rest of the plate with spoonfuls of turnips, beans, and cooked greens. It was a mound of food, and I wondered if I could eat it. I did eat it, relishing each flavor in turn. Not since I left home years before had I enjoyed such cooking, and I cleaned my plate. My hunger was gone and my stomach stuffed to discomfort.

At the finish of the meal, an hour later, the women cleared the table; and the men began cutting tobacco with their sheath knives to fill their pipes. Monk placed a clay pipe and a bit of tobacco on the table before me. "There," he said, "have a smoke. Plenty of weed here so smoke all you like." *Wehe* brought a stick aflame at one end from the fireplace and handed to Monk. He lit his pipe with it; and after taking his first three puffs, he placed his big, rough hands flat on the table before him.

"Now, Tom Skins, I heads the Two Brothers," he announced, "and I am headsman of this mob here. We've been fishing three years, most of us. The first year we fitted out a boat was when Bry got his leg broke. At the end of this last season Williams, who pulled our bow oar, signed on a ship. That put us a man short for the Brothers and we have none at all for the Sisters. Most of the men here about don't know the work 'cept to help cut blubber and boil, but I think they'll soon give it a try like *Ruru* here. You're welcome to stay as long as you like. You may sign on with us here just as on a ship, but you'll find the shares much larger as we whale on our own account. To buy our lines, tools, and goods to trade with, there is two shares kept aside. Then I gets two and a half, Knobby gets one and a half, and its one share apiece for the rest. For you, that will be one out of every ten barrels of oil and the same portion in pounds of bone we take. That's far better than a hundredth or a ninety-fifth lay you'd get from a ship if you were a steersman; even before the rascals had docked you for everything. Here slops, some liquor, and weed is shared out equal. You can have extra booze and weed if you want it, but it has to be paid for or set off 'gainst your lay in a separate counting. We don't charge extra for anything drawn from the stores, just what they cost us from the ships. All is settled up once at the end of the season when we sell our oil and bone.

"Well, you have about four months or more to think about it 'fore any ship arrives. We're parcel whalers for the winter when the fish are in the Strait and parcel farmers for the summer when they're gone. Like now when things is easier. Now let's get you rigged out." He motioned to his wives and pointed toward the north wall.

Maree and *Karee* drew out a chest from the stacks of things along the wall and placed it on the floor next to the end of the table. Monk raised the lid and pulled out a straw hat, which he plopped on my head. "There," he said, "that makes our Tom Skins look a more civilized man in a trice."

The two boys and all the wives charged their pipes and started smoking. The room was large, but the air in it was soon layered with smoke from so many pipes.

They all puffed away at their pleasure while I picked through the clothes in the chest and held up shirts and trousers to estimate their size. I found two sets of clothes that were a bit large, though ones I could alter to fit my frame. I gladly shed my old clothes and slipped into a set of new ones.

After a year's wear my old outfit had molded to the exact shape of my body. I had scraped and sewed for days to make them for warmth and to cover my nakedness. The holes through both knees of the trousers and the elbows of the jacket had grown larger in the last few weeks. Leather around the collar and the sleeve ends was black with a mix of dirt and skin oil. My duckings in the sea had not removed any of the filth; worse yet, the tanning of the leather had been imperfect and when wet they smelled. Added to that odor were those of wood smoke and my sweat. I had become quite used them, but wondered if my new mates nosed it. At least no one had edged upwind from me on the beach at Blind Bay.

There was a pair of pumps in the chest, too fine to wear while working but easy to slip on the feet when there was a need to be shod. I held them up and asked, "Anyone want these?"

Each man shook his head.

"Take them," Monk said with a wave of his hand.

The pumps were a bit tight when I leaned over and pulled them onto my feet, but I knew they would stretch enough for a decent fit. I stood up fully dressed.

Peck tilted his head to one side, grinned, and pointing his pipe stem at me, declared, "Well, Tom Skins, you look less a savage now. Aye, almost civilized. You'll be wantin' to go to church of a Sunday with a lady on your arm."

Monk's wives, smiling in approval, circled about me smoothing the wrinkles in my red-and-white striped shirt.

"So! This calls for a tot all round," Monk exclaimed, and got up and went to a box at the north wall. He pulled out a bottle and gave a nod to *Maree*. From a set of shelves next to the door, she fetched a half dozen tin cups out of the collection of dishes, pots, and kettles. Her smile faded to a stony look as she placed them on the table. Each man took one and held it out to be filled. There was disappointment in the men's faces as they watched their headsman pour little more than a half gill for each one. Monk picked up his own cup and toasted, "To the next season."

"To the next season," each one echoed in turn and took a pull from his cup.

I halted mid swallow and stared up at the lamp, a broken harpoon, and the long oars hanging from the rafters. It felt as if a hot iron were probing into the middle of my chest, and I tilted my head forward to let the liquor still in my mouth to flow back into the cup. I dropped my jaw and breathed in and out, hoping the rush of air would cool my throat.

"To our new mate," Knobby called out.

They all turned to me and raised their cups. "To our new mate," the men repeated in chorus. "Hurrah, mate! Hurrah!" they all cheered and had another swallow of liquor.

"Tom Skins," Monk offered, "there's a bunk here for you as long as you need it." He pointed to the six along the south wall. "When we finish the new storehouse, we'll put a bunk in it for you. We all have our own places. These Indians about here all sleep in one *whare*, all close, jumbled together; but we like it more private."

"Your fears were for naught, lad," Knobby assured me. "When that nob first saw you, there was no other notion in his mind but to sell you to us for a musket."

"I thought for sure I was to be killed when that girl came at me with that razor. I thank you all for buying me out," I said. "I'll work the season and you may have the whole of my share to pay for the musket and powder and these slops, but at the end I want to sign on any ship going back to America."

Monk nodded and said, "That will be more than what's needed. We're now short the one man Williams, and your help will mean we'll be surer of taking our fish. We should have two boats out after a whale. *Kotuku's* boys follow us with the Two Sisters and come in when they're needed. With only one boat fitted out we sometimes lose our fish. You see two boats and crews is needed; then if one is stove we still have a good chance. A man or two may come our way for this next season, but I doubt we could expect enough to crew the Sisters."

Knobby placed his cup on the table and nudged it toward Monk once with his forefinger. The headman caught the movement in the corner of his eye and gave a slight jerk of his head to the left and back. Knobby, noting the refusal, looked innocently past Monk to the window as if he hadn't expected another drink.

The interior of the room was darkening and *Wehe* hopped up on the table to light the lamp with another flaming twig. The old dog, four cats, and four naked toddlers wandered around on the deal floor of the big room. One of the children pulled the dog's tail. The animal looked back at his tormenter with a sad expression and howled a fainthearted complaint.

"Tom Skins," Monk abruptly asked me, "have you noticed the bell by the door?"

"That I have."

"When the lookout is out on the point and sights a fish blow," he explained, "the man runs a blue pennant up the pole there. That's when someone here rings the bell. You hear it ding-ding, ding-ding like its ringing eight bells, then you're to stop what you're doing and head for the boats. It'll be a while yet before the whales arrive, but remember ding-ding, ding-ding. Just like aboard a ship at the watch change. Eight bells."

"Yes, I have it, yes."

"When the pennant is a green one it means a ship is coming in, and we go out and pilot her to the holding ground whether she be a whaler or a trader. It's our only chance to buy our needs and hear the news. Now, there can be times about here when there is danger."

"Danger?" I asked, looking at Monk and then to the other whalers who, for some reason, were inspecting their cups or the top of the table.

"Yes, when there is a chance of a raid by the tribes from across the Strait or down the coast. We're here because we have the leave of these tribes here about.

Karee is a niece of a nob in Blind Bay, Old Scratch's brother, and *Maree* is the daughter of another. That means we're beholden to them, and so their enemies is our enemies. You're on one side or the other out here, Tom Skins; there's no staying out of a war. Now when you're settled in your new place and you hear the bell ringing fast, goin' ding, ding, ding, ding, roll up your blanket and a mat and bring them and a full lantern up here. I'll give you a musket later. We all have one. Be sure to bring it loaded and with extra cartridges. You should make some up when you get it. So."

I was baffled and it must have shown on my face.

The headsman spoke once again, slowly, "I know it sounds daft, lad, but them's my orders." He leaned toward me and added, "When you hear the bell ringing fast like that: ding, ding, ding, YOU COME UP HERE SWIFT." Monk knocked his knuckles on the table with each of his last words giving added force to his instructions.

Such a warning put a new face on our situation. Security at the station was only for the moment, and Monk showed no sign he would reveal more.

All my dismays faded a few minutes later when Peck brought out a scratched and worn fiddle and began playing the instrument he had managed to keep in some sort of repair. One string had snapped and its ends had been hitched together near the bridge. He sat on one of the bunks and sawed away at a reel. In a few seconds the men, their wives and the children began clapping in time with his tune. Knobby John suddenly leaped to his feet and skipped around in the steps of a dance. "Eeyow," he shouted, "eeyow." The toddlers also squealed with delight at his performance and tried to ape him by stomping their feet and twisting from side to side. They turned round and round and when dizzied stumbled back onto their bottoms and giggled. Peck kept playing jigs for an hour; and then seeing the smaller children rubbing their eyes, he slowed and began something close to a lullaby. Little heads began to nod. *Maree* and *Karee* each bedded her child in her bunk. Peck finished a last drawn-out note and put his fiddle back into its bag of heavy canvas.

The other couples gathered up their children and went off to their smaller houses. Bryan, the last one out, slid the door panel closed.

Monk pointed to the upper end bunk, indicating the one to be mine, and then puffed the lamp out. We undressed by the dim glow from the fireplace and climbed into our beds. *Maree* then banked the fire to save a few coals for morning. Each wife climbed into a bunk with her child. Monk settled his big frame with a loud groan into the bunk below me. I was lying there in comfort with a good meal in my stomach. All was quiet in the room save for an infrequent snore.

I could see no choice but to stay and work until a ship of some kind arrived. Had these men not gone to Blind Bay to ransom me, I might never have escaped. I would have been doomed to spend the remainder of my life as a slave. I owed them much and so was bound to the station and hence to the relations of Monk's wives. Except for danger from other Indians, I could see they lived as good a life or even better than many a tradesman in America.

In the morning the babble of *Karee's* little boy awakened me. I lay quietly in my bunk having had my best night's sleep in months without some nightmare of pursuit or disaster.

After a breakfast of cold meat left from the night before, Monk announced, "Today we put up the roof."

He set me, three of the other men, and the two boys to work on the new *whare*. It was a structure handily constructed of poles, sticks, and flag-like materials; but it was also one that once afire would blaze to nothing in minutes.

Bryan's bad leg prevented him from standing for any length of time on a ladder, but he made himself useful passing up the long poles from the stack at the side of the building and handing up pieces of lashings to those who called for them.

In the afternoon a canoe, loaded with what looked like common rushes used for chair bottoms, appeared from around the point. The two Indians in it were cramped by the load and could barely give full swing to their paddles. Bryan watched the vessel gliding in on the water of the cove and called to his boys, "*Wehe, Tokee*, get the *raupo*."

The canoe's bow nosed into the sand. The load, extending far over the hull's sides, was bound in bundles. *Wehe* and *Tokee* waded into the cove and carried each bundle, one-by-one, into the new building and dropped them beside others already there. The men who had brought the load went up to Monk's house and after an hour's visit returned with their pay of tobacco, pipes, and squares of calico.

The *whare* was finished in three days; and we shifted the staves, hoops, mauls, and cooper's tools stored in the other houses into it. Then it became my new home. On one side were two long bundles of whalebone and above them hung a threefold tackle with its fall coiled and neatly tied with rope yarns. During the season there would be other lumber housed in it; yet it was six times better than the soot-blackened dogholes that had been our quarters in the rookeries on Macquarie and Brister's. The floor of my new home was covered with a mat of fern fronds, making it warmer underfoot than bare earth. A window opening had been left in the north wall, and through it the lookout, the sheers, the boat ways, and each point at the entrance of the cove were visible. My bunk, built against the opposite wall, was padded with a layer of *raupo* and topped with a mat *Maree* had woven for me and a new blanket drawn from the station's stores.

The day after the *whare* was finished, Monk sent me and Peck to walk a fence that ran from one shore to the other and blocked off the end of the of the point from the rest of the land.

"What's this fence for?" I asked.

"Pigs," Peck said. "It keeps them out there away from our houses. Otherwise they get into everything. There's about a dozen rooting around. We're to overhaul the fence for any weak places and make any repairs."

We started from the west end of the fence with each of us carrying a bundle of flax leaves in one hand for ties. The fence was constructed by setting two posts in the ground a few inches apart and then spacing a pair every eight or nine feet along the length of the fence. Split saplings and fern trunks had been stacked between the pairs of posts until it was waist high. Binding the top ends of the posts to each other held the horizontals firmly in place.

"Here," Peck said, "pull at the ties to see if any are loose. If you find one; don't spare the leaves, re-tie it snug."

We each gave a post a tug as we passed to see if it was firmly lashed to its mate and the rails were gripped firmly between them.

"Do the pigs break out often?" I inquired.

"Not a common thing. We feed them some, and they find enough fern and such to root around. It's an old boar that gives us a fit now and then by breaking into the gardens. Boney used to chase him, but the dog's too old now. We need a new dog. No, two, three dogs would be even better."

We continued over the top of the hill and down to the other end of the barrier, testing posts and rails and replacing a few ties as we went. On the east shore of the headland, Peck sat on the beach, pulled his pipe from one jacket pocket, and dug into the other one for his tobacco. He minced it on a scrap of wood with his knife to prepare it for a smoke. Slowly and thoughtfully he pressed the charge into the bowl and placed the pipe in his mouth.

"Bryan's leg," I asked, "how did he get so crippled?"

"Flukes," Peck replied. He drew out a box made of thin wood steamed into a round container. He opened it. It held a chip of flint and a steel striker.

"It happened when you were whaling?"

"Aye, we were fast to a fish, a sperm. We were going in to lance when she sweeps her flukes from eye to eye. Tossed the boat arsey versey and broke ol' Bry's leg."

"That was bad luck."

Peck nudged the charred fabric in the box and replied, "Oh, it pains him from time to time, but he can still row good." He struck the flint across the steel a few times and in half a minute had a flame and his pipe lit. He puffed away, looking dreamily at the small offshore islands. "You see you're much needed here, Tom Skins. We need enough men for two boats. It'd be best with three or even four to do it right and not lose a fish."

"I'll be here for all this season. I can't promise more than that."

Peck pulled his straw hat off and ran his hand over his forehead, his straight, brown hair, and down the back of his neck. "There's all a man would ever need right here, Tom. Plenty to eat most of the year. Enough rum. A good *wahine* if you want one. You kiss no man's arse. You carry no boss and landlord on your back. What you earn is yours. Think on it mate. Could you do near as well back home?"

"Aye, if you have no people, those who would miss you, I expect it would be a very good life."

"For sure," agreed Peck. "For sure."

"But I have my father there at home. He didn't wish me to go sealing. If I don't return or get word to him soon, he can only believe I am lost. I don't wish to give him such pain. I want to go back there and work in the shop again. I've had enough adventuring for a while."

Peck nodded. "Well, I have only a cousin in New York, and she don't give a fig about me and wouldn't cry one tear if I was said to be drowned." He drew slowly on his pipe, absorbing pleasure from each mouthful of smoke, and absently watched the puffy clouds drifting over the Strait. The charge in the pipe burned out in a few minutes. He drew it from his mouth and tapped out the ash on a piece of driftwood. While rising to his feet he grunted out, "Ummp, time to see what chore Mr. Monkhouse has for us next, Tom."

We strolled back along our route re-examining the fence for any weak places that we might have missed.

At mid-afternoon we reached the brow of the hill and met a light breeze from the west rippling the water of the cove below. Sunlight sparkled rhythmically from each facet, and farther out they all merged into a single glittering band.

"That's all for the day, lads," Monk called to us before we reached the boat ways. "Time to observe the solemn rites up in my *whare,*" he added. "Bring yourselves and a good appetite. So."

Each time the men, their wives, and their children gathered at Monk's table, the evening meal laid on was generous; and it was enjoyable to watch them eat the food they had grown and gathered. They were the most durable men with no reason to be humble, tough as sole leather, and following a hard, dangerous craft for their families. They had their faults, but they were never niggardly or the least faint of heart. At that moment I might have been a slave to the cannibals had not those men carried a valued musket and powder for miles to Blind Bay for my ransom.

Karee and Sarah took the last plates and bowls away at the end of the meal. In a few minutes the women and children slipped quietly from the *whare.*

Knobby brought out an oily deck of cards from his jacket pocket and spread them on the table, and it took but a minute for the headsman to run his eyes over them to be sure none were missing. Monk got up and rummaged in the stack of boxes and barrels and found two bottles which he placed on the center of the table. Those containers held the solemn rites to be observed, and they were observed by serving them out to all. Knobby finished shuffling the cards, tapped the top of the deck, and with a questioning look asked, "What'll be lads, brag?" The men nodded and the game began.

The evening was to be spent gambling. Not having a thing of value to match their wagers, I sat sipping my vile drink now and then, glad the others were far more interested in their bets and cards than how long my cupful lasted. In an hour they were half drunk; and when they contested the value of the bets on the table, I slipped out the door and returned to my storehouse. Their shouts erupted many times in the night before I dozed off.

The Indians who had brought the load of *raupo* to the cove returned three weeks later in an empty canoe and met with Monk up in his *whare*. They came down two hours later smoking new pipes and carrying some blankets, a kettle, and other smaller trade goods. They loaded those into their hull and paddled away. Our headsman must have traded those goods for something quite valuable; but he never explained what it was.

Monk sent Peck and me to grub up ferns and cut tree roots in the new garden two weeks later. We took a short rest after breaking out a stump and watched the two boys at the other end of the field setting fire to the trees and bush cut a week before. Peck sat on a felled trunk and cut a fill of tobacco for his pipe. When he got it going, I asked, "That was a fair load of goods the Indians fetched the other day. Do you know what it was for, more *raupo*?"

Peck smiled archly and in slow reply chuckled, "Heh, heh, heh. Well, no, not for *raupo* this time. No, Old Scratch is always asking for gifts and always asks for a lot more than he expects to git. If he don't git something now and then he turns considerable moody, but our Monk here, he knows how much will keep him agreeable."

Monk walked about the station in the afternoon inspecting repairs we made and the progress of our land clearing. "Good work, lads," he declared, smiling. "Everyone come up to eat in my *whare* tonight. The women will bring the food up from the cookhouse after eight bells."

There was a good feeling among the men at the station, and they expected to have a large time of it, drinking in good company and playing cards. Monk gave the invitation whenever he was pleased with the progress of the work being done, and it was certain he would bring out the rum bottles for "the solemn rites" after the meal. The men expected to have their liquor in no mean portions as a reward for their good work; and even beyond that some thought of it as a right. Monk, though, always reminded them that once the whaling started the boozing would be allowed only after each fish was boiled down, the oil in the casks and stored away. By ten o'clock I expected Knobby John, Peck, Monk, Bryan, and even *Ruru* would be howling drunk as usual after they ate in the big *whare*. By midnight some would be on the bunks snoring. One or two of them might end up on the floor sleeping amid cast-off jackets and empty bottles. In the morning the lamp would still be burning, wasting good oil; and solemn-faced wives would wake their men and clean up what had been spilled or broken.

The crew, clean-faced and dressed in their newer trousers and shirts, went up to Monk's before I was near ready. Seated on rock a short way up the stream, I washed and then dried off with a remnant of calico that served for a towel. While pulling on my better clothes, I thought of the required toasts they would make to the women, the whales, the boats, and each killing lance in turn. Their rum was the fieriest spirits I had ever put into my mouth. I had soon twigged that to refuse a toast with a goodly tot was an insult among these whaling brethren. No one could play the abstainer there and make them feel less worthy for their drinking. After all were sufficiently fuddled, I would resort to a ruse and go out to piss off the porch; by then they would be too far gone to notice my absence. Thus I would get my night's sleep in the storehouse and not have a sore head or be so ill in the morning. I walked up the slope to Monk's *whare* and went step-by-step up the notched log to the porch. From inside Monk's *whare* came women's and children's voices and the clatter made in the preparations for the meal.

Karee was standing at the side of the door as I entered. Her eyes followed me, and a slight smile touched up the corners of her mouth as I passed by on my way to one of the bone seats at the table. *Maree* avoided my eyes while she walked about placing the plates for the meal; but her daughter, trailing after her, smiled at me. My hand went up to my face. Was there a smear of dirt there I hadn't washed off? I got up and stepped to the looking glass that hung on the post between two of the bunks, but it reflected my face clean of the least smudge. Something was in the wind. In the afternoon each of the men at one time or another had given me a slight sidelong smile as if they were planning to spring some hoax or foolery on me and have a good laugh.

Bryan was sitting at a corner of the table dressing his sheath knife on a whetstone. He dripped a little water from his cup onto the stone and slid the blade back and forth. After working both sides, he wetted his thumbnail and drew the knife-edge lightly across it. "Umph," he grunted and squinted along the length of the blade. "Not a fit job. This is a poor stone, a little coarse. Tom Skins, would you fetch the one down in your *whare*? It's on the head of that cask in the far corner."

"Aye, I know the one. I'll bring it up for you."

"That's a good lad, Tom. It sets my leg to aching most awful when I go up and down those steps more than once a day." The tattooed lines curving around his mouth oddly abetted his smile.

I went out on the porch and paused a few minutes looking over the station and its cleared fields. Twilight was fading from the sky. In the lee of the western point, the smooth water of the cove reflected a dark, inverted shape of the higher ground. The slope on the opposite side was still in a faint glow from the sky, and the first bold star was twinkling above it. Back in the room there was a burst of laughter from the men gathered around the table.

Karee was a step inside the doorway holding a cup for one of the little girls to drink from. Both of the child's hands held the cup to steady it while she drank and looked up to *Karee's* face.

To the west on the far side of Knobby's house, *Wehe* and *Tokee* were in the new field walking from fire to fire and pushing any limbs together to complete their burning.

If I were like these other men, not tied to another place or people, I could live on this beautiful island; but Father was far away back at the Long Point. I had grown up in Yankeeland, a true Jonathan for sure. There had been enough perils and adventures for me. I didn't need more.

I backed down the log, walked north along the path past the cookhouse, and strode across the stream from stone to stone. Overhead several slants of sea birds were returning to their nests from a day's foraging in the Strait. Their return home required only minutes or an hour; mine would take far longer, perhaps an entire year. Nearer the *whare* I saw a faint light coming through a slit in the *raupo* wall up near the eave. Damn! Had the one of the boys, in searching for a tool, taken a lighted lantern into the storehouse and forgotten it? At bedtime my lamp was put out, and in the morning I returned it to the cookhouse where it could be lighted again from the fire or coals. If not returned to the cookhouse, I took great care and made doubly sure it was out when I left. A tipped lantern, a little spilled oil and the rush walls and thatch would roar up in flames in a few minutes. I hurried forward. Nothing could be saved from such a fierce blaze: even bucketing water from the stream would be useless, far too little. The staves for casks, always in short supply, were in there; and as yet we had built no cistern or other place to store excess oil when none were to be had. It had our bundles of bone. Tackles, tubs of line, lances, cooper's winch and plane, and the bag of tools were all in the *whare*, precious items in this wilderness and almost irreplaceable. Damn! Damn! Damn! There will be a sharp word in Monk's ear about the lamp. I rushed forward and, turning the corner, spied light coming from around the edges of the tarpaulin that served as the door. I thrust it aside.

Chapter Six

I held the fabric in my hand, struck aback by what I saw. The lamp, pendent on its hook above, shed a soft glow on a New Zealand girl sitting beside my table. She rose to her feet. I recognized her. I had not forgotten her face or the tattoo on her chin. She was the one who had shaved my beard while I lay bound hand and foot at Blind Bay. Unlike the women around the station who were always in a loose calico dress, the girl wore the flax skirt and a cloak slung loosely over one shoulder. Her black hair, lightly oiled and shiny, was tied back with a red ribbon. She was much cleaner now. Her face, neck, and breasts were an unblemished, golden brown in the lamp light. She looked at me, too shy to speak, waiting to hear my goblin words or see some gesture of welcome. Anticipation was in her eyes, as if in the next moments I would speak those words or give a token of acceptance. Her look was warm, only a shade less than a smile.

On the table were two forks, a pewter plate, and a crockery bowl covered with another plate. She had brought everything in while I was up at Monk's. Damn! I cursed to myself. Damn! Damn! Damn! This was the big mystery. This girl was the reason for all the sly looks and for Bryan sending me to fetch the stone. Monk and the others had struck a bargain with her people and they had her sent up from Blind Bay. So, all the trade goods carried off by the two men after the *whare* was finished were the payment. Everyone else at the station knew she had arrived except me. Damn!

Even if they said I needn't replace what they had given for her, it would only be right to have it come out of my share of oil and bone. If I were to keep her, it would look mean on my part if I did not foot the cost. It was a considerable amount to add to what I felt was owed for my ransom and clothes. They were liberal men one and all and would not deny a man the least they thought he needed, but they were also men who settled their accounts to the shilling and penny. It might take more than a whole season to earn the price of the goods and pay the other debts; then I would have little or nothing due me. Damn! Then it would take me another year fishing to earn enough for passage home.

Ahh! … Yes, yes, yes. To be sure! To be sure. They were making me beholden to them so I would need to sign on for the season after this one. Aye. They knew I would surely honor such a debt to them, my rescuers. Damn, they had slyly laid a snare. And, oh, how well baited! Yes, baited with what they thought I must surely need and certainly desire. They were eager to keep me here darting whales for years in the Two Brothers. What was I to do with her? I could send her back, but that would be as bad as refusing to drink with my new mates … no, no, no, far worse. They would say naught, but they would feel it was ingratitude for all their cost and effort. It was their belief that I should have a woman, aye, very much needed a woman; and at the same time a *wahine* would also serve their end to keep me here pulling the bow oar. So, they had sent for this one since she had shown such interest. Clever, clever … oh, a clever move to bring a girl here who had more on her mind than duty. She may have put herself forward when she heard of the goblins' offer for a wife.

They did not understand my wants. They had no plans or need to return to a home just yet, if at all. Bryan would be flogged hundreds of strokes and have his transportation doubled, or even be hanged, if he went back to Van Dieman's or New South Wales.

To the contrary, I had to meet my own need. Home, Father, my friends at home beckoned more than ever.

If I returned the girl to her people, would they think something was amiss with her? Would she suffer, come to harm in some way? If I kept her, then took her … and I surely would … what then? I had little doubt she would conceive. None of the mates of the whalers were barren, but the very opposite. A child would make a tie to her I would never break any more than one of the others would break from his woman. They prized their wives and their lively, half-Indian children; and that was one reason, aye the chief one, for them to remain whaling. I could neither abandon a child of mine, a part of me, to a life with these savages, perhaps to be killed in a war set afoot by some chief for an imagined insult; nor could I take the child from its mother. So then I too would be bound by a *wahine* and child to this savage place if I could not earn enough in coin to take them back to home port.

I stepped to the table and sat on the bone seat to think afresh what I might do.

The girl watched me with eyes shining, expectant in the lamplight. She uncovered the bowl, gingerly picked out a piece of pork and several small turnips, and placed them on a plate. With her head slightly atilt with an implied a question, she reached forward and offered the filled plate to me with both hands. I expected she wanted to know if the serving was enough. "Oh, this … is … fine. This … is … just … fine," I said.

She stared at me, not comprehending my slow, sarcastic words. I was instantly sorry I had spoken them; she was doing what she thought was right, what would please me. She had left her people and come all the way from Blind Bay to cook and serve me food, to live in my *whare*. I had to respect the girl's honest wish, but how was I ever to do that?

It was awkward. I would not have her stand there like a steward watching my every bite and swallow. "Here," I said softly to amend my first curt tone, "you sit there." I slid the other plate and fork to her side of the table and pointed to the whalebone seat. She hesitated; perhaps fearing to break the *tapu* and eat within a *whare*. I motioned a second time; and then, with an uncertain smile on her face, she sat down. Slowly the girl lifted out a cut of pig, bone and meat together, and laid it on her plate. She looked up at me after each move she made. The girl stabbed her fork into the meat and held it up before her. I suspected the other women of the station had prompted her on how the whaler men ate their food. What to do with the meat next left her baffled.

I drew my sheath knife and offered it to the girl. "Cut it," I mumbled.

She took the knife with her left hand, looked at it and then at the pork impaled on the end of the fork. Unsure about what my words meant, she placed the knife gently on the table, pulled her portion of pig from the fork, and gripped the bone with both hands. She glanced up at me every few seconds while gnawing the meat.

"Tom Skins!" Knobby John bellowed down from Monk's *whare*. "It's time to freshen your hawse and veer out a little cable! Don't be shy now. We're all counting on you to do the right thing … and do it four or five times."

The girl's eyes widened with alarm and she jumped to her feet. I waved my hand to the side and shook my head to show her the shout meant nothing. Once assured that she had not erred, the girl resumed her seat.

I ate slowly, hardly tasting the food in my mouth. Her small face in the soft lamplight drew my gaze, and to avoid staring I glanced at the *raupo* wall beyond.

Did she come only because the goods were given and the bargain made? Certainly not. There was keenness in those dark eyes, not one solely due to curiosity. I recalled the knowing, saucy smile she had given me while straddling my body in the *whare* at Blind Bay. The idea must have been in her mind when she shaved my face. Her words spoken then had no meaning for me, but now I understood she had need to make her wants known to me with speech in addition to her actions.

The image of her, back-lighted in the small doorway of my *whare* prison, and the look she had given me then had clung in my memory like a burr, always there, always calling for heed in the past weeks.

The meal was tense for us both. It was evident she was doing her best to please me and stay in my house; yet she looked as if she feared making some misstep, breaking some unlearned *tapu* of the whaler men.

I pondered again why she had taken the hair from my beard. Had she given it to some *tohunga* to work a spell with? Was I now under some conjuring that held me in my *whare*, allowed me no thought except one of this girl? Did it prevent me from rising to my feet and sending her back to Blind Bay? That look, that simple, desiring look … what magic did she need? None. The spell was in her dark eyes, the curve of her lips, and the swell of her brown breasts.

For the next several moments all the items at the edges of the room, the tools, the bundles of whalebone, and the bunk, faded away. The orb of lamplight held only myself, the table, and the girl.

My last bite was made and swallowed. I rose from my seat and stepped around to the window to ease the tautness. At the table, not a fathom away, she held me with the plea of her eyes. I placed one hand to my right and one to the left on the lower edge of the opening.

Half of the scene outside was the water of the cove mirroring the last light in the sky. The remainder was the slope above the right-hand shore. In the rising shadows, the trees and bushes on it were now murky greens. My view was the cove and shore easing into darkness; but my inward vision overlaid it with the image of the girl as I had first seen her from the doorway. She expelled all else I tried to put in her place. There were faint noises behind me. She was gathering up the remains of the meal. What was I to do? What must I do ... send her away?

A companion was much needed in the fair, favored, but lonely land. Whalers were of little account in the ports of the world, mere hands on long lays; but ashore about the Strait and having trade goods they became something more than poor toads. They would have their women, their quim; and if their own kind were not about, they gladly took the brown Indians to wife. Some, like Monk, even became a relation of the nobs. It was the life of the *tangata bulla*, the men lost or truant from ships and living precariously on the wild coast.

Castor and Pollux were solidly fixed in the night sky with the lesser ones flickering around them. In the gathering gloom the sheer poles, lashed together at their tops, were mere silhouettes a quarter of the way to the lookout. The wistful, two-note call of a night bird echoed over the water.

Having escaped from a dozen deadly perils, I stood in the *whare* unharmed. Only by my resolve to live and much good luck did I look out on the dark water of the cove and the slope of the hill.

Whale ships would arrive once the season began and one might need a hand to help fill before standing for home. I must sign on one for I belonged to Yankeeland, not this wilderness. It was fair and green and without ice or snow about the coasts and hills; yet it was a land of savages, quarrels, and continual raids. Nothing barred my leaving once I repaid my debt to the others. Then I could slip my painter and give it all a good farewell.

What was the strange quality of this girl? Though she was the one who wished for acceptance, I felt helpless, adrift, with her only two or three paces away. She might be called a too forward girl by many at home simply because there was a natural openness and naught of the studied reserve of the girls of the Boro, Norwich, and Mystick. It was much different in a distant, beautiful land where little intervened between a man and a woman, and all was understood without so much bother. At home people gave their smile of approval if required forms were met or, if not, ranted from the pulpit that such a pairing was criminal and illicit intercourse.

Yet, I was sure I should send her back. It was not the right place or time for me. A woman and a child might keep me on the coast for years. Yes, tied to … no … no, not tied to, but encompassed by a family and bound to them by my very wants. Bryan was destined to stay. It appeared Knobby, Monk, and Peck, enjoying a freedom here on this island, even with its perils, would remain for the rest of their lives. Their children would grow up unfettered in mind, handsome and lively in body, and perhaps people a small nation of whalers.

I was tempted to turn and look at her figure again but did not. One more glance … no, no. Even with my back to her and a few paces away there was the taste of her; one savored in my mind and never felt so keenly before.

Yes, better not to watch her moving about. It would be so natural a thing to reach out, draw her to me, and feel her firm, warm body in my embrace. I craved to caress her smooth shoulders and kiss them. There was no one to say I must not; nothing hindering save those reasons I had given myself.

It would be a new manner of life for me if there were a child … sending me over a threshold never to be re-crossed. No doubt she would cleave to me. I knew that without another thought. It was evident in the way she had risen, stood by the table, and had watched me as I paused in the doorway. Surely if I did not send her away that instant, only minutes of sand would fall in a watch glass before I took her in my arms and enjoyed her small, sweet form. With that promise, that longing in her eyes, how could I resist? My mind was teetering on a knife-edge, confused, unable to decide.

I must think of other things … yes, yes, other things … of all the dangers of these past years, my many close escapes … Aye, I need to be thankful for …

In an instant the thought was swept away. She had approached from behind, and her small hands were circling my waist. One slipped up my chest, and the other slid low across my stomach. She hugged my body, pressing the side of her face against my back. I was unable to move … stood simply poised … There was the choice. Should I evade her arms, free myself? I had to decide in that instant. All thoughts of past and future vanished, leaving only the present. The warmth of her cheek and breasts sent a shiver through my body. My hands came up slowly and held hers firmly in place … an embrace that I once meant to refuse. Now, willingly, I accepted. I loosened her hold a little and turned around to face her.

She had snuffed out the lamp. Dim starlight revealed her features only as a blur. Her black hair blended with the darkness. I felt it teasing my face and nudged my nose into it, drawing in her delicious woman scent again and again. She altered the room. It ceased to be a cluttered storehouse but our place alone, one not to be found by any numbers of latitude and longitude. It was …. She squirmed her hips and stomach against my body, against my roger, hard as a fid. There was an insistence in that movement. It was my time … come to me in this rude hut … in this cove ten thousand miles from home. I spread my hands on the small of her back, drew her tighter, but felt no edge of skirt or cloak. They had dropped to the fern mat. She lowered herself to her knees. I followed and we knelt face to face, two indistinct forms in the darkness. Her hand groped forward and found my left hand. She drew it to her and pressed my fingers between her breasts. "*Heke*," she said in a soft voice.

"*Heke*," I repeated, raising my other hand to my forehead in an unseen salute.

She touched my chest and waited a few seconds; then nudged me once more.

I was puzzled for a second until I sensed it was my name she wanted. "It's Thomas," I said.

"Ita Toma," she said.

"No, no it's just Thomas … only one word … ah, no, no here it's Tom or Tom Skins."

Puzzled by so many unknown words, she was a silent and unmoving figure in the gloom.

Ach! I had made a mare's nest of it. I waved a hand from side to side, an almost invisible motion as if to erase all the errors, then spoke the name slowly, distinctly, "Tom … Skins."

"Toma … Kina?" she repeated. "Toma…Kina?"

I pressed my cheek against hers and whispered into her ear, "*Tika, tika.*"

The night bird perched somewhere around the cove was repeating its two-note call each quarter of a minute.

Heke slipped her legs from under her and stretched out on her back. I leaned over and kissed her neck on one side, then the other. I took lingering tastes of her soft, delicate mouth, and went to each breast and down to circle her navel.

Chapter Seven

The squeal of Peck's old fiddle coming from Monk's *whare* wakened me. A rhythmic thumping set the time of the music. All five of them, half seas over or worse, were beating their fists and bottles on the table and stomping on the floor.

Heke was next to me in the bunk, breathing lightly and evenly; and I drifted off listening to its slow, comforting rhythm.

I was aroused once again by the men singing at the limit of their voices.

Haul boys haul, 'fore she runs awa-a-ay
Whiskey an' duff my may-teee
It's whiskey an' duff to-da-a-a-ay
Haul boys haul, 'fore she runs awa-a-a-y
Brandy an' beans my may-teee
It's brandy an' beans too-da-a-a-ay

Through the window opening, the moon was visible with one half of it glowing white and the other half in featureless shadow but still detectable. Weak moonlight was spread in a distorted rectangle across the fronds on the floor.

"Hoo, hoo, hooo, eee," the men bellowed. Their voices and the stomping of their feet echoed from the hillside. They had gone all cock-a-hoop. The celebration was going full and by, and I expected they were now racing around the table waving their bottles.

"Ahoy, Tom! Are you there, Tom Skins?" a voice yelled from Monk's porch. It sounded like Peck's. "D'ye know what yer a-doing? Hee, hee, hee. Have you made a squeaker yet? Keep yer pipe up her thrummy bum 'til you have, m'lad. Hooeee!"

From the thumps on the porch I guessed Peck, enthused with that thought, was doing a dance. "Hooeee! Hooeee!" he shouted again and again.

Muffled shouts came from Monk's *whare*; then a few seconds later a louder thump. Our headsman had probably grabbed Peck by the back of the neck and slammed his faced into a wall. He had done it once before when Peck said something he didn't like. Peck had been so drunk then he couldn't remember what had happened and wondered for days who had blackened his eye and split his nose. Monkhouse could be as coarse as any sealer or whaler with his words, yet there was a sense of fitness in him at times. He knew he could get what he wanted by bellowing his orders, and used his big hands only when his patience was worn away.

Heke stirred a little in the bunk and snuggled her warm back against me. I rose up on my elbow to see that the blanket fully covered her; then I lay back on my left side and cupped my right hand over one of her breasts.

Sleep didn't return while I lay beside my *Heke* there in the Antipodes, the farthest place on earth from home. How had it come to pass? Choice, chance, and nature: which was it? The choice made to go a-sealing had taken me to the Southern Ocean. After the wrecking of the barque on the island there were no choices. Had I been destined from then on by indifferent chance, or was my fortune loaded like a fulham to fall a certain way? Did the seasons of the stars and planets truly decide our fates?

Through the last months we had been, as Monk said, parcel farmers clearing more land and turning the soil in preparation for our new garden.

In the first week in April he announced, "We must look to our property and get it fit for our first fish." Knobby was given the first chore to grease the windless and rig its tackle. He lifted one end and then the other of the thick spar enough to slip a piece of tallow between it and the bracket. To rig the sheers we hoisted the treble block to the top, and *Tokee* climbed up one leg to tie its strap around the lashings. Knobby brought out his irons to straighten their bent shanks and hone their cutting edges. With a thumb brushed lightly across each edge, he tested for sharpness. "There," he stomped a lance on the end of its wood shaft and boasted, "she'll reach to the life of a fish with hardly a push. *Wehe* could do it." The steersman slipped wooden covers over the ends of the irons and tied them on with laces to protect them and also to spare our bare feet, legs, and other parts of our bodies from being slashed during any staving or capsizing. The covers were painted bright red to make them easy to spy in the water after any overset.

Bryan and I cleaned both boats, inspected every nail, and repainted the hulls. Then we loaded the irons, mast and sail, and the rest of the fit-out into the Two

Brothers. Bry placed the two whiffs withtheir flags rolled around their staffs in the bottom of the boat. I expected the line tub was next and waited for someone to help me load it. Bry held up his hand and objected, "No, no, too heavy. Puts too much strain on the boat. Not enough holdin' her up on the ways. We load it after she's launched. Leave it there and be sure the cover is on it, for stout line is dear and hard to come by in these islands. Aye, leave it aside and help me put the oars in." With the whole fit-out aboard the Two Brothers was set to roll off the ways and into the cove.

Monkhouse walked around it, touching and inspecting each item carefully, and growled, "So. The boat's ready, but you're not." He walked over to Knobby, gripped his arm, and snapped, "The lot of you are all soft, soft as tailors and vicars, and it's coming onto the season. Tomorrow we start drills. Everyone here at the boat in the morning."

We launched the Two Brothers at first light and brought it broadside to the beach where we got in, shipped our oars, and sat ready to row. The headsman held the long steer oar in his hand to pull or push the bow quickly in the wanted direction.

Monk asked, "Tom Skins, have you gone after the whale before?"

"No, but I rowed a boat like this more miles than I can remember, and on and off beaches day after day."

"Not the same a'tall. We must turn quick as a swallow, which is why we drill. We must near our fish from fore or aft to stay out of her eye. You mind my every command swift. Never turn and look for'ard till we haul in. Never! I am the eyes for this boat. You hear me. You want something to stare at?" Monk jabbed his right forefinger to the center of his forehead and growled, "Stare at this. Even better, watch your oar." Monk looked at each of us one at a time and then called out, "Down oars!"

Each man grabbed his oar handle out of its cleat but kept the blade just clear of the water. I was slow getting it where it belonged.

"Damnation, Tom Skins!" Monk shouted. "Is that the way you sealers handle a boat? It's damned wondrous you never drowned. Try that again. Apeak. Now … down oars!"

I did better, at least, enough to please Monk.

Then he ordered, "Pull two."

Our two-side oar blades bit into the water. "Back three." he snapped.

The three-side men leaned back, dipped their oar blades into the sea and pushed their handles forward. The boat swept around within its length. The headsman reversed the orders and the whaleboat halted its turning and started in the opposite direction. "Heave up," was his next command and the oar tips rose out of the water. Monk put the steer oar blade in and pushed the handle to stop the hull. He turned the bow toward the Strait and called, "Head all. Give way, give way!" I braced a bare foot ahead, and leaned back on my thwart. The long ash shaft bowed with the strain.

"'Vast two," he shouted. The three-side oars still pulling drove the boat around in a full circle. "Pull two," was his next order; and the vessel straightened and headed north again. "Blast it! Give way! Give way! The lot o' you couldn't best a small steward and a poxed whore."

Monk had used all his insults and swearing by the time the sun fully cleared the hill. The drill lasted for hours and we were miles from the cove before we turned to go back. I could barely pull my oar as the boat entered the cove. I knew the next day my back would be sore, but I was getting the old strength back that I had when rowing about the rookeries.

"More practice tomorrow, boys," the headsman ordered. "It's coming onto the season and we must be ready for it."

The Two Brothers approached the shore and went gliding in with her oars peaked. The bow touched, and we jumped out and prepared her for the ways.

A half dozen men, wrapped up to their noses in their blankets, sat and watched us work. I joined Peck in hauling on the fall of the tackle and asked, "Who are they?"

"Our headsman's relatives."

"What do they come here for?"

"Oh, to visit *Maree* and *Karee* and smoke Monk's weed and eat his food," Peck replied. "Then sleep, eat some more, and smoke some more. And pick up what they can. They're his women's cousins and brothers. You'll see some of *Heke's* people one of these days. You'll have them for awhile and feed them. They'll sleep in your house most of the day. That's part of what's expected. I get my woman's family 'bout four times a year."

Drilling continued even when the weather brewed up and white-fringed waves filled the Strait. Our work-hardened arms and backs sent the whaleboat slicing through the swells faster each day.

Heke rose the next morning at the usual time and went to the cookhouse. I got up a few minutes later, dressed, and stood stretching my arms and arching my back. The drilling would start soon and I stepped toward the door to see if *Heke* was returning with our breakfast. She suddenly threw the tarpaulin aside, stepped in past me, and placed the food on the table. She pushed me to the edge of the bunk and gave me a wide smile that blended into a titter. *Heke* patted her stomach and then held her hands a few inches from it. I was still baffled when she announced, "Keeka, Toma Kina, we meka keeka."

I couldn't puzzle out what she meant until she held both arms as if cradling a baby at her left breast.

"Ah, ah, a squeaker. A squeaker," I blurted out when it finally became clear to me.

Heke took my hand and pressed it on her stomach, "We meka keeka," she repeated and giggled once more. Her right hand raised and swept in an arc overhead. She then held up her left hand with all the fingers extended and then she raised three fingers of her right hand. Eight new moons or thereabout she meant. That was unmistakable.

Heke's announcement changed everything. My child was growing within her. I had expected it, but always nudged the thought into the margins of my mind. This was my life now, fishing for the whale, certainly for all of this season and perhaps for the following one. I needed money if I was to take *Heke* and my child home.

I drew her to me, and while holding her in a long embrace, I knew I must take her home. She would go. She had given me her wide smile with a wordless understanding of that. There was never any question. Now, I must earn enough money, and I could only do that by whaling.

I gazed around the room and tallied what I owned: some clothes, a pair of pumps, two blankets, a lantern, a flint and steel, some tin ware, two forks, a sheath knife, and two pewter spoons. They were my total goods, not much for years of labor in the Southern Ocean. I could carry it all in my arms.

If we took a number of whales this season yielding enough oil and bone, I would have the whole of my share of the next season for passage money. That was all too far in the future, and I had no idea what it might foot to. If not enough for our passage, I might make an agreement with a captain as a redemptioner for the fares; and once home, Father could buy me out of the debt.

At the end of April Monk posted the first lookout and noted that he and Knobby John, by right of their talents, were exempt from that duty while Peck, *Ruru*, Bryan, and I must each stand a watch on the point. Wet or fair day, one of us wrapped up in an old fearnought coat sat on a section of whalebone for a full four hours. Pulling an oar in the rain was uncomfortable, but not as boring as sitting up on the hill. To make the duty more bearable we built a shelter of *raupo* at the foot of the flag pole. Spotting a whale in the rain wasn't likely, but there was always one man on the point with Monk's glass searching for a brief puff rising somewhere just above the dark surface of the Strait.

Late one morning in the second week of May the paired notes of the bell at Monk's rang out for the first time. I sprinted along the path to the ways and there with Peck uncovered and launched the Two Brothers. Monk and *Ruru* waded out with the line tub and loaded it. Knobby drew enough line out to coil a dozen turns on the forward decking, slipped the standing part into the chock, and needled a pin into its hole to keep it in. His hands in swift, practiced motions bent the line to his harpoons. The headsman threw a turn of the line around the loggerhead. We were ready. In three minutes after the sounding of the bell, I was on my thwart holding the bow oar and ready for the first order to pull.

We rowed for an hour out in the strait without seeing the whale's next blowout, and Monk in disgust pulled on the steering oar, swinging the bow back toward the cove. Three days later our luck was better and two spouts were sighted. We launched and headed for the nearer one.

The Two Brothers was about half a cable's length from the last spout, and we were pulling hard, driving the boat swiftly.

"She blows," Monk called out. "Ach! Damn! Heave up!"

We levered our blades from the water and looked at Monk, who was staring ahead. I almost twisted around for a forbidden glance to see the cause of the order. Knobby started a question, "What the …"

"Sperm!" Monk barked out. "For sure a sperm!" A puzzled look on my face brought a response from the headsman. "I saw the blow go fo'ard … sperm! She fights from both ends flukes and jaw. We can't risk it with only one boat. If we're stove, it's a long wait in the water for the boys even when they can see us." The headsman turned and pointed back to the Two Sisters following a half mile away and said, "See there. No, we'll not try for that one. Pull two."

Monk turned the bow toward the farther whale and we overtook it in a half an hour. Before the Two Brothers neared enough for the harpoon, the whale's back bowed up, the tail lifted into the air, and the body slid forward and down. "There go flukes," Monk reported to us and then promised, "We'll dart her on the next rising. Head all." The bow cut through the oily, smoothed patch of sea where the whale had descended. The headsman pulled on his long oar, turning the bow to starboard. After several minutes rowing he said, "About here." The whale's barnacled snout, almost in answer to his forecast, broke from the water a stone's throw to the starboard. Monk swept the bow toward it. There was a loud rush of air. We knew it had spouted. No words were needed; but from habit the headsman whispered, "She blows."

Monk, with pulls on the steering oar and his expert commands, was moving the boat precisely where he wanted it. We rowed quietly aft of the whale, edging the bow in close. "Soft, soft," Monk breathed. He kept his eyes on the whale, then motioned with his right hand for Knobby to stand up. I knew what was happening though I didn't dare turn and look forward. Knobby would slip his oar into its cleat, pick the first iron from the crutch, and heft it high. He would dart it into the animal just behind the fin. "Ha! To the wood," Knobby cried. Out of the corner of my left eye I could see the pole of the second iron lift from the crotch. The whale was plunging beneath the waves, and with no time to dart it, Knobby pitched the useless weapon overboard and the coils of line from the forward decking after it.

Suddenly the line snapped taut and went whizzing forward across the shafts of our oars and out through the chock. Its tremendous power and speed startled me. A man's hand or an arm caught in a bight of it would be ripped off. If it weren't severed, he would be carried overboard to drown. The mere touch of it racing out could rake skin away. Knobby, I knew, would be gripping the hatchet in his hand, watching for any snag.

The animal remained below for a quarter of an hour and then nearly all of its body thrust up out of the sea on our starboard. A white patch on the belly showed as she fell away on her back, dashing up a wall of white spray. She rose again through the froth and ran head out, pulling the Two Brothers along. After cutting through the waves for a mile and a half, the boat began to slow.

"Ha, ha! She tires," Monk crowed. "Aye, she tires. Damn shittin' good luck! That iron has touched the life in her. Haul in, boys."

We turned about and pulled on the line.

"I was right. She bleeds, Knobby," the headsman announced, pointing to stained patches of water as we drew the boat toward the black and white body. "She bleeds slow, but we can lance her soon. She'll be dead within an hour or two. So!"

A bright pool of blood surrounded our prey and reddened the foam stirred up as she rolled over and over. Each time the animal slammed her flukes against the water, they struck with less vigor. Our headsman watched them closely, estimating how much life was left in the animal. "Come aft," he ordered and stepped forward while Knobby started toward the stern. The two men sidled past each other at my thwart. Monk reached the bow, untied the wooden cover from the point of a lance, and held the weapon at head height. He directed Knobby at the steer oar to turn the Two Brothers and bring the bow within a few feet of the whale's body. I could not resist turning my head a little left, but only enough to see Monk's thick arms ram the lance point deep into the animal until the socket was against its skin. He pulled it halfway out and thrust it in again, probing at a different angle, hoping to slice the blade through the heart and lung of the beast. Its flukes suddenly lifted from the sea, scooping a barrel of water into the boat.

"Starn all," Monk shouted and yanked on the lance line, pulling the iron from the whale.

We backed the boat away. The flukes slammed onto the surface once more, dashing bloodied water against our backs and into the boat. For a few seconds the black body shuddered and then began rolling over and over. Each time it came upright, a spray of air and blood spewed from its blowholes. Finally it settled on its right side with the left flipper in the air. Four tight wraps of the line were around the whale. The iron shaft of the harpoon was bent, and the line held the wood handle flat against the black skin.

Peck started bailing out the red-tinted water sloshing fore and aft around our bare feet.

Monk waved a hand toward the lifeless bulk and said, "There you be, Tom Skins, stone dead and fin out. Your first whale and you just got a mite wet. You can thank Knobby for that strike. They aren't taken any easier. We're in luck this time. Let's hope it lasts the season."

The black side of the whale, barely awash at the surface was maybe twice the length of the Two Brothers. It was a wonder that we in our shell of a boat had slain this mountain of flesh and blubber. Six men who together hardly weighed a thousand pounds overcame the fifty or sixty ton giant of the ocean. Monk's thrusts with the lance, needle-like into the enormous animal, had reached and slashed its heart and lungs.

Knobby worked the boat in close to the tail where Monk used the spade to hack away part of each fluke. He hitched a line through a hole cut in one remaining portion, and we began the labor of towing our catch back to the station. There was little wind to help, making our trip to the sheers over four hours of steady pulling. Without a minute's rest despite our fatigue, we warped the whale in under the sheers; and the headsman immediately ordered the cutting-in started. The women had brought out the long spades, knives, skimmer, bailer, and other tools and had them lying ready on the shore.

Bryan's boys pulled on the line to overhaul the lower block down to the cutting stage and, with that done, were sent off in the canoe around the eastern point to find any men to work boiling blubber.

Monk motioned to me to join him on the shore between the sheers and the try pots. "Knobby and me will cut in," he said. "You and the others work the windlass until we have the first blanket piece lying here." The headsman pointed to the oil-soaked earth and ordered, "Then you and *Ruru* will cut it for Bry. He will show you how it's done."

"The same as sea elephant," I said.

Monk repeated, "Aye, same as sea elephant." He joined Knobby out on the narrow stage, and there the two jabbed long-handled spades up and down, slicing the width of blubber wanted. They toggled the first portion to the hook of the block, and our pulls on the handles of the windlass wound up the fall of the tackle, slowly peeling blubber from the carcass as the spades cut it free.

"'Vast there windlass," Knobby called when the two blocks met at the top of the sheers. He cut another hole in the blubber and tied a line through it to prevent the carcass turning in the water.

Monk sliced the long slab loose. It swung in and we lowered it to the beach.

"First blanket," Monk said and then ordered, "*Maree, Kotuku, Heke* take the windlass with Peck while *Ruru* and Thomas cut."

Bryan started his fires in the small wood and old residue of rendered blubber neatly packed beneath the kettles. We cut more blubber than could be boiled, freeing us to step over to help the women turn the windlass.

After two hours of work, one of the women went to the cookhouse and brought down a bottle of rum and a kettle of potatoes and meat. Whenever there was minute free we nipped bites from the kettle and, if we wanted, had a pull from the bottle to fortify us for more labor. Any opportunity to rest was taken, even if it was only a few minutes sitting on a section of whale backbone or simply leaning on the windlass.

A cresset already filled with wood and rendered blubber hung at one end of the cutting stage. At dark, Bry set it afire; and by its flames, sometimes flaring up and sometimes blowing aside, Knobby and Monk could see ends of their long spades plunging into the carcass of the whale. Without the least pause the trying out continued through the night. Bright orange tongues curled from beneath the kettles. Their light reflected from the windlass, the sheer poles, and the smelly cloud of smoke boiling into the sky. In the heat we stripped off our shirts and our glistening bodies moved back and forth, demon-like. Gusts of wind drove the smoke down around us and the try works, giving the scene the look of the nether world.

My legs ached from walking to and fro carrying chunks of blubber for the kettles, but there was some relief while kneeling to cut them from the blanket piece and mincing them on the head of a cask.

Bryan's gamy leg pained him more as he worked; yet he did his best hobbling about to tend the pots and bail oil into the cooling tank. For a seat he stacked two parts of a whale's backbone, and by sitting high on them he could ease the ache for a few minutes and then step closer to the kettles to fork out the rendered pieces. As they were needed, he stuffed them under the pots to keep the fires at the proper heat.

The boys returned about midnight, leading another canoe carrying several Indians who were put to work at the windlass, allowing the women to go off to their bunks. In twilight of the third day the final blanket piece was cut free from the carcass, lowered to the ground, and boiled. Our headsman watched Bry pour out the last dipper of oil to cool and; much pleased, announced, "Leave it all be, lads. We'll cut the bone and pull her out to the Strait later. So."

With a dozen turns of the windlass, we raised the whale's head a foot out of the water and left it hanging, inverted with the feathery baleen pointing upward like a strange hedge. The stripped carcass barely floated, and legged creatures explored its upper surface. Below, fish swarmed in to tear off bits and bolt them.

The bulk of the labor was finished and Monk paid off the Indians with their preferred wages, strings of tobacco. Other goods were accepted, but half of the payment they insisted must be the weed with new pipes in which to smoke it. Coins, except for their use as decorations, were valueless since there were no stores in which to spend them. We had the goods they desired, thus the value of their work was exchanged for those items directly.

Exhausted and with a mind dulled to that of a dray horse, I shambled toward the stream on aching legs, slipped off my trousers, and sat on a rock at the edge of the water, resting many minutes before washing my oily hands in the current. The fingers were set into a hard curl after hours of gripping tools; even at rest they looked as if they still held the handle of the windlass or a mincing knife. Down in the rookeries they had been in like condition from rowing hours every day and swinging the long sealing club. By dipping up fine mud from the edge of the stream and rubbing it on the skin, I washed the dirt, oil, and soot from my body. In my *whare* I dried myself with my old piece of calico. *Heke* laid my clean clothes out on the bunk. "Go fora *kai*," she said and left.

I dressed; then looked around the room. If we took as many whales as our headsman hoped, the bone would fill more than half of the *whare*. Monk, though, had promised that we would add to the other end and make more space for it and some of the gear. I was pacing out the area needed when *Heke* returned from the cookhouse with bowls containing our supper.

Monk allowed us a good night's rest and we began work late the next morning hacking the bone from the jaw. We cleaned it, and stood each one on end against my *whare* to dry, nearly hiding the place behind a screen of frond-like baleen.

Bryan inspected the casks we had filled the day before, now cooled some by the night air. He checked them for leaks; and any loose hoops he drove tight and left them for the boys to roll into the enclosure and cover with wetted *raupo*.

Monk and Knobby John trusted no one else to coil the whale line into its tub. They rove one end through a single block at the top of the sheers, and as the line was drawn down each layer was laid carefully from the outside of the tub to its center. It was the way to assure it would feed out and around the loggerhead. If it fouled and wasn't instantly cut, a sounding whale might pull the boat under and leave us clinging to our oars until the boys in the Two Sisters found us.

Another fish was not sighted by the lookout until one morning a week later. Being so well practiced, we were out of the cove and after it in a few minutes. Monk brought the Two Brothers skillfully alongside. Knobby darted his weapon; then swore it was a poor throw that had only penetrated about a foot. He sent the second iron after it and let us know by more curses it had fallen short. The animal headed off east, towing us toward the far side of the Strait. It went on for two miles, giving us a wonderful ride with our boat pounding from wave to wave and throwing spray to each side. Then the Two Brothers suddenly slowed to a halt.

"Ah, bloody damn," Monk swore. "The iron drawed."

The line lay slack in the water while our prize continued its flight. Monk ordered the line hauled in; and once it was recovered, the Two Brothers with our oars peaked and the sail up, moved in a light wind for an hour.

Bry lifted his left arm, pointed to the north, and called out, "Ahh, there blows."

In that direction there was a small white patch, but it wasn't a spout for it didn't fade away.

Monk put the handle of the steering oar in its loop and reached for his glass. He studied the object for a few seconds and chided, "Your glimms are getting weak, Bry. You're in need of spectacles. That's a schooner coming on to us, a big one. We'll speak her, get the news, and see what she's doing."

ON SOUNDINGS

The sails of the vessel grew in size as it moved steadily on a course that would near our boat. Her fore and aft rig became apparent as she closed. There were no davits and only one boat, which meant she was probably a trader or sealer. Even in the light air, it was evident she was a good sailer. The schooner came to within half a cable's length, and Monk ordered the Two Brothers' sail down and hailed the crew of the vessel. It swept downwind and turned about. Her way was checked, and she came to a halt with sails ashiver. Her jib halyard was let go and the sail slid into its nettings. The headsman had us row the Two Brothers up to her starboard side. Four men were on her deck. A man, with a round, well-tanned face who looked to be an officer from his better dress, stepped to the rail to speak to Monk.

"This is the *Free Settler*, Port Jackson," he said, indicating his vessel with a tilt of the head to his left. "I'm Captain Kyle White. Where is your ship?" he asked, and leaned far over until he was able to shake hands with Monk.

"We have no ship, only this here boat, the Two Brothers. I'm Monk Monkhouse and I heads this boat and I heads our mob."

Captain White scanned the horizon and then looked at the tub of line and the irons in our whaleboat with disbelief. "No ship?" he asked. "You whale out here but have no ship? Where are your quarters, your kettles?"

"Ashore there," Monk answered, pointing southwest.

Another man standing near Captain White was dressed in a black gown with Geneva tabs on his collar. He had topped off his clerical dress with a straw hat that covered much of his thick, gray hair. His rosy-gilled face was newly-shaven; and he peered at Monk though heavy glasses adjusted with a touch of a finger and asked, "Ah, you live on that island do you?"

"Aye, that we do. We have our sheers and *whares* there."

"Then you are just the person to whom I wish to speak. I am the Reverend Josiah Edwards Wooley of the New Worlds Missions. It has been my great honor to be sent here. There is much to do in these islands. I see you have Indians in your crew, Mr. Monkhouse. Are there many about your place?"

Our headsman nodded and replied, "To be sure, the *Rangitani*."

"Captain White," I broke in, "if you speak another ship, please report the barque *Dove* from America has foundered off the west coast of this island. She was a sealer, Tobit master."

"Were you aboard?" the captain asked.

"Yes, I am Thomas Wightman; all were lost save me."

"Ah, sad news for me to carry," the officer said. "I will give it to any I meet and will report it when we return to New South Wales. On the west coast, you say, where?"

"Not on it; but two hundred or so miles from it on a small island."

"Aye," Monk said, "he got here by a canoe. I expect he came onto this island some place about Rocks Point."

"Another island off the coast," Captain White mused. "A strange story, indeed. I've not heard of one about there. Well, rest assured I will give the news to all I meet. You wish to reach Port Jackson?"

I shook my head. "No, I wish to go in the other direction."

"Mr. Monkhouse," the Reverend broke in, "have you a parson bringing you the Gospel and caring for your spiritual well-being?"

"We've heard of none here about, but up in the Bay of Islands there's some."

Wooley held up an open hand and said, "Yes, yes I know of them, but has one called here to join you with your Indian women? I expect you have admitted them to your beds."

Monk nodded and replied, "For sure we have. You're the first parson that ever called on this coast."

Wooley then turned to the officer and said, "In regard to our agreement, Captain White, I wish you to call at this man's place. We must foregather with all souls who live hereabouts and give them the benefits of my presence."

The captain nodded and added, "Aye, our agreement to be sure. And perhaps it will also be to my advantage to call. Mr. Monkhouse, is there flax to be had about the country? That is my business."

"It grows about there, yes, but you mean dressed flax … *muka*? Enough to make a cargo? Well, I can't say. *Ruru*, Bry, is there that much to be had?"

Bryan talked with *Ruru* for a minute. Captain White listened but didn't seem to get the sense of the conversation.

A young New Zealander, also dressed in black, came up through the scuttle and joined the captain and the Reverend at the side of the schooner.

"Ah, my faithful Frederick," Wooley said. "Let me introduce my companion and a teacher who aids me in bringing the blessed word of God to these neglected savages. Frederick, this is Mr. Monkhouse."

Frederick reached down for the headsman's hand.

Monk turned to Captain White and inquired, "Have you been into Blind Bay?"

"Not as yet," the Captain replied. "We have been calling along the coast on the other side of the Strait and found precious little to trade for there."

Bryan spoke up, "It's muskets, Cap'n."

"Yes, what do you mean?"

"They want muskets, powder, and ball," Bryan explained. "You will get no flax but for them, and little else for what you may have to trade."

"They have asked for muskets, yes," the captain said, "but I do not deal in such things. By my agreement I cannot."

Bryan added, "There's a river in the country on t'other side of our cove. You have to have a good pilot there. It's all twists and turns before you reach it. It's said flax grows there aplenty. You might try that, but it's best you first go into Blind Bay."

The Reverend edged closer to the rail and said with an oily smile, "You speak English quite well for a New Zealander. Would you consider being in my employ to do the great work of Christianizing these benighted people?"

"I'm not a New Zealander, sir," Bryan corrected the Reverend in a low voice.

"But your face," Wooley asked, "how is it that you have the ...?" The churchman couldn't find the word or didn't wish to speak it.

Frederick turned to him and said, "*Moko.*"

The curiosity and some latent suspicion of these men had been raised. Captain White, the missionaries, and four of the crew at the rail were watching Bryan. He had forgotten the odd match his marked face made with his speech and blue eyes. He avoided speaking another word, sensing there was danger for him if he could not give a good reason for the whorls and arches cut into his face. He nodded once and shifted his attention to the whale line, coiling a few fakes of it back into the tub and patting them in place with the palm of his hand.

Monk spoke up. "Oh, he's English. Yes, for sure. Another castaway like Tom here, fishing with us. His ship went aground at Poverty Bay and he was taken prisoner and kept for years. He was given his *moko* and then was most fortunate to escape to us here."

The captain tilted his head back and watched Bryan for a few seconds. "What ship were you in?" he asked.

In a pause after that question, the only sounds were the shaking of the sail and the slosh of water alongside.

"*The Prince of Asia*," Bryan replied.

Monk nodded and echoed, "Aye, it was *The Prince of Asia*."

Wooley eyed Bryan and took a half step back, a clue he had no more to say about employment.

Captain White waved his hand toward the land and asked, "Where is your place, Mr. Monkhouse?"

"You see those small islands there. Our cove is just west of them and in from that foreland. You will see a pole there with a blue pennant raised on it. Drop your bower when you're opposite our sheers. So."

The captain ordered the jib up and then spoke to the helmsman. He threw the wheel over and the slow sternway of the schooner edged her bow to larboard. Her sails filled quickly and she fell off, gathering speed.

Monk turned to us and commanded, "Down oars … pull three."

With its sail raised and the wind aft, our boat passed *The Free Settler* despite her greater spread of canvas. We watched her diminish as we drew rapidly ahead.

Chapter Eight

We rounded the Two Brothers into the cove. All the women with their children, seeing us return so early, were gathered on the beach wondering what had gone amiss. Monk ordered us alongside when the schooner arrived to ferry the captain and the elder churchmen to the beach. The Reverend Wooley, carrying two Bibles, stepped off our bow and onto the sand with a lordly air, not even wetting his boots.

I turned to Knobby in the bow and whispered, "I'll lay a brace of sovereigns we're in for a preachment."

"Bring the others up to my *whare*," Monk called to us and turned to lead the visitors up the path.

The two crews, the children, and the women of the station slowly ascended the notched log and nearly filled the large room. Monk offered Captain White and the two churchmen seats at one side of the table. White's first mate, Monk, and Knobby each found a whalebone on which to sit, and the last seats at the table were taken by the crewmen of the schooner. The remainder of us sat on the lower bunks or stood behind those seated. The toddlers, usually all shouts and squeals, were taken by an unknown shyness and peeked wide-eyed from behind their mothers at the newcomers.

Monk introduced each of the women to the captain and Wooley and with that done announced with a smile, "Now a good tot all round." He went to the north wall, got out the bottles, and placed them on the table. *Karee* set a tin cup before those seated at the table and passed out the few left to the men who were standing. The Reverend Wooley, with a sniffy look, waved a disparaging hand at the cup before him making it clear that he would not drink and did not approve of the practice.

"And what news do you have for us?" was Monk's first question.

Captain White looked overhead for a minute and then ventured, "Well, have you heard they have taken the bushranger, Bloody Biggs, in Van Dieman's?"

All those of our station shook their heads.

"We've heard naught, when was that?" Knobby asked.

The captain looked at Wooley and asked, "January, wasn't it, Reverend?"

Wooley thought a moment and replied, "No, I believe it was November or early in December. Yes, yes, it was well before Epiphany if I recall correctly."

Monkhouse showing no interest in Biggs or any bolter new or old, and not caring if the man had been named a magistrate of Hobart Town, asked the captain, "What's the price of oil and bone given now in Port Jackson? We want to know if there's been any advance on what was being paid."

Captain White answered, "When I left, the prices were down, but I can't quote in pounds how much as I rarely deal with it. What is given here?"

Monk shook his head and said, "About a third less than the price at Port Jackson. More from an American ship wanting to fill for home, if they call here. They have no tariff to pay. Bone brings forty, sometimes forty-two pounds for the ton. We have rising fifty barrel of black oil; and of bone we have about five hundredweight. You wish to buy it?"

"I am sent for flax," the captain answered, "but if we haven't a full cargo when I'm ready to sail, I will consider your bone and oil. It will have to be paid for in trade goods. I carry little specie."

"Spreaders, weed and pipes, kettles, tomahawks, cloth," Monk listed. "I can well use those if you have any. Oh, and tin ware, lanterns, fish hooks, and knives are always asked for. Ah, and needles too."

"I have some of those, but I must see what flax I can get for them here," White replied.

Wooley shifted on his seat, impatient with the talk in which he had no interest. He looked at each in turn as they spoke, and at the first pause he thrust his two Bibles out before him and lowered them slowly to the table in a dramatic gesture. "Rejoice, friends, rejoice," he announced, pressing a hand on each Bible. He leaned forward and repeated, "Rejoice! You are not forgotten. I bring the comfort of the Lord here today. Do any of you here possess a Bible?"

There was a murmur of noes and several shook their heads. Wooley stabbed his left forefinger on one Bible and announced, "Then I will leave this one here that you may read it after your labors and gain solace from its words."

The room was quiet except for a few murmurs from the children. All were watching him and waiting for his next sentence.

There was a smile on his pink face as he explained, "There has been a most favorable beginning to my mission. I am greatly pleased. The Lord must be greatly pleased. Thus far I have baptized over twenty children and joined fourteen couples in marriage." He rose to his feet and, beaming to the right and left, declared, "I will sanctify the unions of those who wish it at this very moment and end your sinful cohabitation. I urge you to do so for you must think of your souls and the final judgment that will surely come. I have arrived here to join any and all before God. I give you the means to correct this lapse and begin you on your way to salvation." His audience remained silent as he looked around the circle of faces, expecting couples to step forward. "Come, come," he urged, "there must be some among you in which the religious feelings stir. You know it is right and proper. Think of your children. Would they not want their parents to be properly joined together and themselves baptized? I have arrived here to join any and all before God. I give you the means to fill this need and begin you on your way to salvation." The Reverend scanned the room hopefully once again.

Peck took Amelia's hand, but in the next moment he apparently changed his mind and did not take a step forward. He released his hold and brought his fingers up to scratch a feigned itch on his belly.

Knobby got to his feet slowly and fetched his Sarah forward. Then *Ruru* and *Aihe* joined them. Bryan, sitting on a bunk, shifted a little. Then he rose awkwardly, stepped over to *Kotuku*, and led her by the hand to the end of the table. She stood beside him giving everyone her serene, near smiling look. They appeared an odd pair; yet I was certain those two needed no ceremony, blessing, or listing in any churchman's book to bind them together.

Wooley, heartened by his small victory, let his practiced smile widen, perhaps to hide his distaste for the *moko*, the symbol of the savage on Bryan's face. Pleased and puffed, he picked up his Bible and held it to his chest.

"No others?" the Reverend Wooley queried. "No more to be blessed and joined before God in this good company? No more?" He turned to Monk, expecting the other whalers' choices to be married would prompt the headsman to give way. Monk's left elbow rested on the table with his open hand supporting his chin. His eyes returned only a careless look. The churchman, seeing he would get no response there, shifted his attention to Peck with an inquiring lift of his chin, but Peck parried the invitation with a quick glance up at the unlit lantern above.

The Reverend, who had just arrived, intended to bustle about and use that black book as leverage to order our lives as he saw fit, holding everyone to his unbending moralities. What authority had he been given and from where? Would he appoint himself a magistrate too and deal out floggings? I would not take my *Heke*, she knowing naught of what Wooley would say, and stand before the man. She understood the marriage mat and had made her choice firm and good. That was all that was needed. No amount of words meant anything if they weren't accompanied with a firm intent. *Heke* and I knew each other's mind even without the aid of language. Wooley could speak his words to any number of people whose true feelings he never knew and boast of so many marriages. If any couple decided to part, the words would mean little in these islands.

Josiah Edwards Wooley officiated with gusto and beamed with pride at the couples he was marrying in the same ritual. That completed, the Reverend began his christenings and tacked on an Old Testament name of his choice onto each child in addition to his or her Indian one. Most were unpronounceable by the Indians, and Abraham was turned into Aperahama and Isaiah into Itaiah when they tried out their new names. All the men in the room, save the reverend, hoisted their cups once more and barked out a good cheer; and feeling the spirit of the moment, Monk invited all to remain and eat. Meat and fish hanging inside the chimney were taken out and extra vegetables pulled from the garden. There weren't enough plates and forks for the crowd. By the whalemen's custom of hospitality, guests were given those in Monk's house, plus ones gathered from the other families, leaving some of the station's people and all the children to feed themselves from communal bowls with fingers and sheath knives.

Captain White called his crew from chatting groups an hour after the finish of the meal and ordered them aboard the *Free Settler*.

The Reverend and Frederick remained behind on the porch watching the others back down the notched log to the ground. Wooley watched Peck and noted to which house he went. He then turned to our headsman and began, "Mr. Monkhouse, to be affined to these people is an exceeding good thing; and now if you were to marry your woman, it would guide her people to the church and its great comforts and salvation. It would be a fine example not only to them but to any other men who might come here to whale. It is necessary for good order of society for a man to be committed to his woman in the eyes of God."

Monk looked Wooley up and down and with blandness replied, "Married or not, I am most committed to my women. Ask them."

The Reverend's mouth opened, but he did not speak for a moment. Suddenly his face feathered into an uncertain smile. When he found his voice, the churchman chuckled nervously, "Heh, heh, heh, yes … yes. I take it *cum grano salis*, when you say your women."

"When I say my women, I mean … my women."

Wooley's smile faded into a disturbed stare. Then he frowned, leaned his head forward, and asked, "Do I hear you properly? Do you aver you have more than one mistress?"

"That I did, Reverend. *Maree, Karee* come out here."

The two women came to the door and the headsman took a place between them. "My wives," he declared and put an arm around each one.

The Reverend Josiah Wooley looked at Frederick, back to each of the women, and then at Monk. He drew himself up in a stiff pose and began a rebuke, "This is not a matter of jest, sir. I lately arrived here and have been told of such a practice among the more depraved. You must shed one of them at once."

"Because you say so?"

"Because God does not countenance such. It can be excused in these savages while they are yet in their state of ignorance, but you are not. Or are you? This is the most willful and disgusting sin … fornication! For you, doubly so … more than all the others here … shameless … brazen. You hear me, fornication!"

"If the others choose to be married by you, it only concerns them," Monk said. "They may do as they please. I choose not to." He slipped his arms from around his wives and took a step forward. "This is not New South Wales, Reverend. It's *Tovy Poenamoo* and I heads this mob. I rule here. So!"

Wooley's red face paled. He turned to Frederick and said in a low voice,

"There's nothing more to be done here. Let us go." Frederick began descending the steps.

The Reverend followed his aide, backing down the log, but stopped on the third step. He looked up at Monk's great bulk standing solidly above him. It was an undignified position for the Reverend at the feet of the headsman. His jowly face reddened again and shook with rage. "You are an arrant sinner, an apostate, an infidel," he hissed through his teeth. "Worse than that," he added, "a devil ... incarnate!"

The headsman stared down defiantly at him and took a half step forward. That movement and Monk's right foot, then nearer to the Reverend's face, had their effect. Wooley quickly descended to the ground, spun about, and marched down the path. He fumed and twisted his head to the side a few times to snap a few words back to Frederick who was now close on his heels. The Reverend shook his head and appeared to be mumbling to himself as he paced toward Peck's house.

Heke and I stepped down the log and returned to our *whare*. One glance about inside set me to thinking for several minutes. We had our bunk, our table, and our seats all under a dry roof. Up the trail were the gardens that yielded our potatoes and greens, and in Monk's big chimney pig meat and fish were always smoked. What would Wooley's words add to all that? What would change in our lives after he placed our names in his book and sent another boasting letter to his missionary lords? He would expect to be well hosted and housed each time he visited, meaning that he would live by our labor.

There was a knock at the doorpost. *Heke* stepped over and pulled aside the canvas. The black-frocked Reverend was standing there. She turned to me and announced, "Mihinare, Toma Kina."

I went to the opening. Wooley, with a fresh, charitable smile, greeted me, "Ah, you are Thomas as I recall."

"Aye, Thomas Wightman," I replied slowly, knowing full well the purpose of his visit.

"I noted you and your good lady did not step forward to be married with the others. We are about to leave, but I thought we must come to back and ask you to reconsider. It would be a good example for all here and these innocent savages if you did. How could you have any objection to being married in the eyes of God and the Church? Those not so joined live in sin. You understand that?"

"*Heke* has already been made over to me by her people. It sits well with her. What is more important is what we think of each other. Your words bind no one. You wish us to stand before you while you read from your book. Will that change anything; make me fonder of *Heke* or her of me? Would it make us more loyal?"

"Now, think, son. It is much, much more than that. It is only God who binds. Make no mistake. *Imprimus*, there are your immortal souls to consider. I am speaking of the final judgment. You must be joined properly in the eyes of God. It is your pledge to God and to your wife."

"Who's god? Why not *Heke's atua*, or a Hindoo god? Words, just so many words. *Heke* doesn't know a score of mine, but she understands my intent. A piece of paper is no substitute for that, and it does not add a thing. So, you speak for a minute, write something in your book and somehow everything is far better. Far better for all your wind and ink. I am saved and you have another pair to claim for your little kingdom of kneelers."

Wooley stood silent for a moment, taken aback by my words. He drew himself up for another try and said soberly, "Thomas, it is my duty to labor with you, turn your disbelief aside, for I think you have not been wholly tainted by these people and their ill natures. It is my duty to save you from their sinful example."

"And who gave you that duty?"

"The call comes. One knows it within one's bosom and must choose to answer it."

"So, no one can question your pretension. How convenient."

The Reverend, though piqued, paused and considered another tack. He pointed a finger to the sky and said, "It is a most important part in being a good Christian to be joined to your wife in the Church. Thus you have his blessing for your union and admit to the supremacy of God. You well know there are other obligations. You must be temperate, of steady habits. Here is your great opportunity to help these benighted people about here. These people do so much injury to themselves by their vicious battles. Be wed in the Church, Thomas. Your example and those of others may show them the blessings, the meliorty of our religion. Would it not be a wonderful thing by your marriage to help them to the way of salvation and the joys of peace?"

"Oh, yes. Oh, yes, let us show them the peace the men had at Waterloo. The peace the people in Spain got from a Bonaparte. Yes, all good Christians. The peace of death! You speak with so much authority, but look behind you at what has happened, how the Christian bodies have piled up. Ten thousand times more than here. Yes, I know how these people raid. I don't like it, but I understand it. They live in a different world here where there is no honor in being meek, where being known as a great warrior means more than all other things in life."

"Forget the past: look to the future," Wooley exclaimed with a wave of his hand. "With Christianity as our goal, we will ameliorate their lives. We can dissuade them from their fierceness and frightful, sinful habits. We will ameliorate their lives."

"WE! WE can dissuade them!" I spat out. "WE, you say. You think you can warp me in to work for your mob of preachers?" It was all sounding familiar to me. Then I said, "We all have our trades. Ours here is to fish for whales and sell oil. Yours is to fish for souls and sell salvation."

Shock spread on Wooley's face. He drew back a half step and huffed, "Salvation is not for sale. It is earned by walking in the path of righteousness. Ha! You speak of selling your oil and you take your earnings to buy your women. Yes, they have been sold to you! I have heard of such things. You have purchased them. It is only right for you to marry them in the church and atone for this disgusting, savage practice."

"Did any of them look unhappy to you? Answer me. Did they? True, goods change hands, but any one of them may refuse and another is easily found who is willing to take her place. How many women in England have that choice? Once married, there is no choice for them there. They cannot leave no matter how much they come to dislike the man. Here in this cove, among us a woman's word is tended to far more than in Europe or America. Heaven? That's what you make for yourself wherever you happen to be, if you can. Salvation for these Indians? What does that mean to them? Ha! A good ax, a hoe, or an iron pot is of far better use."

"This is preposterous that I am speaking to you in this manner. It is not for me to defend the true faith here but for you to explain your lack of it. You were raised in a civilized country, yes, a Christian country, and were most fortunate to receive the word of God. Yet you scorn it. In this savage place you may not always have the opportunity to return to the church before you die. I advise you take it now and secure your place in heaven." Reverend Wooley reseated his spectacles on his nose and took a step back. He again pointed a finger to the sky and intoned in a well-practiced speech, "There will come a day when you will regret this life of sin you lead. The final judgment, do not forget that. The final judgment!" He lifted a righteous chin and snapped about with a military step.

I watched him stomp toward the shore, and as I turned away I spied Bryan approaching from the stream.

"He hasn't won you over to his doxy yet?" Bry asked as he neared.

"Ha, I saw you step forward to be spliced, Bry," I bantered with a smile. "I never thought you had such a need for religion."

"Oh, that was *Kotuku's* doing. Oh, she must have us be married by him. The *atua* of the ship people is powerful. She says he gives them spreaders, lanterns, needles, pots, knives, and cloth."

"I don't see the connection, Bry. What has all that truck to do with being married?"

"Why, if you're married by him that brings these good things; his *atua* must be able to make a better job of it, better than her just being made over to me. I did it for her. It makes her most happy, but I have no use for them black flies that march around with their Bibles declaring they're bringing good news and saving everybody from hell. If they didn't have their hellfire and devil, they wouldn't have a damn thing to gally people with."

I looked out toward the *Free Settler* and asked, "What will it be like when more come here, flocks of them?"

Bryan shook his head and said, "Ha, Episcopals, Dippers, Presbyters, Quavers, Craw Thumpers, they'll all be pitching their tents here and scrambling for sinners, preaching on any excuse. Aye, they'll meet, sip their chatter broth, and nip at a biscuit, only with the right people of course and sneer at everyone else. Then they'll start fightin' 'mongst themselves, but all of them ranting in their hum box about how evil us whalers is. Not much that mob won't do for these Indians, but you won't see a stitch done for them above the docks in London. No, not 'less they get to their knees and pray up a squall. Then it's only a mite at a time. No, it's easier to gather up these savages and teach them to sing and crow words they don't understand. They tot up the numbers in their mission house and report it back home. Ho, ho! Look, so many souls saved. For that they get more pledges of money. Aye, easier to do that and more profitable than to tell the people at home why they're poor and hungry. So it goes and those what can't pay up their debts are taken to Newgate prison."

Chapter Nine

A week after the schooner left, three spouts were seen from the lookout. We rowed out again, chasing after the puffs as they appeared and faded in the distance. At two miles from shore we located one of the whales.

"A good-sized cow," Monk muttered as we neared. "I see no calf."

We, facing aft, accepted his word that it was a large right whale without a calf, but perhaps with one not yet born.

"She sounds," Monk reported. With uncanny sense he placed the boat twenty yards from the whale when she breached again just to larboard. Her twin spouts shot up with a loud whoosh and hung in the air for seconds. The sun was on the far side of the whale, begetting a faint rainbow in the exhaled mist. It faded as it settled and dissipated. Monk worked the Two Brothers in close to the black skin of the animal.

At my left shoulder the pole of the first harpoon lifted from the crotch. Seconds later Knobby shouted, "To the wood." Then the next harpoon pole disappeared.

"Both irons," Monk added. "She sounds."

The line whizzed across our oars, through the chock and into the sea. The beast remained below for over a half hour. Suddenly the black head, patterned with barnacles, burst out of the sea just astern of the Two Brothers. The body shot up over half its length out of the water and slammed forward, throwing a wave to each side. The next breaching filled our boat with a foot of water. The bucket, piggin, drugg, and lantern keg floated around in the hull.

"She white waters," Monk called out.

The whale headed toward Cape Stephens for three or four miles, then doubled back, giving Peck time to bail some water from our hull. Its unbroken run toward the Cape and back had tired the animal; and it lay still, drawing and blowing its breath. We rowed the Two Brothers quietly, closing in on the black side of the beast. Monk changed places with Knobby and, once he was there, he had only one chance to plunge the lance in. The flukes lifted from the sea and slammed down on the water, their edge only inches from our bow. The fight was full on again. Our whale made a run toward the Strait and back and thrashed about in a pink froth of blood and seawater for two hours before it finally died.

After the battle the long haul home began, and I wondered if we would ever take a whale within a half mile of the cove. It was always "give way, give way" for hours after a kill. Each time we leaned back bending our oars, the mass barely awash at the end of the tow line didn't appear to move. It felt as if we were tied to a rock. The Two Sisters arrived and with it hitched to the line added the two boys' efforts to the pull. The wind was dead ahead with no advantage to be got from it, and it was late afternoon when we warped the carcass under the shears.

"I do believe this is the largest fish we've taken," Monk said, eying the body from the cutting stage.

Knobby, following him, agreed, "Aye, for sure the longest. Flukes there and her lip reaches to here."

She had a calf and we cut it out of her and boiled it too, making the total yield an unexpected fifty-six barrels. Even with the help of the men who were fetched again to the cove, the trying out required the most of three and a half days. At noon of that final day Bryan fished the last rendered pieces from the kettles and stowed them in an unheaded cask to start rendering the next animal. The fires, no longer fed, died away. *Ruru* dipped the last oil from the cooling vat into a cask and Bryan hammered its bung in tight. The next day Bryan examined all the casks for leaks, and yielded them to us to roll inside the fence and cover with rockweed and *raupo*. On rainless days the boys were tasked to dash buckets of water on them to keep the staves damp and tight.

Late in the afternoon Monk looked out to the Strait for a moment and determining the strength of the wind, ordered, "Launch the boats and bring them to the sheers. We'll tow the carcasses away while the wind is up. Peck and Bry you two row with the boys."

A flock of sea birds, their wings and bodies creamy white in the clear, low sunlight, circled and dipped over the remains of whale and calf. Some landed, forcing others to fluster off. Monk looped the whale line twice over the loggerhead of the Two Brothers, and gave enough slack to Bryan to hitch to the other boat and the carcasses. The headsman pointed the bow of the Two Brothers north.

Dark shoals of fish, which had fed on the stripped bodies for days, followed their moving feast. Small sharks at each side lunged at the flesh and twisted over and over, wrenching off bites. For two hours we leaned forward and lay back, adding our oar strokes to the drive of the sails. Monk estimated the distance back toward the cove, and deciding we had pulled far enough away, ordered, "Peak oars. Douse the sail."

"Sharks will feed on them for days and maybe weeks," Knobby said. "Let's hope the stinking mess don't drift back into the cove."

Monk looked at the water and estimating the current and the effect of the wind declared, "None have yet. They'll sink in a while. We're far enough out now. Unhitch the lines and you can light up, boys."

With the wind against us it was going to be a pull back to the cove; smoking would not be possible or allowed. With the last oil stowed in casks, nothing was pressing unless we spied another whale. Out our pipes came and we filled and lighted them in minutes. It was time to take our ease, smoke, and look at each other's dirty faces and grimy clothes.

"We boiled her down in good time," Monk said. "It's fine, sweet oil. It will fetch a good price, fifteen pound a tun. For the bone, I'd say we'll get fifty pound or more."

"You see, Tom Skins," Knobby pointed out, "we have no ship to keep up and no insurance to pay, no owners to take a third. We own the boats and tools and so keep that third."

Monk then asked me, "Better than even a short lay on a ship isn't it, Tom Skins?"

I nodded, agreeing with him, and replied, "I hope I make enough this season to repay you for rescuing me."

"No need to do that," Monk said. "We were happy to ransom you. You're most needed. We can't fish shorthanded."

"I want to take *Heke* home. I mean to pay you and leave next season."

"Back home you can't make a tenth of what you make here," Peck pointed out.

"Aye, far less than a tenth," Monk added. "Stay here. Only two or three shares are set aside to buy new lines, irons and trade goods. All the rest is divided between us. It might be a good year, and you could earn fifty, sixty, eighty pound in a season. No money to put out for grub and rent. What you earn is all yours."

"It's not home," I said. "I must see my father. He doesn't know what has happened to me. I will stay long enough to pay you and earn passage for myself and *Heke*."

"Well, by that time we might pick up a man," Monk said.

The old problem returned to mind: full ships need no extra hands when filled. If I signed on one still whaling, I might never return to the cove. There must be enough money earned for passage; and if oil and bone were not taken here more quickly, our departure would be put off for two or more seasons.

Tokee and *Wehe* begged a few long puffs from Peck's and Bryan's pipes before we all started the row back to the cove.

We had a blowout of sleep and didn't stir from our bunks until the afternoon of the following day. *Tokee* went around to all families with Monk's invitation to bring all their food up to his big *whare* that evening. One by one we arrived and stepped up the notched log. We, clean shaven for the first time in more than a week and dressed in our best clothes, gathered around the table.

Peck and Knobby John began telling long stories of battles with whales and their ill-usage on some vessels. When Peck ended his last tale he prompted me, "Now your turn, Tom Skins. We told our tales. Let's hear about your sealing."

"It's dull story compared to yours," I said, "but since it is my turn to amuse you a little, I'll tell it. Seals were scarce and we expected it was to be a bad season. We hardly skinned two or three animals in a week, so we were put to lancing sea elephants and boiling them down. We left there and raised a new island where we found the seals covered its beaches, and then it was kill and skin every daylight hour. It wasn't long before we had a full ship. Plenty of seals were still there when we left, maybe tens of thousands; and if I knew where that island lay we could all be rich men in one season. I only know it's far to the south and holds a treasure for whoever finds it again."

Knobby slapped his hand on the table and called out, "Well, that's a story lad. That'll be good for a round or two when you're moored in a tavern back home. Much better than some of the old clankers I've heard in those places."

All afternoon the women had been busy preparing vegetables gathered from the gardens and the fish netted in the cove. *Maree* took some flour down to the cookhouse, made lumps of dough with lard, and fried them in oil. The night before, *Kotuku* had placed a young pig in an earth oven; and we not yet caught up in our eating had savored the prospect of its flesh all day. *Karee* and *Tokee* dug the animal up and brought it into the *whare* at the start of the meal. Peck opened the package of leaves and placed the pig on a square of wood in the center of the table. Its aroma and that of the onions cooked with it filled the room. He poised his sheath knife and a fork above it, waved each in the circle of a mock ritual, and stabbed then into the animal. Then he carved off pieces and apportioned them to the children.

Steam rolled up from the kettles of potatoes and beans the wives placed on the table. One large tin plate was piled with roasted fish and another loaded with *Maree's* fritters.

The toddlers crowded around the table holding their bowls up to receive potatoes, greens, and their slices of pig; then wandered around the room feeding themselves with greasy fingers. Boney, whining and simpering in his best manner, followed one then another of the children and, with a dip of the head and flick of the tongue, begged a scrap of pig from each child. We chewed meat from the bones and bolted servings of the vegetables to restore the energy expended in peeling and boiling the whale. *Aihe* and Sarah sat at the table, and each divided her attention between their infant and their filled plates. The three-and four-year-old children, with faces shiny with grease, returned to Peck for another serving.

I looked at the bones on my plate at the end of the meal and wondered how I could have eaten so much.

Monk slowly exhaled, "Ahhh." He slapped his stomach and boasted, "There that's filled out the wrinkles. Such a feed, mates. Our women have cooked us a king's banquet." He turned and pulled his wives to him, one on his right and the other on his left, and with a squeeze and pat on the bottom sent each back to her chores.

Peck, always the first to bring his pipe out, sliced tobacco from the end of a twist. We followed his lead, rubbing dark shreds of weed in the palm for our smoke. *Kotuku* took a stick from the fireplace, flaming at one end, and passed it to the nearest man. Columns of smoke released from our mouths rose up between the joists and the gear stored on them.

Monk suddenly slapped his big hand on the table and declared, "It was a feast! Aye, a feast! A toast to them. Men, we must make a toast to our women. Each and all." He jumped up, went to a box under the window, and drew out a bottle. He filled cups with liquor for us. Then he filled his own and stomped the bottle loudly on the table. With his drink raised toward *Maree*, he barked, "To *Maree!*"

"To *Maree*," the rest of us chorused. We held our pipes in one hand and hoisted our cups with the other to give each woman a salute. By the time *Heke* was toasted, our cups had been refilled. Monk held out his cup in a jesting offer of a drink to the women.

"No *waipiro*," *Karee* said. Her face twisted into a frown and her hand waved the smell of the liquor away.

"No stinking water for you? Aye, that's my good girls. None for you. So!"

The women lost their smiles and cleared the table. In minutes they filed out the door with the children. It was sure to be a night of drinking for us; and for the women, gathered down in Peck's *whare*, it would be talk while they replaced missing buttons and patched the holes in the elbows of shirt sleeves.

Knobby leaned onto the left cheek of his bottom, lifted his right foot from the floor, and let go with a long ripping noise. "Ahhh … that was my need after that great feast," he said.

"Goddamn, but it wasn't ours," Peck complained, wafting the stink away with a hand. "That was a brewer's fart, grains and all."

Monk doubled his fist, reached across, and bumped it square against Knobby's forehead, knocking it back a bit. "That's enough music from your bumfiddle," he said. "Take it outside next time."

Our toasts resumed with additional ones made to the boats, irons, and the next whale to be brought under the sheers.

Peck brought out his dice, carved from a whale's jawbone. A few shillings, Spanish dollars, and coils of twist tobacco were laid out on the table for the first bets. The men stomped their feet and shouted after each throw of the dice. With more liquor in them, they wagered their valued items. Peck risked his flint and striker and its box against *Ruru's* prized tricorne and lost the roll.

Knobby motioned to *Tokee* and said, "Go to my *whare* and get more tobacco and my ditty bag that has my sewing kit. There's a half dozen silver buttons and some shillings in it." On *Tokee's* return Knobby wagered the coins against Bryan's razor but lost and complained, "This is mere chance. We should use some true skill to decide."

"For sure. Capital idea. Let's dart the iron!" Monk barked. He stepped onto one of the bone seats, then to the table and reached overhead to untie an old harpoon from the rafters. Its head had been snapped off, perhaps in a whale, and the shaft, socket, and pole saved for the day when a blacksmith on a visiting ship could be hired to weld on a new point.

Knobby went to the far corner at the left of the fireplace and wedged a small piece of cloth into a split in the post there. The post had been punched and battered and the clay daub wall on either side of it repaired more than once, good evidence darting the iron was an old game with them.

Monk took the harpoon to the opposite corner of the room. "This will be good drill for you, Tom Skins," he advised me.

"Aye, you must learn to fasten to a fish," Bryan added. "Someday it might be your turn if Knobby gets hurt."

Knobby slapped a hand on the table top and called out, "Lay your bets 'ere! Come, lads, one throw apiece and the closest to the mark takes all. We'll see who can handle the iron."

The bets piled up on the table.

"My wager," Bryan said and put up Knobby's shillings he had just won.

"Mine, two shillings and my knife," Peck offered and placed them on the table.

"No, no, your knife is o … old," Knobby complained. "You put up one more shillin' with it 'gainst my weed, there's near a pound of it."

Monk laid his clasp knife and a whetstone on the table, and we all nodded, agreeing it was equal to the other bets in value. *Ruru* offered Peck's flint and steel with its box and that was accepted. I had nothing of value except my new pumps. I slipped them off and made my bet.

"Ah, 'nother drink 'fore we throw," Knobby proposed, reaching for the bottle. He poured rum into each man's cup until the bottle was drained. Monk went to the boxes under the window and brought out two more.

I delayed drinking much of mine until all the others had downed theirs in a gulp. It was too fiery for me, but I sipped some, knowing that if I didn't it would be noticed by the others and read as an effort to set myself off, put on airs.

Peck picked up the pointless harpoon with his left hand, held it head high, and cupped the butt of the pole in his right hand. With a grunt he pitched it at the rag on the post. It sailed over the table, but missed the target by a foot and a half. The iron shaft went through the wall up to the socket.

"Hee, hee, hee," Knobby snickered. "Hee, hee, hee. Peck, clumsy li'l ... o ... oaf, you'll never shit a ... steersman's turd." He pulled the harpoon from the wall, gave it to *Ruru*, and asked, "Les ... see what you can do with it."

Ruru aped Peck's stance exactly and launched the weapon toward the corner post. It struck closer to the rag but grazed the post and also pierced the wall, cracking out a piece of clay daub. I went forward and retrieved the iron. My try disappointed me as it was no closer than Peck's and punched another hole into the wall.

"Ha, ha," Knobby taunted me. "Monk, les ... show these lads ha ... ow it's done. Without us two, you marines 'ud never strike a fish. It's a gawdamn staunch floor here under you. Whaa'ud you do in the boat pitchin' an' rollin' ... an' flukes ... 'bout ta smash your skull?"

The headsman took the harpoon and launched it, hitting the post a foot below the target with such force the shaft bent. A section of the wall daub the size of a serving platter was shaken loose and shattered on the floor.

Bryan took a swig from his cup and retrieved the weapon. "Here, stand on it, Knobby, while I ben' ... it," he said.

Knobby stepped on the shaft while Bryan brought the soft iron rod back into line. He took his time, hefted the harpoon, and aimed it carefully. His right arm drove the pole smoothly forward. The iron and wood sailed across the room, and the end of the shaft punched into the split in the post two inches above the little swatch of fabric and fell to the floor.

"Ho, ho! Bry!" Peck shouted.

Monk slapped Byran on the back and barked, "A fast fish! Aye, an' maybe deep into the life of ... 'er. No need t' lance."

Knobby was sobered some when he saw Bryan's near perfect throw. Monk retrieved the iron and offered it to Knobby, grinning at him in a smug, wordless challenge to best Bryan. Knobby picked up his cup and drained it slowly.

All were half seas over or more and weaved a bit as they walked around the room. If we continued throwing the old harpoon, it would batter a hole large enough for a door through the back wall of the house.

Knobby took the harpoon and looked at it from one end to the other. Suddenly he lifted it, set his left leg forward as if it were in the notch of a thigh board, and pitched the weapon at the post. It went into the wall even farther from the mark than my try.

We all broke into jeers around Knobby. Bryan stepped to the table and collected all of the wagers.

"Tri … tripped there on tha … edge," Knobby protested. "Th … ere, see."

"Hah! But you got … a … a solid floor here," Peck needled the steersman. "Easier here than dartin' from … boat pitchin' all …ways? Hee, hee, hee."

Knobby's looks turned squally at Peck's gibe.

"A toast for Bry the Brea … uh!" Peck shouted. He grabbed one of the bottles and filled the cups held out to him.

Monk, *Ruru*, and Peck hoisted their cups and repeated the toast, "To Bry the Breakuh. To Bry the Breakuh."

"No. No … no gawdamn to … oast for Bry," Knobby growled. "I steers the Two Brov … ers. An' no gawdamn cove wi' a dumb leg can better me." He weaved toward Bryan with his head slightly canted to one side and his red-veined eyes staring. "I should skin that ugly cann … nibal face of yers," he threatened. "Aye, I'll do that now … peel that gawdamn inky hide off ya."

"'Nother wager," Peck broke in, determined to better Bryan's throw.

"Aye, 'nother trial," Monk seconded, and brought the iron back to the corner for the next throw. "Lay your wagers," he added.

Instead of placing his bet with the others, Knobby seized the neck of a bottle on the table, made a short, quick swing back, and struck Bryan on the head. Bryan staggered back against a bunk and crumpled to the floor. Peck grabbed for the bottle and wrestled it from Knobby's hand, but the steersman scooped Peck up and threw him onto the table. The momentum rolled his small body across it and he tumbled off onto the floor on the far side. Monk clinched with Knobby, pushing him against the table and tilting it up and over. Its thick edge struck a whale bone stool, glanced off, and landed diagonally across Peck's back.

"Eeeacch!" he screamed in pain. Monk kicked Knobby's right leg from under him. With his left hand gripping his neck, he thrust him face down onto the floor and then straddled his big bulk over his back. Monk sat with arms crossed in a nonchalant pose. Knobby raised his head and shouted, "Blast your bal … bal … locks."

"And blast your potato trap," the headsman replied and pushed Knobby's face against the floor with his left hand. "There, that'll give your t … tongue a holiday."

The game was over for a while; and though I had paced my drinking, only sipping at my cup, I was more fuddled than I wanted to be. I felt the pressing need to leak and weaved out the door. At the edge of the porch, I fumbled with my trousers, let fly a good stream over the railing, and waved my roger side to side to wet down the bushes in the dark below. "Ahh. Pisshh on you all … pissh on all captains an' mates," I breathed with relief. It was a good time to make an escape. With more than my limit in me, I surely couldn't hold another swallow of that fierce rum. But there was the log with the line of steps cut into it to be descended one by one. The porch heaved slowly beneath my feet like the deck of a ship in a light swell. How was I to get to the ground without falling? I eased onto my hands and knees, turned around, and backed over the edge of the porch. My right foot found the first step. Then my left foot found the next one, and my right reached one more. I wrapped my arms around the log to slide them lower with each step down. Halfway to the ground, the dark hills and the *whare* started to turn around. "Hol' on, ho … ho … hol' on," I whispered. My grasp on the log wasn't strong enough and I teetered to one side. I tried mightily to right myself; but slipped farther over, lost all support, and landed on the flat of my back. The shock punched the breath out of my lungs. I didn't feel I was badly hurt and decided to lie there and recover while lying under the star-lit sky. A thin streak of white light sped from the zenith half way to the northern horizon. "Ahh … shoo … shooing stah," I slurred. The last time I had watched a sky with such brilliance was when sailing from the little island and still eighty or a hundred miles out at sea. The slim hull had been in endless motion buoying me up and sinking beneath me. The night was far different from those six months before when I suffered thirst, cursed my foolishness, and faced the end of life. Now I was supported by the earth which held me up to scan the arch of the Milky Way and the spread of stars from the crest on the left side of the cove to the one on my right. Argo Navis was to the south in its unending voyage around the sky hidden from me by the hill. Another meteor sent a bright line down in the northeast. "Two shooing ... stah," I counted.

When I left the Boro I could never have imagined what a strange, harrowing adventure my voyage would become. Once driven from the island of the wreck, I could only note the direction of my sailing by the rise and setting of the sun and the stars and hope the wind would drive my wretched little craft to some island of safety.

In the cove there were directions to the world again. Blind Bay was there back through the Gut. From our lookout point the Strait extended east to the Capes, then over to the shore of *Eeka-na-mowee*. Our cove was a known place, even if it was on the opposite side of the world, far from home. *Heke* was there in the *whare* to embrace me warmly when I slipped into our bunk. I was affixed to some part of the charted world again ... hove to on a wild coast for the present but thankful for it ... better off than in the cold, foggy rookeries ... comfortable enough with plenty to eat. Yet a long cruise home had to be made in the coming year or the year after.

"Tree ... fouh." Two more stars streaked to earth, the second only moments after the first.

"Ha! Ha!" Someone yelled and stomped their feet up in the *whare*.

The trial had started again. Knobby would be excluded unless Peck and Bry had quickly forgiven their injuries. Strange. Passing strange how their anger cooled and they were good mates again in an hour or two. The worst offense usually faded in less than a day, revealing a nature in them akin to the Indians' flashes of temper with their equally speedy remission. These men could not remain enemies in the Two Brothers for their living and lives depended on trust and cooperation.

"A fast fish!" Peck shouted from above.

One of the men had made a hit or a near hit with the old harpoon. They were getting drunker, and in the morning not one would remember or care who had won the wagers gathered together on the table. I would have my pumps back.

I had eaten a fill of good food; and my *Heke* was down there in our bed waiting, willing, and even eager to forgive and embrace me. I looked back at all the things that had happened to me; to all the trials I had passed through. A thought came to me that it was inevitable I should fetch up here. From the day I signed on the barque, my course appeared to have been set to carry me to this little cove and to *Heke*. All my ill luck, bad fortune, had changed; but would it remain so? Would I reach home safely with *Heke?*

Far to the east another streak of light plunged behind the hill. "Five … stah," I noted.

I gripped the corner support of the porch, struggled to my feet, and then weaved my way past the gardens and the cookhouse. At the stream I didn't trust my balance on the stones and waded through the water. For a moment I stood at the doorway to my *whare* and in a last glance up at the sky saw another bright streak cut a path across the speckle of stars. "Shix."

Inside, in total darkness, I undressed and fumbled my way to the bunk. *Heke* murmured and shifted aside to give me room. I gave her a gentle nuzzle on the neck, a thankful kiss, and settled onto my back. Stomping continued on the plank floor up in Monk's *whare* resounding drum-like in the quiet air of the night. I, the bunk, and *Heke's* form beside me were wobbling about in black space until I drifted off.

Heke hammering a fist on my back brought me out of a thick sleep. There were muffled screams far out in the darkness.

"Harah, Harah," *Heke* called in my ear.

Her sharp words pained my head. "Damn. How do you know it's Sarah?" I grunted, then rolled out of the bunk and groped around for my trousers. I found them and went outside to slip them on by the starlight. Out there I could hear the screams coming from Knobby's place. It was Sarah!

Someone with a lighted lantern was coming through the door of *Ruru's* place as I ran by. Then I passed Bryan's *whare* and overtook a woman jogging ahead of me. It was *Kotuku*. Monk dashed past us both. When I arrived, Knobby's door was open. I entered the dim interior. *Kotuku* followed me a few seconds later.

The headsman was facing Knobby who stood in the middle of the room.

The lantern burned low. I grabbed the pickwick from the table and worked the wick higher.

Monk shoved the steersman aside. Sarah was crouched in a corner of the room sobbing and holding her child and baby close to her big, bare breasts. She had a red bruise on the side of her face. Her hair, normally well combed and ribboned, was mussed about her head. A small trickle of blood flowed from her nose. Monk turned back to Knobby. The man's face was flushed and perspiring and his eyelids drooped, covering half the pupils and the reddened whites. There was something dark on his upper lip. At a step closer I saw it was dried blood, the result of Monk's pushing his face to the floor. He was very drunk, swaying slightly on his feet, yet sobering some in our presence. A fierce look grew on Monk's big face and Knobby saw he must give an explanation.

"She's dhirty ... look ... dhirty house ... dhirty ...," Knobby's words slid out of his slack mouth. "Can't 'bide ... dhirty house."

The headsman's broad left hand shot forward and seized Knobby's shirt. He lifted the harpooner up by it and shoved his back to the wall.

Monk, with eyes glaring, shouted a foot from his face, "She's dirty? Then ... send ... her back!" He put his right forefinger in the middle of Knobby's stomach and added, "You do this again and I'll run a lance through here and pin you to the wall." He jabbed his thick finger hard against Knobby's gut forcing out a pained grunt.

Kotuku took the baby in one arm and helped Sarah to her feet with the other. She murmured comforting words to the sobbing Sarah as they went toward the door. Bryan limped in and, though still tipsy himself, grasped in a second what had happened. He picked up the bewildered little girl and started after the women.

Monk slammed Knobby over against the bunks. He shouted out, "SO!" His word cut off all reply. Then he waved his right forefinger very slowly at him in a final warning. Having made his will known he turned and strode out the doorway.

Knobby looked around the room and realized that his family was gone. Once I left he would be alone in his *whare*. With no wife bustling about her work and no chatter of children to be heard, the quiet in the house would be unbearable and a constant reminder that what he saw as a messy room was not important.

The pickwick was still in my hand. I stabbed its point into the wood of the table and trailed after Monk down toward the cookhouse.

Heke, Maree, and *Karee,* each wrapped in a blanket, were standing there. *Ruru* held his lantern up, lighting their faces as they listened to Monk relate what had happened in Knobby's *whare*.

Peck was coming up the path with another lantern.

"Monk," I demanded, "you do all the business here. Why do you always buy so much damned whiskey? You see what it does. Knobby's a good man until he drinks."

Monk's face appeared grim in the weak lamplight. He turned to me and replied, "Because, lad, they won't work without it. They have that taste for it, crave it. Oh, they must have their spirits or they'll leave. We can't whale alone, Tom. We're short hands now. Don't fret, it'll not happen again. I rule here. If Sarah is willing to stay, she will tell me how all goes between them. He's most fond of her and his squeakers when he's in his right mind."

I shook my head and put my right arm around *Heke's* shoulders. I pressed her to my side, remembering how she had come to me with such honest desire those few weeks before.

She held the blanket tight around her and looked up at me. "Harah hurta bada?" she asked as we walked.

"No, more scared than hurt. *Kotuku* and Bryan will take care of her and her squeakers for a while."

"He bad man … *kino, kino* Toma Kina," she declared. "*Waipiro kino.*"

"Yes," I admitted, "bad when he's drunk. Sober he's fine."

Chapter Ten

One of *Kotuku's* boys began ringing the bell on Monk's porch in the middle of the morning a week after the big booze bout. Its paired notes, ding-ding, ding-ding, went across the water and echoed from the hillsides around the cove. The green flag had been hoisted on the pole at the point. Far beyond it, miles to the northeast, a three-masted ship with all sails set was heading south. At best guess she was intending to pass through the Strait. We gladly left off our chores and converged on the ways to launch the Two Brothers.

Peck had been at the lookout since daylight and, having spied the vessel and raised the flag, was hurrying down the track. "Whaler!" he called out as he neared. "'Bout three hundred ton ... must lower three, four boats."

Ruru already had the cover off the Two Brothers. I unhitched the fall of the tackle and eased the boat into the water. We climbed aboard and with our five oars sent the boat skimming across the cove and out into the Strait. When we were within a quarter-mile from the ship, she turned and made directly toward us. Monk, seeing its change of course, brought the Two Brothers about with pulls of the steering oar.

A boat hung from each of the ship's davits and a spare one was inverted on her gallows. Spaced evenly in the white strakes along her side were square, black gun ports. The ship altered her course slightly and then slowed. Monk guided the Two Brothers to her starboard side where a crewman waited in the fore chains with a coil of line to cast to us. Knobby caught the end of it and bent it to his thwart. We could see three of the gun ports were real and the other four were false, merely black squares, frauds painted on, which would not fool a child even at forty yards. The ship gave off the rank smell of oil and old whale blood that had soaked into her deck. It was possible they had been many months at sea.

The gunwale of our boat eased against the ship. Monk scrambled up the gangway cleats and through the opening. He turned and beckoned me to come aboard. The deck there was in poor condition; or rather it was the false deck underfoot, badly scored and split by the chimes of many casks. The sooted masts and spars overhead made the ship a strange sight. Our sealer had been kept in far better state even though she had suffered much from the weather during her long voyage.

The crew of the watch, dressed in patched clothes which had absorbed a good deal of oil, soot, and tar, were at their stations holding or coiling lines. They were more interested in Monk and me and stole looks at us as we picked our way aft toward the wheel. Two men stood near the helmsman. The shorter one, with a close-trimmed black beard, called out orders to the men in the rigging. The other man, clean-shaven and better dressed, watched how the crew responded. It was my guess he was the captain.

That officer didn't turn his attention to us until we were two paces away and Monk had extended his hand to be shaken. The man kept both of his clasped behind his back and asked, "And who you be?"

Monk looked miffed and didn't answer at once.

The captain looked to be a man hard of mind and muscle with a straight mouth that had opened only enough to slip out his four words. With head tilted slightly back, his blue-gray eyes ran up and down Monk's large frame and then spared a slight glance at me.

"I'm Monk Monkhouse and this here is Thomas Wightman," Monk said.

"This is the *Achilles* of Sag Harbor. I'm Captain Olyphant. This is Mr. Davis, first officer."

First Mate Davis, though a man in his mid-twenties, had heavy, black eyebrows that shelved over his equally dark eyes. He was a short man but stoutly built. A bear-like stance on deck and a direct, beady stare showed he did not consider his youth or size any disadvantage in ruling his crew.

"Where's your ship?" the captain asked.

"No ship here 'tall," Monk replied. "I heads a station there ashore. There are six of us and we whale on our own account."

"No ship? Ha! Lags then. You have the look of 'em. Don't they look like lags to you, Mr. Davis?" he asked.

Davis made no answer and glumly stared at me and Monk.

"We're no transports here," Monk objected. "All honest men and we have fished here for years. We have some oil and bone to trade or sell."

"Sperm or black?" Olyphant asked.

"All black. No sperm. We only fish for the rights here. It's all sweet, of good color. No mingling with poor oil. We have three quarter ton of bone all scraped and dried and bundled."

Captain Olyphant thought for some moments and then asked, "How much a tun?"

"We're asking 21 pound for the oil. Bone at 60 pound, all cleaned."

"Too much," Davis advised the Captain. "Whaling is good here. We can do better than that."

Olyphant turned to Monk and said, "What I do need is potatoes and garden truck. I could use some at the right price. We've been fishing farther out. Those devils on the other side there want too much for their spuds. Damn their daylights."

"We'll have plenty o' spuds later in the year," Monk offered, "but none now. We have turnips, beans, onions, smoked fish, and salt pork. Yes, and some live pigs."

"How much for your pork and some garden sauce?"

"You will have to come in the cove and make an offer on it."

The captain gave a slight nod, turned to Davis, and said, "Take her in."

"Captain," Monk said, pointing to me, "this man here was on a barque that foundered off the west coast. He wishes you to report it."

"From what port?"

"Stonington," I said quickly. "The *Dove*. Tobit, master. She went down near a year and a half since."

"I will do that," the captain muttered showing no more interest in me.

Crewmen were readying a range of cable for letting go. One man was carrying the lead line forward.

"No need for the lead, eight, nine fathoms there," Monk advised Olyphant, "and good holding ground. A hundred ton brig held here in a gale without letting go a second anchor."

The *Achilles* was under full way again.

Olyphant, without looking at Monk, asked, "Good ground, you say. No rock?"

"None a'tall."

The captain nodded but didn't say another word until the ship was entering between the heads of the cove. Then he asked, "Here?"

Monk pointed forward and said, "There, about a musket shot ahead, that's the place."

The *Achilles* neared the spot. Mr. Davis shouted his order and the chain cable rattled over its roller as the anchor plunged in.

"What will you take in trade?" the captain asked, giving partial attention to Monk as he paced forward to inspect the cable and the furling of the sails.

"There's some things we could use," Monk said. "I'm making a fit-out for another boat. I'll trade what I have for good lines and irons and maybe for some tools and some salt."

The captain gave a short nod and replied, "I'll send Mr. Davis ashore to look at what grub you have and he will bring what gear he can spare for you lags. Get out what you have now. We up anchor first light in the morning." He then turned around and left.

Monk swore an oath under his breath and watched the man stride away.

Some of the crew were stowing away running gear; others were at the larboard waist boat swinging the cranes aside to lower it. The men of the *Achilles* were an odd lot like those on any whaler: an Indian, two Africans, one that looked like a Hindoo. The remainder possibly came from the docks of Boston or New York. Any moment when not in sight of an officer, they glanced over at our *whares* and sheers. Their chanty when hauling on a line seemed listless when compared with the rousers heard on most ships. If I had paid my debt to the others and did not have *Heke* and a child to provide for, I could sign on a whaler; but I would never sign on with that dispirited mob.

"Tom Skins," Monk called me to the gangway. A gam was going on between Bryan, standing in the Two Brothers, and two crewmen leaning over the ship's side. One of the men looked at me with his good right eye. On the left side of his face, a sunken eyelid partially covered what was no longer a full orb. It, paired with a grizzled beard, gave him the look of a longshore brawler.

Monk and I climbed down to the boat. "Let's go," he ordered and stepped to his place at the steering oar. Knobby unbent the line and pushed us away from the ship with the end of his oar.

"He thinks he's a thumping god, blast him," Monk growled. Then he asked Bry, "What did the idlers say?"

Bryan replied with single phrases as he leaned back on each pull of his oar. "They're doing well … taking sperm down south but a sore lot … the single peeper is cook … says most of the first crew took French leave … rest have been signed on along the way… most sorry they did … Cap'n keeps men beyond their watch … lookouts in the crosstrees rain or fog … come in from south with the scurvy … four men down with it."

"Damned blackguard," Monk grumbled.

Brian added, "Three deserted when out for wood an' water… Indians asked five muskets … Cap'n held off, got them back … one musket and sock of powder … the three are about to leave again."

Monk nodded and asked, "Made his own troubles, did he? Are they leery of the people on this side of the Strait?"

"Don't know … told 'em we have no trouble."

"We'll see what they'll give us for some of our grub."

We pulled the Two brothers to shore and hopped out. The boys were waiting there to draw the boat up the ways and cover it.

"*Ruru*," Monk ordered, "roll a couple of casks of pork down here from Tom's *whare*. Take Peck with you."

Davis arrived a half-hour later. We waded in around his boat which held the goods he intended for trading: casks of salt, a killing lance, a tub of line, and three harpoons with shafts straightened too many times and not done well. Except for the irons, line, and the salt, what he brought in the boat were the scraps of leather and bits of hardware that fetched up in the steerage and odd corners of any ship.

Nothing was new except the one lance and some nails. Our headsman leaned in and picked up two rusty files. He gripped them firmly in his hands for a moment and let them drop into the boat. It was certain the chief mate wasn't offering much for the food. "No other tools?" Monk asked. "Saws, planes, mauls?"

"None that I can spare," Davis replied.

"Well then, how long's the line?"

The chief mate thought a second and said, "Ah, two hundred fathom less ten or fifteen we cut off."

The headsman held the end of the line in one hand and ran his other hand across the top layer of fakes in the tub. "Not stranded is it?" he inquired.

Davis shook his head and gave an indifferent, "No."

"A cask of salt pork and some garden greens for the lot," Monk offered. "We corned the pork ourselves this year. All prime meat, not the damned junk provisioners sell."

The mate looked affronted with that offer and protested, "The irons alone are worth more than that."

"Then two pork and half a hundredweight from the garden for all?"

"For that I'll give you the nails and the three old irons with them … salt too. That's four bushels … twelve shillings a bushel, New York price. But not the line though."

We saw the trading wasn't going well. Davis wasn't giving anything away, not even the scraps. Monk looked around at us, then turned back and made one more offer, "Three casks of pork and a hundredweight of garden vegetables for everything here," he said. "Aye, and I want to overhaul the line first."

The mate's frown deepened the furrow between his dark brows. After a few seconds he shook his head once. "No," he muttered, "I need more for it."

"Well, what I have offered is all I can spare, Mr. Davis," Monk replied. "Three of the pork and what is ready from the garden for all but the small stuff, nails, leather, and such."

The mate looked at the items in his boat with his lips pursed deciding whether to accept the deal or not. Then he shook his head.

"I can't give you any better terms than that," Monk growled and motioned for me and Peck to roll the casks of pork back to the storehouse.

The chief mate watched us start up the path and then looked back to the ship for a moment. He knew chances to trade for food did not come that often and he had a big crew to feed. "A bargain!" he suddenly snapped, and beckoned to us to bring the containers of pork back. He turned about and ordered his crew, "Unload the line, the irons, and the salt here."

Two crewmen, one a boy with a pimply face and bearded man several years older, lifted the tub from the whaleboat. They struggled ashore almost dropping it before they placed it where Monk pointed.

"Knobby," Monk ordered, handing him the end of the whale line. "Lay hold of this and run it out up the path. Keep it out of any sand." Knobby paced backward pulling the line from the tub. When the end came out, the headsman announced, "It's worn, but I'll take it. Bry, Peck, show Mr. Davis the gardens and let him choose what he wants." The mate went off with them to the garden plots. Monk watched him until he was a ways up the path and then motioned to the two crewmen who had brought the tub of line ashore to join him several paces from the other *Achilles'* men landing the kegs of salt and the irons.

In a quarter of an hour Bry and Peck returned with baskets filled with turnips, greens and onions. They placed them in the boat and went back for more.

Monk backed away from the two men he was speaking with when he noticed Davis returning.

The mate waded out to his boat, directed the loading of a cask of pork in the boat, and went off with it to the *Achilles*.

Chapter Eleven

I was awakened from sleep early the next morning by a sharp hammering on the door post. The curtain was thrust aside, and Capitan Olyphant burst into the *whare*.

"Where are my men!" he shouted. The officer scanned the interior once and gave me a furious look.

"Aieee," *Heke* screamed and clasped the blanket to her breast.

One crewman from the *Achilles* stood behind the captain with a musket held at the ready.

Bewildered by the sudden awakening, I rolled out of the bunk and stood beside the table, clad only in my shirt and squinting at the light from the window and the open door.

"Damn, but I'll have them back!" Olyphant demanded. He pulled a pistol from his coat pocket and waved it before my face.

"Wha … What men? What is all this about?" I asked.

"God damn you. Don't play the innocent with me. I'm two men short this morning. You're naught but absconders; aye, damned lags that have gotten over here. I'd not scruple shooting the lot of you." He raised his chin a little and stepped forward forcing me back a pace.

Peck suddenly appeared at the door and looked in at the *Achilles's* crewman and Olyphant's back.

"I know nothing of your men," I protested. "I haven't seen them since yesterday."

"Say 'sir' to me, you rascal, and don't give me any of your damn cheek!"

Several voices outside were nearing the *whare*.

Olyphant turned and faced Monk and Knobby as they entered the room. "God damn your daylights, Monkhouse!" he shouted. "You have two of my men here. You enticed them from my ship. I want them back … now!"

The headsman looked at the pistol Olyphant was holding. I noticed then that it was at half cock. Monk's right hand came up and the thumb and forefinger touched his chin in a thoughtful pose for a few seconds. Suddenly it swept down, seizing the barrel of the weapon and wrenching it from the captain's grip. In the next instant Knobby shoved the musket held by the crewman hard against the man's chest; then yanked it back, easily ripping it from his hands.

"You're a covey of rogues here!" the officer bellowed. "Blast and damn every one of you!"

Monk looked calmly at Olyphant and said, "I know nothing of your men. It's not my business what they do. If they have left it is because they don't wish to serve on your ship any longer."

"I had two men desert last night. They have seen your station here. You have offered them work, a place to live, aye, and women. Admit that," the captain demanded.

"I have not," Monk replied, holding a steady gaze at Olyphant's eyes.

"You were talking to them yesterday on the beach. I saw you with that Scutchings, the one with a thick beard and wearing the striped shirt. They call him Scutch. The other one is that silly goose, Gubby."

"I spoke to them, yes. Even so, I have men enough in my mob here. We can take our whales and boil them down too. We have all the Indians about here to help."

Monk pushed the pan cover of the pistol back, raised the weapon to his mouth, and blew the priming from the pan. He looked at the weapon, considering it for a few seconds, and then spat at the touchhole. Knobby took the hint from the headsman and did the same to the musket.

Monk handed the pistol back to the captain butt first and in measured words advised, "Take your ship out of this cove. It's the *Rangitani* and such that own the land hereabout, and you don't have their leave to be here. I heads this station and I do. So!"

"You're naught but lags, damn you. I'll go now, but when I have a full ship I will call at Port Jackson. A government ship will come here, chain you to her deck, and carry you all back to prison. God damn all, but I will see it happen!" Olyphant and his crewman marched out.

Ruru and Bryan, each holding a cocked musket, arrived at the *whare*. Monk and I met them outside, and we all watched Olyphant and his man heading for their boat. All the women, curious about what had happened, gathered in front of *Ruru* and *Aihe's* house and waited there for someone to arrive and report what had passed between Monk and Olyphant.

The captain was rowed back to the *Achilles*. In a half an hour the boat was hoisted up and the ship's cable hove short.

Monk went up to his *whare*. The women returned to the cookhouse to prepare the day's first meal and food for the provision cask if a whale were sighted.

A few minutes later our headsman came out carrying his glass and with it watched the *Achilles* fill away for the Strait. Then he came down to my *whare*. "Take this glass out to the point and watch for that devil," he ordered. "See where he heads. He might turn back and throw a few shot at us."

I took the glass and asked in disbelief, "You think he might do that, fire his cannon at us?"

"Aye, he's in a fury. Fairly burning up. You can see the ilk he is. He's been lord almighty on board that ship for a year or two and probably on a half dozen cruises before this one. That does something in a captain's head and he loses all reason. Yes, I've known one who murdered a man for what he thought was a saucy word. Too much power in their hands for too long and they come to believe they are a grand mogul. Tom Skins, we'll keep a watch in dark and light for two or three days. So."

Monk had the watch kept out on the point at night in addition to the usual search for whales in the daytime. Each of us had to take our shifts scanning the horizon with the glass.

On the morning of the second day after the *Achilles* left, Peck was up on watch. Bryan, *Ruru*, Knobby, and I were gathered at the try works to raise casks from shook. *Ruru* straightened up from his bowed position and looked south. He grunted and pointed to the path that led down from Monk's big *whare*. We saw our headsman along with two men heading toward us. They were dressed in trousers and shirts and didn't appear to be relatives of Monk's wives. As they neared I recognized them as the two crewmen who had brought the tub of line ashore from the *Achilles's* boat.

Monk introduced them, "This here is Scutch and this is Gubby."

The one called Scutch nodded and greeted us. "Mates," he said, and with that word touched a forefinger to the brim of his tarpaulin hat. A smile, possibly one picked from a stable of smiles, formed behind his brown beard and slightly wrinkled the corners of his eyes. It lacked warmth and raised my suspicions. The pale blue eyes, under drooping lids, shifted from one to another as if he were estimating each one's strength.

Gubby, showing less wit than a log, hung back a step behind Scutch, nodded, but said nothing. The Scotch cap on his head was pulled low covering the top half of his ears. He was perhaps 14 or 15 years old and presented a sparsely whiskered chin to the world. Somehow the sun had not tanned his face as it had Scutch's. The boy must have served as a steward aboard and hence perhaps his pale skin; but then again he would have been required to pull lines and stand a watch in the crosstrees while the crews were out in their boats.

So it was very plain. Monk had promised this pair something to get them to desert. Not a hard task, apparently. He had lied to Olyphant, stating to his face he knew nothing of them while they were hidden somewhere out in the hills or around the cove. Monk was that desperate to have the Two Sisters fully manned. Now that he no longer expected the *Achilles* to return, he brought them out.

"Scutch and Gubby are going to whale with us," the headsman explained. "Bry will take Gubby and his two boys in the Two Sisters. With the extra man he will be able to come up to us sooner if we are stove or overset. Scutch has been tub oarsman and will take that thwart. He and Gubby have agreed to a share and a half between them at the end of the season. So."

We looked at each other. We had not been asked to say aye or nay to their joining us, but to accept Monk's decision. We all had trust in Monk to make the right choices for us; but since the blatant lie he had given Olyphant, I had doubts. I knew I didn't like the arrangement. Gubby, standing there with a hanging nether lip, looked to be a numbskull and without enough go in him to earn the three-quarters of a share he would get. He would be in the Two Sisters while we in the Two Brothers would be open to all the peril and would suffer any starvings. I didn't mind Bryan going into the Two Sisters and receiving his full share, for even with his game leg he was strong at the oar and a willing hand at the try works. Bry's two boys would figure in his full share for rowing the second boat and for their labor while cutting in. They were also clearing for the new garden through the day and were always gathering wood for the cookhouse.

Scutch's knowing smile bothered me. He didn't fit with the rest of us and was surely a slacker if I ever saw one, a bad bargain, one of that tribe that always had a sneaking way out of hard work. When men like him were about, things of value disappeared. Scutch didn't have honesty in his look that the men of our station had; and his half-hooded, scheming eyes were not the ones of an eager hand ready to use his strength and wit for the profit of all. What mischief was behind them? The man had just deserted from the *Achilles*, and perhaps he was one of those who had fled before on the other coast of the Strait. Monk was putting too much trust in him.

So far this season we had taken our whales without mishaps. The only bad one had been years before I arrived, when Bry had his leg broken. Our crew worked flawlessly together, each man pulling at the right moment to shoot the boat forward or back or turn it about at Monk's command. Monk's long days of drilling had prepared us well. Now we were to include this new man of doubtful fitness.

Monk had now shown a nature I never thought was in him, but I was new to these brethren of the coast. Perhaps rivalry made it needful and acceptable to tempt men from the ships. Captain Oliphant had certainly given us undeserved scorn, and Monk might have thought stealing these two men was fitting *utu*.

After the casks were finished the next day, Monk ordered the Two Brothers out for a drill, a drill that went as poorly as I expected it would. Scutch sat on the thwart which had been Bryan's beside the line tub, but he didn't dip his oar as deeply as the rest of us. When he leaned back his hands didn't have a taut grip on his oar.

Monk saw that too, and shouted at him, "What are you playing at? Give way, God damn you! Put your back into it." The swearing had no effect and Scutch's oar dipped no deeper and he pulled no harder. "You row like a sick whore. Give way, damn you, give way!" Monk bellowed.

Our headsman watched for a minute to see if his swearing had any effect on the new man. "Heave up," Monk yelled and put the steer oar handle into its loop. He yanked Scutch from his thwart, plunked his bulk in his place, and took up the oar. "Head all," he called. The five oar blades bit into the water at the same instant.

Monk's oar shaft bowed and the white ash gave out a crack when he lay back. With the headsman and me pulling as strongly as the three starboard men, the boat began to turn in that direction. Monk and I were outdoing the other three oars and driving the Two Brothers around in a circle. After a half minute of the demonstration, Monk halted the rowing and changed places with Scutch. "Do that," he said. "If you can't row hearty we'll see if you can swim better."

Scutch exerted himself a mite more, but it was still not equal to anyone else's rowing. He had grasped Monk's need for additional men and was thinking he could ease by with little effort. After four hours of drill in which our headsman threw every curse and insult he knew at Scutch, the man had put a shade more back into his rowing. Monk got out at the boat ways; and, with a deep frown on his forehead and looking regretful of the whole morning's effort, waded past me. He went to Scutch and spoke a few words in tense tones to him. I could not make them out. Scutch didn't appear to be impressed with what the headsman said and looked at him with his indifferent smile.

Monk allotted chores to busy us after each morning's boat drill. *Ruru* and I bundled the dried whalebone and placed it on top of the first two batches that had been moved to take up less space. Knobby honed his irons again, though they were already sharp enough to shave the hair from his forearm.

Gubby and Scutch having no other skills were sent to help the boys enlarge the clearing for the new garden. Monk and I watched from his porch. Monk fumed at the slack efforts of his new crewmen when he saw the long pause after each fall of their axes before they were lifted again. Together they didn't do half as much as one of the boys. At quitting time the two returned from the field in a slow stroll that wasn't any result of their laboring. Monk met the pair when they climbed to the porch and yelled, "Damned lazy dogs! Lobcocks!" Gubby shrank back with a guilty look, but his partner's dreamy eyes mocked the headsman. It was obvious Scutch thought he was clever enough to get by with little effort in the Two Brothers and far less out in the field.

Monk could have struck them both to the floor and flogged them with a rope's end, but they would likely have slipped away in the next few days. He needed them if he was to have a second boat better manned and was left with only harangues and threats to shape them into tolerable crewmen.

Scutch came for the drill clean-shaven one morning, and Bryan stared at him watching his every move. He leaned toward me and whispered, "I know that man for sure now. Even with that beard I was thinking he looked familiar."

"Where from?" I asked.

"Van Diemen's, for sure. He called himself Cornel there. He was a swindler and buz-bloke lagged for seven. You get a look at his back if you can. He was flogged, given his hundred and got his red shirt like me. Aye, he must have bolted into the bush after I got away and then got aboard a sealer or whaler. Monk's picked a sharp cove there. Aye, he's a member of the family. With that mate of his the two will be nothing but grief for us."

"Are you sure it's the same man?"

"Sure as my eyes are mates, lad. I saw him there when he was marched out to the triangle. I've never seen the young'un before, but they're a sure pair of canaries. Keep watch on them."

"That I will."

In mid-afternoon a few days later, *Maree* at the big *whare* rang double notes on the bell. Peck had raised the blue pennant at the lookout and was loping down the path. We all ran from wherever we were toward the boat ways. *Ruru* and I arrived first and had the boat down the ways and the line tub loaded before the others reached us. The last one to step into the boat was Scutch. He paid no attention to Monk's furious glare as he calmly settled himself on his thwart.

"Down oars. Starn all!" Monk shouted. The boat pulled away from the shore about twenty yards. "Back two … pull three," he ordered, and the bow of the Two Brothers swung around toward the Strait. "Head all!" the headsman cried and then asked Peck, "Where away?"

"Towards Cape Stephens … about a point to larboard … one mile, maybe nigh two mile distant."

When out of the cove, Monk drew on his steering oar to bring our bow in line with the course Peck had given.

He snapped out, "Come, lads. Lay out! Give way a'fore she sounds. No fish, no money … then no weed, no rum." He reached a hand forward and helped Peck with a push on his oar handle. The bow of the Two Brothers cleaved a good wave to each side. Peck leaned forward for a stroke. Monk shouted over his head to Scutch, "PULL! Damn your lazy hide … PULL!"

Back at the ways I could see Bryan had the other boat eased down into the water. Gubby and the boys were getting in and shipping their oars. The Two Sisters was our sole saving if the Two Brothers were stove.

We leaned into our work, each stroke of our oars driving the boat north those two miles toward our prey. Scutch though he had to keep pace added the least of all to our speed.

"She blows," Monk announced. "She sounds. Ha! I know where she will come up."

We rowed for a quarter of an hour more. Then Monk ordered, "Heave up. Aye, about here. She'll be up in a few minutes." The Two Brothers glided to the spot where he expected the whale would rise. We sat and waited, not speaking a word for fifteen minutes. Suddenly the black, barnacled nose parted the water two hundred yards astern of us. Twin clouds of vapor shot up and drifted away. Monk turned. Seeing he had overshot his guess, called out, "Pull three, back two … now ahead all … half a cable." He pulled his oar to shape our course to the sinking animal. "Give way or lose fifty barrel o' oil," he warned.

The Two Brothers sliced through light swells.

"Flukes," Monk cried. "A hearty pull, lads."

We rowed about another quarter of a mile.

"She breeches," the headsman whispered. "Row soft now."

We heard the rush of its spout. Droplets of water and mist settled onto us and the boat. There was a strong odor as we passed through the exhaled air. Monk waved a hand downward, a sign for us to row quieter. He pulled his oar to bring the boat to larboard of the great creature. With his right hand lifted and the palm up, he mouthed a silent, "Stand up," to Knobby.

Monk was looking forward over my head. I didn't dare look around; but I heard Knobby slip his oar handle into its cleat. Next he would swing his legs over his thwart and stand facing our fish. At my left the pole of the first iron lifted from the crutch. Knobby, holding it shoulder high, would be tense as we neared.

"'Vast rowing," Monk whispered.

We held our oar blades just above the water, waiting for the next order. Knobby grunted as he pitched the harpoon.

"Ha! We're fast!" Monk yelled.

Knobby with no chance to dart the second iron pitched it overboard.

"Starn all!" Monk shouted.

We leaned back, dipped our oars into the water, and pushed the handles forward.

BLAM! ... flukes slammed the surface of the sea. A blast of water and air struck my back. Knobby's hat and mine flew aft like dried leaves in a gale.

"Heave up," the headsman ordered.

The whale sounded, taking all the slack on the surface, yanking the line lying across our oar handles hard as an iron bar. Each coil spun out of the tub, around the loggerhead, and went whizzing through the chock in the bow. Dense blue-white smoke boiled from under the line as it screeched around the post. Peck dashed water on the line and loggerhead with the piggin. The headsman saw his chance when the line slowed, then slackened for a moment. He threw another turn around the loggerhead. The extra drag had its effect; yet three quarters of the line was drawn out of the tub before the animal wearied and finally halted.

Monk ordered, "Apeak, haul in."

We turned about to pull the line and had only a few fathoms drawn in when the huge, black body shot up almost clear of the water. It landed on its back, throwing whitened waves thirty feet to each side. The animal's powerful flukes drove it ahead pulling all the line back out. It snapped taut, flinging off an arc of water drops.

The Two Brothers, at the end of the arrow-straight line, skimmed over the surface. Menacing thumps came from the bottom that slammed hard against each swell. The bow sliced through, hurling waves to the sides three times as high as the gunwales. We watched the foaming wake aft spread and lengthen. Dashes of water struck our backs and drenched us as the boat burst through each roll of the sea. I feared the boat might be split, sundered at any moment. Peck was bailing constantly. For nearly an hour we were towed toward the Cape, back again and then east into the Strait. At last the exhausted animal slowed and came to a halt.

"Haul in!" Monk ordered.

We pulled the line in, towing our boat toward the motionless mass; and then returned to our thwarts to row. Monk watched with a cautious eye for any sign she would recover. Each rush of the whale's blowout grew louder as we closed in. At thirty yards from the animal, Monk motioned for Knobby to come aft while he started forward. The two, going in opposite directions, sidled past each other. Knobby took up the steering oar. Our headsman forward would be unstowing his killing lance.

"Down oars," Knobby whispered, "and a steady pull, lads … a steady pull." We glided forward, rising and falling with the waves. He then quietly ordered, "Back two …'vast. Now head all … but soft, row soft … bring us to her."

Without a glance forward, I expected Monk had the cover off the lance blade. Its honed edges would glint in the sunlight.

"Heave up," Knobby hissed. The bow of the Two Brothers was paces from touching the whale's skin. The headsman had selected his spot and grunted as he plunged the lance into the body. He would quickly draw it back part way and thrust it in at another angle, levering the end of the pole handle up and down, slicing the blade around inside the body.

The whale bowed up and rolled over. "Lay off! Lay off!" Monk shouted.

Scutch stood up from his thwart and twisted left. He stared at the whale, terrified. In rising and turning, his right arm swung his oar handle forward. I leaned back to get my oar blade aft. It came down on Scutch's blade. I pushed to back the boat, but the oar twisted in my hands. My blade skidded across the water, and I pitched forward. *Ruru* and Peck were pushing on their oars to force the boat astern. Without my oar or Scutch's drawing aft, the oars on the other side swerved the bow under the rising flukes. Monk, then *Ruru* dived into the water on the larboard side. The flukes were lifting higher, blacking out a quarter of the sky. Even its edge would shatter my spine like a twig. I threw my oar down, jumped from my thwart onto the next and was in mid-leap over the gunwale when I heard the flukes smash the bow and slam the sea. A blast of water hit my side as I plunged head first. I turned up and reached the surface. The broad tail was lifting. The great animal was feeling for our boat in its blind spot. Knobby swung the bow away from the flukes with the steering oar before they struck again. Peck and Scutch were struggling to back the boat.

Monk bobbed up and grabbed the gunwale. "God damn you, Scutch!" he bellowed. "God damn you! You funked!" Scutch's face went white when he heard the fierce cursing. Guilt spread across it. He knew he had caused the smashing of the boat.

Knobby managed to keep the Two Brothers from danger. The flukes slammed down again lashing us with more spray.

Ruru and I got aboard and sat next to the loggerhead to raise the bow, but water was still pouring in. Monk pulled himself along the side under Scutch's oar shaft and hoisted himself up next to Knobby. His weight with ours brought the stern down, lifting the bow even more. Less water ran in through the shattered strakes. The boat was safe from foundering for the moment. Each wave spilled some water in, but Peck's quick bailing kept it down.

The whale's head broke the surface. Twin sprays of blood and air shot from its spouts and was carried by the breeze to rain on us, the thwarts, and the gunwales. Everything was instantly gory. Blood and seawater sloshed under the thwarts in the boat. The animal spouted again and again spewing her life out through her blowholes. Foam whipped up by the thrashing flukes swirled in colors, pink to carmine. She was dying in a pool of her own blood. Our clothes were soaked with the spray. It dripped from our hands and arms. A red drizzle kept settling on us and the boat. Trickles of blood ran down our faces as we watched the animal twist and turn in agony.

The blubber casing of the animal held the harpoon fast. Its wooden pole flailed from side to side with each roll and finally pulled from its socket. The tail rose slowly one more time and smacked the surface. The body lay lifeless rising and falling with the waves. Bloody water and froth washed across the black skin.

Our headsman leaned over the aft thwart and punched his right fist against Scutch's chest laying him almost flat. Then he roared, "You're no whaler! You're nothing but a goddamned lazy dog. No! Not even that. Only a dog's turd!" Scutch sat up again. Monk prodded his thick finger in his face and growled, "Most likely we'll lose this fish because of you. Fifty barrel of oil, sixty barrel. God damn you! I'll settle up with you when we get ashore."

Monk put a hand on Peck's shoulder and stepped up onto his thwart to scan landward.

"Can you see Bry's boat?" Knobby asked.

"Aye, but it's no bigger than a flea on Boney's ear. It'll be an hour before he gets here. Damn! We'll not sit here doing nothing. Haul in the rest of that line. Put it forward. Tom, pull all that gear in, those oars and the lance. Scutch! Git your goddamned useless arse down here in front of Peck!"

The man quickly stepped over the thwart.

The headsman pounded Scutch on the top of the head with his fist, driving him to his knees, and growled out, "Bail, damn you! Keep bailing 'til I tell you to stop."

The man crouched in the cramped space between Peck's and Knobby's feet and was reaching for the piggin when Monk slapped his open hand against the side of his blood-covered head. Scutch made no response except to shield himself from another blow with his arms.

Long before the Two Sisters arrived, we had all the line in and the oars, the lance, and the second iron fished out of the bloody water.

Monk would not permit Scutch to clean himself and kept him at the after thwart, bailing with the piggin, even if he could not get a cup of water in a scoop. When he slowed the headsman hammered his head down to his knees and shouted, "I'm going to cut your stones off and cook 'em! … split your scurvy belly open … see your damned guts spill on the ground!" Monk spoke no more, yet his deep frown and tense jaw showed that rage boiled white hot within him.

He ordered some weight shifted aft to allow Peck to go forward and slide a square of tarred canvas under and around the shattered strakes. He tacked it to the gunwales at each side but was unable to reach underneath and drive tacks there to make a better seal. It slowed the flow of water coming in.

Monk trimmed the whale's flukes with the spade and cut the hole for the tow line. "It's too late to take her in," he said. "We're too far away to think of it. With this boat stove we'd have to row with the Sisters the whole of the night and part of tomorrow to get her to the sheers. We'll waif her. Draw us alongside."

Knobby pulled on the line and brought the gunwale of the Two Brothers up to the whale. Peck leaped onto the broad back with the whiff to fix it into the animal. Once it was done, Peck grasped the end of an oar I held out to him for balance and in one long stride stepped across and landed on a thwart.

Knobby unbent the line from the harpoon. That iron in the body with the letters T B filed on it was our sure claim to the catch; at least it was considered so by American whalemen.

Monk studied the problem of our damaged boat. To keep as much of the water out as possible, he rigged a noose around the boat and worked it around so it would tow from the bottom and lift the bow some.

It took more than the whole hour the headsman had guessed before the Two Sisters arrived. Bryan lowered his sail and brought the Two Sisters alongside. He hitched the jury-rigged tow line to the loggerhead of his boat and said not a word about the damage to the bow of the Two Brothers or the bloody coating over all of us.

"Tom and Peck, you stay with me," Monk ordered. "*Ruru* and Knobby into the other boat and row with Bry. Scutch, you stay there and don't stop bailing or I'll pitch your worthless skin overboard. Now, down oars and pull. It's a long ways to go and it'll be dark soon."

The towline from the Two Sisters lifted the bow of the Two Brothers some as we started for the cove.

Bry set our course toward the hills about our station, lighted by the final bit of sunlight. In an hour and a half twilight faded and stars appeared in the unclouded parts of the sky. Bry had to make his choice of a heading from them. While rowing, constantly leaning fore and aft, we didn't speak. There was only the gurgle of two moving hulls and the oar blades to be heard. Once in a while the call of a sea bird pierced the night. With the sweep of our oars and the sail of the Two Sisters drawing, we were making good headway. After another hour of rowing Monk asked me, "You have young eyes, Tom. Is that a light I see there 'bout a half point to larboard?"

I turned about and spotted it at the horizon. "Aye, not much of a light, but a light … not a star," I said.

The headsman called forward to the Two Sisters, "Bry, do you see the light a little to larboard?"

"Aye, that I do," he answered.

"I'm sure that's the cove. Make for it," Monk said. To us in the Two Brothers he added, "Ah, the women have made a fire on the point. We won't to be goin' around in circles all night. Tomorrow I want this boat mended first thing. First thing, you hear. I'll be damned if I'll lose that fish. I want to have both boats to tow it in."

"How we going to do that?" Peck asked. "There's two strakes each side smashed and the next two are split open."

"We will patch what we can," Monk explained, "and tack a bigger tarpaulin over the whole damned mess."

"That's chancy. She'll leak for sure," Peck objected.

"Then we bail, damn all!" Monk snapped. "We bail! That's good oil and bone out there floatin' around and I'll be goddamned if I'll let it spoil or drift away. We'd be towing the fish in now if we didn't have this stinking scab in our boat." Monk took his right hand from the sweep, leaned over, and boxed the side of Scutch's head. Scutch rolled with the blow, but kept bailing.

A half hour later Bryan shouted, "Coo … wee." The sound ranged into the darkness ahead. "Coo … wee," he repeated and waited for several moments for an answer. From the direction of the light, came a weaker and higher pitched "Coo … wee." Bryan called back to the headsman, "There's the other light."

"They make another fire there by the sheers," Peck called to me. "We head for it now."

Bryan steered for the second light. It grew brighter and figures became visible moving about, tossing limbs onto a blaze between the sheers and the boat ways. The sheer poles were dimly lighted at their tops by a lantern. *Heke*, standing near one pole, veered out some line to lower the light. *Karee* and *Maree*, each carrying a lantern, were approaching the shore.

The bow of the Two Sisters glided toward them. Bryan untied the towline between the two boats, and we drew each up its ways.

All of us who had been in the Two Brothers stripped off our clothes and waded into knee-deep water to wash the whale's blood from our bodies and out of our hair. Monk stomped among us to Scutch. He seized the man's right shoulder with his left hand.

"You humbugged me!" he shouted into his face. "You're no whaler! You an' Gubby'll leave here and never come back. I'll cut you in half with a spade if I see you in this cove again!"

The women carrying their lanterns edged nearer the two.

Scutch looked up at Monk terrified; knowing no trick or excuse would deflect the headsman's anger.

"But, Mister Monkhouse," he pleaded, "we will row and boil."

"Row! You row? Ha! My arse on a band box!"

"We signed on here to fish. We were given nothing, no advance. You cannot begrudge us a chance to make a shilling or two before we leave."

"A shilling or two!" Monk, screamed. "Not a penny, you lazy wretch!" Monk kept his grip on Scutch's shoulder, drew his right fist back, and punched it square into his face. The crewman, driven from his feet, fell backward full length into the water. He was scrambling to get up; but our headsman stepped forward, gripped his throat, and shoved his head down. Scutch's arms and legs were thrashing desperately, but Monk held his head under water for a full minute. He surely meant to drown him. Gubby was frozen in place, wide-eyed, mouth agape, too terrified to move a finger or speak. I waded forward to beg Monk to release him. With his right hand he pulled Scutch to his feet and shook him. With his left hand he pointed to the top of the hill above the sheers.

He spit out one word. "GO!"

Blood streamed from Scutch's nose and ran into his mouth. He coughed out a mix of it and water and gasped. Each expired breath spluttered away the blood from his nose and upper lip. After a half dozen heaves for air, he shook his head once and dashed off. His pale back and buttocks grew smaller as he ran up the hill, then faded into the bushes.

Gubby's jaw still hung open; his body was fixed as a post driven into the sand. Monk glared at him and pointed to the clothes lying on the sand. Gubby roused himself and, with shaking hands, gathered up Scutch's blood-soaked trousers and shirt and sprinted off after his mate. We stood silent in the light of the fire and watched Gubby disappear into the darkness.

"*Tutae*," Bryan said quietly. "No loss there. They'll not live long."

Without speaking another word, those of us from the Two Brothers finished washing our bodies, picked up our clothes, and walked naked up the path toward our houses. I gave *Heke* my wet clothes and slipped up the line to walk behind Bryan.

"*Tutae?*" I asked. "Bry, what does that mean?"

Bryan turned his head slightly and said, "Shit. A nobody. One who has no courage. Worse than a *kukie*."

"A *kukie*?"

"It means a man who has no *mana*, no craft, can only dig and fetch and carry loads. He deserves no respect."

I thought for a moment, then asked, "Why did you say they won't live long?"

"These Indians can see what kind of men they are and what they are not. Those two have little value for them. Hardly as much as a grunter … and they eat grunters. They were in luck when they were ransomed the first time. If Olyphant doesn't buy them back again, they'll be made slaves … or worse; and I think he's had his fill of that pair by now."

I walked along behind Bryan, thinking that Scutch had doomed Gubby and himself to some terrible fate.

At our *whare* Heke had some cold potatoes put aside. I ate them for a short meal, blew out the lamp, and rolled into the bunk. The long day had been exhausting; and there was an even longer one to begin in the morning, another hard pull at the oars. The whale must be boiled as soon as possible before it began to swell.

At the first show of morning light someone began ringing the bell; and not the least eager for the day's labor, I rolled out of my bunk and dressed. There was a curse, a wish in my head to have the lazy, cunning Scutch end as a slave and never leave the island.

From the tool bag in the corner of the *whare*, I selected what tools would be needed to repair the Two Brothers. Bryan and I stripped off the canvas and broke away the shattered remains of the thigh board and box. What Monk wanted was a quick repair to make the boat watertight enough to help tow the whale in. Two boats with their sails up and all the men and boys rowing could tow our catch in sooner, providing we found it. We braced out the remaining frames to keep them spread and wrapped a tarpaulin bandage over the broken strakes. With the fabric tacked tightly to the wood, and tar daubed over it, we had an ugly, misshapen bow.

Monk had gone to the lookout to search for our whale and was returning along the footpath to the ways. "There," he said, indicating the direction with his glass. "I think nor'east by east. I'm not certain, but I think I see the waif out there."

"She's ready," Bryan reported, pointing to the boat.

The headsman looked the repair over and gave a nod. "So. Get them both in the water," he ordered. "One line to tow, but no tub or irons. No need for them today."

Tokee and *Wehe* eased the Two Brothers down the ways. A trickle of water oozed through the patch.

"Tom Skins," Monk said, "you, *Ruru*, and *Wehe* go with me in the Two Brothers. Bry, *Tokee* and Peck will go in the Two Sisters with Knobby. That gives each boat four men apiece when we tow our fish."

Our boats turned together and headed out of the cove and into the Strait, fully lighted by the sun.

It took the bulk of the day to locate the whale and tow it to the cove. The wind failed the last few miles, and it was almost dark when we pulled the great animal under the sheers.

"No time to spare, lads," Monk announced. "We've lost a whole day and a half. Our fish will be spoiling soon. Have a bite to eat and come back here when I ring the bell."

Monk turned to *Tokee* and *Wehe* and said, "Eat a mite and then go for our help. We will need six or seven men; promise plenty of weed for their work."

The boys hopped into the canoe and paddled away into the darkness.

Monk rang the bell after our quick meal, and though exhausted we gathered at the sheers to cut in and begin the tryout.

Tokee and *Wehe* returned in two hours leading a canoe filled with men recruited from the next inlet to the south. Our band with our helpers reduced the animal to oil and cut out its bone a bit faster than usual, and Monk pleased with the speedy tryout allowed us a day and a half to catch up on our sleep. Then we were invited to his *whare* to eat and observe the solemn rites.

Bryan and I chose to forgo the solemn rites and began a proper repair of the Two Brothers by backing up its broken strakes and nailing on new parts. Despite our careful fitting and caulking, it leaked. It could never withstand the pounding while being towed through the waves by a whale going head out; thus it became our second boat, fit only to come in and pick us up if the Two Sisters were stove. Monk ran his hands over the finished job and said, "About the best we can do. We'll buy another one when a full ship calls over in Cloudy Bay. We'll leave word there with the Indians. Eight or ten pounds should get us one that will serve well enough."

The next morning the sun ruddled the high, thin clouds directly overhead, then cleared the crests of the hills to the east. The lightest airs ruffling the surface of the cove turned the reflections of the slope of the far shore into blurred patches on the water. By all those marks it would be a fair day for my watch at the lookout.

Kotuku was coming out of her door when something drew her attention to the northern edge of the cove. I followed her gaze and saw a long, dark object moving in the shadow of the right headland. Then another three appeared, following it. Four canoes filled with paddlers were approaching in a line with one more sweeping around the point. She stared at them for a second and shrieked, "*Taua! Tokee! Pryanee! Waka! Waka! Taua!*" Her screams echoed around the cove.

Chapter Twelve

Before the next canoe appeared, I dashed back to the *whare*. Inside, *Heke*, terrified, was at the window watching the line of canoes coming in from the Strait. The chanting of the rowers broke the quiet of the cove. "Quick, roll up *parankiti*, mats. Go to Monk's!" I shouted.

She spun about and began rolling the bedding. I knelt beneath the bunk and pawed into extra *raupo* piled next to the wall of the house. I pulled out my powder and the musket wrapped in its oiled canvas and stood by the table to load the weapon.

Heke was starting for the door.

"Here, lantern," I snapped, reached up and took it from its hook. She grabbed it and went out the door.

My hands shook a little as I dribbled powder into the pan, closed the cover, and turned the musket on end to dump the charge into the muzzle.

Someone started ringing the bell. Ding! Ding! Ding! Ding! Its frantic sounds started Boney howling, adding to the alarm.

I rammed the paper and ball down, replaced the rod, and dashed out the door. To the north where the pig fence met the water, the first canoe was nearing the shore. In a quarter of a minute I had reached the stream and skipped across on the stones. Just ahead of me, Bryan, with his musket, hobbled along behind *Kotuku* and her two boys, who were carrying bedding and lanterns. At the cookhouse they turned toward Monk's *whare*. Amelia with her baby and *Aihe* with hers and one child were running up the hill ahead of them. From the other direction Knobby was loping down from his *whare* with his weapon and blankets.

Monk's wives, kneeling at the edge of the porch, reached down for the babies being passed up. Sarah's two-year-old and *Aihe's* four-year-old were each pulled up by one arm. Their mothers handed bedding and lanterns up after them.

Monk stood on the porch watching the canoes entering the cove and driving closer to the beach. Their fearsome song with each dip of their paddles was echoing louder around the cove.

How had Monk planned for our defense? It was baffling. It didn't make sense to retreat to his house. Even if we had more guns and powder than the raiders, we couldn't hold them off for more than a half hour at most. For sure the New Zealanders would work higher on the hill and fling torches onto the roof. That would fire the thatch and the whole *whare* would be ablaze in minutes. Why the blankets, mats, and lanterns? It was mad. What use could they be now?

Bryan passed up the last musket. Boney howled and ran between the women and children reaching the deck and those crowding through the doorway. When they were all inside, he circled around the porch whining, knowing by his animal sense things were awry.

I climbed the log after the others. Before entering the door I looked north. A canoe plowed into the beach at the boat ways. All the raiders, naked and carrying only their clubs and guns, leaped from the hull and dashed ashore screaming their battle cries. The next canoe landed at my *whare*.

Everyone inside Monk's place was in the south half of the room. The headsman and Knobby were on the opposite side pulling boxes and kegs from along the north wall. The two men pitched all the clothes, bolts of cloth, rope, and fishing nets onto the table. Once the floor was cleared, they flipped three unpegged floorboards aside. Monk jumped through the opening to the ground below. "Bry," he called, "come down here with a pot and a lantern."

Bryan grabbed the items and eased his body into the hole.

I went out and looked north again. Raiders were dashing across the stream; and from the line of them two or three men, bellowing their war whoops, turned aside to each *whare*.

Monk hoisted himself out of the opening and ordered, "*Wehe, Tokee*, down there with Bry." Then he shouted, "Thomas, get in here! Take our oil and spread it all around the walls and on the table!"

I entered and demanded, "You mean to fire the house? We'll be roasted like pigs."

"Do it!" Monk shouted and slammed his big hand across my back. The blow knocked the wind out of me and pitched me a step forward.

Suicide? Self-murder? What was the man thinking? No, no, it wasn't Monk's way. He would fight to the last breath. Still baffled, I grabbed the keg and wrenched the spigot out. I shoved people aside. Oil chugged from the container and splashed on the walls, bunks, and floor.

"Knobby, where are you?" Monk demanded.

"Here, behind you," he replied.

"The powder … pry the bung out of one of the kegs … put a rag over it to keep any sparks off. Then pass the rest of the lanterns down to Bry and the boys."

Knobby drew his sheath knife and worked its point in around the bung.

Monk stepped back to the opening in the floor and called down, "Bry, Are you through?"

"Aye," he answered. "We're making it bigger. I've got the boys working on the inside."

"Down here," the headsman commanded and pointed to the opening. "Everyone under the floor." They hesitated, unsure of what to do.

"NOW! NOW!" he shouted. "Get down there!"

They began to move.

Peck and *Ruru* helped the women and children down through the opening; then passed the rolls of blankets and mats to hands reaching up for them.

Monk must have had some plan or gone wholly mad. But what else was I to do but slosh oil onto the table and the walls as he ordered? I passed near the door and spotted a half dozen men dashing up the path from the cookhouse. "They're here!" I shouted.

Monk grabbed a musket and dashed onto the porch. I dropped my keg and looked about for another weapon. I found one and stepped out the door. The first man sped up the steps of the narrow log screaming his war whoop. He was at the top of the log with his club raised when Monk fired a yard from his face. The ball carried away the left part of his jaw and tore his neck open. Blood gushed out splattering the next raider below. The man peeled off the log and fell to the ground. A second man leaped onto the deck with eyes glaring. He howled as he raised his weapon to smash Monk's head. I pulled my trigger, but the weapon misfired. Monk parried the club to one side with his musket and kicked the man square in the crotch. The kick lifted him off the porch and he fell back onto the next two men, tumbling with them into a heap below.

"Tom, give a hand here!" Monk cried and dropped to his knees. Together we worked the end of the notched log from its support and cast it aside. It fell on the men below, and then rolled down the slope.

Raiders had climbed up the hill to the other end of the *whare,* and beaten a hole through the back wall right of the fireplace. From the porch and through the door, I could see two raiders pulling away the wattled sticks and dried mud to enlarge the breach. Knobby slewed a musket toward it and fired into the chest of one man. The impact of the ball tipped him backward. His partner fled around the corner. The enemy below had retreated a short way down the path to wait for more men before their next charge. Knobby rushed onto the porch with another musket and pointed it at them. Most scattered, looking for cover, but one man holding an old fowling piece at his hip came forward a few steps. He fired but the shot went wild. Seeing he had hit nothing, he turned and ran. Knobby rested his musket on the railing, aimed, and pulled the trigger. The weapon dropped from the raider's hands as he plunged forward onto his face with no effort to break his fall.

Near the shore bright orange flames were eating through the walls of Bry's *whare* and a thick, white smoke was rising from its thatch.

Monk dashed inside and yelled back, "Knobby, Tom, come in here. Down under the floor!"

Knobby ran in, dropped his musket, and leaped into the opening. I followed expecting all the others to be crowded below. Only Peck and Knobby were hunched over in the space under the floor. Peck got to his knees to crawl into a hole in the hillside. Knobby was waiting to follow him. That was how the others had escaped.

Monk was still on the floor above. He pulled the bottles of arrack and whiskey from their box and smashed them together on the table. Then he seized the powder keg and strode around the room casting its contents right and left. He led a narrow train of it back to the edge of the opening. Monk tossed the keg aside and grabbed Knobby's discharged musket.

The Indians were back at the rear wall, hammering to enlarge their hole.

Monk leaped down beside me. With the gun held on its side next to the trail of powder, he set the cock and pulled the trigger. The spark was weak and failed to fire the powder. He cocked it again and once more it failed. "Damnation!" the headsman cursed and vaulted up onto the floor. One raider was already shouldering his way through the wall. Monk stepped over and smashed the musket stock in half across his head. He tossed the broken weapon aside, ducked low to grab a stick from the fireplace, and blew on its glowing end. Monk returned to the hole and jumped in. One touch of his stick to the powder and an intense, white light hissed and flared along the trail of powder.

Another raider was forcing his way in and was almost through the hole at the back.

WHOOSH! The entire room above instantly filled with flame. A blast of hot air struck my face, though I was bending low. Monk, still erect, staggered back a pace. His eyebrows were gone and his hair was singed off as far back as his ears. The strong stink of burned powder and hair came in my next breath. Most of the flame died away, leaving the space filled with thick, white smoke. It rose revealing the curtains and the bunks were now afire. A raider, with hair aflame, rolled on the floor, shrieking in pain. Another man was backing out of the hole in the wall. Boney leaped right and left out on the porch, howling miserably. Separate blazes were growing higher around the edges of the room. Monk and I watched the flames on the bunks roll up and lick at the walls. All the boxes, gear, and nets on the table were feeding a column of fire. Heat was building by the second, forcing us to crouch lower. The thatch of the roof was beginning to blaze overhead. Fire followed the lamp oil and liquor leaking through the cracks of the floor, and it spread in sheets of blue and orange flames across the underside of the wood. From them meteors of burning oil fell to earth.

Monk pointed and commanded, "Into that hole."

He followed as I crawled in. We halted and listened to fire roaring and the wood of the walls and roof cracking and popping. Monk announced with a slight smile, "Time to fill it up, lad, and we're safe for a while. I pulled all this earth in here when I found this hole. Now we can push it back and plug the way with it."

We set to work by the light of the flaming *whare*. I found the pot and scooped dirt up with it. Monk emptied it to fill the entrance.

"After the *whare* burns down, won't they poke about and discover this hole?" I asked.

"We will have it chock full of earth, and all the charred wood and clay from the chimney above will fall and hide any sign of it. They have no reason to suspect it's here and I'll wager they'll not look too close when they cannot find our skulls. Them about the Strait all know Bry's here. Ha, if they see naught of our bones they'll think the old wizard worked his magic and shifted us off to Sidney Cove. They have the veriest fear of him. It was a damned good reason to have Bryan here at the station."

"So, you had it all planned to hide in here if any Indians came here to raid?"

"Aye, I found this cave under a bush and I filled it in with a little soil so no one would know it was here; then I built my *whare* over it. I didn't tell anyone about it 'cause some people, most people, can't keep a secret. Now, Tom, fetch one of the lanterns. It's getting too dark to see what we're doing."

I crawled twenty yards farther back where the tunnel widened out and the rock overhead allowed an upright stance. Everyone was sitting on the floor of the cave, unmoving in the light of two lanterns. The women held their children close to them. They were silent except for Sarah's little girl, who pressed her face to her mother's side and simpered. In the weak light I could see everyone was stunned by the sudden attack.

"Where's *Heke?*" Bryan asked when he saw me.

I looked at each of the faces by the lantern's light. "Not here?" I asked. Then I went past the others and shouted into the darkness, "*Heke! Heke!*"

"No need to call," Bryan said. "She's not back there. No one saw her in the *whare*. We thought she was following you."

I felt my heart skip, then turned about and demanded, "*Aihe*, Amelia, did you see *Heke* on the path?"

Each woman shook her head.

"Everybody was busy with the little ones and the bedding, muskets, and all," Knobby explained. "Perhaps she was so gallied she ran off into the bush?"

"No, no, no, she knew we were to come up here. She could see where everyone was going." I felt an uneasy void in my stomach. It was a mystery. I took one of the lanterns back with me and reported to Monk, "*Heke's* missing."

"Not there?"

"I have to go out and find her. Dig it back out," I demanded and pressed forward to get past Monk.

The headsman blocked my way with an arm. "Are you mad, Tom?" he asked. "No going back out this hole. Nothing but fire out there, fierce fire. When it dies they will be all around the cove gathering up what they fancy and searching for slaves."

"Is there no other way?"

"Aye, but it's at the other end. You have to go near half mile or so through this hill. The sea covers that way out except at low water, and to keep out of sight we must wait for dark to go outside. There's naught we can do now, lad. Unless she has found a good place to hide, they've taken her. If they carry her down the coast or across the Strait, most likely you'll never see her again. Sorry, lad. That's the way it is out here. You will find another."

"I want no other. I want her. She carries my child."

"Oh, that's bad luck, but it's not to be helped. You're not in Yankeeland, Tom Skins. There is a chance she might have hid away somewhere. Well, we've given them the slip for a while at least."

There was no other choice at the moment and I could only hope that *Heke* had escaped. Monk was packing the earth into the opening and pounding it in firmly with rocks.

A muffled blast shook the earth beneath and around us. Bits of soil and small rocks fell from the roof the cave.

"What was that?" I asked.

Monk looked up. "That was the last of our dust, a full keg. There can't be much of the *whare* left up there."

We finished and crawled back on our hands and knees to the larger portion of the cave. Monk put the lantern down and seated himself.

Each one sat there without speaking. Anger had replaced the puzzled look on the faces of the men. Above ground our homes were being looted and burned. In twenty or twenty-five minutes, the raiders had driven us from our beds and houses. Those were only possessions, things that could be replaced. I had lost much more, everything, my little *Heke* and our child.

"Well, lads and lassies," Monk began, "we're in a scrape, though I much doubt they can find us in here. *Heke's* outside somewhere, but she might be safe if she's found a good place to hide."

Bryan was sitting just behind *Kotuku* and moved his head slowly from side to side. He who knew the nature of these Indians better than anyone doubted *Heke* had escaped, but I had to have some hope.

"The boats and all the tools, irons and spades will be taken," the headsman continued. "If we return, we'll find nothing but charred wood in the whole station."

"But how do we get out?" Peck asked. "How long will we have to stay in here?"

"As to getting out, don't worry, there's a way," Monk said. Then he added, "How long we'll be in here? That all depends on them. It may be one, two, three days. That's why we have brought our blankets and mats. If it's longer than that, we'll have to slip out some night from the other end and go down the inside way to Blind Bay. If they've taken Ol' Scratch's village there, then we make for Queen Charlotte's and Cloudy Bay. We're most likely done for if they get that far before us. I've followed this cave through the hill and found its other end is at the other shore, but under water. It's a little open only at low tide. You have to wade to get out so there's small chance they'll ever find it. There are two casks of hard bread stored in here. It's ahead there a ways. We can last awhile."

"Water?" Peck asked, holding up a finger. "We must have water."

"There's some that comes down through the rock all along the way to the other end. We're not in so bad a way. Now make up your bundles so you can carry them easy. There are some narrow places ahead."

All the bedding and mats were retied into tighter rolls by the men and taken as their loads. Each woman held a small child in one arm and led one that could walk with her other hand. Monk placed *Tokee*, carrying one lantern, in the middle of the line of marchers and put *Wehe* with another one near the end. He carried one in the lead, and the light was spread along our line of people.

"Now put out all the other lanterns," Monk ordered. "We must save all the oil we can."

We started off slowly.

"How long have you known of this cave?" Knobby asked Monk.

"About four ... five year." Monk stopped and held his lantern up. "See there in the mud," he said. "I made those footprints we're following when I overhauled this cave."

"And what are those other marks there in the muck? It looks like something's been dragged in or out."

"Some small logs. You'll see why when we get farther on."

Monk paused along the way a few minutes later and pointed to two kegs sitting at the side of the cave. He stepped over, patted one of them, and said, "Tack. That will stay us for a while. We'll come back and get them later. We have enough to carry for now."

Each one in the line moved slowly over the uneven cave floor, placing one foot after the other with care. In places, rocks had fallen from above and the tots had to be helped, sometimes lifted over boulders and set on their feet again. Where the roof was low, we were forced onto all fours and dragged our rolls of bedding behind us. The narrow passages were more difficult for the women with babies, and to go through each held her child with one arm and hopped ahead on knees and one hand.

Water dripped from the rock above, gathered on the uneven floor in pools, and reflected the light of our lanterns as they were carried past. The pools fed into a small, erratic stream running in the direction of our march. At a few places the cave enlarged into vaulty rooms where the roof and walls were barely indicated by our lamp light.

An eerie, echoing noise came from ahead and slowly increased in volume as we advanced. It might have been wind blowing about the far entrance of the cave, but when we were closer it became recognizable as water splashing into a pool.

Monk stopped. I could have sworn we had already traveled the half mile length of the cave, yet there was no light of an entrance ahead.

He raised his lantern higher and warned, "Take care, everyone. There's a bad spot here."

I dropped my load and stepped up beside Monk. A large, black void blocked our way ahead. There was no place for the slimmest passage around it. The stream of water spilled over the edge of a steep-walled hole, and the noise rose from its splashing into a pool somewhere far below. At the left side the distance across the void was only twelve or fourteen feet. The gap was wider to the right, farther from the wall. Three slim logs, hardly more than saplings, had been placed across the narrow part of the gap to form a rude bridge to the far side. It barely spanned the opening at that point. At each end of the logs, the shaft an old blubber spade or lance had been driven into a crevice to prevent logs from working away from the cave wall and slipping off the supporting rock. A coil of old whale line lay on the logs where it would remain dry.

The odd streaks along the way had been made when Monk had dragged those logs in to bridge the hole.

Monk passed his lantern to *Maree* and reached down for the whale line. He handed its end to Peck and ordered, "Go across with this line around you and then hold it taut for us to use for safety. Don't be uneasy about it. You're small and if you slip off we can haul you up. Tom and Bry, tail onto this with me."

Peck took the end of the line and, though he knew he must do it, he gave Monk a worried look.

Monk reassured Peck, "I put the logs there and went across them twice when I overhauled this cave, and I did it without a line. They will hold you. We're carrying loads and squeakers across and will need a hand on that line for balance and assurance." He turned and called, "You back there with those other lanterns, bring them up for more light here."

Peck wrapped the line under his arms and around his chest and knotted himself into a bowline. His right hand gripped the hemp, and his left kept touch with the rock wall as he moved each muddied foot forward. He tested each step before he placed his entire weight on it. Near the middle of the makeshift bridge there was a projection of the rock wall at shoulder height. Peck halted and eyed it, considering how to get by. He stooped over, inched his feet ahead slowly, and passed under the obstacle. At the other side, he positioned himself ten or twelve feet from the edge of the hole and held the line taut.

Monk started across with two rolls of blankets and a lantern, moving as Peck had with shuffling steps. The logs bent when he was in the middle, threatening to snap under his weight, but he kept going. He bowed over as he passed by the jut of stone and reached the safety of the far rim. There he put his load and lantern down and took the end of the line from Peck. "Peck," he said, "you stand there at the end of the logs and give a hand to the women as they come over."

The women with babies crossed one at a time, each holding her child in one arm and sliding her free hand along the line. Peck grabbed each woman's hand as she made it across. Knobby and the other women each led one toddler across. *Ruru* picked up a roll of blankets and guided *Tokee* over. He returned for *Wehe* and one more load.

Monk called to Knobby, "You, Tom, and *Ruru*, bring the rest of the bedding over and then go back for the bread."

Kotuku, with one lantern, started farther into the cave leading the women and children. Their light dimmed and winked out as they disappeared around a corner.

I took my load across and shuffled back over the gaping hole to join the others waiting to go for the kegs of tack.

Knobby was holding the lantern in his hand.

"Do you have your flint and striker?" I asked him. "We'd be in a fine mess if our light went out."

"Oh, yes, I have it," he answered, "right here in my jacket. I was thinking the same thing. There, I can feel it to make sure."

With only the one lantern, we picked our way along within its glow that dimly lighted the sides of the cave. In the larger cavities it barely indicated the nearer wall. Without the light, only the touch of a hand on the rock would keep us going in the right direction, and at some place we might not be able to keep that contact. Then we would have no idea in which direction we were heading. We continued on and reached the place where the bread had been cached. Knobby pointed to the few small rocks on which the kegs rested. "Ah, look there," he said. "He's set them so the heads would stay dry and not rot."

"Monk studied it close," I agreed. "I could never guess why he wanted us to go up to his *whare* when there was danger. If it were not for this cave, we'd be slaves or dead."

"You never know what will come to pass in this country," Knobby said. "Monk has got us through a lot of scrapes. Well, let's be on our way."

Knobby and I each shouldered a keg and followed *Ruru* who led the way with the lantern.

With the weight on my shoulder, it was tricky to walk on the slippery and uneven floor. In the low passages we were forced to travel on hands and knees and roll the kegs before us. We made several stops along the way to rest. The lantern was then exchanged for one of the kegs, giving each man a spell from carrying his load.

The light of Monk's lantern appeared dimly ahead when we rounded a turn. Bryan still held the nearer end of the line at the bridge of logs, and on the other side Monk had his end gripped in his big hands. Knobby was the first to cross with his keg held before him. He shuffled his muddy feet crab-wise on the logs, carefully moving each one hardly a foot at a time. *Ruru* was next with his container, but he walked across with his usual stride until he met the projection. He ducked under it and paraded off the end of the logs.

Monk called across, "Tom, take that end of the line while Bry comes over. It'll be hard for him with that gammy leg of his."

Bryan handed me the end of the line and I leaned back to hold it taut for him. He took his time sidling along the logs, favoring his bad leg, and keeping both hands on the line. He stopped at the overhang in the middle and looked down into the blackness below. Then with a shake of his head, he leaned low enough to pass under the rock and continued on to the safety of the other side.

"Tom Skins, it's your turn now," Monk called to me. "We'll keep a stout hold here."

Just as Peck had, I made a bowline under my arms and around my chest. For added security I held onto the line above the knot with my right hand and held the lantern in my left hand. I stepped onto the logs. My left shoulder touching the rock wall was no assurance. The first trip across had been precarious enough; but with no line, nothing between me and that great black emptiness, it was much worse. Being a topman on the barque had accustomed me to heights, but that was two years since. On a ship's yard there was the jackstay to be gripped and the footrope below. Men had fallen from the rigging and caught a line or landed in the belly of a sail. Some almost as fortunate had landed in the sea; but here there was rock and whatever else below. Even if I struck water, I might never get out. With only the whale line about me and the slippery logs to support me, I felt a greater danger of falling. The lantern lighted the rock to my left and very little beneath my feet. To the right was the velvet blackness that would mean death if I fell and the line parted. I brought a foot forward and put it down securely, then lifted the next one. To pass the rock that jutted out, I bent slightly toward the pit and inched sideways. Six feet from the end I made two long strides in eagerness to get over. My right foot missed the center of the muddy log. The ankle turned. I was going over! Instantly my grip tightened on the line. Shouts from the others echoed in the hole. The line was ripped from my right hand and snapped taut. The bowline cut across my back and under my arms, jerking my body to a stop. I swung in, slamming the left side of my chest against the rock. Pain shot across my ribs. The lantern jerked from my grasp, banged against the stone below and glanced off, hitting the other side. A second later it splashed into the water below.

I was swinging, twisting in the utter darkness. The right side of my chest and then my back bumped against the rock wall.

"Hang on, lad, we'll pull you up!" Monk bellowed.

I could feel the line lifting me and looked up. There was a light above. Peck was holding the other lantern out as far as he could reach. Only his face was visible. The other men were farther back from the lip, pulling on the line. It was sliding up across six or seven feet of rough rock and was being abraded, peeling a yarn away.

"Stop!" I yelled.

"What's the matter?" Monk asked.

"The rock is cutting the line. Make a bowline in other end and let it down to me. Don't haul on either line yet. I will have to shift from one to the other."

"Right, lad," Monk called back.

The other end came down over the rock. I grabbed it with my left hand and slipped my left foot into to the loop. "Far enough. Now hold it there. Are you ready? I'm putting my weight on it."

"Yes, we have it," Peck said.

I raised myself up on that leg and kept my weight there. "Now, pull the other end up a foot and hold it."

By shifting my weight from one line, then to the other, I was able to rise a foot at a time until I felt the men's hands slipping beneath my arms and gripping the line around my chest. They drew me up over the edge to safety.

"Are you alright, lad?" Knobby asked.

My heart was pounding and I was panting from the strain. I let out a long sigh and rubbed my right hand lightly over my side. "Ahhh," I groaned, "I think I broke a rib … and nearly shit my trousers."

Peck held the light closer, and Knobby lifted my shirt and touched my ribs with his fingers.

"Ah! Ah! That hurts," I cried.

"Ho! That was a fright," Monk gasped. "We thought you were lost. For the trouble we're in, we need every man. You take a minute, Tom."

Knobby stared at the void and the logs that spanned it and asked, "How did you get them across and in place? I don't see how it could be done with one man alone."

Monk pointed up on the rock which protruded above and asked, "There, you see that stone that pokes out there?"

"Aye," Knobby replied, looking upward.

"I threw a line with a weight over it; reached it back with a long stick. With the end of the first spar hitched to it, I pushed to it the other side. Then it was easy to slide the other two across on it. I've been through all parts of this cave. Now there is just the one way out from here. You fit to go now, Tom Skins"?

"Sore, but ready," I replied.

The others picked up the kegs and lanterns; and we started down a sloping, uneven floor leading toward the other end of the cave. There were a few openings which led off to the sides.

"Monk, do any of those go anywhere?" Knobby asked.

"No," the headsman replied, "I've tried them all and they become too small to follow or just end."

A vague light appeared ahead before we reached the women and children. After another fifty yards of travel we found them huddled together on their mats. None of them, wet and smeared with mud, spoke a word. Their lantern had been blown out, yet watery patterns of light squiggled on the roof of the cave. Their source was from a pool of water five to six feet lower than the rock on which the women rested. Morning sunlight struck the bottom just outside the cave and reflected up to play across the rock ceiling.

Small waves sent surges in through the flooded entrance, giving a constant rise and fall to the pool. Monk pointed to it. "There's our way out," he said. "At low ebb there's about a foot or two of air between the rock and water. We can wade out with a few steps. How long we will have to keep in here, I can't say. How many of them raiders was killed? Three, four? That might be a discouragement to them. After they get all the iron they might leave, or Scratch might drive them off. Tomorrow we'll send *Ruru* to look. If the raiders are still about, I don't know what we'll do. The far side of Cloudy Bay or Cape Campbell is too long a trip. I count twenty-one of us, squeakers and all. We must travel only at night and it will be slow. The best we can hope for is to find a ship that will take us aboard, one that might carry us as far as the Bay of Islands."

"Even if these savages are gone and we go back to the cove, whaling's all done for us," Peck pointed out. "We can never fish without boats and irons and line."

The headsman held up a finger and said, "Ah, my dears, don't despair yet. We don't know what we'll find. If the try pots are still there and perhaps the sheers and windlass, we can start again. Boats can be got from a full ship going home. I have hidden gold and silver about the cove, my share and the shares for the trade goods; perhaps we can buy another fit-out. What do you say, lads? Will you fish with me again?"

There was the offer. We had been doing well with whales enough before the attack and earning shares far larger than on any ship. To build it all up again meant gathering together each item from the whale boats and irons to the mincing knives. Even if we were able to assemble all of it again, we might lose it in another raid. Worse yet, not escape with our lives twice.

If enough men were to settle at the station and about it, that might make us strong enough to forestall another attack. Then we might continue to whale, but that was not likely for years, if at all. The islands had a bad reputation everywhere.

Much was different now, but worse for me than the others. Where was my *Heke*, now pregnant with my child? Was there the least chance for me to find her? Might I discover her in the next few days in some cove where she had hidden away? Then again, she might have been kidnapped and carried far off. I must find her and earn enough in pounds in some manner to see her and our child home. If I did not find her, what use was it for me to start again?

Bryan, sitting next to his wife, looked up at Monk and said, "I see no prospect for me and *Kotuku* anyplace but hereabout. I'll start again if there's any others who will stay."

Knobby asked *Ruru,* "Did you hear of *korero?* Any talk of men gathering … canoes coming up the coast?"

Ruru replied, "No, *korero?* No talka."

"I see a cloven hoof in this," Bryan said. "Wherever they came from, they had no good cause to raid us."

"I'm not sure," Peck offered, "but I thought I saw a white man with them that was raiding."

"Where?" Monk demanded.

"When I came out of my house, I saw one canoe pull in between Tom's place and the sheers. One of them that got out looked odd. He had his hair all done up with feathers like the rest of them, but he looked lighter."

"Did you think it was Scutch or Gubby?"

"I doubt it, but I had no time for looking. There were a half dozen canoes landing at once and raiders running all about."

"Damnation," our headsman swore. "I could expect Scutch to do this if he could. He and Gubby might have stirred up those somewhere down the coast. He told them there was plenty booty to be had here. If I find he's had a part in this and I lay hands on him, I'll split him open like a shoat and let the people here cook and eat 'em. I'll own it was a bad choice to let them hide here and sign on."

Peck then pointed out, "Remember, he said you had no right sending him away and he should get something for signing on since he got no advance."

"Advance, ha!" Monk spat out. "There is no advance given with us. No need for it. I told him so. I should have given them both a damned good flogging for an advance."

Knobby nodded and said, "If Scutch got them to raid us, he won't get a thing out of it, not a damn scrap now 'less he saved it from the fires. Them that burned us will pick up the iron and want to be off somewhere. If they did leave the oil and bone behind and a ship calls, the Indians will take all the goods he trades it for. If he was part of this, he'll never get away. For sure he didn't think it out to the end."

"Aye," Peck agreed, "those two will have to mend muskets and fight with the others; and if he and Gubby won't fight they'll be no more than slaves. It'll be turning ground for potatoes and gathering wood and fetching water for Gubby. He's not got the spirit for anything more. Scutch might make a *toa*. But I doubt it. He's not one for bravery. Likes to do everything on the sly … and he's likely to stumble into some *tapu* and then he'll get a knock on the head and end up in the oven."

Monk nodded and grumbled, "Better for all if he had done a dance on air in Van Dieman's. I'd give them boiled lobsters over there six fathom o' rope to see it was done proper."

Bryan slowly shook his head as he listened to the others. "No, no," he objected, "I doubt it was them two that got the raid started. Gubby's a cod's head. Scutch has that sneaky way about him, not the kind of man they like. And he wouldn't know six words that might stir 'em up and do this. No, the one that got them going was someone with position."

"Then who was it?" I asked.

"It had to be someone with big *mana*. I expect it was Olyphant."

"Aye, he's a damned tetchy one!" Monk burst out. "Aye, I could believe that even more."

"You see, he has a ship, is a captain," Bryan went on, "and that gives him a kind of *mana*. It's not the same as a chief's *mana* or a *toa's mana*, but it gets plenty influence with them. He's told some lies to get them to raid us. I can see how it could be done. The ground where they bury their dead is most *tapu* than anything. Olyphant could have sent someone ashore to knock over the markers or even dig it up there. He might have told them we took out bones and made fish hooks and whistles out of them. That would put them in a rage, and only killing for *utu* could even things up. They would believe him if he said we did it, he being some like a *rangatira*, a white chief. Then they must raid and have their *utu*. Olyphant would encourage that. He surely told them there was plenty of iron and muskets to be had here."

Monk slapped his thigh and spat out, "Damnation, but that makes sense. For sure, that devil would do it if he could."

"In a day or so the *Achilles* will call in if it's not already here," Bryan said. "Olyphant will want to see for sure that they burned us down. It may be he planned to get our oil and bone."

Monk's voice dropped in tone and he growled, "I know the cast of his mind and he'd take it, given the chance. Aye, he thinks we're all lags here. I'm going to see for myself. If I find Olyphant caused this, I'll sink the *Achilles* or burn it to the water."

"That will take some doing," Peck objected.

"No doubtin' that," Monk replied, "but I'll find a way. Cut his cable and let his ship run ashore or some such mischief. Olyphant knew Scutch and Gubby were slackers, not worth their grub. They would have deserted from his ship sooner or later. It was no good reason to set the Indians on us to burn the station. It was all just spite over two worthless rascals. Tonight I'm going out. Damn! I want to see what's going on out there. What have you in your jackets, lads? Take everything out."

"I have my sheath knife," Peck said and laid it on the rock.

"I have mine too," Knobby added, "with my flint and striker."

"Bry," Monk asked, "what have you?"

Bryan placed his knife and a small ditty box beside the headsman and replied, "My cartridges I made up."

Monk opened the box and held it close to him. "Six," he said and poked them about with his finger. "No good without a musket. Thomas, *Ruru*. Have you anything?"

Ruru shook his head.

I held my open hands at each side. In my haste leaving the *whare*, I had thought only of *Heke* and the musket and left my sheath knife lying on the table.

Monk's jaw was set firmly, and he pursed his lips while he looked at the items on the rock. Then he muttered, "So, lads, not much to avenge ourselves with."

Chapter Thirteen

It was a tangle of events. It had been a good living in the cove, though the whaling was dangerous. It was Monk's wish for more men that had brought on the wrath of Olyphant. He might well be the one who was behind the raid. What was to be done? Without the boats, irons, lines, and other tools, we were helpless and had no means to make money. Even if Olyphant were not the one who had caused the raid, he might poison other captains' minds against signing me on. He believed or wanted to believe we were all transports, bolters from New Holland.

Bryan knew the tongue and could easily trade between the ships and Scratch's people. He would live well enough with *Kotuku* and her boys. *Ruru* will go back with his relatives. Peck, Monk, and Knobby could set up with their wives' relations and raise spuds and grunters; yet that, with gathering flax to trade, would hardly do more than keep them in slops, booze, and tobacco. I would have to do the same if I found my *Heke* and then despair of ever returning home.

Without her I was adrift. I hoped she was somewhere close by the station; yet the unease returned that she had been carried to the south beyond Cape Campbell or across the Strait.

The women were arranging blankets, comforting crying children, and cleaning the babies' messes.

My mind drifted from item to item but always returned to consider anything I might do to find *Heke*. If she were not in one of the dozens of small coves there back toward Blind Bay, how could I search for her across the Strait? How could I get about, find her, and free her in a land filled with ten thousand savages? I knew a few words of the speech, yet even if I knew it well I could not move unnoticed among those down the east coast or on the other side of the Strait. Rumor would fly before me once I was seen. Without many blankets, muskets, and powder, ransom was impossible. There appeared to be no practical way for rescue.

Monk turned to me and asked, "You want to go out with me tonight to discover what's afoot? *Ruru* will come too. I want to see what's there and be sure they have no curiosity in what's left of my *whare*. Don't want 'em to be poking about much."

I nodded quickly. If I went out I might learn something of *Heke* or perhaps even find her.

"Then get some sleep for now," Monk advised. "We'll be out for a while, maybe most of the night."

Time in the cave could not be measured. The light filtering in through the flooded entrance was only a sign that the sun was still high up.

There was no position that was not painful while I lay on the rock. My injury kept sleep fragmented, allowing only short naps. At each awakening people were talking. No shapeless lights wobbled on the rock overhead. Thoughts of *Heke* returned. Was she alive and a prisoner, or had she found a place to hide and was waiting to return when it was safe?

I fell asleep again and later was aroused by a hammering. It was dark and one of the lanterns had been relit. The tongue of flame lighted only a portion of the rock wall and Knobby on his knees before a keg of tack, knocking on its head with a rock.

"We're going to break up some of this and wet it," Knobby said. "There's a little sweet water I've found back there."

Monk stood near the pool, now totally dark. "Hear that jabbling sound?" he asked.

Several voices responded with, "Aye."

"It's nearing low water," the headsman said. "See how far it's gone down? In an hour we can wade out with our clothes on our heads. Then we can dress outside and be dry. Douse the lantern when we go. If you re-light it, be sure to keep it shaded from the opening. It might be seen outside at slack water."

We watched the level in the pool and when it reached its lowest, *Ruru*, Monk, and I each slipped off our shirt and trousers. The headsman felt his way down, eased into the water, and held his bundle of clothes on the top of his head. I followed and placed my free hand on Monk's shoulder and *Ruru* in turn held onto mine. We moved toward the opening in half steps over a bottom that was a jumble of rocks. The water rose and fell from the level of our chests to our chins. Monk halted outside the entrance and searched around by the starlight. Behind us in the cave one of the women was shushing and comforting a crying baby.

"Come ahead," Monk whispered.

Outside, the rocks of the shore were gray-black shapes outlined by a little foam on the water sloshing around them. Monk waded along until he found a way up. He turned to *Ruru* and me and whispered, "We'll go up over the hill and come down near my *whare*."

We dressed and with Monk leading, started up through the bushes. The headsman stopped every thirty or forty yards to listen and to scan ahead. As the last one, I took a careful look behind us at the halts. Each step up the hill caused a pain in my side, and I was thankful for the slow pace and each rest.

"Damned savages. Do you smell it, Tom?" Monk whispered.

"Yes, smoke. They must have burned everything, even our oil and bone."

On the crest of the hill the odor increased. Little was visible on the other side except for a starlit layer of smoke hanging over the cove and a red glow from the place where the cookhouse was located. We worked our way farther down the slope until we saw the half-burned supports of Monk's house outlined against the light smoke above. "Just as I thought," Monk said, "no one's touched it. They fear it. There's no one stirring about. *Ruru*, you go ahead there north."

We followed him, waded the stream, and passed above the boat ways through the bushes. The ways were intact, but the Two Brothers and the Two Sisters had been taken. Beyond the ways, the tall sheers showed black against the stars. *Ruru* continued on to the fence that surrounded the casks of oil. Monk tapped his shoulder to halt him there.

The headsman worked a hand under the rushes. "Yes, for sure," he whispered. "The oil is still here. Those Indians have left them all safe here for that rascal Olyphant, or else they would have broken them apart for the hoops."

"You wait. I go close, hear talka," *Ruru* said.

"Not too close," Monk warned.

He crept toward the shore and near the path that led back toward the stream.

Monk and I watched from behind the corner of the fence. *Ruru* was the only one who could chance it. If challenged he could answer in their tongue and pass himself off as one of the raiders in the dark. We waited for what was perhaps a few minutes, but it felt like an hour. He could be discovered as not being one of them, and we could be surprised by some raiders wandering about.

Monk nudged me and pointed to a black shape moving toward our concealment. I recognized it as *Ruru*.

He approached and whispered, "Dey reepi here all nighty. Go backa udda ride."

"If they don't go back 'till tomorrow, what do we do now?" I asked.

"Wait," Monk replied. "We wait until they do go. We wait and see if Olyphant shows up."

"You're sure he will?"

"Why is this oil still here? Because Olyphant wants it. I'll lay every shilling I ever earned on that. And I'll lay the bone's not been burned but kept for him too."

"Olyphant did all this because Scutch and Gubby deserted to us?"

"He thinks of us as lags, and anything a lag has he can take. Any injury he can do us is a favor to Port Jackson. No one there will question it."

"Well, I expect he didn't ask if Scutch and Gubby were lags when they went on board the *Achilles*."

Monk agreed, "Aye, he needed them to row a boat and to cut blubber. Once he had a full ship, he meant to maroon them somewhere, as Bry's ship did him."

"I go mora, *kapitana*," *Ruru* offered. "I go, hear mora."

"No, no," Monk warned, "too much danger. Come, we'll go up and sit in the bush where we can see all around the cove."

We slipped away from the casks and climbed up through the low trees along the pig fence to the crest of the hill. There we settled down in a patch of small ferns to sleep until daylight. *Ruru* dozed off and was snoring in a minute, but Monk and I had only short naps and were awake before dawn lightened the sky.

That first diffuse light revealed Monk's reddened face with turgid blisters on his forehead and nose. The smell of burnt hair hung about him. I had crouched lower and escaped the flash of the burning powder that had shot across the floor of the *whare*.

I had my injury, though, a large patch over my ribs turning blue. Each breath I took caused me more hurt. The skin under my arms was raw, with red scrapes where the line had stopped my fall.

Monk rose up behind a tree and peeked around its trunk to see what was left of our station. I got to my feet and joined him. Thin columns of smoke were still rising from the charred remains of the houses, feeding the misty layer hanging over the entire cove. The raiders were stirring about, loading their canoes in the shadow before the sun lifted over the hill and touched the beach.

The headsman pointed to some bundles stacked on the shore. "Look there, Tom Skins," he hissed, "that's our bone. They took it out before they burned your *whare*. They left it there on the shore to be loaded on the *Achilles*. Olyphant's behind all this for sure. Damn him to hell! I'll slit him like a pig … send his ship chock to the bottom!"

I scanned the beach and the entire cove, hoping to see any prisoner. "Do you see *Heke?*" I asked.

"No," Monk replied. "If they caught her, she's been carried away. See the canoes there? Count them. I'm sure more came than are there now. Some have gone."

"To where?"

"Across the Strait, like *Ruru* said. We heard nothing of this raid. If they came up from below Cloudy Bay, I think *Maree's* people would have learned of it, and we would have been warned a day or two before, maybe even sooner."

"What if Old Scarhead came across from the west coast and kept it a good secret?"

"No, No," *Ruru* protested, pointing directly east. "Froma dera."

Monk agreed, "*Ruru's* right, they're from the other side. They must get themselves worked up for a raid. There's a lot of fuss and talk. No end to the speeches about the insults and what they'll do when they get at their enemies. They're in hot spirits for days before they set off. Everything has to be made ready, spears, canoes, and spuds. Any talk of getting that all together would have reached us if they came from Cloudy Bay or from anyplace on this side."

"We go back now?" I asked.

Monk shook his head. "No, no. We watch for what happens; see when the *Achilles* comes here. Besides, we shouldn't go back until dark. Someone might spy us between here and the cave."

We were dressed only in our shirts and trousers, but the sun warmed us and we stretched out between the ferns to spend the day sleeping.

Ruru roused me just after midday and pointed to the north.

Monk was already up, looking in that direction from between the limbs of the tree. "So. Just as I thought," he said. "The blackguard was hiding somewhere, probably just this side of the Cape. There, see that?" He pointed to a sail on the horizon.

"You think it's the *Achilles*?" I asked.

"What else? Mark me now, lad, he'll be loading our oil and bone in two hours. Damnation!"

"He steals our property and there is naught we can do?"

"Naught."

"This is foul piracy."

"Ha! Justice. You want justice out here? You make your own with a musket and a club. I'll get *utu*. Oh yes, I'll have *utu*. I will square accounts with that devil. Before he leaves this island, I'll see him beg for his life."

As Monk predicted, in little more than an hour the ship was entering our cove.

"See that mended fore topsail?" Monk asked. "You remember it? No doubt, that's the *Achilles*."

Monk pulled a branch down a little to better view the ship through the leaves. "Keep well hidden," he warned. "He'll be searching all about with his glass."

The men of the *Achilles* lowered two boats. Once ashore one crew began loading their boat with bundles of our bone. Crewmen from the other boat rolled our oil casks into the water and tied them together, to be rafted to the *Achilles*.

Monk stared at the thieving with eyes afire. He doubled his left fist and pounded the trunk of the tree. Suddenly he plumped to the ground, closed his eyes, and for the better part of a half hour remained there thinking. He grunted once and stood up to study the ship again. Tackle had been rigged to hoist the oil casks from the water and lower them into the hold.

Monk asked, "Thomas, what did Olyphant want? What did the *Achilles* first come here for? Spuds, lad. What garden greens we traded to them won't last but a few days for that crew, and he needs spuds, onions something that will keep for a while." He turned to *Ruru* and questioned, "You have people in the next cove?"

Ruru nodded. "Nina, tena." He held up both hands and splayed the fingers. "Alla go dera, fisha."

"One man's enough. Tell him to go to the ship and say there's many potatoes down at Scratch's village. *Nui, nui, nui kumera.* One nail will fetch two dozen baskets. But the ship must stay two day … three day for the potatoes to be all brought in. Understand?

"Never say anything of our cave. Never! Tell anyone who asks that we were trapped in my *whare* and we all fell asleep. Then we awoke on the beach somewhere. Bry worked his magic, his *mataku.*"

Ruru grinned. He saw some plan for *utu* in Monk's message, some clever deception. Then he repeated, "*Nui, nui, kumera.*"

"Keep out of sight as much as you can. Then you stay with them till we come there. Tell them we need a canoe to go to Scratch's. We must get there before the ship and have Scratch keep it there all tomorrow night."

Ruru slipped down through the trees. Monk smiled as he watched him. "We lay a trap, Tom," he confided. "Oh yes, my boy, we lay a trap; and if all goes well we will have all our property back and then some."

For the remainder of the day we studied the raiders still in the cove. Some remained ashore and a few more paddled out to the *Achilles* expecting to wheedle an ax or a knife from Olyphant. Monk watched every move the crew made on the deck of the ship until the last cask of our oil was hoisted and lowered through the hatch. It was late afternoon, but on the vessel no preparations were made to leave the anchorage.

Monk took one last look at the whaler, nodded, and then said, "We can rebuild some of our *whares* in a week or two and then we can fish again. If Olyphant doesn't take or break up our kettles and windlass … but then again, if he does take them … if he's that goddamn mean?" He was silent for half a minute, then ordered, "Tom Skins, come with me."

We went back to the pig fence and traveled farther east along it for fifty yards. An outcropping of rock was half hidden in the bushes three dozen paces or so from the fence. Monk walked up to it and said, "Let's hope Olyphant needs the potatoes so much he will go down the coast for them. Now, what do the men always want?"

"Weed."

"And? Something more than weed?"

I followed his hint and replied, "Ah, yes, rum, arrack, whiskey, gin, booze of any kind."

"If Olyphant takes the *Achilles* to Blind Bay for the potatoes, I'll promise Old Scratch tobacco, spreaders, tools, if he will trade rum to the crew."

"Where will he get any rum or whiskey?"

Monk pointed to a slot between two rocks about three feet in width and nearly filled with a mat of dead leaves. "There are two full kegs of rum in here. You'll see," he explained and began digging out the leaves and uncovering the kegs. He lifted each one out and handed it to me to place on the ground.

"Tom Skins, you're a good lad," he said in a nearly apologetic tone; one he had never used before. Monk's voice was at its best barking orders, and when pleased his laughter always burst out boisterous, unstinted. His big face had lost its habitually confident look. It was calm, no longer ruffled by his fierce anger. He put a hand on my shoulder and in a soft voice added, "Aye, lad. You're in a savage place. It takes men of our mark to live here, deserters, lags. You're some different than this lot, Tom. Come with me."

Monk circled around the edge of the rock and stopped before another crevice only a few inches wide. "I've caused this raid by my fool idea to get more hands. If this plan doesn't carry out and I'm killed, I want you to get away, get back to your home." He pointed to the crevice and explained, "My ditty bag is buried in there. It's near full of Spanish Dollars, some cut, some whole, and maybe two dozen gold sovereigns, Rupees and Guilders too."

I looked at the slot, also filled with spent leaves, a place I would have overlooked in any search for valuables.

"It's what I saved from my shares. Take what you need to get passage and see that *Maree* and *Karee* have the rest. You know enough to say naught. Knobby John and Peck would buy booze with it all, if I was gone and they found it. We're on this coast 'cause we're daft and don't fit nowheres else. It's all too dull at home for our likes. We whale for we can't do without the chasing, killing the fish, and having our grand booze-up after. 'Cept maybe for Bry. He don't need it much anymore. No, he's found his place and his woman. Bless the ol' bastard and his *Kotuku*. Now, the money I've kept to buy goods and our lines and such is buried in that hole where we store the potatoes. We can't get to that now, but it should be shared out equal if things come to an end here."

This was the first time I had seen Monk unsure of the future. Before the raid he always bellowed his orders and demanded an instant response. Now he was gentle in his motions and thoughts, perhaps thinking of the danger that was ahead and the chance his plan might go awry.

"I promise," I said. "I'll see they get the money if I can."

"Sure you will, lad. I'd never doubt that. We might get our oil and fit-out back or we might not; but I make a solemn promise to you, Tom Skins, we will find *Heke* and bring her here. I can see another won't do for you. You've got a good woman there, one that will stick no matter what happens."

I didn't wish to picture in my mind a scene in which the raiders seized her and forced her into one of their canoes to be carried into slavery or for a thing far worse. They might not have taken her; yet *Heke's* disappearance fed a suspicion, an uneasiness that increased to a wordless dread at times. It settled over my thoughts until at intervals my mind rebelled and replaced it with the more welcome idea that she had slipped away to the south into that maze of twisting inlets with their dozens of secret coves. She could be hiding somewhere in the underwood or traveling to Blind Bay by some secret route.

Monk suddenly said, "It's getting dark enough to travel. Let's make shift and discover if my scheme will set us to whaling again." He led me back around the rock, shouldered one of the kegs, and started off.

An attempt to hoist my keg like Monk caused a sharp pain in my injured side. I could only grip it by the chimes and carry it before me.

We worked our way in the growing darkness down to the edge of the bushes at the shoreline. I doubted we had arrived anywhere near the opening to the cave, but Monk confidently plunked his keg onto the ground.

"Wait here," he ordered, "while I fetch Peck and Knobby." He stripped off his clothes and slipped down between the boulders.

I then recognized the entrance to our hideout we had left from the night before. For a quarter of an hour I crouched in the bushes by the liquor, watching in all directions and listening for the least sound not made by the wind or a bird. Monk finally came out, leading the two men carrying their clothes in their hands.

"Well, Tom ..." Knobby began.

"Whist!" Monk whispered. "Peck, Knobby. Get dressed quick and take one of these."

"What's that?" Peck asked.

"Booze," I replied.

Knobby inquired, "What's it for?"

"To stupefy, as it always is," Monk answered. "Just take it and be quiet."

"Damn. Where we going with it?" Peck asked as he dressed.

"We're taking it to Blind Bay," Monk said, "but by the inside route."

Peck was still puzzled and questioned Monk, "So we take it there and do what with it, have a big booze-up?"

"Yes, hopefully there will be a big booze-up, but not for us. I think I have a way to get back our oil, bone, property, and then some. What choice do you have now that we've lost our boats and irons? Will you raise a patch of spuds and a few grunters with your wives' people?"

"For sure we don't have much choice," Knobby replied, "but you've always brought us through and got us the best price for our oil and bone. I'll go if you think we have one chance in two for it to work."

"That's about it, lads," Monk explained, "one chance in two. Olyphant will pay for this raid one way or 'nother. Damnation, but I'll give him a bumper of trouble! Are you with me?"

Knobby and Peck mumbled their ayes; and each picked up a keg, though they had no exact idea what our headsman had in mind.

Monk set a fast pace to the southwest, angling up the slope toward the crest of the hill. At the top Knobby dropped his load and complained, "It's a man-killing pace, Monk. Why the hurry?"

"We have nine, ten mile to paddle tonight to the neck. Then we push our canoe over it and paddle another twenty mile to Scratch's *whares*. We have to make it there before the sun is up. Olyphant might break his bower out tonight. He won't know about the Gut and would never try it if he did; but with a fresh wind after doubling the Cape he may overtake us when we come out into Blind Bay. We must get to Scratch first and get his help with my plan. The *Achilles* will have to be kept in the bay for all of tomorrow night for this to work."

"How are you going to do that?" Peck asked.

"Aha, Olyphant wants his potatoes," Monk said, "and we'll make him wait for them."

"But we haven't a pistol and not more than a penny's worth o' dust."

"Old Scratch does and he has muskets. First we must reach Blind Bay before Olyphant. If we do, my plan will work. At Scratch's we mustn't say how we squeaked out of the raid without hardly a nick. Not a word about the cave to anyone. That must always stay a secret, you understand? I'll say no more till we're there and the *Achilles* drops her bower. We can't waste a minute. Me and Tom will take the booze now and give you a rest."

Monk and I started off again down the trail on the other side of the hill with Peck and Knobby hurrying after us. I was glad to drop my keg beside Monk's when we arrived at the shore. My arms ached; my side hurt more than ever. I couldn't last another ten yards. Monk would not allow a rest and sent us off looking for *Ruru* and his friends. We found them a few minutes later beside a little stream near the shore.

Monk arrived and demanded, "Did a man go to the *Achilles?*"

Ruru nodded and assured him, "Aye, he go. He terra kapitana *kumera nui, nui* dera."

"Ah, good. Now we must have one of their canoes. I'll give them a half pound of weed to use it and they can have it back in one or two days."

Ruru made the offer, but the men raised objections.

"Dey wanta *parankiti,* pounda tobacco anda pipe alla five-a man," *Ruru* reported to us.

"Damn!" Monk swore in a low, breathy voice. "No blankets. I'll give one pound of weed to share between them ALL! Nothing more."

Ruru relayed the new deal to the others, and that started another dispute among them that lasted for several minutes.

"Wanta mora," *Ruru* replied.

Monk stomped a few paces down the shore and came back. "Damn, damn, damn," he growled. "We've got to be on our way. A pound and a half of weed and a new pipe each. That ought to satisfy them. That's ten times what the wretched thing is worth. They can go and get their canoe and weed from Scratch in two or three days."

The men wrangled over the latest offer. Some were willing to take it, but others were not. That kept the shouts going for several minutes. The ones thinking of the pleasure in a pound and a half of weed pestered the holdouts to accept. At last the deal was made.

Monk clapped his hands onto one of the dugouts and began dragging it toward the water. Peck, Knobby, and I ran up alongside to help him to get it afloat. *Ruru* gathered up some paddles and a bailer and tossed them into the hull. In a minute we were in the canoe with our kegs of rum and gliding out across the black water.

Stars between the crest of the islands close around us yielded a faint light by which to navigate. The headlands we paddled past in the next hour were dark profiles; and between them the little bays were soft, sable voids that never yielded a single glint of a fire. Once we were beyond the last foreland, the shore tended away to the west. A large bay opened out and only black, empty water showed ahead and to each side.

"Dera," *Ruru* said, "dera." He pointed to a star in the southwest and steered for it. In a half hour land appeared, and *Ruru* kept us gliding along the dark mass just off to our starboard. Another black, featureless hill appeared on the other side, enclosing us in an arm of water. The sides narrowed and came together in a low saddle of land that blocked our way.

"Ah, the neck," Monk whispered. "We're about a third of the way, boys."

He leaped out at the shore. "Take a spell," he ordered. "I'm going to look over the other side." The headsman ran up to search beyond the barrier, and we, thankful for the chance, walked about to work the stiffness out of our legs.

A few minutes later Monk returned and spoke in a low voice. "It's clear all about. Let's get her over."

We gripped the gunwale and shoved the hull foot by foot across the beach and up through low, scraggly bushes. Shallow furrows had been cut into the earth by many other canoes pushed across into the next inlet. At the top we halted for a rest and peered into the murk, hoping to pick out faint shapes in the darkness of the next passage ahead.

"How much farther now?" Knobby asked.

"I guess another quarter hour down to the water," Monk said. "Then it's about twenty mile more of paddling. We must get to Scratch's before the *Achilles* if you want to get the oil and bone back. We're running late and it might break light by the time we get out into Blind Bay."

It took less effort going down slope, and we kept the canoe sliding along without a stop until we reached the water.

From the portage our course was out into a widening channel and then into a bay three to four miles across. In the gray, morning light, small islands appeared as dark patches on the horizon.

Monk pointed and said, "There, beyond them, that's Blind Bay."

We skirted south of the islands and paddled out into the wider expanse of Blind Bay. The canoe began lifting and falling on swells from the west.

The sun edged up into a partially clouded sky. Monk wobbled to full height for a few seconds to search to the north for the *Achilles*. "No sign of her yet," he said, and knelt again in the canoe. He turned about and warned *Ruru*, "Keep a good watch back there. If you see any sail let us know. If Olyphant shows within a mile or two, we'll have to paddle ashore and take to the bushes. If he sees us in his glass wearing shirts and jackets, he will suspect something amiss and might not go to Scratch's."

Monk guided our canoe around the west headland and held a course within a hundred yards of the shore. We made it around the last point and came within sight of Scratch's village. There was no ship or boat of any kind off the village or out in the bay.

Knobby looked back along the coast toward the Cape and asked, "Isn't Olyphant coming?"

"He's a devil," Monk said, "but he's no fool. He doesn't know the sea and the land about here. If he decided on going to Scratch's for spuds, he waited for the first light before leaving."

With no sign of the *Achilles*, Monk allowed us a slower pace. After an entire night of constant labor, we were exhausted and plunged our paddles in and pulled with less effort. Men, women, and children were coming down and gathering on the shore when we were still a quarter mile away. They began the usual "*Haere mai. Haere mai*," and waved their mats in welcome as we drew closer. Monk hopped out before the bow of the canoe touched the shore. He strode through the crowd with the rest of us in his wake. Several men were wrapped in blankets and seated on the ground farther back. "*Haere mai*," they mumbled over and over. I spotted Scratch's two feathered topknots on one of the heads. Monk pressed noses first with him and then others. I followed him, greeted each in turn, and then asked Scratch, "Has anyone seen *Heke?*"

Ruru came to my side and asked Scratch the same question. I knew the answer the second after Scratch's short reply of a few words and his blank expression. It proved he knew nothing of *Heke*.

"*Heke* no coma," *Ruru* explained.

I had hoped for a better answer. Still, if she weren't there it was no proof that she had been taken.

Ruru then started shouting, waving his arms, and running back and forth before the nobs. He became more excited by the minute.

Peck nudged my arm and said, "Oh, they love to do that. For sure he's telling them how we were raided and a big story of how Bry's magic saved us from the fire. These people never trusted them on the other side of the Strait, always telling us they were bad people, so they will believe it all."

Anger hardened Scratch's looks as he listened; and his eyes blazed as he considered the *utu* he must have for the raid on his niece and her husband, and for taking a woman for a slave from his people. The sachem growled out an order, and all the children and women quickly left.

Monk laid out his plan for revenge. "If the *Achilles* comes in we must keep it here all night," he explained. "You tell the kapitana he will have his potatoes or whatever he wants, but he must wait. It will all come from far away. You know *taihoa, taihoa.* By and by they will bring them here ready to load tomorrow." Monk paused and then added, "We have brought *waipiro.* They must trade it at night, but to the men only, not the kapitana or mates. Ask much for it so they will not suspect some trick. If the crew gets their hands on it, they will be drunk in two hours, anchor watch and all."

Ruru listened carefully to Monk to be certain how the deception was to be worked on the *Achilles* if it came into the bay. He repeated the plan to Scratch and the other nobs.

When *Ruru* was finished, Monk added, "Tell them if they help us, there will be goods, axes, *parankiti*, and for certain, plenty tobacco. *Nui, nui.*"

At the mention of trade goods they would receive, they all clamored a full approval. Such *utu* was to their liking. There must be payment for wrongs and insults. Everyone shouted approval, even though they might not agree how it would be done.

Monk smiled, pleased that they were all willing; and then he listed some things he needed. "We must have some dress to look like these people when we go aboard, and we must have the loan of any muskets and all the powder they have. Then two canoes."

Old Scratch's eyes narrowed. The grooved skin of his face slowly shaped into a pleased smile as he pictured in his mind the great treasure in the hold of the ship that would be his. The old warrior also considered that there would be a good fight; and he would like nothing better than to show his skill with his weapons, to feint and dodge with his staff or flail about with his *patu*. Trickery and a fight. It was something they all would do for *utu*. Scratch sent his people out to gather the things Monk had asked for.

Knobby and Peck cleaned the muskets and tested their locks and flints for proper sparks. From their keg of powder, over three-quarters full, Peck loaded them and made extra cartridges. He placed the weapons in a *whare* with our disguises.

Monk paced along the shore and watched for the ship all day. Perhaps he doubted that Olyphant had taken the bait; but in late afternoon a lookout stationed on the hillside called the news down to the village that he had spied a sail. It approached from the right direction, northerly; and in an hour we could see the boats mounted on her sides showing her to be a whaler and most certainly the *Achilles*.

Knobby stared at it and said, "That's her for sure."

"*Ruru*, you put on that kilt thing and …" Monk ordered, but didn't finish his sentence. Instead, he tilted his head to his right and tugged the ear lobe with his thumb and forefinger. *Ruru* gathered his meaning that he was to be a spy and went off to change his clothes.

He returned an hour or so later with his hair twisted into a knot on the top of his head and looked to be a genuine man of the village. Monk nodded a quick approval and said, "Go with the others to trade and hear what they have to say. You must appear most friendly. Speak to the crew only, no kapitana, no mates. Say there will be good rum to be traded, but it will come late tonight."

Ruru listened, grinning at the thought of playing a part in a clever stratagem that meant *utu*.

Monk led Knobby, Peck, and me outside of the palisade and behind some bushes on a little rise. From there we could observe the *Achilles* and not be seen by anyone on the ship.

He explained more details of his plan. "Scratch's people will be out there trading for what they can get. *Ruru* will promise the crew he will bring rum tonight. That will get them thinking about it and thirsting for it, but it won't be taken out till after eight bells."

"You think they'll all get so drunk we can slip aboard?" I asked.

"It's a certainty."

Peck shook his head and objected to Monk, "Aye, the crew; but will the anchor watch and perhaps a mate with them get drunk? They're leery of these Indians."

"Even if some are not drunk, you and Knobby will draw them to one side and Tom and I will get aboard from the other side in the dark. In all, there will be five of us with Scratch and all his men. If we want what they robbed of us, we might need to split a skull or two. What do you say, lads?"

"*Utu!*" Knobby snapped. "Olyphant didn't care if we were taken for slaves or killed and eaten. Let's settle up accounts with that rascal."

"We will get aboard the *Achilles* quiet as we can," Monk continued. "We must not rouse Olyphant or Davis. I want Scratch's powder and any more we can find aboard spread on her false deck, then covered with sails from their boats. I want you to find every bucket, kid, kettle, and dipper and pass them down off the *Achilles*. The pump must be disabled too, and make no noise while you're about it."

The orders puzzled us.

"Why the powder on the deck?" Peck asked. "And why break their pump?"

"Ha! You see how they must obey us strictly?" he boasted. "If there is the least move, any attempt to rush us, we will fire the powder and all they have worked for on this cruise will be ablaze. They will have naught to put it out. Olyphant will be in a worse state than he put us into. We will make them ferry our oil and bone ashore and some of theirs too for good measure. We will take their trade goods, their tools, their irons and all the gear we need to fish again. So!"

To board the *Achilles* was my only hope. If we did not get our fit-out back, all our coin would be needed to buy boats, irons, and line. It would be two, no … three, four seasons of work before I earned enough money for passage. Perhaps it would be five years before I reached home. If I signed on a whaler still fishing, there would be no searching for *Heke*. Betwixt such choices, I would rather fight to get our gear, then whale and have time to search for her. So I must board with the others and take all the risks.

It would be justice to take back what had been stolen from us. *Tika*, aye, *tika*. Damn, but I was thinking with *Heke's* words. I could well say *utu*. Payment, yes, we deserved payment for such a crime; and out in these islands where there were no laws, no magistrates, one had to look to oneself to gain justice. I sat and considered what might happen when Knobby, Monk, *Ruru*, Peck, and I went up through the gangway of the *Achilles*. We must not make the least sound boarding and moving about the deck. If we were discovered too soon there might be a terrible end to it all.

We watched more than a dozen canoes crowd up to the side of the ship at her gangway. All the remainder of the day, Davis allowed only six or seven traders on board at any one time. We studied every detail of their exchanges. A small pig was hoisted aboard after a haggling session between Davis and the animal's owner. Olyphant walked about viewing the trading, and in the early evening he disappeared down the companionway. Davis kept to the deck until the twilight began to fade, then ended trade by sending everyone away. He made a last turn around the deck and went below.

Monk tapped a finger toward the ship, smiled, and then said, "If Olyphant left the anchor watch to the men, he must feel safe in this bay. There may be something else on his mind at the moment. It's dark enough now and they can't see us moving about."

He led us from the rise into the palisade and to the *whare* where our clothes and muskets were placed. Several partially burned limbs were lying in the ashes of a shallow fire pit before it.

The headsman then raised his shirt and ran a hand across his belly. "We're a shade light to be these Indians. We must be darker if we're to be them for tonight or they will suspect something." He picked up one of the charred sticks and said," I think this will stain our skin enough. Strip off your clothes."

We stripped off. Each of us picked up a limb, crumbled charcoal from it and rubbed it on ourselves and each other, blackening faces, legs, and backs and making sure no places were left uncolored.

"That's good, boys," Monk said. "It will be much darker when we go out. Now let's see how the dress fits us."

Peck crawled into the *whare* and passed out the Indian kilts. With them wrapped around our waists, we walked about, inspecting each other front and back.

"It won't fool a child," I said.

"In the dark, paddling around the *Achilles*, it will do fine," Monk said. "As long as they see us as Indians they will be just wary; but if they see us as whalers, see who we are, then it will be musket balls. Once we're aboard for a few minutes and have the dust spread on deck it won't matter. We'll have them. They daren't make a move or we fire the dust."

Knobby chuckled, "Hee, hee, hee. No need for muskets. We'll do a war dance, stomp and scream an' frighten Olyphant and his crew off the ship."

"One way or another we'll do it," Monk promised. "Let's get what sleep we can. We will be going out an hour or two before light in the morning."

I followed the others inside and stretched out on a mat. There was no foretelling what the night would bring. It might all go awry. If we are discovered too early, muskets will be fired at us. I had seen what a ball will do. One or two or even all of us could be killed.

The material wrapped around my middle scratched my skin. It was an hour before I first fell asleep; then I awoke and dozed again and again. Between each nap my thoughts always returned to *Heke*. We had traveled from the station in one night and she could have been hidden in one of the many dark coves passed by. She might still be on her way and arrive in the next few days. That was a slim hope. If she had been taken, she was on the other side of the Strait.

Chapter Fourteen

Something awakened me. I felt I had been asleep for only a few minutes, but it had possibly been hours.

"Kapitana?" a hushed voice questioned. A faint light from outside indicated the low opening, and I saw an indistinct figure crouching to enter it.

"Kapitana?" the voice repeated. *Ruru* was at the door.

"Yes," Monk answered.

"*Waipiro* go."

"Good. They took kegs?"

"Two-a go."

"Hear that, boys, they took the rum out. We'll give them two or three hours to soak it up. Now back to sleep for a while."

I tried to sleep again but felt tension in the *whare*. It was too quiet. I expected none of the others were sleeping and, like me, were only lying there thinking of the raid. There was no slow, deep respiration of tired and resting men. No one snored.

Anything could happen when we boarded the *Achilles*. Someone might take a musket ball or be skewered with a lance. That one might be me. Despite the great risks it appeared we were fated to board the vessel and take back our stolen tools and property. What else could we do? What else could I do? I would not desert them now after they had shown such liberality, such welcome. Also, I could not forget Monk's promise to help find and rescue *Heke*. My future was bound to theirs by that promise. Then again we might take the *Achilles* without a peep from a thoroughly sodden crew. With that thought I fell asleep.

I awoke next when I felt Monk's big hand shaking my shoulder.

"Time to go, lad," the headsman said. "Tom Skins, you and I will go out first in a canoe to the larboard side."

"Knobby, *Ruru*, and Peck you go out next and take the powder and a musket.

Be sure to cover them with a mat so they can't be seen. Then go out to the ship and call to the anchor watch at the gangway. If they're awake, that will draw them to that side. We must find how many there are. Offer to bring women and trade more rum to them."

We felt about, found our weapons, and crawled through the low door.

Beyond the log palisade the hull and rigging of the *Achilles* was silhouetted by a cantle of moon in the west and star shine. Men were holding two canoes ready for us at the water's edge.

"Knobby give us about a quarter hour before you leave," Monk whispered. "We must go the long way 'round." We placed our muskets in our dugout and shoved off.

The headsman headed out in a wide circle around the bow of the *Achilles* to its larboard side. From that point the hull was indistinct, merging with the inky mass of the hills ashore. The masts and yards were barely visible against clouds lighted by the first hint of dawn. Monk turned the canoe and headed directly toward the ship using its mainmast as a guide. We closed in alongside the hull just under the waist boat. Monk tied the canoe to a slide board with a cord. Using the supports of the board, he climbed to the channel and crouched there between the rail and the hull of the boat. It was the best place to hide. The guard would be looking over the side for a swimmer or a canoe nearing the *Achilles*; and the places to search from were between each set of davits. The boats on them blocked a good view of the water. Monk was crouched low, waiting for the man on watch and listening for his footsteps. A half minute later he whispered, "Muskets." I passed both up and then climbed to join him. We looked over the rail and could barely see the length of the deck fore and aft. All was silent save for the faint slap of the longer halyards moving in a slight breeze.

"All drunk?" I whispered.

"The crew maybe," Monk replied.

"Knobby should be close by now."

"Whist, there by the windlass."

The dark figure of a crewman, carrying a musket, moved between the windlass and the side of the ship.

He stepped to the rail, peered idly over at the water, and started aft toward us. We hunkered down out of sight and heard the light brush of the man's bare feet on the deck as he passed. A few seconds went by and we peeked over the rail again. The figure was now moving near the quarter boat davits.

Monk whispered, "Quick, get on the deck there by the pump. Then we'll see what happens when Knobby gets here."

We climbed over the rail and slipped across to the mainmast where we could see anyone approaching the gangway. The man of the watch came from aft, walking slowly and looking over the side for any savage who might be attempting to board the vessel. A few minutes later he came around once again, always looking overboard. The eastern sky was showing some light; and had he looked in our direction, he would have seen us.

"One man only," Monk whispered after the guard passed by.

He was coming from aft for the third time when there was a knock at the gangway. The watchman trotted forward and peered over the side. A dark figure ran from somewhere aft. By the cap and smudge of beard there was no mistaking the first mate, Davis.

He leaned over the rail and swore, "Ah, there you are, you damned swine! You sent that goddamn liquor aboard! I'll settle with you lot of heathens now!" He raised a pistol gripped in his right hand and was lowering it to aim when Monk dashed across to Davis and struck his head with the butt of his musket. The officer slumped to the deck with his pistol still in his hand. The man of the watch turned from the rail. I prodded the muzzle of my musket into his face. His hands opened and his weapon fell, but I caught it before the butt hit the deck. He held his shaking hands toward me, dumb show that he would make no resistance. Monk opened the gangway and waved the men in the canoe to come aboard. Then he knelt beside the mate's body to tie his hands.

Peck came aboard last and Monk whispered to him, "Take Tom's musket and watch the companionway for Olyphant." Then he handed me the mate's pistol and said, "Davis was up here keeping an eye on the anchor watch. There's just this one man and only one. That means the whole crew must be well corned. Go into the steerage and bring any weapons they have and their lantern up to me."

I went down through the hatch, feeling for each step in turn with my toes. I peered about. The light of the lantern, hanging from a beam, dimly revealed a complete mess. Two tin cups lay on their sides at the foot of the steps. The air in the steerage was charged with the odors of rum, dirty clothes, and the oil burning in the lantern. To the right and left men were stretched out on their bunks, some with an arm or leg over the side. One crewman was lying in the middle of the floor with his head near a patch of vomit. From a dark corner came a loud, continuous snoring. The keg of rum traded to the crew had been up-ended on a roll of cordage, allowing it to be tipped to pour out its contents. I rocked it back and forth but there was no sloshing. Every drop was gone.

There were no spades or lances lying about which might be used in a fight with the New Zealanders. They battled close in with their *patus* making any long weapons awkward, nearly useless. Not one man looked as if he could face the Indians or our muskets on a crowded deck. I went around and drew each man's knife from its sheath. One of the crewmen looking up at me from beneath half closed eyelids, showed no alarm at me dressed as an Indian, smudged with charcoal, and carrying a pistol. The man was senseless as if he had taken laudanum. One keg had afforded him and all the others a jolly booze-up. Monk had guessed correctly that the crew, even the headsmen, would get thoroughly drunk before the captain or mate learned the rum was aboard. I tilted the keg to one side and dropped the knives inside the coil of cordage. On my way up to the deck I reached over and took the lamp from its hook, leaving the steerage in darkness.

The sky was now a bit lighter. The mate Davis and the man of the anchor watch were each tied hand and foot, gagged, and placed face down on the deck.

Ruru and Knobby were by the try works, spreading powder from the keg across the false deck.

Monk, aft with Peck by the cabin companionway, looked up when I arrived and asked, "How is it below? Any weapons?"

"Nothing. I hid their knives and the men will all pass for dead until noon."

Monk nodded and took the pistol from me. "Same in the fo'c's'le," he said, and slipped the barrel of the weapon into his waistband. "Peck, give your musket back to Thomas. He will keep a good watch here. You and Knobby get the sails from the boats and cover the powder to keep off any wind and dampness. Once they're spread and secure, we've got them."

Knobby and Peck drew the masts from one of the boats and set about covering the powder.

I set the lantern at one side of the companionway and held the musket at the ready.

Landward, gray streaks were spreading in the eastern sky above the crests of the dark mountains; and in the faint light reflecting from the water several canoes were visible coming out of the shadow of the land and moving toward the ship. Minutes later the first Indians reached the *Achilles* and were climbing quietly up through the gangway.

Monk came aft carrying a large, oily rag, possibly one used to wipe the handles of the blubber forks and dippers. I stepped forward to open the latch. The headsman shook his head and whispered, "No, he's too wary. For sure the man will have a pistol or two with him. I'll bring him up swift." He knelt on the deck, opened the lantern, and drew the frayed edges of the fabric through the flame. They began to glow red. He rose to his feet and waved the rag around to increase the white smoke coming from it.

"Now, ready?" Monk asked.

I nodded, took a step back, and aimed the muzzle of my weapon at the door. Monk turned the latch and eased the door open. He listened for a few seconds and leaned in. His fingers holding the smoking rag out at arm's length slowly opened, and the rag dropped.

Ten seconds later the first few wisps of smoke spilled out of the opening. Monk banged his fist against the side of the companionway and shouted, "Fire! Fire! Fire!" He drew out his pistol, cocked it, and stood opposite me. We waited for Olyphant to come up, but the captain did not appear or make any sound below. Monk stood motionless for a few seconds and then hammered again, calling out, "We're afire! We're afire!"

It remained quiet below, and I wondered if the captain might be elsewhere in the ship. Suddenly someone was stomping up the steps. Olyphant jumped out onto the deck, coughing and wreathed in smoke. He stood there bareheaded, barefooted, stripped to the waist. Monk aimed his pistol at the center of his chest. Olyphant retreated a pace, but he halted when he felt the muzzle of my musket touch his back. The captain showed no look of surprise except that his mouth hung slightly open. He eyed Monk's face and body smudged with charcoal; then looked beyond him to the deck forward, filled with New Zealanders squabbling over hatchets they had found in the boats. Some of them gripped their stone or bone clubs in their hands. Others had staffs.

Peck and Knobby were near the mainmast looking aft at us.

"We've had enough of your foul game, Olyphant," Monk snapped. "You caused all our *whares* to be burned and stole our oil and bone. We've got naught left. We were near killed. All that over two worthless rascals. We're here to square accounts. Damn your guts!"

The sound of feet thumping up the steps again came from the companionway. I stepped back and swung the muzzle of the musket to cover the doorway. A plump woman, naked from the top of her head to the soles of her feet, burst out through the smoke. Her dugs bounced at each stride as she rushed forward to the gangway.

Monk shifted his gaze to me for a second, smiled, and squeezed his right eye into a wink that wrinkled up half his face. Then, without turning his head, he shouted, "Peck, fetch a line here and tie him up." Peck searched about for a minute and came back to the quarterdeck with a short piece. I held Olyphant's arms while Peck tied his wrists behind him.

Monk held up a forefinger and motioned for the captain to follow him. He led him forward to the try-works and stopped at one of the sails laid across the deck. He stooped, lifted its edge, and looked back to the captain. His forehead wrinkled with a pretended concern, one not quite hiding a smirk. "Dust ... powder, Mr. Olyphant," he said. "There's near a whole keg of it spread here." Monk tilted his head slightly, and with raised eyebrows asked, "What if it caught fire, was lit it by someone? Can you see what would happen?"

All there could picture how the furious, white blaze of burning powder would boil out the oil which had seeped for months under the false deck and into the cuts and splits of the wood. In a minute everything around the try works and the forward part of the ship from rail to rail would be a roaring blaze. Next, the tarred shrouds and stays would catch fire; and the flames would quickly rise up the mast. Olyphant stared down at the powder while a slight breeze moved his mussed and thinning hair. His sullen expression did not change and he gave no hint he would answer our headsman.

Monk straightened up and threatened, "If there is one move by your men to take the ship back I'll put the lock of this pistol over that dust and pull the trigger.

Ha! You won't be able to put it out. We've not left a bucket or one thing aboard that will hold water. They have all been pitched over the side, and we have broken your pump. Well, now, you might bail water in your hat to staunch the fire and order every man aboard to piss on it; but I wouldn't give you much hope there. Here is what I ask, and I know you won't deny me." A pleased smile was on Monk's face as he continued, "We will take all our bone and oil you stole and add some of yours for good measure. Also, we will have some of your spermaceti, all your muskets and powder, and the lines and irons we lost. Our boats have gone missing so we will take your best two."

Those of us from the station stood at the edges of the sails listening to Monk list the items to be taken.

"Oh, yes, and staves, ours have been burned. We must have them and hoops and your cooper's tools. I'll need any deals you have aboard. To pay for their bother, these friends of ours will have your trade goods and whatever else they fancy."

Olyphant remained silent, staring at the device of sails and powder that if ignited could leave his entire vessel burned to the waterline.

Monk looked at the captain; and with his right hand held athwart his hip and his upper body bent forward in a bow, he mocked, "Well, naught to say, your lordship?"

I stepped forward demanded, "Do you know if they took a hostage, a woman?"

Olyphant stared blankly at the deck, not giving the least indication that he had heard my question.

I rammed the butt of my musket against the captain's shoulder, almost knocking him off his feet.

"My *Heke* is missing," I shouted. "Have they taken her?"

Olyphant turned to me. His slot of a mouth curved into the beginning of a smile and he nodded his head once.

I felt a mix of feelings, outrage that *Heke* had been made a prisoner and probably a slave, but also some relief that she might be alive.

Monk grabbed my arm and led me back toward the quarterdeck.

"He lies," Monk advised in a low voice. "He knows nothing of her. He could see it might help him if you thought he knew where she was taken." Monk grabbed the musket from me and ordered, "Get below and find his trade goods. They're most likely all down there with his money where he can keep an eye on them. First thing, put that rag overboard before all is afire."

At the companionway I took a breath and held it as I went down through the smudge, but could not keep the air in my lungs after reaching the cabin. I took another breath. That started a fit of coughing and I couldn't stop it until I had both stern lights open. Fresh air entered and carried the smoke up through the companionway, slowly clearing the cabin. The rag had fallen behind the steps. I leaned in, snatched up the smoking wad, and tossed it out one of the openings.

To find Olyphant's goods, I tried the first narrow door on the larboard side of the cabin. That proved to be the captain's privy, but in a cabinet above it were some boxes. The first contained dozens of clay pipes. The second held fishhooks of four different sizes and papers filled with needles and pins. Behind them were horn combs, looking glasses, spools of thread, knives, and bags of glass beads. Another bag was full of dressed flints for gunlocks. It was a stock of small items, but it was of tremendous value on the coast and would buy anything more readily than gold or silver coin from any country. The narrow door on the starboard was padlocked. Two of my good kicks and the panels splintered and fell in, revealing a cuddy filled with blankets, axes, spades, rolls of calico, and half a dozen muskets. Under all that were four casks of tobacco. One had the head taken off and half its weed removed. Olyphant had learned what was best to trade for food and stores and had prepared well for his voyage.

Knowing any money would be well hidden, I opened every cabinet and drawer in the cabin and stomped my feet on the deck to reveal any loose boards there. The cabin's paneled parts sounded solid under my hammering. I threw the bedding on the bunk back … nothing there. Under the bunk and behind some extra blankets and clothes, there were some kegs,… the officers' supply of brandy or some sort of liquor. Still no money, though. Even Davis might not know where the specie was cached, and he certainly would deny it if he did. It would not be in the obvious places, but even so, I turned around and lifted the top of the desk. The account book was there and on its pages was a list of the monies paid out in different ports. A balance of 645 pounds 12 shillings was still aboard. Yes. Oh, yes. There was money on board, if it were a true counting, but where? Not outside the cabin. Olyphant must surely keep it concealed in a place under his eye at all times.

The sum divided into six shares would mean each of us would receive about 107 pounds, the same as the shares of two or three good years whaling. If I had that much in hand I might leave as soon as I had recovered *Heke*, or perhaps without her if she had been slain. We had all suffered from the raid and all should have a share for recompense. It would be just punishment for Olyphant to have it taken from him. All of us at the station might have been clubbed, cooked, and eaten had it not been for the secret cave and Monk's foresight. Yet in my search I had found no money, and Olyphant, even with the muzzle of a cocked pistol pressed into his ear would never reveal its place. A dead man could not reveal where the money was concealed. There was even a possibility the pounds and shillings were falsely entered into the account book for some scheming reason.

But if it were in the cabin, would it be wise to find it? What would the men do with such a windfall? Knobby and Peck and even Monk might be tempted to leave; to take their 107 pounds with this year's pay to Port Jackson, Hobart Town, or to the Bay of Islands and resume their old habits. Have a right royal booze-up. Drink it all up in a week's time maybe? Perhaps to be robbed in those places or even slain there for their money? It would all be for nothing and they would be worse off for having that much placed in their hands. Odd things befell people when they came onto a great sum of money. When all their coins were spent and they were sleeping rough on the beach, what might they do then? They would sign on some ship and not earn a twentieth of what they did from their shore whaling. Would they ever return to the station to whale there again?

If they didn't, *Ruru* and *Aihe* would go back to their people. Bryan would stay with his *Kotuku* on the island, even had he a choice to go elsewhere. I could not imagine that pair separated after watching them walk together along the shore of the cove of an evening. They were much alike, she mellow and grandmotherly to all the children, and he, calm and measured in his speech even when very drunk. I could see the whaling from the cove might possibly end. There would be no *whares*, no wives, no bright, lively little sons and daughters for the men if they, penniless in those ports, were forced to sign on a ship.

If the others left the cove, there would be no one to help me find and rescue *Heke*. Then any gold and silver would do me little good. I stopped looking.

It was better that the men continue the chase of the animals from the shore.

It was in their blood. If the ship's treasure were not discovered, they would not be tempted to leave; and they could have their drinking bouts at the station without fear of being murdered for their money.

Monk could then keep his pledge to me, and *Heke* might be found and ransomed or rescued from life as a slave. I hurried up the steps to report what I had found and not found.

Peck and Knobby were rigging a tackle to hoist the casks from the hold.

Two of the *Achilles* crew had come up from the steerage, blinking in the light and gawking at the strange scene on deck. Both men moved softly, cautious of any step that might jar their aching heads; and watched the crowd of Indians shouting at each other, arguing, and tossing clothes and tools to their mates in the canoes drawn in alongside.

"Goods are there all right," I reported to Monk. "Not a great store, but fine goods."

"Muskets?" the headsman asked.

"Six and some spreaders. Much weed, steamers, axes, fish hooks."

"We will take the muskets, spreaders, any slops, and half the weed; and leave the rest for Scratch."

I leaned my head toward Monk's as I stepped past to obey the order and whispered, "Found no coin."

By late afternoon the spermaceti, the oil, the bone, and all the other items our headsman had sworn he would take in reprisal had been ferried or floated ashore. Ten sobering, suffering members of the whaler's crew had been rowing the boats between the ship and the beach. Without their sheath knives or any weapon, they watched the New Zealanders with distrust. Their eyes focused on the club each one had in his belt or held by its thong. The *Achilles* crewmen could do nothing except obey Monk's orders. If the powder were fired, any oil and bone remaining aboard, the product of their hard labor, would be gone. They would have no ship on which they could resume whaling. The owners would collect the insurance, but the crew, not sharing in the payment, would be far poorer than the day they signed on. Worst of all they would be marooned on a savage coast. Silence and obedience were the only responses they could give.

Scratch was in his glory, chattering and grinning widely while his share was carried up the companionway to be whisked off and stored in his *whare*. He could trade with the goods and be generous with prized gifts. Such would raise his *mana* high.

"Knobby, find the ship's powder, all of it," Monk ordered. "Then send it ashore.

Knobby cornered the youngest of the crew and poked his musket under his chin. "Tell where your powder is," he demanded, "or I'll blow your head off."

The lad's bulging eyes rolled down, straining to see Knobby's finger on the trigger.

"Speak!" Knobby shouted and pushed the barrel up, forcing his victim's head back.

"Or … Orlop," he stuttered. "Larboard. Fo … forward of the hatch, sir."

"Lead me to it or be the first to die here."

The boy trotted to the steerage companionway, with Knobby close after him. A few minutes later four of the *Achilles* crewmen came up on deck, each with a keg of powder. Knobby had them load it with the last of the trade items into the next boat that arrived back from shore.

The two whaleboats drew in below the gangway on their return from their last trips. Monk leaned over and ordered, "You *Achilles* men, back up on board. We will take Mr. Olyphant with us for a hostage till we are safely ashore. The Indians will return him to you later."

Davis with his gag removed demanded, "How do you expect him to get down with his hands bound?"

"Why, we will lower him as befits his station," the headsman replied. "You, Peck, overhaul that block."

Peck pulled enough slack through to bring the block down to the gangway. Monk grabbed a length of rope and passed it twice around Olyphant's chest, and quickly bent the ends together. Peck saw what was to be done and slipped the line onto the hook of the block.

Knobby and Peck grabbed the fall and hoisted the captain into the air. He swung to and fro as he was lowered over the side. *Ruru* scrambled down to guide him to a thwart in the boat and unhook the block.

Davis's coal-dark eyes glared at Monk. He was furious but helpless. His crew had been dulled with drink and disarmed. With one small spark as Monk had threatened the ship would be ablaze. Scratch's men, armed with their flat, sharpened clubs, crowded the deck; and those weapons swung with any speed could cleave a man's head and break arms. He shuddered with rage as the New Zealanders came from below wearing trousers and coats, probably some of his, and carrying the last few articles they fancied.

"Peck, Knobby, down in the boat with Olyphant and *Ruru*," Monk ordered, "and, Tom Skins, bring the other boat." He turned to Davis, stared fiercely into his eyes, and aimed a finger at him almost touching his nose. "*Utu*," he growled. "*Utu.*"

Monk climbed down into the stern of his boat. "Head all," he called and they pulled for the shore.

With a dumb show of rowing, I motioned for two New Zealanders to go with me in the next boat. Once we were aboard I swept the bow around to follow our headsman.

The crew lined along the rail to watch us leave. I wondered if they mistrusted Olyphant's reasons, if he had given any, for loading our oil and bone onto the *Achilles*. They had seen our burned *whares*. He might have told them some tale to conceal his scheming. He might have claimed the Indians had sold him the oil and bone for goods. Oh yes, all honestly done; but the crew could now see that we, the true owners, were still alive and much in charge of all. Guilt and chagrin tinged their faces as my boat pulled away. In their minds it was now more than a suspicion that their captain had incited the Indians on the east side of the Strait.

The oil and bone he had robbed from our station was retaken and they had lost some of theirs. Worst yet, their irons and tools, the most needed items, we carried away in their two best boats. There was only one choice for them if they were to whale: go to Port Jackson or the Bay of Islands and replace the lost property. Any concealed specie, if any were there, must be used to buy the missing gear, or some of their remaining oil must be traded for it. That would set them back many months or a year before they filled for home. Monk had cleverly given them a punishment that would last for a long while. We had our *utu* in good measure.

Monk's boat pulled to the shore just before mine. Half a dozen Indians joined him to hustle Olyphant into the stockade.

"What do we do with all the oil and spermaceti?" Knobby asked when Monk returned. "We can't tow it all back to the cove."

"I have made a deal with Scratch. All the oil will be stored here, and when a ship comes to trade we shall sell it from this shore. His *kukies* will keep it wetted."

It was nearing sundown. Seeing the Indians had not brought Olyphant from the stockade or readied a canoe to carry him back, my suspicion grew that Monk had never intended to return him, though he had promised that. There was nothing to gain by keeping Olyphant longer. He had no means to injure us more.

No one said a thing about it until the *Achilles* lowered a boat.

"He comes for Olyphant," Monk muttered. He went into the stockade and came back carrying a musket.

Davis guided the boat toward the beach.

"No farther!" Monkhouse yelled and cocked the musket. "You have no need to land here."

"Where's our captain?" the mate called out.

"He's gone on holiday."

"You send him to us now. You gave your word those savages would bring him back."

"Well, now, I didn't say exactly when, did I?"

"Damn, but you cannot hold him. I'm coming there to get him."

The headsman raised the musket to his shoulder and sighted down the barrel at the mate's chest. Davis had plenty of courage but he certainly was no fool. There were no weapons left on the *Achilles*, and he instantly saw a demand alone would not work with Monk. The two men stood facing each other across twenty yards of water. Our headsman kept the weapon up, steady, and ready to fire. The mate of the *Achilles*, standing in the stern of the boat, stared at the muzzle at a loss of what to do next.

Gradually Monk lowered the musket a little and warned, "You will leave here and not come back. If you show within fifty mile of the Strait I'll know of it. These people hereabouts are my relatives, and they would like to board you again when you have more to take. I should have burned your ship, but I don't want your scum about this shore. We've had enough of you and them."

"I will fetch a government ship from Port Jackson," Davis threatened. "You are all bolters here."

Monk smiled and said, "This here is not a parcel of New South Wales. Who do you expect will help? The governor is no friend of American captains, and he has no cause to send his men and arrest anyone on your word alone. You're blocked there."

"What's to happen with our captain?" Davis asked.

Monk lowered his musket more and growled, "'Tonement. It's called 'tonement. We have squared our accounts with him. So!"

The mate leaned over and conferred in whispers with his rowers for a minute. He glanced up at Monk while still listening to what his men had to say. Then he straightened up and ordered, "Pull three." The boat swung about and started back to the *Achilles*.

"Break your bower out before tonight!" the headsman shouted after him. He rested the butt of his musket on the sand, but kept his eyes on the whaleboat as it was pulled to the side of the ship. Monk watched the boat being hoisted and every move of the crew readying the *Achilles* for sea.

What puzzled me was what might happen to Olyphant. Monk had certainly studied it much and had decided on all beforehand. There was no point in even asking him. The scowl on his face meant he was in no mood to reveal his intentions.

Davis had no choice but to leave without his captain. The *Achilles* had been disarmed. In minutes it could be surrounded with dozens of canoes filled with Indians firing muskets and then beset by others climbing aboard, swinging clubs. A defense would have to be made with any knives, gaffs, and spades we had missed and left aboard. The mate sent men forward to the windlass, and the clicking of the pawl was continuous until the cable was vertical.

Davis then shouted his order, "Break 'er out."

We remained on the beach until the *Achilles* was far out into Blind Bay.

Utu had been taken justly. Olyphant had caused the villainous attack on us. It was not deserved, though Monk had lured Scutch and Gubby from the *Achilles*. Those two proved to be of little value in shore whaling and surely were no better aboard the ship. Their desertion was of no great loss to the *Achilles*, even a benefit, for their lays were forfeit and would be shared by its owners. It was the hurt to his vanity Olyphant could not bear. As almighty lord of his little domain, he could not suffer a traverse by anyone, certainly not by one he deemed a lag. He saw his men's desertion, abetted by Monk, as weakening his authority over his crew. To accuse everyone of being a lag at our station was his flimsy excuse for the raid. Only Bryan of us all was a convict, and he was not the least danger to a soul now or ever had been.

Olyphant had much to do with *Heke's* disappearance; and though it was not directly done, he deserved to answer for it. My wife might be a slave or dead. I would not ask Monk where the captain was to be taken or what might happen to him. Olyphant must rue his mischief. He had sorely miscalculated Monkhouse and us.

Monk and *Ruru* talked to Old Scratch and others for over an hour. When their *korero* was ended it looked as if they had settled on something.

Chapter Fifteen

"He's agreed," Monk said when he returned to us. "They will send grub to stay us and will send some of their *kukies* to help us raise our *whares* again. So."

At the dawn of the second day after the *Achilles* left, Scratch's slaves began stirring about the village and launched three canoes loaded with mats, baskets of potatoes and cooked food.

We pushed the *Achilles*' boats into deeper water, and freighted them with the tools and muskets taken from the ship. Monkhouse boarded one, pointed its bow northeast, and led the other whaleboat and the canoes in a straggling line up the coast.

Clouds drifted over the sky, shadowing the water of the bay to a dismal gray and darkening the greenery of the hillsides. With the clouds came a wind and a poppling sea that rolled and pitched the boats and canoes as we moved north. We rowed all day, and at times, when there was a wind from aft, raised the sail. It was a much different trip toward Admiralty Bay than the one I had first made when ransomed. A slow rain began dotting us and veiling the hills to the east. Monk led the line closer inshore. We were miserable in our wet clothes. The *kukies* were wearing capes, but I doubted they were any drier than we were. We halted at the Gut for two hours until the tide turned to carry us through. In the late afternoon we rounded the headland of our cove and crossed to its far shore.

"We can whale again!" Monk called out to us. "Our sheers, kettles, and windlass are still here. Enough of the season is left. With luck we might take three or four whales."

I had a quick look forward and saw those items were untouched, but there were only a few charred remnants of our *whares*.

The boats' bows touched the sand; and the headsman shouted, "Unload." We emptied them of everything, dragged them higher on the shore, and worked them parallel to the beach. Monk walked around each one and, satisfied they were well-placed, ordered, "Capsize!"

Our entire crew grabbed the gunwale of our boat and rolled over until it was bottom up. Peck slipped the water butt under one side, propping it up for an opening. The other boat was inverted next and the crews slithered under one or the other to get out of the rain.

Though wet and shivering, I ran to where my *whare* once stood, where I had lived for months, some very happy months, with *Heke*. The image of her face smiled impishly in my mind. Only the charred stumps of posts, ashes, and some charcoal marked the rectangle of ground our house had once covered. The table and the bunk had burned; and every tool, hoop, and bit of metal had been found and carried away. It was dismal, my wandering in the rain, searching for some sign or mark that she had returned while we were at Blind Bay. A long, charred stick leaned across the top of one of the burned stumps. One end rested on the ground and the raised end pointed to the small offshore islands. Could that be a sign? Could she have placed it there as a clue? No. It was silly to have some desperate hope she was nearby. That stick had simply fallen there by chance. If she had not been taken, she would have fled in the opposite direction back toward her people in Blind Bay or into those many inlets between the islands to the south.

Might Scutch and Gubby be in those hidden coves or in the higher hills to the southwest? Not likely. I didn't care, for those two were of no concern to me or any of us.

I ran back to join the others under one of the boats. There we had to lie on the damp sand; but at least we were shielded from the chilling wind and the dog's soup pouring down. Each of us had a small space between the thwarts where there was room to sit up. I had spent many nights in the sealing islands lodged in that fashion. Out on the cove and beyond, just visible under the gunwale, the rain dashed in sheets across a gray surface lined with white-lipped waves.

My mind kept going back to *Heke*. Surely if free she would have tried to reach Blind Bay. Yet, if she had chosen to hide nearby she would be watching the cove for our return. I had to face it: most likely she had been seized. If taken alive she might be set to digging in the gardens and carrying loads even though she was *rangatira.* If she had been cudgeled, she would have been carried off for another purpose. I tried to block the idea from my mind, but it always returned to nag at me. The recurring vision of her headless body being dumped into a canoe was sickening. But was she taken? I had watched her leave with the roll of blankets and the lantern and thought I had seen her with the others going toward Monk's porch. It was baffling. While I was loading the musket, had one of the raiders snatched her and dragged her behind the *whare*? Those across the Strait will surely boast of their great victory, of their *utu*, of all the iron and tools taken as booty. If they show her as a slave word of her capture should reach me. What might I do to fetch her back if she were still alive? It was an impossible task. The other side of the Strait was an unknown coast to me, filled with hostile tribes. I could never land there unnoticed and cross into that country. Discovery would mean death if they guessed where I came from and my purpose. How could I search her out if I could not reveal myself or speak the language?

The constant chatter of two New Zealanders under the overturned boat was annoying to me. Even the rain and the dismal view outside did not affect them. They were too happy to suit my thoughts.

There was a whining at the gunwale; and there was Boney, wet and shivering, in a crouch begging entrance. One of the *kukies* pulled the smelly old creature under the boat. In the days after the raid, the dog hadn't found much to eat, and his ribs showed beneath his fur.

Evening closed down and I rested my head on the sand and listened to the recurring talk and snores. I tried to get some sleep, but there wasn't much room and a shifting arm or foot always nudged me awake. There was only an impenetrable blackness to be seen, never for a moment relieved by a light.

In the morning we crawled from beneath the boats and looked up to the sky, one clouded but yielding no rain.

"Everything is soaked," Monk said, "so we'll have no fire until the sun comes out and dries some wood. I want all of you to find any posts of our old houses not badly burned, and later we'll cut some new trees. That effort will warm us a bit. I plan to have the first new *whare* there where Thomas's was." The headsman started up the trail and then turned to say, "I'm going for Bry and the women. Keep a good watch."

He hadn't been gone more than a few minutes when calls of "Coo … ee" came from the hillside.

Bryan was hobbling his way down through the trees, calling and waving an arm as he descended. Monk met him a quarter of the way up. The rest of us rushed up to join them.

"Aye, lads, aye," Bryan greeted us, "I see you have gotten some new gear. Even from the top I could see those were not our boats."

"They're not, but are even better and will serve well," Peck said. "We had our pick of the best ones on the *Achilles*."

"When she anchored at Scratch's village," Knobby broke in, "we got the whole crew drunk as David's sow and slipped aboard without a squeak. Took the ship easy."

"We spread dust over her deck," Peck added. "One twitch from the crew and that would have been the end of her in half an hour."

"We can fish again," Knobby boasted. "We took our oil and bone and those boats with all the irons we need. We got the lot."

"How did you get Olyphant to go there?" Bryan asked.

Monk explained, "I had one of *Ruru's* people tell him there were plenty of spuds to trade for in Blind Bay. He took the bait and went out around by the Cape."

"Hee, hee, hee. It was nuts for us," Peck chuckled. "It couldn't have gone better. We caught Olyphant asleep with a heifer. Got all we lost and more and gallied ol' Davis enough to send him out of the Strait. I'll lay a pound or two he'll not return."

Bryan looked puzzled for moment and asked, "Davis? What happened to Olyphant? Isn't he in the *Achilles*?"

Monk ignored the question and asked, "Are all our people safe?"

Bryan groaned as he sat on a low limb to rest his leg and answered, "Oh, yes, safe enough. Me and *Kotuku* have been keeping a good watch up there. When we saw the *Achilles* leave we brought them out of the cave. It was hard to keep them in. I could see we were safe if we stayed on that side of the hill. We've built a shelter of sorts under the trees. Been fishing some, too. I saw you come in yesterday, but thought it best to wait for the thick weather to clear."

"That was a good choice," I said. "We spent a damp, cold night under the boats."

"And where's Olyphant now?" Bry asked.

Monk put his hand on Peck's shoulder and ordered, "Run over to the other side and bring the women and children here."

"Oh, no need to do that," Bryan said. "They're all up at the top. Most likely on their way down now. I told them to wait quiet while I got closer to see if all was right here. When I called out, they were to start. Now, where's Olyphant got to?"

"He's a guest with Scratch," Monk breathed out, and parried Bryan's curiosity with a look to the horizon.

Bryan's expression didn't alter an iota; yet I saw an understanding grow in his eyes. The man instantly sensed he was never to ask again.

Tokee and *Wehe* ran down the path, followed by the smaller children squealing with delight.

Monk scooped up a child in each arm. With his laughter mixing with theirs, he turned around and around in an impromptu dance.

A few minutes later the women arrived. After greeting them the headsman faced the cove and watched Scratch's *kukies* working on the shore below. "All gather about now and mark me well," he ordered. "Those that raided us will tell how we went into my *whare* and never came out and must have been burned. Yet here we are alive. We must never speak of how we escaped the fire to anyone. Not anyone! The wives are not to tell their relations. You little ones are to say naught about a cave. Do you understand me, no one must know? That we all escaped the fire is our protection from those who would raid us because to them it was magic, powerful magic. *Mataku!* We will be most *tapu* if they never learn the secret."

The women understood more or less what Monk was saying, yet Bryan repeated the warning to the wives and children in their own speech that they were never to reveal the existence of the cave beneath the hill.

Tales told by the New Zealanders of people wasting away and dying after breaking a *tapu*, and the same happening from the effect of *mataku*, were never doubted. The great power of *tapu* and *mataku* over the New Zealanders was known to all sealers and whalers. We saw our vanishing in the fire and re-appearing was a boon for us; and if the secret of the cave were never revealed, another raid might be prevented by the Indians' fear of Bryan's magic.

Ruru repeated the tale of magic to Scratch's slaves. Though they must have heard the tale several times at Blind Bay, they could now see the remains of Monk's *whare*, the very place where the magic had occurred. The burns on our headsman's face were proof to them that we had been in the *whare* when it was afire, and they had just seen the women and children appear out of the trees and bushes unharmed. It was surely an unequaled piece of magic to save so many people from a certain death. In their minds Bryan was the greatest of wizards, all powerful and not one to be the least crossed. It was the best security we could have.

Scratch's *kukies* wandered over parts of the burned station, cutting trees and gathering what could be salvaged. They could see it had been a swift raid with all the *whares* fired and one woman missing. If Bryan came near them as they worked, they became uneasy and watched him with wide eyes.

When asked to cut trees near the ruins of Monk's house, they looked with awe and suspicion at the charred poles still standing on the hillside and refused. *Ruru* explained to Monk, "Dey no go. Dey cuta tree here, bringa *raupo* here, but no go upa dera. *Mataku, kino, kino.*"

"No matter," the headsman said. "It's surely to our good. I doubt they would discover anything, yet it's best they stay clear. They will keep more respect if they don't get near it."

A few canoes arrived from *Anakoha* and Point Jackson. The people there had learned of the miraculous return of the station's people and now they felt it was safe to travel about. Relatives came to be assured *Ruru* and *Aihe* were still alive. A grand *tangi* followed with all the tears, cutting of skin, blood, and endless wailing. Others wished to see the whalers and their families who had been saved by the wizard and were walking about hale and not the least harmed except for Monk, who had the seared face.

Scabs on his nose and forehead were hard, dark, and ready to peel off; even some hair was sprouting where it had been singed from his head and eyebrows.

Three trips with both whaleboats were required to ferry up all the tubs of whale line, hoops, and the staves taken from the *Achilles*. The casks were sorely needed. With no place to store the oil only the bone could be saved, and thus the work and danger of talking a whale would only give small return.

Ruru heard the story of Bryan's powerful magic had spread over to Queen

Charlotte Sound. There was endless talk, he reported, about the wondrous event when any of the New Zealanders met.

"One *tohunga* say we go up wita smoke," *Ruru* explained. "Go ovah dera. By an' by alla man, woman coma here."

Several canoes of New Zealanders came to the station two weeks later. From the moment they landed, the children were on the lookout for Bryan. They scattered at his approach and peeked at him from around the corner of a *whare* or from the cover of a bush.

"You see that, Tom Skins?" Knobby asked me one day.

"See what?"

"Those Indians, the ones visiting here … they're most wary when he's about. No one ever touches a thing of his or crosses in front of him; and some won't even look at him and for sure not into his eyes. They think he can make a man drop dead. *Kotuku* and her two boys, they're magic too. They will do anything for them; give them anything they ask for."

Bryan spent some days with *Wehe* and *Tokee* raising casks from the staves, knowing they would be undisturbed at the sheers while they fed fuel to the cresset, heated the staves, and hammered hoops home. Bry had a cooper's eye and trued a stave with a single pass over the joiner, and sealed a poorly cut head with a bit of flag inserted around its edge.

Tokee discovered the station's bell lying halfway to the shore of the cove, where the blast of the powder keg had thrown it. He tied it to a tree limb where its clapper could send out its message of a whale sighting, a visitor, or a danger.

With a few weeks left of the season, Monk had hopes of taking more whales and kept one of the women or one of the boys posted at the lookout while we finished our *whares*. We had the framework of the headsman's house raised and were working on the thatch one morning, but our work was halted by the ding-ding, ding-ding, ding-ding of the bell echoing around the cove. *Wehe* out at the point had raised the blue pennant and was sprinting toward the boats.

We scrambled off the roof of the *whare* and rushed down to the boat ways. The old excitement of the chase was on us, and we launched our boat and pulled for the Strait. We quickly outdistanced the second boat, which had only the two boys to propel it. The whale, a small one, was taken in few hours and we had it towed to the sheers by dark.

After the tryout Monk announced, "With that one and what oil we took back from Olyphant and stored at Blind Bay, I tally twenty-three tuns of black oil, two tuns of sperm oil, and one of spermaceti. That's plus the bone. Now we must look to sell it soon before all the ships leave."

One of the boys was at the lookout each day searching from north around to the east with the glass for whales or any ship that might look in to wood and water and might buy our oil and bone. In a week they spied only two sails, but they were miles away, heading south through the Strait, nowhere near our cove. Monk grew anxious and at last summoned us to the try works one morning. He paced back and forth for a minute and finally said, "Lads, I believe the ships have been warned off us. Damn that Davis. I'd swear he's told some lies to keep the ships from calling here. We must sell our oil and bone for more goods. Most of all, we must have more casks."

Monk was also thinking of the men's need for liquor. We had tobacco enough, but our rum had been lost in the fire and the two kegs had been traded to the *Achilles* to befuddle her crew. Olyphant's supply of brandy taken from the *Achilles* would be gone in another week or two and Monk, given the opportunity, must surely buy or trade for more. That was understood between him and the men. No whaler ashore could be expected to work without his daily pipes and his rum.

The headsman declared, "If they won't come to us, then damn it, we will go to them. *Ruru*, I want you to go to Cloudy Bay. There must be a ship or two there that needs to fill. Will anyone go with him?"

I instantly stepped forward, thinking I might learn news of *Heke* along the way.

"Ah, Tom Skins. Good lad. You and *Ruru* take a boat and start now. It's near the end of the season, and we must find a ship before they are all gone. I can't spare another man to go. I must keep the others here if Davis comes back."

All nodded, agreeing that only we two must go to Cloudy Bay.

Ruru and I eased one of the boats down its ways, hoisted the mast, and hitched the shrouds. We worked at our oars until we caught a moderate breeze from the northwest. It took most of the day to sail past the ends of the slim points of land thrusting into the Strait, and the light faded before we reached the last cape. Under a partial moon it showed only as a featureless mass with its slopes reduced to unvarying black. We doubled it, made the turn toward Cloudy Bay; and then it was a mere run to the south and southwest. With a middling wind blowing I yielded the steer oar to *Ruru* and lay along the length of a thwart to sleep.

At first light I awakened and saw we were skirting high hills three to four miles to starboard. Their folded slopes met the sea, forming little coves and inlets. To the southwest, a low-lying coast, the shore of Cloudy Bay was a good ten miles farther on.

In the afternoon the wind weakened; and the sky became overcast, giving a gray, listless look to the Bay. *Ruru* pointed ahead and then held up three fingers, indicating three sets of masts showing in the light mist. The vessels were anchored off the low ground and all less than a quarter mile from each other. The one nearest to us was a brig and next was a large schooner. The third vessel I guessed was about three hundred fifty tons or more, and davits and boats on her sides showed her to be a whaler.

"The smaller ones could only be colonials," I said. "We'll try the far one first. She could be English or a Yankee, being so large. She would need more to fill her. Aye, she'll be the best choice of the three, nearer what we need."

Four men were gathered at the starboard quarter of the whaler watching us approach. We pulled around far enough to read on her sternboard that she was the *Sagittarius* and her port was Salem. Ha, I was right. Yankee ships having to travel so far for oil were always much larger. The four crewmen moved ahead to the gangway as we rowed toward it. Two of the men aboard were armed with muskets. With the ships anchored near each other and with an alert guard, they were on the *qui vive* for some reason.

"Are you a full ship?" I called to them.

One of the men stepped closer to the rail and asked, "And who wishes to know?"

"Thomas Wightman," I called back.

"Where are you anchored?"

"Admiralty Bay, north of here."

The crewmen whispered a few words between them. The man who had asked the questions leaned over the rail, pointed to me and said, "You. You can come aboard but leave that Indian of yours there."

We rowed the boat in closer to the hull. Men in the patched and stained dress of whalers opened the gangway and lowered a ladder of trunnels. The one who had done all the talking was a little better dressed and offered a hand up. He wore no beard as the others did, but his chin, not lately shaven, bristled with brown whiskers. Taking a half step back and raising his head slightly, he looked me over. "What's your ship? Who's master?" he inquired.

"No ship. Six of us are whaling on our own account from shore."

"No ship then … well, well no ship," the man repeated in a low voice and then offered a hand. "I'm Mr. Daniels, third mate. Come below. You must speak to Captain Jones."

I followed the mate to the companionway, and as we went I had a quick look at the deck and the rigging overhead. The *Sagittarius* lowered four boats like *Achilles*, but was by far a better kept vessel.

Daniels knocked on the cabin door and preceded me when we were permitted in by the captain's sharp-spoken, "Enter."

The cabin interior was paneled in well-matched, varnished hardwood like the parlors of a few larger houses in Stonington. In many months of living in a fo'c'sle, hovels on shore, and *whares* I had forgotten such comfortable, civilized places existed. With my bare feet and in patched sailor's clothes, I was ill at ease. No tarpaulin like me ever lived in such a space even ashore.

The captain, in trousers and shirtsleeves, sat at his desk.

The third mate pointed to me and announced, "This here man is Thomas Wightman, Cap'n. Came out here in a whaleboat with an Indian. Says he's in no ship, but whales from shore."

The captain wore a neatly trimmed beard, yet I saw he was a younger man than the mate, perhaps only in his late twenties. He had an open, honest look as he leaned back and tapped his fingers on his desktop.

His eyes went from my head to my bare feet and back again, assessing me thoroughly.

The captain smiled lightly and asked, "Just how did you arrive here in these islands? Transported by the generosity of the King of England?"

"No, I came here sealing and was shipwrecked."

"You will call me captain and say sir to me!" the captain snapped and sat higher in his chair. The officer touched the fingers of his right hand to his chest twice and then snapped, "Captain Simeon Jones! Do you understand that?"

I was taken a little aback by the demand for the "sir." Since working at the station with Monkhouse, I had forgotten all officers' need of that respectful address. In my condition as a castaway and a seaman, I could not object to the requirement. Also, recalling that a buyer was needed for our oil, I responded with a respectful, "Yes, sir, Captain Jones. I was sealing on the barque *Dove* and I wish you to report the loss of it when you return. I alone survived from it."

"You alone? No one else? Not another man?"

"It's a long tale, sir. All due to our captain's fool ideas and a lee shore."

Captain Jones's body stiffened a little in his chair, and his look chilled when he heard the last sentence. I knew I should not have spoken it. Officers would not openly admit a fault in themselves or any brother officer. An accusation of a failure or error, if only implied, was a hint of a possible mutiny in their touchy minds. The least show of discontent, even a sullen look, might be punished in some way. Each little incident aboard was always well examined to see if any sign of a cabal might be found in it, and I knew those suspicions went to absurd lengths at times.

The captain shook his head and said, "I have heard naught of your *Dove*, but I will report your misfortune. We have been fourteen months out and expect to be about six to nine months more. I will report it to any ships I speak. So, now, you are looking for a berth for home?"

"No, sir, I cannot leave as yet. There is one I must find and take with me. We are oiling a ways this side of Admiralty Bay. We take right whales near some small islands there. Our headsman wants to sell our oil and bone."

"Ah, then, somewhere near the Strait?" Jones asked. "We heard from the Indians there was trouble there."

"Trouble? Yes, sir, that's true," I explained. "A whaler called and when two of their crew deserted to us, the captain caused some raiders to burn our *whares*. We're sure it happened so, for he came there the next day and took all our oil and bone aboard." Damn! I instantly regretted giving those details. That was another thing Jones might take amiss, a charge of theft by an officer; yet I had to speak of it to tell what truly happened.

Captain Jones showed no pique at that accusation, but pursed his lips and looked idly around the paneled cabin. Then he ventured the name, "Olyphant?"

"Aye sir," I said and confirmed his guess.

The captain tapped his fingers again on the desk. He glanced up at the third mate and their eyes met in a knowing look. "Ol-y-phant," Jones said again, slowly testing the name on the tongue.

"You have met him, sir?" I asked.

"Umph, no," the captain answered. Then he asked idly, "Oil and bone, you say?"

"Aye sir, twenty-three tun black, two tun sperm. All sweet oil. About one tun of spermaceti and one and a half ton of bone cleaned and dried. All the best."

"That would bring us to … three, four months closer to filling," Daniels suggested.

"Ah yes, but what does he want for it?" Captain Jones asked and looked to me for a reply.

"Mr. Monkhouse heads our station and will take 21 pounds a tun for black oil, 50 pounds for sperm, and 60 for the spermaceti. He'll take 62 pounds a ton for the bone, Captain."

"Ha! Does he now? Black oil is down to 28 pounds in London at last report. Even if he carried it to Port Jackson, he could not sell it there. Anyone entering it in the home country would have to pay the tariff on it as colonial caught or foreign oil. Oil from New Zealand is considered foreign caught and the duty on a tun of sperm is over 24 pound. For black oil, it's over eight pounds. Bone is even more. Your Mr. Monkhouse knows he must find an English ship willing to buy it and so entered by them as English caught. That is if he can find one that will risk it. He dreams, he dreams. I might take it, but not at those prices. Perhaps we may come to some agreement as I will sell it in New York."

"Some of it is at our station but most is at Blind Bay, sir," I explained.

Jones ran the fingers of his right hand through his head of thick, dark hair and offered, "I will overhaul it. If it is good oil as you say, I will make an offer. You came here in your own boat?"

"Yes sir."

The captain turned to Daniels and ordered, "Hoist it aboard, and call Mr. Abbot to the quarterdeck. Well, Wightman, we will see your Mr. Monkhouse and test his oil."

I climbed down to the boat and with *Ruru* unshipped the mast. Then we scrambled up to help the crew hoist the boat and swing it inboard.

Mr. Abbot, a lanky and slow-speaking first mate, called out his orders and his crew had the topsails sheeted home, the yards mastheaded, and the bower hove in minutes.

Outwardly, by dress, the men looked to be the same sort as those of the *Achilles*, but their spirits were far better and they worked with a will.

By midday the barque was moving northeast four or five miles from the hills we had passed coming in.

I approached one of the crewman, a short, stout lad coiling away some of the running gear, and asked, "The officers appear to know Olyphant of the *Achilles*. Have you ever spoke her crew?"

The sailor scanned the sails and state of the running gear. He had heard my question, but first satisfied himself that all was stowed properly before he turned to give me his answer. "No, we haven't, but we met one of her deserters months ago at the Molyneux."

"Ah, a deserter. Did he have some tale to tell?"

"Not a long one, only that Olyphant is a hard citizen. Trouble follows the man."

"Aye, more likely he carries it about with him. I could swear to that."

The men off watch were curious about me, a man they thought daft or desperate enough to live ashore with the cannibals.

"D'ye sleep with one eye open?" one man asked.

"Not now," I replied, "but I had a frightful scare when they first captured me and again when those from the other side of the Strait raided us."

Another man overhearing us added, "Well we heard the stories about these Indians and keep a sharp watch when we're anchored here. I'd not trust any of them any time."

Danny, the steward, a boy about thirteen, kept staring at me and at last asked, "Have you ever seen them eat people?"

"No, lad, and I don't expect to. I mean to leave before long … perhaps after next season."

The wind was fitful, and the ship was worked farther into the Strait and up along the headlands. It was sunset of the next day when she passed the small islands and left them off her quarter. From them I took my bearings and spotted the pole at the lookout. "Just there," I said, pointing it out to Mr. Abbot, "our station is in there beyond that point."

At twilight the *Sagittarius's* bower plunged into the water of the cove; the crew ungripped our boat and lowered it over the side. Captain Jones joined us to be rowed ashore, and the instant the bow touched the beach the officer hopped from its forward decking to the beach. Our headsman came forward and offered his hand to the Captain. "Monk Monkhouse," he announced. "I heads this mob."

"Captain Simeon Jones of the *Sagittarius*," the officer replied, shaking his hand. "Your man Wightman has reported you have oil and bone to sell."

"Oh, aye, that we do. The best. Now, here are my other men. This is Peter Peck, Knobby John Shea here, and Bryan Reed with the *moko*."

"I would take him for an Indian," the Captain said.

"Most do. He is one now in some ways, being wrecked out here many years past. Well let's be at our ease, Captain."

Monk led Captain Jones up to Knobby's new *whare*. There, seated on whalebone sections, they began to dicker about the value of the oil and bone. The rest of us remained just outside the door in the spilling lamplight, waiting for any agreement on prices.

"He will get a good price," Peck assured us. "He has his own method of dealing for prices and we have the sweetest oil about the Strait."

Chapter Sixteen

At the end of half an hour Monk stepped out and announced, "I have agreed to 12 pound and 10 for the tun of black oil with an extra pound if it proves the sweetest, 40 pound for sperm, and 21 pound for bone. Each cask taken to be replaced with another or shakes and hoops to raise a new one."

No man took the time to cypher the total amount due him. "Eyow! Huzza! A good round deal!" they shouted, knowing it was a fine sale and a good profit to be made simply by the prices given.

Maree and *Karee* had brought two bottles of liquor and several cups in which to drink it. The deal was sealed with several toasts. Our headsman proposed one to the *Sagittarius,* one to the oil, and one to Captain Jones.

After tossing off the last one, Knobby held his cup up to be filled again and called out, "To Mrs. Jones."

The Captain had not referred to any wife. It was Knobby's not so sly way to get another drink since to veto the toast would show poor manners, wife or no wife. Monk smiled at the steersman and poured only a meager spoonful into his cup. He gave the rest of us a bit more.

Knobby swigged down that allotment for the toast and proposed yet another one, "To the *Sagittarius* again."

Monk, still smiling at the steersman, slowly dribbled a half dozen drops into his cup. Knobby aware it was the end of his foolery sipped the mite of liquor with a smack of his lips.

Captain Jones wasn't about to let anyone get to the windward of him in his dealings, and in the morning he ordered the bundles of bone opened and spread to be assured that it had all been properly scraped and dried. Monk had Bryan tap around the bung of each barrel with his hammer to loosen it and permit the captain to gauge the contents of the casks.

"Two and a half inches down," Jones noted.

"Aye, ready to be taken across the line," Monk said. "They'll not leak."

Jones next lowered his thief into the container and raised it up to the light.

"Ah, yes, a good light color," he said and sniffed it. "Sweet. I'll pay the extra pound for this lot."

We knew it to be fine oil. With only six men we could take but one fish at a time, and each had to be cut in and boiled with the Indians' help before we thought of chasing another. I suspected the oil taken from the *Achilles* and stored at Blind Bay might not be as fine.

After the *Sagittarius* finished loading at the cove, Monk and I went aboard to guide her around the cape to Scratch's village.

We landed and went through the usual greeting by the in-laws, but I left them as soon as I could get away and went to our stored oil. With the rush covering pulled off the casks, I quickly noted some of them were missing. "We're four short," I pointed out to Monk when he arrived. "I remember the count for sure. Where have they got to?"

The headsman walked to the casks and looked over their uncovered bilges. "Old Scratch," Monk murmured, "he has taken his share."

"His share? Four? Why?"

"It's understood, lad. We have to expect it. You can think of the cove as let to us and the oil and such other goods we give him as the rent. He will trade those four on his own account."

So it was part of the give and take. We needed the station on the cove; and Scratch collecting his "rent" supplied his people with gifts of goods and weed. Such generosity made good *mana* for him; and all benefited from the whales we took and boiled out at their cove.

I tapped the barrels and loosened the bungs, and found three containers had leaked even while covered with the wet *raupo*. About a quarter of one barrel had soaked into the sand.

"We can bear the loss," Monk declared when he measured what remained. "Not that much to grieve over."

Captain Jones again inspected the quality of the oil in each cask before he allowed it to be towed out and hoisted aboard the *Sagittarius*. The oil of the *Achilles*, as I suspected, proved a bit darker and less sweet.

It was all stowed in the *Sagittarius*, and the next day we headed north to double the Cape and return to our cove.

Settling the terms of payment was to be done on board. Jones offered, "I can give you about a third to a half in specie, and I can give goods to the value of the remainder. Let's go below and you may make your choice."

The captain led us to a storage room just off the main cabin. The mate held up a lantern, and by its light Jones unlocked the door and pointed to the items stacked there. "Tobacco in hands or twists, rum, knives, lanterns, what will you have?" Jones asked.

Monk looked it over and replied, "A cask of weed for sure, two of spirits, two dozen knives, four or five lanterns. Two hundred weight of wheat flour and deals or other sawn lumber you may have. My *whare* needs a new floor and I need to make a table, too."

"That is forward in the blubber room," Mr. Abbot said. We followed him, and there he indicated the wood stowed behind some bundles of shakes next to the ribs of the vessel. "I'll give you two-thirds of what's here," he offered. "I can spare it more than anything else."

Monk looked it over and made a quick calculation. "It'll do for my floor in any lengths you can give me," he said.

Mr. Abbot tallied the lumber and the amount of trade goods taken on a sheet of paper; and the captain, and Monkhouse stood on the deck to settle the deal. Captain Jones knew he had bought good oil and bone. Monk, pleased with the price given for it, haggled but little on the price of the goods. For the remainder of the value of the oil and bone, the captain agreed to pay in silver and gold coin.

Mr. Abbot and the captain came down and looked over a few casks standing in the forward part of the blubber room.

"What do you say, about another three months?" Jones asked his first mate.

"Yes, maybe just two months in the off-shore grounds will fill us. Then it's off for home."

It was possible the ship could be in New York in less in half a year. I craved to be aboard; yet I need not ask for a berth. Somewhere in the dark hills across the Strait, *Heke* might still be alive, and I could not think of leaving without an attempt to rescue her and the child she was to bear.

The next day the *Sagittarius* left and the cove was empty again. In two or three weeks the whales would desert the Strait and not return until the next May. Perhaps no other ship except one in need of wood or water, or a trader like *The Free Settler*, would call in the cove before the next season began.

I tallied what a man needed to become a trader in the country: a *whare*, of course, stocked with all the knives, kettles, cloth, fish hooks, muskets, powder, and tomahawks the New Zealanders prized. They could not resist tobacco, the fogus; the wonderful weed was the one item always in demand. Hogsheads of it were necessary for trade. The sale of grunters and spuds to whalers would yield specie and more goods. There could be a future in it except for the raiding. There was the woeful snag for the enemies of *Heke's* relations were my enemies. I was affixed to her people and must share in their fate whatever it might be. At the least it might be mere robbery or at worst to be chased and slain. I well knew there was always danger, and the raid just made on us might be repeated at any time. It might happen if I became a trader. No, a life in this land where war was made on a whim or a slight to some chief was too risky. It was not home. Home is where your people are. I had been away a long time; and if I find *Heke* I must take her and our child home. There was no question but she would go.

The Indians, so Bryan had told me, continually planned raids for booty and slaves. Others were made for *utu* to avenge an insult, real or imagined. It was in their nature to raid; or was it that they reveled in the excitement of contriving it and then in the battles themselves. Perhaps they found their lives were too dull when no such escapade was hinted in the future; and once they were caught up in one there was no thought of retreat for the *toa*, the fighting man. Perhaps to miss the fight, to miss flailing about with spear and club, was not tolerable. Recitals of past raids, of taking slaves and killing, enlivened their days. Long orations listing their victories impressed the crowd of listeners and swelled the speaker's reputation. Bryan called it all "bounce" in the Bayside jargon. Younger men, on hearing how much loot was seized, saw it as glory, the only glory acceptable. Far better to die fighting one's enemies in battle, to be a great warrior, to be legend, than live as a contemptible *kukie*.

Something akin to that could be said of men on the coast around The Mystick and New London. During the war a high fever for action and great profit seized them when preparing to run the blockade despite the risks of injury, capture, or death. At that time I had been only a year or two younger than some boys who helped man the cutters and schooners that carried cargoes by night and in thick weather. Those crews knew all the places where they might hide their vessels by day and what shoal water they could pass through at night along that indented coast. Each time they showed their heels to the Royal Navy or privateers, the men boasted of it at the inn, raising a thrill in their listeners. They chuckled when they told and retold stories of their close scrapes fleeing their pursuers as round shot ripped the air close overhead. If one punched a hole through their sails, it was a proud mark of their sauciness, their contempt of danger and the King.

Despite his wide grins and ready laughter, Monk must have a boding of the future. Our little group of houses in the cove, with its wealth of iron and desirable things, could be open to more raids if the secret of the cave got out. Visiting Indians reported plenty of muskets and powder being traded to the tribes far to the north where they were used with good effect. Those who could trade for the new weapons then held the power in their hands to settle old injuries from their neighbors. *Utu* was sought with interest. Payment was taken in weapons, slaves, and corpses. Even under the protection of Scratch or a more powerful sachem, it was an uncertain future for us at the cove. That was surely why Monk had revealed the location of the money to me.

On a day that commenced with dark clouds, a shower, and a promise of heavier rain, Monkhouse ordered the deals taken from the *Achilles* and those bartered from Captain Jones carried up to his *whare*. It was nearly completed, but its floor of saplings, even covered with fern fronds and mats, was lumpy and a trial to walk on.

The sawn lumber was laid out and we estimated there was enough to replace three quarters of the saplings. Knobby and Peck set up the long cooper's joiner to plane the deals for closer fits. The two men pulled up small portions of the floor, replaced it with deals, and pegged them down. It was my job to ram a boat spade along at a low angle to the floor, nipping off any pegs not driven flush.

The house interior was now nearly restored to what it had been before the fire. Monk pointed to the south side of the room and ordered, "Tomorrow, lads, we'll raise the bunks."

Two cats wandered along sniffing at the edges and corners of the room for any rat foolish enough to enter it. The small children, delighted by the wide, uncluttered space and the scent of the freshly cut wood, stomped through the rolls of shavings. They chased each other about squealing their loudest. How could it be otherwise with them; with such vitality bubbling in their hale, half-caste bodies?

I went to the window and watched the rainwater spilling from the thatch. Before it had fallen two feet the gusting wind dashed it away, at times against the walls of the *whare*. The downpour grayed away the entire cove and all of but the nearest portion of the shore.

Ardent calls of the children could not divert me from my uneasy thoughts; and the question always returned to me, "What had happened to my *Heke?*" The image of her face came to me as it did every morning when I awoke. In the past weeks I could have done nothing, not knowing where to look. I needed some rumor of her whereabouts. Bryan had assured me more than once it would come in time.

Ruru's naked little boy, filled with the simple delight of being alive, was pulling at my trouser leg. His face was dirty and snotty, but it bore a wide smile. I might have a child like him in the days ahead, but would I ever learn of him or ever see him?

Monkhouse came to the window beside me and looked out. "Sure to be wet all the rest of the day and tomorrow, lad," he said and then asked, "Thinking on her?"

I nodded.

"Don't give over hope yet, mate. We'll find her. They're fond of talking. That's part of the game, spouting about what they did. Oh, they can't keep still about how they robbed and burned us. Aye, and got their *utu*. Oh, they love that. When we hear of her, we'll think of some way to get her back. Trick them. That's the only way I see it can be done."

The next day Bryan and the boys cut and fitted together a table from the scraps left from the flooring. By driving little wedges into the ends of its through tenons, they made a heavy and rigid piece of furniture.

It was centered in the room and on it the headsman placed a bottle of liquor for each man. He emptied the leather sack of coins he had received from Captain Jones and spread them out. We poured drinks into our cups and watched the division begin. Monk first set a portion of the coins aside and explained, "This here, Tom Skins, is the shares for what we must buy from ships: lines, irons, slops, and such. Sometimes if we trade for them with our oil, they only take it at a discount, not the full value. They say the oil is not the best which is a thundering lie. We have the sweetest oil in the Strait. With gold or silver they can't argue their value down, and it's better for us. If you leave here you get your share of all trade goods of the station, and we will buy any trade goods accounted to you as your pay. Better than a mate's lay on a ship wouldn't you say?"

I nodded, knowing it was far better.

Monk then figured the amount due each man in coin and placed it in a stack before each one according to his share. Most were Spanish coins stamped with the likeness of their king and some were the Port Jackson dollars, the same ones with a dump punched out of their centers. There were dozens of shillings, some sovereigns, Rix Dollars, and Rupees in the stacks. "There, men," the headsman explained, "that's all we can settle up now. When we sell more we'll divide again."

I counted the various values of the coins and summed my share to twenty-one pounds English money. I pushed my coins toward Monk and said, "You must take from this or the goods accounted to me, the price of the ransom, the muskets, my slops, and all that was given to *Heke's* father."

The men around the table murmured objections to my offer.

"No need for that. You well-earned your share lad," Bryan said.

Knobby, sitting across from me, slapped his right hand on the table and barked out, "Aye. You're a dab hand in the boat and a damn good man boiling. It's worth those goods given to have you here."

Peck took a pull from his cup, swallowed it, and added, "Keep mine too."

I shook my head and replied, "I could never feel at ease if I didn't return what I owe you. It was my good fortune to be spared and find such mates here. Who knows what they would have done with me?"

Knobby leaned back and snickered, "Hee, hee, hee. Oh, you wouldn't have come to any grief with that titter by your side."

"Take what it cost you for my ransom, my slops, and all the goods for *Heke*," I insisted again.

Monk spread the coins in an arc on the table; and estimating the cost of the musket, powder, blankets, tobacco, and other goods, picked out what amounted to their value. "No," he said, "better I take it from your share paid to you in goods and put it in with what is held in common for the station. You can keep the coin. So."

I figured I still had to make twice that much in coin again or maybe more for passage money.

We picked up our coins to clear the table for the division of the tobacco. Knobby measured out half fathom lengths and cut two for each and then replaced the head of the barrel.

"More when you're low again. Now a new steamer each," the headsman announced, placing six clean, white clay pipes on the table.

He opened the bundles of clothing next, spread the contents out on the floor and said, "Each takes what best fits him."

The others picked through the jackets, trousers, and shirts and found some that matched their frames, but Monk's wives would have to add to the largest ones to fit them over his great bulk.

With no whales to pursue, no heavy labor to cut blubber, and no try pot to feed, the men walked about restless and bored while they tended to the simple chores of the station. In their idle minds they must have been anticipating their next big booze-up. The drams taken in the morning and afternoon were no substitute but more of a reminder of their last spree.

Monk's *whare* had been finished. The new floor was all laid and the bunks and table built. It was the end of the season, and without a word spoken between them, the men understood more of the liquor from the *Sagittarius* would be shared out. It was their due. Monk knew how much rum he might dole at a time that would satisfy his crew and not result in too much damage to bodies or *whare*. On the next rainy day when no work was ordered, we gathered around Monk's new table to throw dice and drink.

Knobby drank his share in an hour and a half; then his voice grew loud and his remarks sarcastic. He leaned toward one, then the other of the two sitting next to him and, with a damp, flushed face, cited his gripes as they came to mind. "I fasten to fish … do more than alla you," he complained. "Need 'nother half share." With a loud thump of his fist on the table he demanded, "I need bigger *whare* … not *raupo* … one … like this … timber … sawed lumber floor … no gaw-damned dirt. No *raupo*." When he could think of no other complaint, he jollied the headsman, "Eh, more rum? … eh. More rum? … jus' a 'nother cup? See jus' that much. See there."

Monk shook his head in refusal without even looking at Knobby.

Now that that try failed, the boatsteerer sat sulking, soured that he could not have more rum when he had the money to pay for it or if he didn't, to have it set against his share of goods.

"Gaw-damn. I'll up killick …'n leave," he swore as he staggered up from the game. "Aye … go where … I can … have aw … all … I … I … want. My money … unerstan' … my money. I'll sign … uhh … next shii … hip."

It was seen as a sham threat by the others and they ignored him. Knobby sat on a bunk, then stretched out full length and began snoring. When he awoke he never remembered how irked he had been when Monk refused him more liquor.

"Knobby and Peck will never sign on a whaler," Bryan assured me the next day. "They know they're far better off here. There's dangers and misadventures on whale ships and more work for far less pay. No, they'll never leave here 'less these Indians drive them off."

Monk, Peck, and Knobby John had fetched up on the shore of the cove by accidents and their restless natures, but they were held there by their love of independence. *Ruru* was drawn by the thrill of whaling and the opportunity to get the wonderful goods from the ships. Bryan, as a convict, could not go to back to New Holland, and he could never return to England and to what his life had been there. Here he possibly had come by a far better one; for certain he would never leave his *Kotuku*.

Bryan had been drinking less as the months went by. I expected it was *Kotuku's* cooing voice making the change in him, for she knew her man and knew the way to lessen his drinking the *waipiro* was not by endless carping but by persuasion. Now he drank only when we gathered up at Monk's.

With the season over we took the tackle from the sheers, stowed all the irons and line away, and covered the windlass and the try kettles with their tarpaulin covers to keep off the rain. Knobby and Peck began repainting both boats with the same colors as their original ones and re-leathering their wearing parts. As months would pass before the whales arrived again in the Strait, we did not rush the work.

Whaling required the senses to be continually alert while the dull work about the station, weeding the gardens and repairs to their fences, allowed time for fretted thoughts of *Heke* and to imagine a variety of fates for her. Bryan said to be a slave was barely tolerable in peacetime, and in wartime it was much worse. There was always work and heavy carrying to do. Some slaves gained favor if they had skills. Some rose in rank as Bryan did, but for most it was a miserable life forever doing the same digging and fetching for years. Escape was chancy. Groups of them were said to be living up in the mountains, hidden from any villages. It was particularly dangerous to be taken as a slave during a war for if not slain after the battle, one's life was ever in peril, forfeit to the whim of one's captor.

Ransoming *Heke* for powder and muskets might be possible, yet not an exchange to be made from a boat pulled inshore. New Zealanders so tempted would simply rush forward and take boat and muskets and make slaves of the crew. Ransom must be managed from a ship, heavily armed, with each of its canons and swivels loaded with a sack of musket balls. There was no ship of that power about. If one called here my small mite of coins were not near enough to hire it. Then again, *Heke* might have been traded or given to another tribe far to the north where wars were rumored and where she would surely be beyond recovery. What fancies. What wild fancies! I must lay them aside. She most likely was there eight or ten leagues across the Strait. I imagined her figure, large with child, far out in the fields or forest where she would be gathering wood, digging fern root, or carrying loads of flax for her captors.

I was helpless. Monk's idea to use trickery or stealth was the only way we might fetch her back. Yes, pluck her swiftly from them by some ruse. But how?

No trouble from across the Strait had been rumored in the passing weeks. The usual gossip brought no hint about any planned raid, and that was a mite of assurance. If the Indians remained peaceable, there was less chance *Heke* would suffer in some bad event, ill treatment, or such.

Ruru announced to us all that he, *Aihe*, and their children were to visit relations in *Anakoha*. Before the pair departed Monk cautioned them once more,

"Never speak of going through the cave. Tell all we fell asleep, then awoke in the woods. If you hear anything of *Heke*, send word to us."

Ruru nodded that he understood.

The headsman nodded in return and grunted, "So."

They were to return in five days; and I waited impatiently for them, hoping for some news. More than a week and a half went by, yet they didn't arrive. That was their nature. Time for them was much different, not to be divided precisely by a timepiece or calendar. It was marked by the arrivals of the seasons: the planting and harvesting of potatoes, when eels were to be caught in the streams, and when young birds could be taken from their nests. Then there was the time for hunting rats and the lean season to be got through.

I had to have patience. There was no other choice. Chatter and gossip were the only sources from which to learn of *Heke*. In time the Indians' habit to discuss every event as they moved from village to village should turn up some news.

At certain times *Ruru's* people packed up and took themselves off in their canoes to visit places back in the turning reaches or Queen Charlotte Sound or even to Blind Bay. So much the better, I reasoned; they might hear more from others farther away.

Three weeks after he had left, *Ruru* came around the point with three men in his canoe, but had no *Aihe* or child with him. All of us at the station were waiting on the shore when he waded out of the water and named each of the men, his relations, as they came forward. The face of one man, bearing a half-finished *moko*, was called *Te Ao* and he showed some likeness to *Ruru* with his wide-eyed look.

The women crowded about and questioned *Ruru* about *Aihe*.

"*Keeka coma*," he explained to them, pointing overhead and sweeping his hand across the sky. It was a good guess that in a month or little more *Aihe's* baby would arrive. *Ruru* confirmed that when he pointed over the hill and said, "*Aihe* wita ... *matua wahine* ... ovah dera." His wife would remain with her mother for that month.

In the evening the women prepared a large meal and brought it up to us in Monk's house. *Ruru's* relatives, well-filled with food, rolled up in their blankets along a wall and snored. Monk had kept his eye on *Ruru* throughout the evening and now that his companions were asleep he motioned to him to go out onto the porch. We filed through the doorway after him and gathered into a circle in the last of the twilight with the first stars appearing overhead.

We suspected *Ruru's* return with his relatives and without *Aihe* was a sign that he had learned some news of *Heke*. Monk had carefully held his questions until *Ruru's* relatives fell asleep. If they saw our interest in *Heke's* whereabouts at the station, they would chatter about it wherever they went. Monk was using much caution so any plan we made remained secret.

"*Porirua*," *Ruru* announced proudly, "*Porirua* here, *Heke* dera." He held his hands side by side with the thumbs up, meaning *Heke* was near or at the place called *Porirua*. He touched his finger to his right eye and added, "*Te Ao*. He rooki dera."

"He saw *Heke*?" I asked.

Ruru shook his head and answered, "No, no, he rooki *whare*. Alla *kainga*. Alla people dera."

Bryan began questioning him. After a few exchanges he translated *Ruru's* answers.

"His cousin *Te Ao* visits there," Bryan explained. "He's married to a woman from that country around *Porirua*. He's been there many times. I think I know which people are about that place. They have gone some ways along the Strait to fish or visit relations and have put up their little huts by a river. He is sure that *Heke* is with them."

Monk, apparently in deep thought, bowed his head and looked at the deck at his feet. "Ah ... are they now camped near the shore ... very near?" he asked.

Bryan put the question to *Ruru*; but not quite satisfied with his answer, spoke to him again. He thought for a moment, then explained, "I figure it's not rising fifty or sixty yards from the river bank. What he says makes it about that. You come in from the Strait and go up a river where there's *raupo* and flax. It's there on a low rise by the river."

"Will you and your cousin go to show us the way?" our headsman asked *Ruru* directly.

Ruru nodded, then said, "I aska *tohunga*. He tay aye, I go dera."

"He can't do that!" Monk snapped to Bryan. "The *tohunga* will be tattling it all around. Word will get out we intend to go there. Everyone will know what we're up to in two days." He turned to *Ruru* and warned, "Don't say a word to the *tohunga*. He knows no more than I do or anyone else about what to do. He guesses."

Bryan nodded and said, "They all put too much faith in them *tohungas*. Can't plant a potato without them singing a song over it. Same with everything they do. For years I did it myself. They'd ask if they should go hunt birds or take a trip in a canoe. I always thought beforehand how I could get clear of my advice if it went wrong. I always looked for something to blame first."

Monk faced *Ruru* and asked, "When we got out of my old *whare* when it burned, was that magic?"

Ruru shook his head.

"No, it wasn't magic," Monk continued, "but to all others it was. They didn't know of the cave. Magic is just what you want to believe and they thought it was so." Then, aware he was talking in English, the headsman turned to Bryan and said, "Repeat that to *Ruru* and make sure he understands he must not talk to any *tohunga*."

There was doubt in *Ruru's* wide eyes. He may have been recalling the prophecies he had heard over many years. Perhaps some of them might have been suspect and the *tohunga* might have strained logic to explain any outcome the reverse of his prediction. Yet it was difficult for *Ruru* to abandon the beliefs of a lifetime when he had never heard a thing spoken to the contrary. He had been told about *tohungas* and their power when he was a child, and from that first day he could only believe they could foretell events. Now we goblins claimed seeing the future was all a sham.

Monk added another point to the argument. "You see *tapu* do us harm or strike us? We don't believe it; therefore it can do us no hurt. So."

Ruru slowly nodded, seeing the logic; but it was obvious he wasn't wholly convinced. The power of the past was on him. It would take more than those few words to dispel his belief that *tohungas* could see the future. Their show of balancing sticks and pebbles and poking into the guts of a man or beast still held some sway in his mind.

"Not a word to the *tohunga* or anyone about our going across the Strait," Monk warned.

Bryan repeated the sentence to *Ruru*, and the man responded with a few words.

"He'll not talk to a *tohunga*," Bryan promised.

Ruru left us and re-entered the *whare*.

"They're a leaky lot," Knobby said. "I've seen them ready to bust open when they had some gossip they wanted to tell, but some of them can keep a secret … when they surely want to."

Peck spoke up, "Let's hope he can keep this to himself. That woman of mine is working her tongue the instant I get in the door. I just keep nodding and don't listen to a tenth of her blether."

Knobby, Peck, and Bryan headed back inside the *whare*.

Monk remained on the deck and leaned his head back to scan the constellations. "Summer," he said, "summer is upon us."

I knew what he was thinking and raised my eyes to the sky too. Winter winds had come up many times and forced us back from pursuing the whale. "Aye, better weather coming and it will be needed to cross," I said.

"Even more to return," Monk added. "We must be able to come back the instant we have *Heke*. If the wind makes against us, we could be taken. They will have two dozen canoes out if they spy us, but with a good wind aft or on the quarter we can walk away from them for all their paddling."

"How can we find *Heke*? How can we get her away? I can't think how it's to be done … slip in quietly?"

Weak light from the lantern hanging inside the *whare* struck the uneven floor of the porch marking a distorted outline of the open door. Stars were the only other lights to be seen. The hills around the cove were black, lumpy margins against the lower sky.

Monk was a dusky figure leaning against the wall. "What will draw them out?" he asked. "What would send them running about in confusion a good way from their huts?"

I could think of nothing.

After having posed the question, he then answered it. "Enemies, Tom Skins, and enemies they crave to fight; but they run away like cowards. Ah. Then they give chase, expecting to knock them on the head."

"Are we to become an army? We can't multiply into hundreds."

"We will become as many as we wish," Monk boasted.

"We surely can't overpower them," I pointed out. "You and I and two or three others are to become an army? Sheer folly. I thought we were to trick them."

"We shall do both. Trick them and overcome their numbers. Our army will be out in the dark somewhere. Here, and then there, and again over yonder." The headsman swept one hand to the right and one to the left, indicating soldiers moving back and forth, and laughed, "Ha, ha, ha, a will-o-the-wisp. A phantom a regiment. You see, it will be where they think it is." He reached out and slapped my shoulder. "Hee, hee, hee, what do you think of that, lad?" he asked. "Hee, hee, hee, shall we make fools of them, my boy? Yes, fools. We will work a mischief with them, and you shall have your *wahine* back. You shall have her and your squeaker with you in your *whare*."

I was trying to imagine how we were to conjure ranks of men, even false ones. "How can we do that?" I asked.

"Ummp, well, it must be at night, on a very dark night. We will make musket fire aplenty. The men will come out to chase the raiders. Then the muskets retreat. They follow them into the underwood and trees. While they are gone, we find your *Heke* and carry her away. So."

For a several seconds I tried to imagine the scene; then objected, "Muskets? We have half a dozen. How can we reload them while running through the woods? That's a mad idea."

Chapter Seventeen

"It is not mad. We don't fire muskets. It's not muskets they hear," Monk explained. "Oh, we put a ball or two through the thatch of their *whare* first to get them roused out, then it's a dozen or two squibs set off with slow matches farther and farther away. We will have *Heke* and be gone before they learn they've been gulled. Perhaps we will also start a fire to confound them more." Monk was proud of his clever scheme and punched my shoulder again and asked, "Well, what do think of that, lad? Do we make an army out of a little powder and cord?"

"If it will work ... the squibs, I mean. Can we devise such a thing and make good, slow matches? Will they serve for musket fire?"

"I have done it. I know how to make them well. We have enough dust to make hundreds. But we won't need so many. We need to go across one night without a moon. *Te Ao* must be with us to lead us to their camp."

"How can we be sure *Ruru* and *Te Ao* will say nothing before we leave?"

"I'll promise those two they will have spreaders and weed aplenty; that is, if they say not a word to anyone and we return with *Heke*."

The next morning I eyed one of the boats taken from the *Achilles* in the raid. It was now named the Two Brothers. I imagined how I, Monk, and *Ruru* and his cousin would approach the eastern shore of the Strait. A whale boat sat low on the water, but its white sail might be seen as we neared the dangerous coast. If we had to flee with aid of the sail, it would be a mark for any pursuing canoes to follow even at night. But, if it were made very dark it would blend into the night and give little hint as to where we headed. It might be dyed as the Indians dyed the parts of their dress.

"Tom Skins, you're thinking right there," Monk said when I suggested it to him. "Aye, let *Ruru* take it to his relatives. They can make it a good dark color. In a few days it should be done. So."

I took the sail from the boat and gave it to *Ruru* to carry to *Anakoha*. "Ah, blacka," he said, agreeing with the idea. "Meka gooda, you see. Arra blacka." He loaded the sail into his canoe. "Seven, eighta day," he promised, holding up all his fingers but no thumbs, and set off with *Te Ao* around the headland.

Monk invited the crew of the station to have their next supper in the big *whare*. With the meal finished and the table cleared, we drew tobacco from our pockets and began mincing it. Monk spoke less than usual, and the women sensed from that and a slow casting of his looks about the room that it was time for them to leave. They gathered up their children and led them out the door.

Monk watched them and said, "Less mouths to tell tales. Now, if we are to rescue *Heke*, we must have nitre to make slow matches. The slow match is the key. We will make squibs and each one will have a slow match. Me and Tom Skins will place them out about that camp of the Indians over there and then return near the huts. When they explode one after the other, the Indians will chase off after them and so give us time to find *Heke*."

"We have our dust," Bryan suggested. "It can be leached from it. Soak it in water and it will make a crust as it dries. That will be the nitre."

"Then we will try it," Monk ordered. "Knobby, tomorrow you stir some of our powder with water. Now to make squibs we need paper to wrap them up tightly. We have the Bible, but lack some glue or gum."

Knobby then proposed, "Better to make them of wood. I've seen that done. Cut a piece of a small limb about the length of a finger. Bind it round with some marline, and drill a hole half way down the center of it. Powder held in it tight with clay should make a good report."

"You're thinking, lads, for sure you're thinking," Monk said. "I count two dozen are needed … maybe three dozen. There should be at least that number for some might misfire. Tom Skins, plait some flax for the slow match. Make it about the size of a heavy yarn. Two fathom of it will do unless it burns faster than what I expect."

All the parts were readied in less than a week: the plait soaked in nitre and dried, the powder, and the drilled pieces of wood. Monk fitted them together for the first squib, and we went to the sheers to see a test of it on the head of a cask. He puffed on the glowing end of a lighted piece of the match and touched it to the short tail of the squib. The glow caught and smoldered for half a minute.

BANG! Two fragments of shattered wood flew up over our heads, and a puff of white smoke drifted away in the breeze. It had made a sharp report, surely one good as a musket.

Peck cried out, "Well, you've done it."

"Not near finished yet," Monk replied. "There's two dozen or more to make and each must be wrapped in a piece of tarpaulin to keep it dry. There might be dew on the ground. Oh, yes, much work to be done, lads."

Ruru and *Te Ao* returned with the sail, still wet from its treatment. It looked peculiar when hoisted on the mast and billowing in the wind. After drying it remained mostly a dull black with some blotchy, lighter patches.

Whatever the danger, I must go. I wanted *Heke* safe back in my *whare* and was determined to rescue her by any way. Was it a fair thing, though, to ask these men to risk injury and capture to recover *Heke*? Monk had offered his help knowing that his conspiring with Scutch and Gubby was a blunder that most likely caused the raid and *Heke's* loss. He must feel guilt for that, and he also must know that if *Heke* were not recovered he might soon lose a crewman. *Ruru* had declared he was for the game without a second thought. Perhaps he looked upon it as something to ease the dull days now that chasing the whale was finished; yet, if he were taken on that other shore he might become a slave or be killed.

The one moonless night was nearing when the four of us planned to cross the Strait. On that one night we must sail over to the other side, hoping *Te Ao* could guide us to where *Heke* was held. The false attack must be arranged and the squibs set out after seeing the place for the first time. Perhaps we might find the rescue could not be done, or we might be discovered and driven off. It depended on how stealthily we moved about and how much luck was ours.

All men were at the boat ways the morning we were to leave. The boat was ready. The boys had smeared its hull with a mix of fat and charcoal. Four paddles were loaded in addition to the oars. The all-important squibs were wrapped in pieces of tarpaulin and placed in a bucket with a flint and steel and a length of slow match. Monk had stowed two muskets and a box of cartridges in the bow and covered them with our jackets.

"One musket," Monk said, "we will fire through the top of one hut to convince them there is a real enemy attacking. *Te Ao* has laid out what we must do. We will take the boat near *Koamaroo* to a place he knows of 'til near sunset. Then we cross and make for the other side as it becomes dark."

"It will be better if I go too," Knobby offered. "One more musket will make it surer."

"And I'll add another," Peck declared and raised his hand.

"It's not to be a battle," Monk pointed out. "It's craft we must use now and with fewer men it will be easier and the risk less. You two and Bry are to keep a constant watch here 'til we return. If we're discovered and they give chase, we will lead them somewhere else; but they may come here. Have all your muskets loaded and your cartridges made."

We set off. Monk guided the boat past the points of land along the Strait and in the late afternoon reached the cove *Te Ao* had selected. Monk and I put on kilts and blackened our exposed skin as we had done in Blind Bay.

The twilight dimmed. "Time to go," Monk announced and poled the boat away from the shore. Facing aft, I watched the brighter stars appear and noted the ones which would be near to setting on the western horizon before the first light of morning. They would be our guide back to the west, but they could not be wholly depended on. Clouds might cover them. With no compass we might be lost, rowing about blindly until daylight, only to find ourselves within sight of our enemies.

It was near midnight when we reached the other side of the Strait. *Te Ao* turned about to study the dark outline and pointed a little north of east. In another hour sailing we heard the muttering of low breakers ahead.

"Where to now?" Monk asked.

Te Ao waved a hand farther to the larboard. The headsman swung the boat in that direction, and ordered, "Dowse the sail and mast." We lowered and stowed them, and resumed pulling the oars until off a rocky headland. *Ruru* whispered to his cousin. *Te Ao* gave a one word reply and motioned to Monk to head farther north. Dark masses of hills blocked most of the stars just along the eastern horizon. We skirted the point and then turned toward shore.

"Paddles," Monk whispered and slipped the handle of the steering oar into its loop.

We laid our oars along the gunwales and turned about to use our paddles.

We moved between two patches of surf. On the larboard was a black mass of a hill and on the other side low land. Monk's stronger pull steered the boat closer to the starboard side. In a quarter of an hour we could make out dark patches of something along the shore. *Te Ao* spoke one word to *Ruru* and pointed ahead to a light. A small fire flickered there, faded out, and flickered again.

The banks on each side encroached on the stream increasing its current and slowing our headway. *Te Ao* stopped paddling and pointed toward the starboard bank. Long, dark shapes just visible in the starlight appeared to be canoes drawn ashore. Just above them the fire we had seen was now only a small red glow. *Te Ao* waved a hand back downstream. The Two Brothers turned about in the current and headed toward a dark patch at the shore. *Te Ao* pulled for it. We could see there were flags growing thickly along the shore and guessed he meant to hide the boat in them. The bow slipped in. We got out and forced the boat into the flags. *Te Ao* peeked from the cover of the growth to the right and left and listened. Satisfied it was safe, he went out several paces farther and searched again. He came back, muttered to *Ruru*, and pointed up the slope.

Ruru turned to us and whispered, "Upa dera."

The fire flared up into a brighter light and then faded again to little more than a glow.

Our bare feet sank into the soft mud and sucked out as we followed Monk several yards upstream along the shore. We neared the shapes we had seen from the Two Brothers and found they were canoes. Monk began pushing one of them into the stream. All of us helped shove it and all the others off the bank; and as each one became fully afloat, Monk gave it a final push that sent it into the current and gliding off into the darkness. We could not be pursued unless there were other canoes drawn ashore farther up.

"*Ruru, Te Ao*," Monk whispered, "you go wait by the boat and be ready to set off when Tom and I come back." He gripped my arm and leaned close. "Get the squibs," he said, "and light your match."

I followed *Ruru* and his cousin to the boat. At the stern and I felt around for the bucket with the squibs, flint, and steel. I placed the tinder and the slow match on one of the thwarts and struck the flint across the steel twice. The light, glancing strikes seemed loud; yet the few weak sparks did not lodge in the charred cloth. A dog howled once. To strike harder would make a noise the dog might hear and start him in a fit of barking. It would surely waken the Indians. But the squibs had to be laid and lighted. I waited with the steel and flint in my hands, debating whether to strike them again. There was a slosh of legs moving in the water. Monk's large, black shape neared.

"What's amiss, Tom?" he whispered.

"The noise. It's plaguey loud. It'll surely wake their dogs."

"Oh, no, not that little click. They're far away. Strike again harder. Do it now. We must have the match lit."

I whipped the flint twice more down across the steel. There were good sparks but they died out as I blew on them.

"It's dampness," Monk said and rummaged around in the bow of the boat. He bent over the thwart for a moment.

"There, try it again."

I struck another spark. Instantly there was a flash of white light that blinded me for a second. Monk had broken a cartridge open and dropped a pinch of powder on the tinder. My sight gradually returned and I could see a red glow. Monk had the match lighted and the tinder snuffed out.

The dog began howling again. Monk and I waded to the edge of the flags and peeked through them up to the glow of the fire. Two voices were exchanging muffled words. A minute later flames blazed up and revealed a man tossing wood onto the fire and looking all about. In the wavering light, several low bush shelters were visible. The ground between them and the flags was clear of any bush, and in the firelight not even a cat could approach unnoticed. In several minutes the man turned and dropped to his hands and knees to enter one of the little huts.

"So, not their nature to be much disturbed by a few yelps," Monk breathed. "We will set our squibs on the far side of the huts. We want to place them in the underwood where they can't see well and will take plenty care moving about. That will draw them away from the stream. Once we have stirred them up, let them come out and search about over there while we find *Heke*." Monk went to the boat and returned with one of the muskets and the bucket. "Now, let's be on our way," he whispered. "Here, you bring all the charges and the match."

He walked east along the bank for several minutes, and then turned south. We kept a good distance from the huts to avoid rousing the dog. The ground sloped up gradually as if we were starting up a hill in that direction. We passed through patches of small trees and bushes.

Monk then stopped and said, "The first one here."

I touched the slow match to the first squib and another small, red light glowed in the dark. Monk placed the charge on a limb. On our return we set squibs fifteen paces to twenty paces apart on rocks, logs, or in the crotch of low limbs. The first reports would draw the men away from the shore, then north.

I lighted the last one and tapped Monk's shoulder.

"That all?" he asked.

"Yes, every one gone."

"Good, we must hurry," he said, and started back, slipping through the bushes, always keeping a good distance from the cleared ground and huts.

Monk halted and touched my shoulder. I stopped. He knelt on the earth and whispered, "Here Tom, down here."

He was only a dark figure next to a bush.

"Give me your match," he said.

I handed the cord to him and watched the red glow moving near the ground. Monk rose to his feet.

"What was that?" I asked.

"I propped the musket there in that bush and laid the match across the pan. It will fire over their little nests there. If they find it, it will be a sure sign their enemy is close about. Hurry now, the match has only a short way to burn."

We returned to the flags near our boat. The fire by the bush shelters was now only a few coals again. Monk whispered into my ear, "Ready, Tom Skins?"

"Yes."

"Then we will lie here and wait. When they come out, you watch for *Heke*. It will be mad, confusion all 'round. Bring her to the boat and we'll be away before they know she's gone."

It seemed a half hour had passed while we were watching the huts, but it was probably only eight or ten minutes. I thought there was a chance that the slow matches had gone out. If they had it would be a calamity after all our effort and risk.

The dog began his howling again. Then another joined him.

Several men with clubs in their hands crawled out of the huts and stood up, searching the darkness. Two of them were building up the fire. Its flames were rising. We might be seen lying at the edge of the flags, and they would rush down to smash our skulls.

BANG! Just then the musket fired, jetting its flame toward the shelters. The blast brought howls from the men and screams from women inside the huts. They spilled out, searching in all directions. Three men charged in the direction of the musket report. A minute later, one of them returned waving the weapon. Moments later after he arrived our first squib exploded. Its sound echoed around the slope of the hill. More people crawled from the huts and once on their feet looked in that direction. Several dogs howled and scampered around the shelters and running figures. Two squibs farther away went off in quick succession, setting off a renewed round of screaming and yelling. Some of the men started off but halted, unable to make up their minds if it was a wise thing to do. Suddenly one of them rushed into the dark waving his club, and others heartened by his boldness followed him. The New Zealanders were in a panic by what they thought was musket fire from some enemy making a raid. Dogs were howling; mothers rushed around the huts shouting for children. Men scrabbling for weapons made it a total confusion.

A very pregnant woman was crawling from one of the huts. I jumped to my feet and rushed forward, hoping it was *Heke* and she would recognize me in the dim light though I was dressed in the flax kilt and smeared with charcoal. I was nearly up to her when another squib exploded. The woman turned toward the report echoing from the far side of the huts. I reached her and put my hand on her shoulder. She jerked about. It was *Heke*! She looked terrified and shrank from me.

"*Heke*," I whispered and seized her arm.

She stared wide-eyed at me, unable to answer.

"It's me, Tom Skins, Toma Kina!"

For several seconds she stood bewildered, unmoving. Then she smiled slightly and started with me down the slope. She was walking too slowly. I pulled on her arm to speed her waddle over the uneven ground. We were halfway to the patch of flags when a stout, gray-haired woman, shrieking wildly, charged down after us. She grabbed *Heke's* other arm and tugged her back a step. Monk ran up and seized the old woman by her nape with his big hand. She released *Heke's* arm, then stumbled and fell backward when Monk let her go. At that moment two more noise-makers went off in the distance, BANG! … BANG! Women dashing about the huts renewed their screaming at a higher pitch. We urged *Heke* toward our hidden boat. She tripped but I caught her before she fell. Back up the slope the old woman was on her feet again shouting, giving the alarm that their slave was escaping. Monk reached the flags. He turned, scooped *Heke* up, and carried her to the boat. We shoved off from the shore and hoisted ourselves in. A black shape came bulling through the flags toward the canoe. I raised an oar and thrust the blade toward it. There was a grunt. Someone began thrashing about in the water. I rammed again at the noise. The current caught the boat when it was out of the flags and moved us downstream.

Monk allowed the Two Brothers to drift for a half minute and then whispered, "Paddles."

We headed down the inlet, paddling gently to make the least noise. The Indians on the shore kept shouting, spurring the dogs to add more howls to the chaos. Our headsman slipped his paddle into the bottom of the boat and ordered, "Oars." He turned about on the aft thwart to ship the stroke oar.

In a few minutes we were near the inlet's opening where surf showed as a vague, white band on each side. We heard no canoe following.

"'Vast rowing," the headsman commanded. "We ship the mast."

Monk and *Te Ao* slid it from under the thwarts and passed the end to me and *Ruru* to fit it into the step and hitch the shrouds.

After it was up, *Te Ao* remained standing. He was silent for some seconds and then whispered, "*Waka.*"

"Whist," Monk breathed and stood motionless.

We sat still on our thwarts, listening for a sound from any direction. Only the dim lines of surf and a few stars above could be seen in the blackness.

The rescue had gone well so far. The woman who saw *Heke* being taken was the only flaw. Except for her we would have slipped away through the flags without notice. That tribe now knew their slave from across the Strait had not simply run off in the confusion but had been carried away.

The strike of a paddle against the side of a canoe came out of the darkness aft. Then it sounded again. Monk hissed, "Musket."

I stepped over the next thwart to the bow, slipped the weapon out of its wrap, and passed it back to the headsman. I heard the click of the cock. The shot rang out. White light flashed in the weapon's pan and flame shot from the muzzle. The partial images of Monk with musket at his hip and *Heke* sitting on a thwart persisted in my eyes for a second. Out in the blackness several voices spat out words like curses. We remained unmoving, listening for any noise that would reveal they were still pursuing us. The sound of their Babel drifted away astern. The Indians facing an unknown number of enemies armed with muskets had given up the chase. Monk whispered, "Hoist the sail." He ran out the steering oar and ordered, "Down oars. Head all, but soft." The pull of the oars and some press of the sail moved the boat smoothly into the darkness.

I leaned forward for my next stroke and turned to glimpse the star that should be near the horizon in the west. It had already set or was hidden by a cloud. Monk was holding the boat beam to the wind, and making a guess of a course that would put us as far as possible from the east side of the Strait before the first light. It was strange sailing toward nothing and over nearly unseen waves. The smudged hull and the blackened sail were probably invisible at fifty yards distance.

At the graying of the sky Monk pointed to the horizon. "Point Jackson 'bout two, three mile away there," he said. "We've done pretty well, Tom Skins. It's about twenty mile to our cove."

"I'd say so."

The headsman looked at the sail going slack in the failing breeze. For now only our rowing would get us home.

Heke, sitting on the tub thwart, looked about the boat and at Monk and me with our blackened faces. She was bewildered, having been roused from sleep by musket fire and carried off in a boat in the middle of the night. Her hair was mussed and dirty. She appeared tired. The work demanded of her must have left her too fatigued to groom herself. She looked forward once more and smiled. I could not go to her at the moment and comfort her. It pained me that she had been so ill-used. Our rescue had been delayed. Yet, I could have done nothing before we learned where she had been taken.

"Apeak," Monk said. "Grub."

We peaked our oars. He reached under the aft decking and brought out the cask. There was the usual basket of smoked pork in it which he passed forward. "I'll lay there will be a want of wind for a while," he said. "We must make our own breeze with oars for some time before we fetch the cove; and we'll need our guts full to stay us for the day."

I stepped over the thwarts, took a seat beside *Heke*, and hugged her. Her fingers touched my face. There was little wonder that with my skin smeared with the mixture of grease and charcoal and in the New Zealand dress she did not know me at first look. She nudged her face against my chest and began to sob. I could do nothing more to comfort her than hold her in my tight embrace.

"There, Tom Skins," Monk said and pointed to the basket being passed around. I took it and offered some meat to *Heke*. She picked out one piece of pork. The headsman filled a cup with water for us to share. We chewed the flesh from the bones and pitched them into the sea. No word was spoken between us.

"Take *Heke* forward," Monk said. I helped her step over the thwarts to the harpooner's seat. Then remembering the jackets stuffed into the bows, I pulled one out, slipped it over *Heke's* shoulders, and gave her another long hug. She then looked around in the colorless light at the boat and the Cape.

I wanted to stay beside her but Monk ordered, "Down oars and head all, lads. We have to put more distance between us and them before it becomes much lighter."

Heke in the bow was facing my back as I rowed. When I first looked around she was very drowsy, and in the next few minutes she was asleep on the thwart with her knees drawn up to her large belly.

A few breezes came to aid us in the morning, but none lasted long and for most of the day our oars bit into the water and propelled the boat through the chop off the long capes that pointed into the Strait. In late afternoon we passed the offshore islands, only two miles distant from our cove.

A flag had been hoisted on the pole. The boys must have been up at the lookout from first light searching. They could now see us closing in. There came faint "Coo-ees" from shore.

We rounded the headland, and *Heke* hearing the distant calls of the women eased her bulk upright on the thwart. The wives and children were gathered at the boat ways. *Maree*, *Kotuku*, and *Karee*, each crying loudly, rushed into the water before the bow touched the shore. They lifted *Heke* out and carried her to the beach. All the sobs and wailing of the women lessened for a few seconds, just long enough for them to ask questions.

I leaped out and watched the knot of children and women move up the path to the *whares*.

Peck, Knobby, and Bryan crowded around us to learn the details of the rescue. "So it all went well?" Knobby asked.

"Aye, fooled the lot of them," our headsman replied. "They ran there and about and shouted. Bedlam it was. No trouble a'tall to get *Heke*. Now, Tom Skins and me want to wash this grease off us and get dressed. Knobby, you and Peck see to the boat. Haul it up and tomorrow clean all that muck from her sides."

At the stream Monk and I took turns scrubbing each other's back. A half hour later, in my *whare* dried and dressed, the whole world about seemed far better. *Heke's* fate had been a constant worry to me by day. When awake at night it was far worse. When we learned where she was, it appeared an impossible task to rescue her; but with luck and trickery we had done it.

A few minutes later the women, still crying and not having stopped for a minute, brought *Heke* to me. She had been bathed and her hair oiled and combed. The mite of soap, the comb, and one of *Kotuku's* loose calico dresses fitted over her large belly had made her look neat as ever. I slipped my arms around her and we remained in our embrace, standing beside the table in the center of the room. The women withdrew, each trailing a stream of words as she went.

At first I meant to ask how she had been used after being taken, but it might renew terrible thoughts. There was no reason for that now she was in our *whare* again. Her life on the other side of the Strait could be guessed. Hard work had been her lot. It was certain that she had gathered and carried many bundles of firewood while there. Many mats and other lumber must have been strapped to her back when the tribe moved from their village to their camp near the shore.

After a short lament those taken in raids usually accepted their fate. So Bryan had said. Many times she might have despaired that I could ever rescue her.

Heke looked up to me. Having been snatched from her captors and swiftly returned home again showed as a great relief in her look. Though tears ran from her eyes, she smiled, putting all that happened to her in the last months from her mind.

"*Keeka* coma. *Keeka* coma toon-ah," she purred.

I gave her an added squeeze and reached down with a hand to feel for the life quickening in her belly. Her breasts were larger and her time was nearing; the women were probably talking about it when they left. The birth of our child would be one good fortune; and it also reminded me that my wife and child had to be transported back home. It was a problem to be put aside for a while.

New Zealanders had watched whalers and traders bring all sorts of treasures from ships and knew that far across the sea there was an endless supply. Those valuables could be traded for, but it took many pigs, baskets of potatoes, and hundredweights of *muka* to get them. Yet in a few years at the cove, the wives of the whalers had gained a wealth of useful and desirable things. *Ruru* and *Aihe* had clothes from the ships to wear during the day and warm blankets to cover them at night. He had an ax, many fishhooks of all sizes; and she possessed a lantern, knives, spoons, pots, and a goashore. *Ruru* also kept a good supply of tobacco which he shared with his friends. His relatives, seeing what useful goods could be gained by chasing the whale, had asked to join the station.

Ruru loaded his family and *Te Ao* into his canoe and they returned to their inlet. He said they would stay a month, but a few days later he came around the point in his canoe with some other men. That was a surprise for we had expected they would stay a month and maybe with a week or two added. Monk, Peck, and I, working at the boat ways, went to the shore to greet *Ruru* and help draw his canoe up the beach.

Monk first asked him, "Your men come next season to fish?"

He shook his head and reported, "Dey no coma here."

Our headsman appeared baffled by their sudden change of mind. It was wholly unexpected that they now chose not to whale. He had looked forward to training the men for they could be fine watermen as *Ruru's* work in the boat had shown. He was not afraid of the thrashing flukes of a whale, even relished each chase, each battle. There was some new thing that caused him and the others to reconsider.

"They could earn nigh twenty-five or even thirty pound in goods in three months," the headsman pointed out to *Ruru*. "That's much tobacco, pipes, axes. And there's *parankitis*, calico for their wives. *Nui, nui*. Why won't they come next season?"

Ruru was tardy in answering as if he didn't wish to reveal the cause. At last he pointed across the Strait and muttered, "Dey coma backa."

"Them that raided us?" Monk asked.

Ruru nodded, pointed at his ear, and replied, "*Te Ao* heara."

Monk then beckoned for him to follow, and led us all up the path toward the *whares*. Knobby saw us coming up and joined in as we passed.

"What's the news?" Knobby asked.

Monk turned half about and grumbled one word. "Trouble." He continued past the gardens and the cookhouse to Bryan's *whare*.

Bryan and *Kotuku* sat on sections of whale backbone at the front of their house, where it was their old habit to rest at midday and enjoy any breeze offering.

Ruru began speaking to Bryan immediately and pointed out to the Strait. Bryan listened for a minute and asked him questions. He sat thinking a bit, then translated *Ruru's* message.

"*Te Ao* has heard from his people on the other side," he began. "The nob you took *Heke* from was made to look a big fool, being led off the wrong way by a few noisemakers. The others laugh at him now, call him a *wahine*. He's a tetchy sort. Well, damn, but they all are. He could take a good drubbin' in a fight, ah … but not gibes, never. There's no secret about who did it and he swears he's coming across to here and kill us all. Since you went to such trouble to get *Heke* back, he's thinking she has some sort of extra value. He's rounding up help now. It'll be a bigger *taua* this time if he gets all his help. More relatives, maybe even another tribe or two."

Monkhouse nodded and asked, "Could we hide in the cave again?"

"They won't leave so soon this time. He might choose to stay here about and Scratch might not be able to drive him away. Then he'd find us when we came out."

"Old Scratch will help us though? For our wives … his relations and all?"

Bryan nodded and replied, "Aye 'cept we're out here where it's hard to defend. Even if we had a *pah* to run to, they'd starve us out. Scratch will want to fight on his own ground back there by his village. That means we have to give up the station and carry everything back through the Gut."

"Then they'll burn all our *whares* again," Monk groaned. "Damn this plaguey country. Damn! Damn! I didn't think they would try to get *utu* for just one slave."

"It's not just her he's after," Bryan explained, "though he will crack her skull open for spite if he finds her. It's the tauntin' that hurts him most. He can't abide that. Even if we offered to pay for *Heke*, like a big ransom, he won't take it. He thinks a raid, burning our place again, killing, and taking more slaves is the only way he can get *utu* and his respect back. He must have respect, prove he still has *mana*."

Monk asked, "What do you think, Bry, should we leave now?"

Bryan pursed his lips for a moment and then released a sigh. He was weighing the situation, drawing from the years he had spent among the tribes on the other coast. He hummed a short note and replied, "He's telling everyone we're not *tapu* anymore and hoping they'll believe it. Sure to be bluffing some, making speeches and bragging what he'll do. He mayn't get enough people to follow him. I would say wait. It will take some time to get a number of them together and they're a superstitious lot. There will be a lot of foretelling the future and casting lots to see if it's the right time. A *tohunga* might see a sign and say we're still *tapu* here and it won't go well. Then they might decide not to try. I think we can wait 'til we hear some more. Send *Te Ao* some more tobacco and fishhooks and such. That will keep his ears in our service. Might be well to send a spreader to his wife."

A week after *Ruru*'s return, *Heke* eased out of our bunk only an hour after she had gotten into it. The movement awakened me. She wrapped one of the blankets around her and whispered, "*Keeka* coma. I go *Kotuku*." I held my arm around her as we walked up the path. At Bryan's, *Heke* called out, "*Kotuku*." In a few seconds the woman slid the door panel open, and there was a short exchange of words. *Kotuku* reached out and drew *Heke* into the *whare*. Bryan was inside striking his flint and steel. In a minute he had the lantern going. *Kotuku* turned and pushed me back a step and ordered, "She *tapu*. You go, Toma Kina."

I had no choice. *Tapu* was *tapu*. Better I not insist staying there, and though sleep wasn't my intent, I returned to my bunk and lay there thinking. Later the women, whose voices carried well in the quiet of the night, were singing and chanting the words for the birth.

It was the odd meeting of two nations of people. Each day the Indians could see that we, the other beings, didn't believe in charms and were not harmed by any *tapu*. Sometimes we took fish where it was *tapued* to fish and no harm came to us. Yet near the *kaingas* it was wise for the English and Yankees not to break the most serious ones or tread near the sacred ground of the dead. Nevertheless, we didn't give a fig for any of it. The *tohungas* were all humbugs, giving the most childish performances to impress the innocents. It had become a mixture of beliefs for these people. In some places they declared they would become *mihinare* and welcome the *mihinare* to live with them. How much of it did they understand? Months before *Kotuku* had asked to be married by that black coat in the name of the new *atua*. Now she was back to singing the old charms for the birth of a child.

I finally dozed off, but was awakened in the early morning by Bryan throwing back the tarpaulin at the door. There was a smile wrinkling his *moko*.

"You have a son now, Tom Skins," he announced. "Did you hear him? A banging strong fellow."

Though not fully awake I shook my head and mumbled, "No, fast asleep."

"Well, come up and see him."

I rolled out of the bunk still dressed in my shirt and trousers and walked with Bryan up the path.

At Bryan's call at the door, *Kotuku* brought the naked child out for us to view. *Maree* came out after her and pointed to the child's little roger and grinned proudly. Our boy had much dark hair and a little pink tab of tongue poked from between his lips, but his eyes were hidden under puffy lids. I touched my thumb to the boy's fingers and the tiny hand gripped it with good strength and held on. *Kotuku* hoisted the baby up a little and he mewed. Our squeaker, I had repeated to myself many times when I stroked *Heke's* growing belly. Now my boy was born, a certain fact which altered everything for me.

Had we not heard *Te Ao's* warnings of a suspected raid, *Heke* and I and our child might remain in the cove and feel safe for the next season or two. Now there was a threat hanging over us all. There was need to find a way to leave sooner, perhaps in the next few weeks.

I took one step to enter the door. *Maree* pushed me back.

"*Heke tapu*, Toma Kina," she objected.

Tapu, tapu, I repeated to myself. They will mumble their silly verses for a few days. Best I not interfere. It will do no harm to wait. *Heke* believed in *tapu* herself.

Giving respect for most of their beliefs was wise. The station was on their land; and if we displeased Scratch too often we could all be sent away, though that was unlikely to happen as two of the wives were his nieces and some were the sisters and daughters of others in his village.

The nobs also got their payment and liked nothing better than to sit wrapped in their warm blankets and light up their steamers. Their sole supply of tobacco came from the holds of the ships. The seeds also brought to them had been very welcome. Beans, peas, onions, and pumpkins were additions to the potatoes and turnips in their gardens. With vegetables which would keep, there was less of the grumbling time when other food was scarce.

Each vessel that dropped its bower into the bay carried axes, knives and chisels. Iron was the wondrous thing, the magical thing to them, hard as the hardest rock but unbreakable. Stone would not cut near as well as the poorest steel. The goblins had it in abundance and so were welcome and forgiven for many of their lapses and blunders.

Kotuku declared the *tapu* removed when she decided it was the proper day, and all the women gathered to escort *Heke* down the path to our *whare*. I heard their chattering approach, pulled the tarpaulin aside and stepped outside, meeting them under the overhang of the roof.

"*Titiro*," *Maree* said as she pointed to my child in *Heke's* arms.

"*Titiro*," I muttered as I took the baby from her. In my hardened hands he looked tender and vulnerable.

Maree pointed to the hills, to the cove, and the sky. "*Titiro*," she repeated and waved her arm to include everything. "All rooki dera, rooki dera."

"Rooki," I echoed, feeling like a parrot in repeating her words. What kind of a name was that? *Titiro?* Rooki?

Maree saw I was puzzled and pointed to her right eye with her right forefinger and to her left eye with her left finger. Ah. Look about. Yes. Of course. Look around. I was holding *Titiro* Wightman. Was that *Heke's* choice for our son, or had they all haggled over names and finally agreed on *Titiro?* It was as good a name as any I might have chosen, and it could be shortened to *Tiro* which was handier and I liked even better. I followed *Heke* into the *whare*. Inside she turned and seated herself on the bunk. I sat beside her and she leaned against my shoulder and smiled up at me.

"Hava keeka, Toma Kina," she purred. "You-a-happy?"

"Yes, *Heke*. Most happy we have our keeka."

I had to think more of the future, the near future. If raiders came again from across the Strait, what would we do? If it was a big *taua* Scratch and his warriors, even with our help, might not be able to fight them off; so there was no assured safety in a retreat to Blind Bay. Bryan had told stories of what happened when a *pah* or village was overrun, when the raiders' blood was hot and they bludgeoned their enemies as they ran. Few were spared. Quite believable as I had seen their eyes, wild and fierce, during the raid and heard their battle cries.

Could we escape from Blind Bay to the east and thence to Cloudy Bay? I imagined slipping through the bush with *Heke* and our little son to cross over the mountains to a trading brig on the far shore of the Island. Could we carry enough food? There was little to be gathered along the way. It would be a parlous trip, for any people we met might be enemies. They had to be avoided. Could we follow the tracks without fear of ambush, or might we have to force our way through underwood and trees? That wasn't what I wanted, to be always fleeing from one place to another. The raiders would expect us to go to Scratch's village since we were under his protection. Ahh, but what if we did not go in that direction but went by boat or canoe somewhere else? Not out in the Strait where we would be easily discovered.

From off the capes the many inlets could be seen twisting one way, then another, narrowing, and enlarging into bays far back between the mountainous islands. Trees and bushes on their steep slopes grew near the water's edge, and in a few places a canoe might be pulled in and hidden under overhanging limbs. If we went back into those winding reaches, we might conceal ourselves or even find a way to some safe haven. There could be more security in that direction, and it would be far easier to travel with *Heke* and *Tiro* by canoe. I must make an end of the danger and get them to New Holland or Van Dieman's or at least into a ship.

I was imagining the worst that could happen, yet there was no need to suppose the nob and his men could cross the Strait and fall upon our station unawares. It would not be like the attack set afoot by Olyphant in only a few days. Bryan was sure reports would precede the raiders. As yet, the first rumor of a raid had not been followed by another about the readying of canoes and the gathering of weapons. Each day a growing feel of security sank my worries a little more.

"It's the *mataku* that keeps them away," Bryan explained. "They are afraid of what magic can be worked on them. If all of us could disappear and reappear, well then we might send them to where a *taniwha* lives. He's the bad 'un. Does anybody in he can get his hands on."

Monk agreed with Bry and kept us at work gathering materials to erect a new *whare* in which to store our shook, lines, tools, and the bone we hoped to gather in the next season. For the women it was always weeding the gardens and washing clothes. For two weeks little changed around the station, and everything went on in a quiet routine until one night I was jolted from sleep by a hammering on the doorpost of my *whare*.

Chapter Eighteen

Peck outside shouted, "Wake up, Tom! Wake up! We hear they're coming!"

Heke and I were instantly awake. I swung my legs out of the bunk and stumbled in the dark to the doorway. I threw the tarpaulin aside, admitted Peck, and then turned to feel around on the table for my flint and striker. "Who's coming?" I asked.

"Them from across the Strait!" Peck snapped out. "That nob has got his people together, a lot of them. He's on his way here."

Two quick strikes and I puffed a spark into a flame. Peck held out the lantern and I lighted the wick with a sliver of wood. The glow increased about the room and revealed *Heke* sitting up in our bunk watching wide-eyed.

"Are you sure of that?" I demanded.

"*Te Ao* is here. He thinks the raiders will be here at first light and he's maybe three hours ahead of the first canoes. Monk says we're to pack up and leave now. We're to bring what we can in a few minutes. He wants to be gone in time to make it through the Gut with the tide."

"Damn short time," I groaned, and pulled on my trousers and slipped my knife into its sheath.

"We don't want to get caught. Remember how close it was when they came the first time."

"Where's Monk now?"

"He's bringing muskets, powder, and some of the grub to the shore. Knobby and *Ruru* have the boats near the cookhouse to load them."

Heke, wide-eyed with fear, was staring at us. She caught the import of our words though she didn't understand them all.

"Bring your blankets and Monk wants just the small tools and the boat spade," Peck said. "We can't take anything big." He picked up the lantern and held it while I gathered up the bag of tools.

"You take the spade," I said and started for the door.

"Coma back, Toma?" *Heke* asked anxiously.

"Yes, yes," I assured her and nodded toward the bunk. "Roll *parankiti,* mat. Be ready to leave."

Peck placed the lantern on the table and followed me out the door.

At the beach below the cookhouse, the women, all talking at once, were crowded about with their children and babies. *Wehe* and *Tokee* held lanterns for Monk while he slipped baskets and a spare sail under the thwarts of one boat. *Ruru* was stowing muskets into the bow of the second boat.

Peck and I arrived with our loads. "Put those in Bry's boat," our headsman called out.

I handed the tools to *Ruru* and went to Monk.

"Well, Tom Skins, they're on their way," he said. "Maybe twenty, thirty canoes full of 'em. Go get *Heke* and *Tiro.* Be sure to bring your musket here, too."

"Is *Ruru* going with you?"

Monk looked up, puzzled. "Aye," he replied, "why shouldn't he?"

"Then he won't need his canoe. I mean to try for Cloudy Bay."

The headsman stopped his loading and turned to warn me, "Oh, dangerous, lad. You must be quick about it. They came across at Point Jackson and the last time they were seen was this side of the next point. That's why *Ruru* is coming with us. All at his village have left already."

"Still, I want to go back that way. I think I can make it through."

"You're meaning to find a ship and sign on? Well, if you're of that mind I can't stop you, but there's much risk that way, lad."

"It's a risk everywhere."

"Aye, you're right about that; but it's a mite safer if we're all together. Well, Tom, you'd better have this." Monk waded to the stern of his boat and pawed around under the cuddy decking. He straightened up and handed me a heavy leather pouch and explained, "I settled up for each of us out of what was left of the specie and added some of mine. Your share's upwards of fifty pound. With what you've saved already it should get passage for you both. Go east to the Horn if you find a ship making for there. Too much fever going through the Indies, and those damned Dutch aren't to be trusted. Don't risk it that way."

"I'll go east if I can. We'll be on our way in minutes."

"Take some grub," the headsman offered, pointing to several baskets placed beside the bow of the boat.

I grabbed one, then went back to Bryan's boat and found the tool bag. I pulled a hatchet from it and held it up for Monk to see. The headsman nodded a yes, and I ran back toward my *whare*.

Heke was dressed, with her shawl cut from an old blanket on her shoulders, and sitting on the bunk waiting. She held *Tiro* in her arms. The blankets and the mats were rolled, tied, and ready to load. I dumped the food and hatchet onto the table. "Wait here," I said.

"*Toma Kina*," she called after me, but I had already ducked out the door and was on my way to the boat ways to get *Ruru's* canoe. In a few minutes I had it towed opposite the *whare* and was loading wads of *raupo* and our mats for padding. We might spend entire days and nights in the canoe. *Heke*, with *Tiro* in her arms, got into the bow. I put in blankets, the hatchet, and the basket of food.

My cache of coins, musket, and powder were hidden under our bunk. I went in and brought them out. The musket, easily wetted in our canoe, might become simply a long club. Even if kept dry, a single ball fired at a canoe full of raiders could not help much. I knew it would serve the others better.

The canoe held all that we needed, but I raised the lantern and looked from end to end to be sure. A bailer! There must be something to bail with, something better than my old tarpaulin hat. Ah! … the tin basin on the box at the end of the bunk would do. I rushed in, snatched it up, and was back out in seconds.

We were ready to go. Yet, I had to take the musket to Monk; and *Heke* must say her farewell to everyone, hopefully a quick one. Lights were moving back and forth on the beach below the cookhouse. I stepped into the canoe and swung the bow towards the lanterns and followed their slim reflections on the black water. All the women waded toward the canoe and started their wailing *tangi* as we neared. Damn, such a to-do, I thought, and stepped out to carry the musket to *Ruru*.

The men stopped their loading and gathered around me.

"Take care," Knobby John cautioned and gave my hand a hard grip.

Monk's big, rough face took on a sad look when he stepped forward. "If for some reason you don't get passage, Tom," he said softly, "listen to what they are saying about there in Cloudy Bay. This raid might fail if they see a bad sign or get to quarreling and turn back. We could start fishing again."

That wasn't likely, I thought. They were already too close. I nodded and turned to Peck waiting to speak to me.

"Well, Tom Skins, all good luck for you, *Heke,* and your son," he said and shook my hand. His left hand slapped my shoulder, putting more force into his words.

Bryan was asking *Ruru* questions, but stopped and said, "I was wrong about them over there, Tom Skins. I thought we had them gallied enough, but maybe someone talked and they learned of the cave. If that's happened we're not *tapu* anymore. Now to get to Cloudy Bay, *Ruru* says turn in at the first passage, then go southwest and keep the big island close to larboard for two or three hours paddling."

I nodded and said, "Yes, I know it. I was near its end once fishing."

"You pass three coves on its west side; and when you reach the other end go due south. You round a long, low point on your starboard and keep going. Stay in the middle and go in with the flood tide. On the ebb, go to one side and against it. You come to a reach that goes a distance east. Oh, a long way, he says. He can't say how many miles, but many, maybe three, four hours paddling. Then from there you must climb over a hill and you'll be in Queen Charlotte. That's the best I can do, lad."

"It's enough, Bry. I'll make it through somehow," I assured him. I climbed into the canoe and began backing it away from the shore. The women had quieted a little, but their cries burst out anew as the bow swung around by the sweep of my paddle. We could stay no longer.

I pulled the canoe to the mouth of the cove. From there the lanterns were only yellow specks in the distance.

Once around the point I paddled as fast as I was able to carry us away from the Strait and the expected raiders. A dark shore was to the starboard for three or four miles, and then it ended. The larger island appeared on the larboard, and we would pass along it to enter the reach leading to Queen Charlotte. I selected a star low in the sky to lead me to the last cove. That would be in two hours, about what remained of the night and the least time in which we might get there.

For an hour I kept an even pace and passed by two coves. An unexpected shape appeared, blocking the lower stars ahead. That had to be the point north of the third inlet. I had drifted east some and turned west to skirt it.

It was getting light. *Heke,* holding *Tiro* and wrapped in a blanket, showed as a motionless lump in the bow of the canoe.

It was time to go ashore. I paddled around the end of the point and into the third cove. No light yet penetrated to the back of that inlet and it remained a velvety darkness. On the left, the meeting of the nearer slope and sea was dimly detectable. Off to starboard, away from the bulk of the island, a faint light mirrored from the water of the cove. No canoes were on it. That was a good sign, and I continued along the shore, searching for a place in which to hide.

Light increased in the next half hour and revealed a narrow valley leading from the coast up into the hills. Its upper end was veiled in a morning mist back-lighted by the predawn glow. The stream from it made a turn just before it flowed into the cove. I paddled into it and found the canoe could be hidden behind the bushes on the bank. It would not be detectable to searchers unless they came close to the shore where they could see around the end of the bushes.

I stretched out in the hull and covered myself with the other blanket. Rest for my arms was most needed just then, and I should have an entire day of sleep to recruit my strength.

Doubts came to me now that I was no longer paddling and searching for pursuers. Was it the right choice to go through the maze of isles and inlets ahead? Was it possible to carry my family through to Cloudy Bay? My greatest wish at that moment was to have them aboard a ship sailing to Cape Horn. I would have even settled for Port Jackson.

The *raupo* and mat under me were passably comfortable and sleep finally came.

It was the growing light or the baby's mewling that awakened me. The sun was edging over the hills and the air was warming. *Heke* was putting *Tiro* to her breast to nurse him. I stepped from the canoe and waded far enough out to search the entire cove. Its surface was now a blue unruffled by any breeze, save for a little in the center and out between the heads. There were no canoes.

In the evening just before darkness, we had to slip out of the cove and take bearings on that next point. It was all I had to guide me.

If the islands were farther apart, I might take a sight on a peak and by it determine our course; but here in this tatter of mountains and sea, in this maze, we might go astray very shortly. Wooded slopes hid the higher mountains farther back that might have served as marks by which to navigate. One hillside ahead, covered with trees and ferns, looked much like one just passed. The next cove reached was nearly a twin of the last. My choice of a course through the winding waterways could mean escape or ... ach! I didn't wish to think more of it.

We fell asleep again, but were awakened by the beams of the mid-morning sun shining directly on our faces.

Breakfast was pieces of smoked fish, with a drink scooped in a hand from the stream. Once more I drifted off to recoup my lost sleep.

The sun was an hour or more past noon when I awoke. At the bow of the canoe *Heke* was still dozing. *Tiro*, comfortable on her warm bosom, made only little mewling sounds now and again.

I had to relieve myself and waded ashore to find a place to squat. It was wise to hide our turds carefully and to leave no sign of our passage. We were fleeing; and men, dozens of them, might be searching for us at that very moment. I pawed the dead leaves aside to make a small hole.

Something odd was lying in the soil like a straight root. Its surface was smooth and had been white once but now was stained tawny by the rotting litter. It wasn't a root for it came out of the earth freely. With a finger I wiped the dirt away from its ends and discovered it was a long bone, a leg bone far too large for a dog or even a good sized pig. For sure it was one from a man. I gently raked more leaves aside uncovering ribs and a curving line of backbone segments. A mass of disturbed ants seethed over them. Ten feet away the skull, severed from the body, was lying on its side, half-buried with the jaw open in a grotesque yawn. Its one visible eye socket was fixed on me in an empty stare. I scanned along the ground farther away and picked out the shapes of more bones with bits of dark, dried sinew still clinging to them. The white orb of another skull rested in the shadow at the base of a tree. It was smaller, that of a child. I went up, touched it lightly to roll it over, and discovered its thin bone had been smashed in at the back. Here were the remains of maybe a half dozen people. Some instance of *utu* had been taken in this small cove. Within the past three or four years these peoples had been alive. Perhaps the child had been cradled in its mother's arms at the very instant of its death. Somewhere about the Strait there must be many who knew of these killings.

All the tales of *utu* taken in two or three hundred years could be recited by some ancient Indian living within these twisting arms of the sea. Their memories were a wonder. A listing of their ancestors and the battles they had fought might take hours. With no books, no writing, memory was their only history.

I did not want my bones or those of *Heke* or *Tiro* added to them. If we were to reach safety, I must use all my wits and be chary of each move we made. For the remainder of the daylight hours we had to stay hidden.

I dug another hole to squat over and returned to the canoe.

There was a long pull ahead to reach Queen Charlotte, and I managed a good, restful sleep until late afternoon. When awake again I went out to search the inlet. A sudden spasm seized my chest. A canoe was coming in swiftly, skirting the shore from the northern point. It was already half way around to our hiding place. I went back to the canoe, nudged *Heke*, and jabbed a finger twice to the north. She instantly twigged there was danger and her eyes searched all about.

She cradled *Tiro* in her arms and followed me ashore. I took a route up along the edge of the stream. The bush on the banks became too thick and tangled to be pushed aside, and we were forced into the flow of water. We waded around the rocks in the stream for a hundred yards and then turned up into a patch of ferns on one slope. I motioned for her to sit and held a finger to my lips. If *Tiro* awoke the noise of the water pouring over the rocks would cover his little cries, and they could not be heard at the shore. She was fearful, but I knew I had to leave her and start back along the stream.

I returned and found a place behind a screen of branches and leaves from which I could see the entire bay. The canoe with six men paddling approached at a good pace. It followed the shoreline, keeping within thirty yards of it. If they discovered the canoe there behind the bushes, we would have no chance at all. We could not escape into the dense thicket covering the slopes or hop over the rocks of the stream. It would be slow travel. To flee up there with *Heke* and *Tiro* was impossible. The raiders, carrying only their weapons, could force a way through the tangle of bush and trees and leap over obstacles. I might fight off one of them for a minute with nothing more at hand than a tree limb and my sheath knife; against two or more

I could not last but seconds. Yet those warriors might hold back in their attack, allowing me some small advantages to keep the fight going, taunting me for their amusement. They drilled continually and were expert with their weapons. Perhaps after they killed me they would not look further up the valley and *Heke* might escape. No. No. That was a vain hope. They would search well, very well.

The men ceased paddling and allowed their canoe to drift to a halt. Each face bore a full *moko*. Though they were near a hundred yards from my cover, I stopped in mid-breath as if they might hear the sound of it. My heart thumped. An argument started between the two men in the aft of the hull. I could not distinguish their words let alone understand them; yet it was plain they disagreed. One pointed to the stream and argued with the other. The man in the aft of the canoe stood up for a better view of the rocks and bushes and, satisfied their quarry was not there, waved them on. Luckily they had not detected the canoe as they came around from the north. They began paddling again, but the man who had differed with the leader did not take his eyes off the shore. I breathed deeply again as the canoe diminished and finally disappeared around the south head of the cove.

There was no doubt they were searching for someone. They might not have been the raiders but men sent to tell us the attack had not occurred, or that the raiders had burned our *whares* again, considered it fit *utu*, and left. The odds were much against that. Their appearance and strong paddling were hints their intent was *utu*. Friend or enemy, it made no difference. I was done with whaling, never to pull the bow oar of a boat again. There could be no turning back. There must be no delay now that we were on our way home.

For a good hour I watched the cove for a return of the canoe and then returned up the stream. *Heke's* eyes were still filled with fright when she looked up from the ferns. "Toma, dey go?" she asked in a shaking whisper.

"Yes, for now," I replied, raising her to her feet to give her a kiss and a long embrace.

I took *Heke* and *Tiro* back to the canoe where they could sleep more. For the remainder of the day I watched for a return of the canoe. Those men, I suspected, might retrace their way and catch us unawares.

Clouds, thick and leaden, slowly closed over the entire sky, masking the last reds or pinks of the sunset. They allowed little twilight. It was time to leave, and we set off for the south head, keeping near the shore and edging slowly forward. I pointed a finger to my right eye and then to the water ahead. *Heke* understood. She could see a bit more beyond the south head with each pull of my paddle, and I could backwater quickly out of sight if she spotted danger. On rounding it fully, two passages came into view, one leading east and another west. No searchers' canoe or any vessel was on their darkening surfaces. Their canoe might have gone into one of those wide openings or south around the foreland I was to double. That black finger of land was there, two or three miles away. I pulled hard with my paddle and we turned around its end in a half hour. In the deepening darkness, no fire, no *whare* showed on its other side. There were no stars. It was murky all about with no clues, no indications of the passage farther south. We moved in a void, dark as a pocket. The only comparison was to be struck blind. It was bad enough, but then rain drops began to pat … pat … pat slowly on the painted canvas of my hat. Now a thorough wetting was a misery to be added to the loss of starlight. I cursed my foolish choice to continue after doubling that last headland. I should have pulled in to the shore and waited for the clouds to clear off. Impatience again!

I labored at the paddle only enough to keep warm. *Heke* had both blankets over her and denied that she was cold. I wished we had oilskins, but then, if wishes were horses …. Even if we had some I would instantly trade mine for any sign that would guide me in the proper direction.

Keep to the middle of the channel on the flood, Bryan had said. But damn! Where was the middle? Where were the shores? In the inkwell of night we might have turned about and were returning to the Strait or a current was carrying us one way or another. We might enter the wrong arm and would lose hours retracing the way. I ceased paddling, for there was no choice but to wait for light and hope we were not carried too far by the tide. It was to be an interminable night with naught to do but sit there miserably wet and listen for any swish of paddles or warriors' chant. I didn't even risk a whisper to *Heke*. The sound might carry over the water despite the hiss of the rain.

Chapter Nineteen

It ceased raining after several hours. A small glow in the east grew enough to give shape to the nearest shore, the long, low point we had doubled. I paddled slowly toward it. In the clearing air a small cove was visible where it joined the larger portion of the island, but it offered little concealment when revealed fully. I pulled onto its narrow beach and, being wet and exhausted, made no attempt to hide the canoe behind the few bushes and plants there. We wrung the water from the blankets and huddled together beneath them, hoping to keep *Tiro* warm with our shivering bodies and also to get some sleep.

A few hours later the clouds parted and allowed rays of the sun through in places. My first thought was, any pursuers in sight? I stood up and scanned the reach and the slopes of each side. No canoe was on the water; no *whare* or *pah* was to be seen on the shores in any direction. Our course was open to the south a full mile and a half wide.

There were two choices for us. We might risk travel in daylight or rest and start off in the evening, though the night might become the same dense darkness.

Heke stood up and swept the damp strings of hair from her face. She searched around for several minutes, and said, "Dey no cuma heera."

With her assurance, though I thought it a doubtful one, I decided to go on in daylight when the set of the tide could be seen. In following *Ruru's* directions, the back of the inlets had to be seen to discover that one long reach that led eastward. There were too many openings, one after the other, and at night darkness would conceal all that lay within them. We might enter one and travel miles before we found there was no passage through and all effort would be wasted. For sure our journey now had to be in daylight. I hoped an ever increasing distance might baffle any pursuers.

I bailed the rainwater out of the canoe. *Heke*, holding *Tiro*, got in; and I shoved us away from the narrow strip of sand. My entire body ached and my arms were stiff when I leaned forward and plunged my paddle into the water.

The appearance of the land and the reach about us was little different than that of Admiralty Bay, where hills and mountains covered with greenery rose up from the water's edge. There was almost no level ground, only scant bits of a beach. Forelands at each side of the channel masked the distant mountains, except for a crest or two hazed in blue. Each point we passed on our larboard did not reveal the passage *Ruru* had said led east for hours of paddling. Openings in that direction proved to be mere coves a mile or so deep.

A few raveled bits of clouds lingered about the higher peaks. After midday patches of bright sunlight and cloud shadows drifted across the steep, wrinkled slopes. Stray breezes riffled the water in the distance, darkening some swaths in sharp contrast with the bright reflections of untouched surfaces.

Our canoe, if seen from miles away, would show only as a speck edging along one side of the broad channel at ebb tide, but any of the sharp-eyed Indians could certainly spy it. After each half dozen strokes I looked back, knowing we might be followed.

We reached a headland that blocked the view further south, and I paddled cautiously around its end, gradually revealing the way. A wide inlet led far off to the west but ended in a small bay. More of the channel opened directly south for four or five miles.

By twilight we had made over ten miles; and I, very tired, selected a narrow beach and pulled in. The heat of the sun bearing down all day had dried the blankets, and that night we huddled beneath them comfortably.

Noises in the underwood aroused me a few times. I listened uneasily to them; but they stopped after a few seconds. They might have been the scurryings of birds or rats; so I declared them to be each time and dozed off again. Near daybreak when unable to sleep more, I looked all about. Our blankets were damp again, only this time lightly beaded with dew. The ridges of the hills all about were dark, irregular outlines against a paling sky. *Heke* was still asleep, breathing lightly and evenly. *Tiro's* head, resting against her breast, was partially covered by the edge of the blanket; and I gently pulled it aside to reveal his smooth face, untroubled, unaware of any peril. Hopefully we would carry him away from these islands that he might never know violence here.

I slipped from beneath the covers and walked to the water's edge to search the reach north and south. No canoe moved on its blue-gray surface. Rays of the sun struck the tops of the mountains; and the indirect light from them and the sky gave shapes to the trees on the opposite shore. Birds began their sweet twitters, lessening my fears.

Perhaps safety was at hand. From the station we had traveled along twenty miles of coast, ten on each side, where we might have hidden. All the coves and forelands would have made it ten times that distance to be searched. Our pursuers would have to look under the trees, around bushes and rock projections to be certain we had not taken refuge in some crevice. I doubted they had such patience.

Heke awakened and we ate a small meal. Now that we were far from the Strait, I felt secure enough to allow rest for my arms until midday. Then we started south, and in an hour reached a junction with an opening that led off to the east. It was the deepest one so far and looked as if it might be miles in length to its end, but I wasn't sure we had gone far enough south to change course. Was that the true way now offering to the east? Both it and the way south were open for a good distance, for two to three hours of travel at least. Should I turn there or continue south? I made the choice to turn into the east channel. It appeared wide enough. Each few minutes as I paddled, a bit more of it was revealed. There might be a connection with the Strait at the far end and the raiders could bring their canoes in with ease. With that danger in mind I slowed paddling and kept close the south shore, advancing cautiously around every little bulge to spot any canoe first. *Heke* pointed across to a rocky projection of the far shore. A *pah* had been built on it, using the water on three sides as its protecting moat. She took a long look and advised, "Dey gone. No *waka* dera, alla gone." It did look abandoned, even partially derelict; and I resumed paddling, but advanced cautiously as the shores to the right and left were revealed.

By late afternoon we had covered six or seven miles to the east, and I was convinced we were in the wanted inlet. The few beaches passed were short, slim borders to the reach. Overhanging limbs in other places inshore shadowed the water to a well-like darkness. We eased around one point and all thoughts of raiders instantly fled. We heard children's voices. My pulls with the paddle opened a snug little cove to our sight in the south shore. An inverted image of the hills, lighted by the low sun, reflected from the smooth, green-tinted water. Beneath the trees back from the shore were several of the low huts the people fashioned quickly when away from their villages. Smoke from a small fire filtered up through the trees and spread as a hazy layer along the face of the hills.

Chapter Twenty

Three canoes were drawn up, partially out of the water. A few people were moving around the fire, the first people we had seen since the men in the canoe passed by the first day. Women with noisy children could not be raiders, not part of a swift-moving *taua* bent on *utu*. *Heke* called out and brought them all hurrying to the shore to watch us land. Boys and girls darted back and forth chattering to each other. I swung the canoe toward the beach and our bow's vee ripple was pulled across the entire cove and into the transparent water near the shore.

"*Haere mai. Haere mai*," the words came across to us as I paddled closer. "*Haere mai. Haere mai*," they repeated many times while waving their arms and mats. There were about two dozen of them, children and men and women of all ages with only curiosity and openness in their manner. Several dogs ran back and forth at the edge of the water and, wishing to be part of the event, howled but idly without giving welcome or threat. The bow hadn't yet touched the shore when a boy and a girl standing in the water seized it and pulled it in. Immediately they began their questions.

Heke, carrying *Tiro*, waded up the beach and began a lively conversation with those who gathered around her. Each woman in turn insisted on having a peek at the baby. *Heke* then stepped back to me and announced, "*Mihinare* heera, Toma Kina. He cuma ovah dera." She pointed to the hill behind the encampment.

A half minute later a white man, probably in his mid-twenties, with brown hair that reached halfway to his shoulders came forward. He wasn't in the black dress I expected of a churchman, but wore dark blue trousers and lacked any form of hat or shoes. An Indian cloak was pulled over his shoulders, and he was without a shirt to cover his slight build.

"Ah, my good people," the man eagerly greeted us. "How do you do?"

There was something of the woman about him, long eyelashes, a narrow face, and a thin voice; yet he was male in his movements and had a month's worth of beard on his face.

He extended his hand and explained, "I must humbly apologize for my rude appearance. It's not meet for a man of the church to appear half dressed, but they have taken all my things from me. I am the Reverend Benjamin Hughes."

"And I am Thomas Wightman," I answered and shook his hand. "I belong to Connecticut in America." I motioned to *Heke* and added, "This is my wife, *Heke*, from Blind Bay and our son *Tiro*."

"I am so very glad to meet you and *Heke* and your little child. Of course my possessions were nothing, only cloth and paper; but people expect the black dress, the tabs, and such. It gives more authority to the words for some, Mr. Wightman."

"There's no handle to my name, Reverend," I noted. "I have been a mere sealer, a whaler, and a foremast hand, so I am only Thomas."

"Well, handles to names should be well-earned and not merely given, but it's a way of the world that may never change."

I looked around the snug little camp, back to the reverend and asked, "How did you come to be here?"

"Oh, sent here of course. I was landed over in Queen Charlotte from the *Hussar*, a trading schooner, Captain Fredericks. I fear I have not done so well in my efforts … to be a missionary here I mean."

"No need for despair yet. These people are taking your measure, for there are no fools amongst them. They want to know what manner of man you are. You pass muster and you may get most of your things returned, maybe all of them."

"And you have come here for …?" Hughes left his question unfinished for me to answer.

"Shipwrecked. I have been in this part of the world sealing or whaling since the first of 1819. On the way to China our ship struck on a lee shore, but I finally reached the coast of this island. Now there's trouble to the north and we wish to reach Cloudy Bay."

"Oh, quite a tale indeed, Mr. Wightman. You say there is trouble up there?"

"Yes, about Admiralty Bay. A whaler came in and stirred up a hornet's nest. Raids and such." I pointed up the hill and asked, "So, is Queen Charlotte Sound just over there?"

"Yes, it is. I was left there at Cannibal Cove to make my way to some place of my choosing to begin a mission. I have been traveling here and there for three weeks, nearly a month. I wish for a place where the people can gather with ease."

"You arrived from where?"

"I boarded the *Hussar* at Port Jackson. It called at Cloudy Bay first. We touched at a place there called *Bookatea* or *Pookatea*. That's where you need to go to find any ships. I was told many whalers anchor about there. Then they carried me to Queen Charlotte."

"Ah, now! Cloudy Bay. Were there any other vessels there?"

"None, and none called in while we were anchored, which was but four days."

"That's where we're bound. I hoped there would be a whaler or two full up or nearly so and ready to stand for home. We mean to go there tomorrow, and if there are no ships, we will wait."

"It will take you two, maybe three days to reach it."

"Three days you say?"

"That is my guess at the very least, perhaps more."

The sun had settled behind a high mountain to the west and the small huts were in shadow. To lessen the gloom under the thick trees, the women had built up the fire.

All the while we were talking; the men and women had crowded around listening to our speech though they lacked any understanding of it.

"Let's go to the fire," the Reverend suggested. "I feel a little chill." He led the way and the entire group followed. I turned back to the canoe to get the basin, the hatchet, the blankets, and the bag of coins. Coins, particularly the gold ones, were prized as pendants; but they would be more tempted to take the blankets and the hatchet. I had seen them eying those items in the hull. The hatchet was one thing I must keep close. It might be sorely needed.

Hughes had seated himself by the blazing wood.

I joined him and asked, "Do you remember any other ship there in Port Jackson that advertised for Cloudy Bay?"

"Shipping and whaling were never my province, Thomas. There were two or three preparing to sail, but I fear I took little notice of where they were bound.

"Would you consider staying here awhile? You know much more of the

New Zealanders than I do, and your wife would be of great help to teach me the language. I have lists of their words, but I find them of no use. I can't seem to make them understand. Very little of it seems to match their speech from the way it is set down."

"You say you have no knowledge of whaling, Reverend; and I have little of your business."

"My meaning was that you have been here for some time and understand them. I look at the work differently from some of my colleagues. They set too much value on appearances. Our purpose must not be set aside or delayed by small details as it sometimes is; and I am loath to say even by vanities. I think we should do better by uniting our efforts and be less concerned with the names of our various churches, if you know what I intend."

"I believe I do. If you can stop some of the raiding, so much to the good Reverend. It would be false of me to pretend I know their true minds. I can only say, always treat them as equals and you may win them over. Have much patience. Let them make up their own minds. That's the end of my short wisdom. Some of them are now my enemies and are hunting for me and my wife so I cannot spend more than the night here. Now, can we reach the Strait by going farther east from here in our canoe?"

"No, it ends in mountains. The only way out by water is the way you came in."

"Is there a good way over this hill?"

"Oh, yes," Hughes replied. "I came over it. These people travel it back and forth and have made it a good track."

"Good, and are they trusty and even-tempered over there?"

"They were well disposed to me, yet I cannot say they are always so."

"Is it possible to get our canoe over?"

The Reverend shook his head and said, "It would be a trial and take time with the small number of men who are here. You might chance to get another canoe on the far side. If you can, there is a shorter way, a passage to Cloudy Bay without going the whole length of Queen Charlotte and then doubling the point. None of this island to the north and west of here is laid down rightly on my map."

We ate our supper by the firelight. Once I finished my meal, I told my story to the Reverend.

"I was shipwrecked, and had to sail in a canoe to reach the far side of this island. On my way to Cook's Strait I was taken prisoner even before I had got half the distance there."

"Ah, yes, that was a misadventure for sure."

I poked at the fire with a stick and continued, "I was carried from the coast to Blind Bay. Aye, then I was given or traded to *Heke's* people." I smiled at her. She returned the smile and looked down at *Tiro* in her arms.

"Whalers came from Admiralty Bay to ransom me, and in all I fished and worked about ten months with them. The season was almost over when the trouble started and we were raided. They took *Heke* as a slave, but we rescued her. They were coming again for another raid so I thought it best we go to Cloudy Bay. That is all there is to tell."

Heke repeated the tale to the others crowded around her in the firelight and listening intently. They asked questions at each pause she made. They were disappointed that the story ended and pestered *Heke* for more details, probably about the raid and the ruse we used to fool her captors. It was a fine story for them to talk about for the rest of the night.

"Well, I'm for sleeping," I declared and searched about for a place to spread our mat and blankets.

I was roused at first light by *Heke* tending to the baby and the children running and calling back and forth.

At the fire I met Hughes and offered, "If we don't return in a two or three days the canoe is yours."

"I thank you. I shall use it to find a good situation here."

"Keep a close watch, Reverend. Who knows what will come to pass about here? Listen to these people and you will learn their speech in a short while."

"I wish you could stay longer," Hughes half-begged as he shook my hand. "I must admit it's quite lonely here without anyone to talk with."

"We would like to, but it's not possible. It was a risk for us to stay the night, and so we must be on our way. Goodbye, Reverend."

Several children ran ahead guiding *Heke* and me to the beginning of the track.

I turned for a last look at the cove and its little cluster of New Zealanders. Hughes among them was still waving his goodbye. Our brief visit had reminded him that he was to be a *mihinare* alone among these savages and charged to save their souls for the *atua* of the ship people. While considering the mission in some office in Britain, it had the look of adventure, honor; but now on the shore of that long channel the greater depth of the task was plain. I wondered if he still considered himself strong enough. There would be many nights in a crowded *whare* when he would miss the talk of a countryman.

How might the man judge himself once he had spent years in service among these people? Might he plume himself as a great savior? Men had ways to make even small offices into little kingdoms.

The path was soft mud in places. Higher up it became firmer, yet steeper, and it slowed us. *Heke* had *Tiro*, and I carried the food, bedding, and other items.

The hatchet in my hand was the most valuable item we had and the best one to bargain with. Some Indian over in Queen Charlotte I hoped might agree to carry us to Cloudy Bay for it.

Part way up the hill *Heke* and I halted and looked to the west along the reach we had entered and paddled through the day before. It had been the right choice, and continued more miles to the east. Without *Ruru's* directions we might not have found it. On the opposite shore the sunlight had edged halfway down the slopes. Three children were in our canoe paddling about on the dark water within the shadow of the hill.

The trail continued up in a twisting route to the top of the ridge. We paused to rest there for several minutes amid chest-high ferns. From the ridge the path went down the other side into the trees and by an unseen way to the shore of an inlet below. Its calm water, near two miles in length, reflected sky and broken clouds. At its farther end it merged into a broader expanse of deep blue water which could only be Queen Charlotte Sound. Beyond its south shore, still in morning shadows, and over the mountains was Cloudy Bay. The view was blocked and there was no guessing how far we were from our goal.

Smoke rose out of the trees on one side of the cove below and thinned to a haze. Indians were certainly there. The Reverend Hughes had said they were of good disposition, but was it possible that others had come from across the Strait in the last few days? We had to approach them with caution.

Once rested, we started off on the route down to the cove, dodging under or pushing aside branches and fronds. Our feet slid in the wet places; mud oozed between the toes. I turned now and again to see how *Heke* was managing with *Tiro*. Near the bottom I slowed our pace and motioned *Heke* to keep back a ways. I eased around each bend, watching for what was revealed at each next step. Then I halted to peer through the trees and ferns as far ahead as possible, hoping to discover any people before we were seen. At the shore the track parted and went to the right and left. We chose to continue on to the right. The smoke seen from the ridge above meant people were on that side. Hopefully, the ones there would prove as friendly as those with the Reverend Hughes.

Laughter and high pitched voices filtered through the trees. *Heke* came forward to listen, and after a few seconds she moved on a dozen yards, intent on the voices. She looked back at me and, smiling, said, "We rooki more."

We edged forward on the track. Beyond some ferns four naked children, three girls and a boy, were skipping stones across the water in a game of ducks and drakes. The children spied us, instantly left off their play, and waited quietly for us to approach. *Heke* spoke a few words, and they in turn asked her questions and pointed to the hatchet and basin I was holding.

Ahead through the trees I saw an old man, his thin frame bowed a little with age, approaching on the path. A fringe of white whiskers along the line of his jaw partially hid his *moko*. He greeted us with a smile and gentle eyes as he neared. *Heke* spoke first; then an exchange of words went on for a minute. All the while I watched the faces of the children and the old man, and now and again cast my eye on the track ahead and behind. The ancient turned to walk back along the path. *Heke* smiled at me and gave a lift of her chin, a gesture for us to follow the man. Suddenly the children shouted and dashed past us to take the lead along the path.

A few minutes later we approached a low slope cleared of trees and bushes. On it, a line of palings encircled a few houses and a *whata*. Several canoes, large and small, were drawn up on the gravelly shore twenty yards away. All the people left what they were doing and crowded around us. *Heke* was busy replying to questions from the right and left; but she managed to name me by touching my chest and pronouncing, "Toma Kina." They repeated the name two or three times trying for the sound. "Toma Kina," I heard from left and right. A short man, one with broad shoulders and the assured look and stride of a nob approached. The deference given him by others confirmed my notion that he was the chief of the place.

Heke spoke to him and pointed across the water to the far shore and to the hatchet in my hand. I displayed the hatchet to the nob blade up and brushed my thumb lightly across the well-honed edge. It held everyone's eyes, a tool worth far more than the best canoe there, perhaps all of them. There was no other object they desired more from the ships except a musket. The hatchet was the best thing we had to trade. Our blankets were needed for more nights on the way and even for use aboard a ship, as I would not buy blankets from a vessel at three or four times their value. Our coins, gold and silver, might be used for that, but I reserved them only for passage money.

The nob took the hatchet from my hand, walked to an old log, and struck it with a good swing. On his second stroke a good sized chip flew up. He looked the tool over well, examining the fine steel of its cutting edge and the wood of the handle, worn smooth and oily by much use at the station. *Heke* said a few words to him, perhaps to help the trade go forward. He gave her a short answer.

"He take-ah you, me dera," she said.

"To the other side there or on to Cloudy Bay?" I asked. "We must reach *Bookatea* as soon as we can."

Heke spoke again with the nob. "No, dera, dera," *Heke* replied, pointing to the far shore. "No more for axa."

"I am not a fool!" I spat out.

I could see the man dearly wanted the hatchet, yet he would carry us no farther than the other side of Queen Charlotte, just two or three hours of paddling. Ha! He must do much better than that, I thought, and took the tool from him. The other men crowded in and reached forward to run their fingers over the haft and steel head, a precious thing they all wished to own. Nothing could be more useful in shaping a canoe or building a *whare*, and far better than their stone tools to clear new ground for potato gardens. The nob, seeing that one of the others might offer to take us to Blind Bay and claim the hatchet, spoke a few words to *Heke*.

"He go," she said.

"Now? To Blind Bay?" I asked.

"Now-a, we go."

The nob turned around and ordered some of the men to push a large canoe into the water.

I led *Heke* to the canoe and ordered, "Get in."

I tossed the blankets, mats, and basin into the canoe. I wasn't giving the nob a half minute to change his mind.

Another man got in to help paddle.

We passed down the inlet with our three blades pulling and fetched the opposite shore of the Queen Charlotte by afternoon. The nob turned, went along it for miles, and entered a narrow passage. That evening was spent in a small village, and early the next morning we paddled out onto the Strait. The dark coast of *Eeka-na-mowee* was miles away to the east on other side. I recognized the scalloped shore close on our starboard as the one *Ruru* and I had passed weeks before in the Two Brothers and then in the *Sagittarius*.

Ahead was the broad sweep of Cloudy Bay. I turned and nodded to *Heke*. She looked forward and, seeing our goal in sight, gave me a wide smile.

No ships were anchored on its expanse and no sails were to be seen on the horizon. The season in the Strait was over; but I hoped some ship whaling out at sea might look in for potatoes or to wood and water.

The wind blew fresh in the afternoon, raising a swell. Now and then a bit of sea lipped over the gunwale. A two inch wave of water began chasing back and forth from one end of the hull to the other, wetting feet and the edges of the blankets. Traveling partly beam to the weather gave the narrow hull a rolling motion that threatened to overset it, but the nob and his rower kept going and never showed the least concern.

We arrived offshore and waited just outside the surf, riding high and low, watching the break of waves. Our canoe had been seen far offshore and a crowd was gathering on the beach. A few children, anxious for the canoe to touch the shore, waved their arms and ran into the surf up to their waists.

We timed the waves and at the right moment started in. On landing we had many hands help run the canoe up beyond the reach of the waves.

More people were coming through the dunes and gathering around *Heke* and me. They talked without pause while they escorted us from the beach toward a group of *whares* inland. More were joining from every direction; and as we neared the houses we led a noisy parade of men, women, children and dogs.

The chief of the village listened intently to *Heke* as she told the story of the raid and our escape through the long reaches and islands. At any pause he grunted a word or two, though his face showed no change.

Her tale seemed too long to describe what had happened to us, but I knew the reason was the people loved a good story. Heke was telling every detail, waving her arms, and maybe adding a little to make it more dramatic. They were disappointed when she ended it.

I urged her, "Ask if a ship has been here."

Heke relayed the question and answers came from several people at once.

"Dey cuma here, tena day bye, tena day bye," *Heke* said while holding her open hands out before her. She closed them to fists and spayed the fingers again.

That meant the last ship called there twenty days before. "A big ship, *nui, nui?*" I asked.

Heke pondered the question for a moment and then inquired about the size of the vessel.

"*Iti, iti,*" the chief replied, posing his hands a few inches apart to indicate its size.

It would be a good guess that it had been a small trader of forty or fifty ton, a colonial like the *Free Settler*; but what we needed was a three hundred and fifty to a four hundred ton ship, one of the larger English or American ships that was full up with oil and in fit condition to run east in the high latitude of the Horn.

We waited at the village, hoping such a vessel would call soon, and twice each day I climbed to the highest dune and scanned the horizon for any indication of a sail. In the opposite direction, north along the coast, there was a chance, though a small one, of a war party appearing there. At the end of a month, a brig came in from the east for wood and water. It was a whaler from the off-shore grounds with only two hundred barrels of oil aboard, and the captain expected to be out another six or eight months. Ten days later a large schooner looked in for potatoes and flax. It needed only two or three weeks to fill and return to Port Jackson. I considered taking passage on her with the thought of finding a ship for America in that port, but she was cramped both in the cabin and fo'c'sle, with little room for two more and a baby.

"How much for the fare to New Holland?" I asked the mate.

The gruff and unkempt man replied, "Eight pound."

It was not a reasonable price, but we were on the far side of the world and not in a position to chaffer over the amount.

I was about to accept when the fellow added, "That's eight pound each. Sixteen pound and the squeaker can go free."

"Even eight pounds is dear for the fourteen or fifteen hundred miles there. You will make it in two or three weeks."

"We have yet to fill, and then come back maybe three or four hundred mile to pick you up. It's sixteen pound, ipso facto."

That settled the matter right there. The mate, knowing the fix we were in, was trying to squeeze all he could from us.

Even if we took passage on the schooner, a proper vessel might not be found for some time after we arrived in Port Jackson; thus it was better to wait in Cloudy Bay for another month or two and not miss any opportunity to go east. Many vessels leaving Port Jackson called in China to get a return freight, adding months to their passage; and then they still had to make it through the Dutch Islands. The mate's demand for sixteen pounds and Monk's warning renewed my determination to go east.

Several weeks after the schooner left, the village again erupted in noise and bustle. The cause of the activity was a sail on the southeastern horizon. The vessel was making long boards, beating her way in. Near midday she was close enough to be recognized as a whaler, barque-rigged; yet only one set of her davits carried a boat. The others were oddly empty. Had all of her other boats been stove by whales? There was something familiar about the hull of that vessel. Before her bower was let go, I rushed to get a canoe out onto the Bay. Three lads, being as anxious as I was to board the visitor, helped me run it down to the water. We leaped into the hull and picked up our paddles. Several other canoes loaded with mats, vegetables, and baskets of dried fish pushed off a few minutes later. The barque was riding a little low in the water. Upon nearing I knew I had seen that hull before. It was the *Sagittarius!* Ha! So she had filled! She must be a full ship. That was why there was only one boat on her cranes and another stowed inboard, inverted, and held by its gripes. The others must have been sold to ships still fishing. The *Sagittarius* was certainly on her way home. Her course back to New York could only be by the Horn and with a swift passage, downwind all the way to that Cape.

The boys were surprised when I turned the canoe about and headed back to the beach. I leaped out as it nosed into the sand. *Heke*, holding *Tiro*, was standing with the crowd watching the crew climb about the ship's rigging.

"*Heke*," I called to her, "we go!" I ran to get our blankets and mats from the *whare* where we slept. In a few minutes *Heke*, the baby, and our bedding were in the canoe and we were paddling for the *Sagittarius*.

The captain had not allowed trading to begin, and there was a cluster of canoes at the side of the barque. Two of the crew stood at the closed gangway waiting for the command to open it.

We pulled alongside and I hailed them, "Ahoy there, *Sagittarius!*"

"Who's that?" one of the crew called down.

I waved my paddle and answered, "Wightman here, the shore whaler."

They opened the gangway and quickly lowered a ladder. *Heke* tied *Tiro* onto her back with her square of blanket and started up. I followed close behind to give them some security. At the top two crewmen reached for *Heke* and lifted her onto the deck.

Between main and foremast the deck was oddly clear. The try works was gone; the bricks most likely had been sold or pitched overboard and the kettles lowered below. That meant every cask in the hold was stowed full, bung up, and the barque was ready to quit the coast. Overhead some new lines had been rove in the rigging. Soot had been washed from the foremast and its yards, and some tarring had been started on the shrouds and stays.

Mr. Daniels approached and asked, "Well, Thomas, what cheer? You have more oil to sell?"

"Not a pint, I whale no more."

"Aha, made your fortune, have you?"

"No fortune," I replied. "Our station is probably no more at this moment and what oil we had gone. There were raiders coming again, perhaps an hour or two away when we left. It's all most likely taken away or burned long since."

Mr. Abbot stepped into the circle of men around me and asked, "The same attacked you again?"

"Aye, only more of them this time. There were twenty or thirty canoes coming from the other island. I must see Captain Jones now."

"Back to work, all of you," Mr. Abbot ordered and motioned for me to follow him aft. The men backed out of our way. Captain Jones was coming forward to meet us.

"Well, Wightman, what news?" he inquired.

"None to the good, sir. We were about to be raided again when we left. I need to reach Boston or New York. Are you leaving soon and going east?"

The Captain slowly nodded his head and explained, "Yes, but I cannot give you a berth. You see our empty davits. We're finished here. I have more than enough men aboard to work the ship. I cannot even pay a wage."

"I mean passage. I have all my pay and want to make an agreement as to the fare. Here is my wife and child and I wish to take them to America."

"Ah, a wife and child," Mr. Abbot said, grinning. "Been quite busy otherwise?"

Captain Jones smiled lightly at the mate's words and asked, "Well, well. Where will I put you? I cannot give you a cabin unless you make an arraignment with Mr. Daniels or Mr. Abbot, and they would be too crowded if they went together." He shook his head and added, "You might stay here a few weeks longer and find a ship that could give you better quarters than I. Three were cruising off the Banks and the *Molyneux* and will come north as we did. I spoke all three. Two of them meant to look in here on their way."

I shook my head and explained, "We want to leave now. I have been in this part of the world for three and a half years, one entire year as castaway and almost a year living with these cannibals. I lost my whole lay of the skins. Any money I made was only in these last months."

"You might go north to the Bay of Islands. Many ships call there," Jones suggested.

"No, it is time for me to return. I want no delay in getting to sea and on my way."

"Then it will have to be the steerage and you will have to share it with the idlers and the boatsteerers. It will be cramped. There are some casks in it, too."

"We can travel the steerage," I offered. "We will manage."

"I will have a bunk made over the cask heads and give you a little straw."

"That will be as good as what we have had these last weeks, perhaps better."

"Come below," the captain said and strode aft.

Heke and I followed him down the narrow steps into the cabin.

Heke's dress was now showing wear and had been torn in our traveling. She had nothing to change to since we left the station and must have something new, providing Jones had it. She would also need a jacket for the colder weather as we would be going by way of the Horn.

Captain Jones seated himself at his desk and looked at the beams overhead as he calculated the cost of the passage. "The only passengers I have carried were those who had interest in the *Sagittarius* and then for only a short distance," he said. "I will base the fare on the allowance of the Navy which is six dollars a month for the mess. To that I must add about five dollars. The owners will want that for the ship and I must account to them for it. Two of you would be twenty-two dollars a month and it foots to eighty-eight dollars for the voyage. I will leave it at that, though it may take a week or two longer to reach New York. Is that agreeable to you?"

The figures seemed very favorable for a voyage of four, maybe four and a half months. The schooner's mate had asked sixteen pounds to carry us to Port Jackson, a high fare indeed to carry two passengers fourteen or fifteen hundred miles. On some vessels, Bry had said it was rising that. The *Sagittarius* would be traveling thirteen or fourteen thousand miles. Jones, I believe, was favoring us on the fare. I nodded my assent to the Captain's terms. From inside my blouse, I drew the pouch and counted out the agreed sum in sovereigns and silver on the desk.

The officer turned each of the coins over in his hand and rejected one of the sovereigns. "Shaved," he declared and placed it back on the desk top. I offered one more, and he inspected it and nodded acceptance.

Captain Jones looked up, smiled, and announced, "Now that you are a pay-passenger, I can put a handle to your name and call you Mr. Wightman."

"No need for that. I've been without one for the whole of my life."

"So you have put aside fishing for the whale here."

"That decision was made for me. My wife and I had to find our way here while being chased by men who would kill us in a trice. They take offense quickly here and are a peevish lot if they feel insulted. I fear that has come about without our intending it."

The Captain picked up his dividers, placed them at the front edge of the desk, and said, "Well, I make it we will fetch New York about the first of July."

That was just what I wanted to hear from the captain. *Heke*, *Tiro*, and I were beyond the reach of the raiders; and soon the *Sagittarius* would be running east in high latitudes before the gales and half gales of the Southern Ocean.

Though Jones had been chafed about his title when we first met, I had a liking for the man. He had a pleasing address, and there was the look of fairness in his expression. No snarly suspicions of Olyphant would darken his looks, which were those of a younger man not hardened by the business. He must have started his trade sitting on a boat thwart and remembered the aches after long turns at an oar. As a captain he knew what discipline was needed and what service was due. Anything beyond those was seen as hazing and yielded only resentment and trouble.

The *Sagittarius's* crew, active and willing, contrasted with the dispirited men of the *Achilles*. Jones and Abbot to their credit kept their vessel in far better repair.

"One more item," I said to the Captain. "My wife *Heke* will need something warm to wear for the high latitudes."

"Yes, I still have some clothing. No frocks, you understand, though we did have a few at one time with the trade goods. Once we are under way tomorrow, bring her here and she can try on some ducks and shirts. Now, let's get you settled. Come above."

Jones preceded us up the steps. On deck, New Zealanders were bringing baskets of potatoes aboard and haggling with the cook over their quality and price. A pig, squealing and wiggling in a piece of netting, was being raised above the rail by a gun tackle with three men on the fall. One man held a line tied to the hook of the block and pulled the animal inboard. The remainder of the crew were hoisting water casks and stowing away bundles of firewood.

"Mr. Daniels," the Captain called out as he neared the second mate, "Mr.

Wightman and his family are to be our passengers. Show him what we have in the steerage and have Chips knock up something for quarters."

The steerage was cramped with the men already bunked there. The carpenter laid deals across the heads of some casks of biscuit. I used the straw given us and the mats and the two blankets we owned to make our bunk. The carpenter found an old sail which, weakened by rot, had ripped along its reef band. Part of it he nailed to the beams and carlings overhead, and it gave some privacy except that every word in the steerage, even whispered ones, could be overheard. *Heke* was used to crowding and was quite pleased with our cubby. She had always slept higgledy-piggledy in the *whares* with a dog or two, so such closeness would not bother her.

Young Danny, the steward, the cooper, Chips, and Fernando the Portuguese cook bunked there with Joshua, the African boatsteerer, and the third mate. With *Heke* and me eight were housed in that space. *Tiro* was the ninth but he needed little more room than his mother's arms. We could have all spread farther apart except for the casks stored there.

By evening the loading was finished and only a half dozen Indians remained aboard offering their mats and some carvings in trade with the crewmen.

Heke, holding *Tiro*, stood beside me in the waist of the *Sagittarius*. We both looked to the shore and the few points of light, fires outside the houses that brightened and waned. All else there was grading into deep shadow. The mountains were a line of black crests sharp against the evening sky. Far above them, long streaks of clouds were losing the pink blush of twilight. Nearly a year before I had discovered the fringe of snow on the mountains of *Tovy Poenamoo*; but that was on its other side, more than a hundred or so miles from where we were.

I put my arm around *Heke*. "Afraid?" I asked.

She looked up at me and answered, "Me no fraidy. *Tapu* to you alla time-a. Go wita you alla place. Alrighty, no fraidy." Then she nuzzled her head against my chest.

For sure, I always knew what her answer would be and needn't have asked. It did not matter to me how we were brought together, that she had been traded for goods. It seemed only a formality now, a reverse dowry gladly given. She, in turn, had offered herself and her loyalty. There had been no ceremony observed;

indeed, I would not have allowed Wooley to mouth his words and foot up another marriage to his credit. Aye, I had even avoided it, for she was my wife because I declared she was. In turn she would have said the same if she knew enough English words. I had no doubt that the night she entered my *whare* her first want was to lie with me and make a keeka. She was *tapued* to me, and a child would bind me to her.

What might become of the country beyond that shore? Would the New Zealanders leave off their feuding when they had the benefit of new plants and animals and there was no more grumbling time? The problem was more of pride and *utu* and it had little to do with food. There men raided for *utu* after any injury or insult, and they taught their sons to do the same. It was tradition, hundreds of years of it; and in that wild place Hughes would have to change that, dissuade them from raiding and their endless cravings for revenge. I wished the man well.

Wooley, always aware of his footing as a missionary in his home country, was prepared to keep it at any cost by preaching to the Indians, declaring their souls saved, and listing them in his book. He had little idea of how much those who claimed they were *mihinare* understood of scripture. It was that outward show he was pleased with, so many christenings, so many marriages to list and boast of to his superiors in each letter home.

The Indians saw something useful in becoming *mihinare*, though they didn't compass all of it. The idea of forgiving did not fit the least with *utu*. To exact payment for a wrong was far more satisfying and it firmly restored one's honor. The *arikis* might also object when they learned that the meanest slaves were their equals before the Christian *atua* and they could no longer keep them. Did they understand being *mihinare* meant more than not working Sunday? Would being *mihinare* be of small account to them, they declaring they were so one week, then not the next when it did not suit their wants? Wooley assumed their first words showed belief and never asked if they were aware of all that being a Christian meant.

All of us fishing from the cove had gained far more from our labor than we would have on a ship at sea. Though there were whales aplenty, it was too risky to follow the trade any longer while living ashore. Fishing for the whale would surely continue from the ships. The sale of the oil and bone that filled the hold of the

Sagittarius might double the money of her investors. Nothing short of an armada would stop the whalers from returning as long as ships carried great profits back to their owners. Such men will find any way honest or devious to seize the fortunes. They will send ships to fish the season in the Strait and when the whales depart, follow them and continue the chase in their offshore grounds.

Chapter Twenty-one

"Heave hearty, ho! Heave hearty, ho!" In the first glow of daylight, the crewmen timed their pulls on the bars of the windlass with those words. The clank of the pawl after each phrase marked a partial turn of the barrel and the links of the chain cable brought aboard. I climbed the steps to the deck and into the cool morning air to watch the sails being cast loose. I had gone up the shrouds endless times as a topman; but now I could watch it not obligated to clamber up the shrouds and slide my feet along the footrope. With the bower chained in place and the yards braced, the *Sagittarius* bore away on a broad reach. Her jib boom aimed spear-like at Cape Horn.

At midday the vessel was under a full press of sail, and the last, faint blue mountain sank below the horizon aft marking the end of terrifying, yet sometimes pleasurable adventures for me. I had arrived on the coast of *Tovy Poenamoo* almost dead from thirst. Now I was fleeing from the island in a far better condition with my wife and child.

Heke and I went into the cabin and selected trousers and shirts for her to wear. She also had to have a watch coat for we would reach latitudes even higher than the seal rookeries. It would soon grow cold. The price I paid for the slops was at least two and a half times what it would have been in New York, but we were in the Southern Ocean and the nearest emporium was near two thousand miles away in Port Jackson. *Heke* was pleased with her clothes, especially the red and white striped shirt that had caught her eye. She would have no other and paraded around in it and her duck trousers for my approval. From the back she resembled one of the crewmen.

After the last cask of oil had been lowered into the hold of the *Sagittarius*, the crew must have cheered and cast their stained trousers and ragged shirts overboard. They now wore cleaner ones bearing fewer patches. Day after day the barque made good progress on its southerly course. Crewmen feeling the colder wind added woolen shirts under their jackets and wore boots on their feet.

On the second day out Mr. Abbot had ordered the foretopsail sent down and a newer one of heavier material bent in its place. At the end of three days, several more were changed. Much of the rigging had already been repaired and tarred, and the mate opined to all that it should give no problems or give way.

The wind increased by the day, driving long swells eastward. It was comforting to feel each rise and fall of the hull taking us nearer home. The *Sagittarius* heeled, giving a better view of the sea rushing past at the speed of a race horse. Driven by the steady press on the sails, the bow tumbled white water aside; and the log line spun out, measuring an unbroken string of good runs. If the barque had been beating in the other direction with bowlines taut, the foredeck would have been continually awash and the wind a howl in the rigging.

In the cabin Captain Jones walked his dividers across the chart and marked the progress of the barque toward the fifty-sixth parallel and the seventy-first meridian.

Each night the men off watch crowded into the steerage where the entertainment was the retelling of old yarns. My offerings were the tales of the sealing voyage, the flight from the island in the canoe, my capture, and the raid on our station. Those had fascinated the crew as I first told them months before. Even when repeated they found them just as entertaining. New ones were the prizes. I added the rescue of *Heke* from *Eeka-na-mowee* and our final escape through the twisting channels and islands. Because it was new they asked for any details to make it longer. After that one ended I resorted to the suspect ones told on the sealing grounds. None of the men cared much about the truth of them as long as they were exciting.

Tiro was always on the minds of the men of the Sagittarius, and anytime *Heke* brought him on deck, they peeked at him and asked after his health. Those bunked in the steerage moved about quietly and spoke in whispers when they knew he was asleep. Once awake, he had the attention of one or two of the crewmen. They looked wistfully at *Tiro* as he smiled, babbled words, and gripped any finger presented to him.

Joshua had been spending much of his time in the steerage, sewing on a red wool shirt. No one paid much attention to his chore, as other men were busy repairing clothes for the expected cold of the high latitudes. They were puzzled when he finished his work and held up not a repaired shirt but an exact miniature of one.

He presented it to *Heke* and said, "For de baby, you put dat on him an' he look like a steersman, a headsman. Yessir, an' it keep him warm, too."

"Tanka you, Totua. O, Tanka you," *Heke* replied to Joshua. She slipped the little shirt on *Tiro* and found it was a fine fit. It surprised me that Joshua, never having taken a measurement, made a garment that came out so well-tailored to the child. He had a fine eye for distance and measurement that must have served him well when darting his irons at the whale.

Daylight spanned many hours, but its strength much of the time was diminished by clouds or a thin mist. At the higher latitudes we met stronger winds which drove a mizzling rain along the length of the vessel, keeping the lines, gear, and deck forever wet. It soon grew heavier. Water ran down the masts and shrouds and small streams drained from the clews of the sails to be whipped away into drops again. The constant press of wind on the heavy, wet sails kept them turgid and shivering at their leaches.

The men of the watch coming down from the deck hung their oilskins on hooks in the steerage; their dripping kept the deck there continually wet. Everything in the space remained damp; even the blankets never felt quite dry.

Since she had no need to go on deck, *Heke* stayed below. She did venture to the top of the steps whenever the rain stopped and some bit of sun broke through to brighten the view of swells sweeping eastward with the wind.

Mr. Abbot took his sightings when some breaks in the clouds permitted, but they were not near as often as he needed. He relied more on the log line to confirm the greater portion of our progress and added estimates of how much the current increased it.

Each night after the mate finished the log I read it to learn how much closer we were to home. Under the date, the officer always began, "Commences with" … and then noted the direction and strength of the wind. The final words at the end of each entry were always the same, "So ends this day." Those were followed by the coordinates of our last figured position.

Nights became colder; and at times a frigid air suddenly enveloped the

Sagittarius for half an hour or more. It was released just as quickly from that sudden chill and the temperature rose a few degrees.

"Ice?" I asked Mr. Abbot.

"Yes, ice islands there to the windward of us. I've felt them many a time. They chill the wind and it chills us. Captain Jones is expecting to overtake some, so we are to shorten sail at night and double the watch."

None of those dangers were spotted ahead, though the episodes of cold air were repeated.

A long, low coast, slightly darker than the gray sky above it, appeared on the northern horizon one morning. Captain Jones announced that it was an island near the Cape and instructed Mr. Abbott to keep a good offing. In a few hours that margin of land, with no more detail than a water stain on the edge of a book page, slipped away in our wake.

The *Sagittarius* was pressed by the wind and carried by the scend and fall of the sea many leagues past the Horn and the Falklands before the captain set a course north. A new feeling arose in the crew when the barque turned from the driving swells of that passage. They moved more quickly about the deck and their work. Every day put us farther from the wet and constant half gale and into drier weather. We looked forward to bathing, washing our clothes and drying them properly.

Mr. Abbot had taken the men off the repairs of the *Sagittarius* while she was running in the thick weather, but as the air warmed he started the work again. The mate sent two of the crew up to finish tarring the standing rigging and others to paint parts about the ship and the remaining two boats.

The crews of the *Achilles* and the *Sagittarius* were alike: a few marlinspike sailors, boys from farms, and men from other parts in the world. The difference was that, with a nearly identical crew, Jones had the better ordered ship. Anyone could see it was simply the methods of the captains. Under Jones the men knew the usages and obeyed them. They knew the punishment for breaking them and accepted it, knowing it would be justly applied. In the short time I was aboard the *Achilles*, I saw Olyphant had a way of treating everyone with contempt. What words he spoke always had a disagreeable tinge that turned his men sour and sullen. Perhaps he thought it should be so, the natural result of discipline aptly applied. Anything less would be a sign of weakness. The crew of the *Achilles* saw only continual hazing by the officers until the end of the voyage. There would be little profit if any when all was settled up. More men would have left the *Achilles* had they not feared the New Zealanders. Davis must have repeated the story of the *Boyd* and wild cannibal feasts to discourage them from slipping ashore.

Fair treatment alone would have surely changed their attitude. That was the key.

Mr. Abbot surprised the ship's company one evening at the dog watch when he announced the *Sagittarius* would call at Rio de Janeiro to exchange some of the black oil for coffee. That news sat very well with the crew, they having seen nothing but rolling sea and the faint tip of the continent since leaving Cloudy Bay. Now they had a visit to look forward to and it enlivened their talk.

"Ah, the senhoritas," one crewman crooned, closing his eyes and leaning his head back in his sweet memory of a previous visit. "Ah, the senhoritas there," he repeated, "they are all beautiful. All colors, some black as my boots, but all beautiful."

The next day some men appeared with their faces shaved, and a day after that more came on deck without their whiskers. I felt my own chin. It had not been shaved in three months. I would borrow a razor from one of the mates before we reached New York.

At noon three days after the mate's announcement, Danny's young eyes saw something on the horizon; and he climbed onto the windlass barrel for a better look. "Land ho!" he squeaked in his young voice. "Land ho, everyone!" he rejoiced, jumped to the deck, and ran aft to tell Captain Jones.

The call went through the vessel that the Kingdom of Brazil was sighted, and that news brought everyone to the rail to study an uneven lavender strip at the horizon.

It was a mite rainy, yet a glorious day with patterns of sunlight alternating with portending shadows beneath thunderheads drifting across the ocean. Clouds were sharp-edged masses of white, visibly swelling up into clean blue sky. It was an even a grander day for us when we saw the land rise higher from the sea and reveal slopes covered with rain-freshened greenery and slim palms standing behind the beaches. The barque moved north and turned toward the entrance.

"There," I said to *Heke*, and pointed to the great stone monolith, "that's the sure mark of the River of January."

She stared at the shoreline as the *Sagittarius* passed between the heads. Inside them the hillsides were almost covered with large buildings and white houses two and three stories high. Boats and ships were sailing across the harbor in all directions. *Heke* had heard that such wonders existed in Port Jackson, yet she may not have believed such tales. She probably had never seen more than two or three hundred people gathered in one place; but on that shore crowds of people were passing to and fro on the streets between the houses. That great world beyond the horizon from where the sealers and whalers came was there before her, the source of the warm blankets, lanterns, pots, knives, and calico which filled the holds of the ships. New Zealanders had their tales of islands lying far across the sea, but in their recollections they were little different than the ones on which they lived. This was a huge extent of land, far beyond her imagining. What had they thought when they were told that such things as continents existed and were filled with masses of strange people?

"*Kingi riva dera?*" *Heke* eagerly asked as she searched the shore and buildings from the rail.

"Not the English kingi," I replied. "He lives in England, in London. That's far away, thousands of miles away from this place. There are many kingis in Europe. Here they have a kingi from Portugal."

She suddenly pointed to the shore and stared wide-eyed.

A heavy cart, drawn by a pair of oxen, had come out of a side street and was moving along the shore. It was a double mystery for her, never having seen a wheeled device. With a man riding on it and the large, unknown animals pulling it, the sight was hardly to be believed. It might be an apparition to her, one not to be counted as real. A sow was the only large animal she had seen at our station.

I smiled and said, "You will see many carts and wagons; and you will see more animals like those: horses, mules, cows, and sheep. I will take you to a menagerie where they have a much greater one we call an elephant. It is many times the size of that beast there. Oh, *nui, nui, nui.*"

It was too much for *Heke* to puzzle out. She shook her head, baffled by all the strange things she could see ashore and my explanations.

There was nothing new or the least improvement since my visit there years earlier; the same blacks in their decrepit bumboats came alongside to hawk their fruit, birds, and monkeys in their sing-song touts.

The parrots offered were sheathed in brilliant feathers, but in shape they resembled the drabber birds familiar to *Heke*. The monkeys, however, astonished her. "Nota *kuri?*" she asked.

"No, no. Not a *kuri*. Not a dog," I chuckled. "They live in the trees. They climb up like this." I pulled myself up the shrouds a short way to show *Heke* how the animal clambered up trees and swung from limb to limb.

The oxen and the monkeys were the extraordinary animals of a new world she had just entered.

Heke was fascinated by the black women on the bumboats and the crews on the small vessels crossing near the *Sagittarius*. She had seen two Africans on the *Achilles* from a distance; and there was Joshua, who shared the steerage with us and another in the fo'c's'le; but here, around the shores of the bay, there lived an entire nation of jet-skinned men and women.

I bought bananas, oranges, and other fruits from the boats for Heke to try; and their fresh, sweet tastes were another revelation for on *Tovy Poenamoo* there were no fruits, only a few berries which could not be eaten but could be squeezed to yield juice. Rio was filled with wonders.

Port officials saw no reason to accommodate visiting ship captains or make the least change to their slow, casual routine which might detract from the dignity of their fine uniforms and hats, or the power of their offices. They dawdled for two days before pratique was granted to the *Sagittarius*; but once it was, our crew quickly rigged a tackle over the main hatch, hoisted casks of oil from the blubber room, and lowered them into the lighters alongside. On their return the boats brought barrels of fresh water and bundled firewood, but the coffee was slow in being loaded at different warehouses and little of it arrived alongside that night.

Captain Jones seeing he could hardly deny leave allowed nearly half of the crew to go to the city.

When I had first gone ashore there years ago, the black and mulatto women had sidled up and smiled broadly at me as they had to my mates. A few were quite beautiful, showing bright white teeth when they laughed; and they walked along the streets with a silky grace and insinuated their expert trade with a familiar arm slipped around the waist. It had cast me off balance and I had drawn from them, feeling loutish, awkward, and far out of my walk. Beyond my lack of their Portuguese, such unexpected boldness put me ill at ease; and I could not imagine following them into some little shanty as my mates eagerly did, ignoring the risk of the pox and gleet.

Joshua did not ask for leave. I made a note of that, knowing the man would take no risk, for a black face was a slave's face ashore, and no protection he might carry or amount of protest to any official could avail him if he were taken while on land. He might be spirited out into the country to cut sugar cane, and all inquiries for him would be met with blank or indifferent looks. Joshua stood at the rail perhaps having learned caution from sore experience; so not tempted to go ashore, he merely watched the people and carriages moving along the streets.

The exchange of cargo was completed in two days, four days after we had first entered the harbor. In the place of the casks of oil, there were now two hundred bags of coffee beans stowed on fresh dunnage in the hold.

The *Sagittarius* worked out to sea and farther up the coast where the steerage, even with the scuttle open day and night, became nothing more than a baking box. On deck the drilling heat of the sun was a reminder of my passage through that ocean years before.

With not a waif cloud in the sky, there were sharply cut borders between the patterns of sunlight and shadows cast by the sails and lines. All items in sight were starkly lighted with no half lights which would have softened the scene. *Heke* and I found places in the shade and leaned our backs against the coils of line hanging from the belays. We spent our day on deck moving from one shadow to the next as the sun traveled the sky or the ship was brought to the wind or ran before it. The *Sagittarius* worked north past the Leeward Islands, and there dog watches were the pleasantest part of the day. Some of the heat was over; and the crew gathered on the foredeck, the favored place on the ship whether there was the least breeze or not. They passed by the galley, lighted their pipes from the failing embers of the fire, and sat on the fore hatch to smoke. Later arrivals made do by leaning against the rail. Talk was mostly hopes about the progress of the vessel and what each would do with his money after the voyage had been settled up.

On the clear nights there was the slow change in the star patterns to watch. I pointed out the constellations rising in the northern sky that were unfamiliar to *Heke*.

"Ah, Toma Kina, arra new," she said as she studied them. "More cuma dere?"

"Aye, there will many more new ones," I replied. "See, those stars that were once far to the north are now right overhead."

For days the wind remained a warm exhaling which bellied out all sails set, without a shake at their leaches. We glided nor'west listening to the creak of blocks, the slap of long halyards, and the splash of the bow cleaving the sea. The deck, lighted under a full or gibbous moon and the ever-present stars, was a comfortable place to sleep. The entire watch ended up there rather than suffer the oppressive heat in the steerage or fo'c'sle. *Heke*, *Tiro*, and I joined them.

"If you sleep on deck," Danny advised me, "be sure you pick one of the softer planks."

"So, you will be the ship's clown?" I asked and yanked his hat down to cover his eyes.

We slept well there but never discovered any of Danny's soft planks.

On some nights lightning flashes blanched the deck and sails; and the harshly lighted images persisted in the eyes for a few seconds. Our vessel sailed beneath black clouds; and at times deluges of large, splatting drops drove us into the refuge below.

Chapter Twenty-two

At daybreak ten days later Mr. Abbot had the men in their places at the side of the barque and ordered, "Heave away." The man at the bow heaved the deep sea lead forward. It made its long pendulum swing, plunged in, and pulled the line rapidly down. A sounding was got. Men of the watch shouted, "Yankeeland! Aye, Yankeeland!" We had less than a hundred fathoms beneath our keel. We were within one or two day's sail of port.

The next afternoon the *Sagittarius* hove to off Sandy Hook to pick up the pilot. A tall, thin man dressed in black stood in the boat below the gangway gripping a trunnel of the ladder. We watched him from the gangway and the rail. Before he started up, he studied each one of us. His gaze went from face to face as if he were searching for one particular man.

"Where from? How long from your last port?" the pilot called up.

"Rio de Janeiro," Mr. Abbot answered. "Forty-six days."

"Other calls? Surinam? Cuba? The Carolinas?"

"None," the officer assured him.

"You swear to that."

"I do."

The pilot was still cautious, even after he had passed through the gangway. On deck he inspected each of the crew from head to foot. He looked the whole length of the vessel and even scanned the main and foretops and the sails shaking in the breeze. He then took his position near the helm to cun the *Sagittarius* into the port.

At the Narrows the yards were backed again for customs and health. Two men came aboard; and one of them with a pinched and doubtful look proclaimed he was the health officer and repeated the same questions the pilot had made.

"Has anyone died aboard your vessel since your last call?" he inquired.

"No one has died aboard during two years, the whole of the cruise," Captain

Jones replied. "We have not looked in anywhere after we left Rio, forty six days since."

"Fever," the officer explained. "There's fever in the city again. It was very bad last year. We need no other additions to it." He and his companion were thorough and inspected the fo'c'sle, the steerage, and even the hold for any one ill and stowed away before allowing us to proceed up the bay.

The *Sagittarius* neared the Battery; and ahead along the shoreline was a tall, intricate mass which appeared to be a thick pine forest stripped of its needles. At closer range it resolved into the masts of ships that were crowded against the docks. A few had sails hanging from their yards to dry. Boats and ships of all sizes were crossing the water and going up the broad river off to the east or returning from errands there.

Mr. Abbot set his watch to get up a warping line and carry it to the pier. Bit by bit the line was drawn in by the windlass until the *Sagittarius* was within its slip and her jib boom, like all those of the other ships, extended over the street that marked the sharp barrier between land and bay.

Early the next morning the unloading began.

New York was a dismaying mix of strange sights and noises for *Heke* and a more amazing piece of the world than Brazil had been. She stood at the rail of the *Sagittarius* holding *Tiro* and watched wagons loaded with casks and boxes being drawn along the thoroughfare by stomping horses. Men pushing hand carts trotted to cut in front of them to get to one side or the other. She gawked at the animals only a few yards away. In Rio de Janeiro she had seen the asses and oxen only from a distance, but on the dock the large creatures were near enough to see all the details of their hooves, tails, and manes.

I had not met with those smells, the sweating animals, their piss and fresh dung, in years and now the stinks seemed stronger than any memory. When the barque was still a mile from its berth, I had caught a whiff of them and other land odors.

Heke stared up at the brick facades of the buildings that lined the far side of the street from the docks. In Rio the structures could not have appeared so tall to her when viewed from the deck of the *Sagittarius* anchored a quarter mile distant.

We bid our farewells to Danny, Joshua, Fernando, Daniels, and the others of the crew who were busy setting up the tackle to hoist out the bundles of bone from the hold.

I picked up our roll of mats, jackets, and blankets and stood at the gangway with *Heke* at my side.

"No more sea for you, lad?" Mr. Abbot asked.

"I've had quite enough for a while," I replied. "I must see how my father has been these last years."

Captain Jones shook my hand and offered, "If you have a change of mind and wish a cruise in the next month, apply at Misters Leggit and Mason's counting house. I'll recommend you to the owners for a berth in any of their ships."

"No, thank you. I chased and boiled enough whales. No, now I have my *Heke* and my son. So I'm for the land for a while, thank you. I wish you good fortune."

I motioned to *Heke* to follow and started out through the gangway. Behind us a bundle of baleen was being raised from the hold. Men's yells and curses came from up and down the landing. Once we reached the edge of the street, *Heke* clutched *Tiro* more securely and shrank back at the sight of a pair of large, heavy-hoofed draft horses snorting and clomping toward us. I put my free arm around her shoulders and said, "They'll not hurt you. Keep close to me."

Despite my words that they were harmless, her eyes were still fearful. A man shouted, damning everyone in his way, as he attempted to back his dray. His dog ran back and forth on the empty bed and barked incessantly at another hound on the pavement leaping up and yelping in dispute. On the dock I weaved on a course around the stacks of boxes and bundled cargo. *Heke* kept close to me and looked right and left at the confused mix of men and wagons working their way in one direction or the other. We waited for several drays to pass before we could cross to the opposite side.

Heke and I placed our bare feet carefully on the street, making long steps and detours to avoid the fresh, wet horse turds already drawing swirls of flies. A vagrant breeze brought another stink to the nose, one from the oily, trash-filled water surging around the pilings below the piers.

On board the *Sagittarius*, shoes from its slops sold at three times the New York price. Like many of the crew, *Heke* and I had paced the deck barefooted; but to walk on streets with dirt and filth underfoot, shoes were needed. I made an inquiry of a man idling at the first corner and was directed to a slop shop located two blocks away. Following his instruction, I led *Heke* along the front of the buildings which faced the harbor. The pounding of hammers came from a large shop ahead. A haze of smoke spilled from the top of its doorway and went upward, leading my eye to the white letters, "Samuel Smithson, Cooperage," painted on the brick wall above the opening. Two men within the shadowy interior stood on each side of a large cask and were driving a hoop down, compressing its staves. A heating cresset inside the partially finished container was the source of the smoke. A few yards on we came to a smaller door standing partially open. Six feet of cable, thick as a man's arm, was nailed to a post at one side of the shop. Each end of it had been neatly seized and snaked with log line to prevent raveling. Beside the door a sign listed the types of cordage for sale inside: whale line, cables, rope hawser-laid and shroud-laid, small stuff, nettings. An enormous, damaged treble block fit for a first rate rested against the wall below the sign.

We turned at the corner of the street and walked away from the harbor. I turned to speak to *Heke* and discovered she had stopped several steps back and was staring at a window. She touched one of the panes of glass and slid her finger up and down on the slick surface. It was a puzzling thing for her, something very smooth like the looking glasses she had used at Blind Bay; but the pane was larger and one she could see through like smooth water. There were two small stern lights on the *Sagittarius* in the captain's cabin, but they had been propped open and hardly noticeable the few times she was there. These many panes covering a space six by four feet and facing the street were a novel thing. A man on the other side the window, repeatedly passing a serving mallet around a piece of rigging, looked up for a second, nodded once, and returned to his task. I touched *Heke's* shoulder; and she, alerted that I was moving on, followed, but twice looked back at the window.

We found the slop shop and stepped into its dark, stuffy interior smelling of new oilskins hung on the walls. In addition to the oilskins, clothes, tin ware, sheath knives, needles, and spools of thread were offered for sale. It was a small place with all the items jumbled together. *Heke* gazed wide-eyed at the treasure stored there, the masses of jackets, the shirts, and the woolen underwear piled on top of blankets and those in turn stacked on sea chests.

A thin, old man sat at a desk writing in an account book.

"Good day to you, sir," I began. "You have ready for sale shoes? I need a pair for my companion here and myself."

"On that far side in the hogsheads. All sizes," the man replied, turning slightly to me to make his answer.

From one container I chose some thick-heeled pumps for *Heke,* and from another I pulled out a pair of work shoes. I inspected the leather and sewing closely before buying them. If there were things I knew well, it was properly cured hides and good stitching. The thread had been well-waxed and seated tightly in the feather cut into the soles. Good stockings had to be next. A pair each would do until we reached home. I drew a pair of stockings on *Heke's* feet and slipped her shoes over them. "A good fit?" I asked. She nodded and turned one foot to admire each side of the blacked and waxed leather.

I asked the proprietor, "Do you know where we might find a seamstress, a dress shop?"

The man raised half out of his chair, tilted his face a little forward, and squinted over his glasses at *Heke.* After considering the odd match of her sailor's clothes with her hair and the baby in her arms, he squeaked out, "Ah! Ah! Bless me, it's a woman. Bless me!" The old man thought for a moment. "Well, I've never been asked for such before," he answered, shaking his head of white hair, "but over there on the next street and up three streets you will find Mrs. Phillips' shop. Sign over the blue door. Nothing Frenchy 'bout her place. Very plain stock she makes. Except some Sunday gowns."

I replied, "Such will do."

The cost of the shoes and stockings was a third of what it would have been from the slops on any ship; still it was not any bargain. Sailors fitting out just prior to leaving port sometimes had little time to look for gear at lower prices, and the shopkeepers near the waterfront, aware of that, charged more than those farther uptown.

As she strode along out on the street, *Heke* kept looking down at her new pumps. She was proud of them. They were possibly the first pair of shoes that ever covered her feet, as there was scant need even for flax sandals on the paths around Blind Bay.

The noises of the loading and unloading faded away as we walked farther from the busy waterfront. Traffic, though, was almost as heavy with carts and chaises clattering up and down the streets. The clop-clop of hooves and the squinching of iron tires on the stones never ceased.

Ahead was a tavern with a sign over its entrance that announced it was The Bowsprit. Loud, bullying voices and the strong smell of liquor spilled from its open door. Many of the words yelled inside were profanity. In front of the establishment, three men sat on kegs placed against the wall and smoked their pipes. I nodded to the men, each red-faced from much drink, and said, "A good day to you."

One man mumbled the same greeting in return as we passed by.

The seamstress's dark blue door could be easily seen from the end of the block, and a large window had been framed in beside it for the display of a few dresses and bonnets. *Heke* stepped close and tapped on one of the panes, still baffled by the water-like but solid quality of it. Then she peered through the glass at the dresses inside. A little bell tinkled as the door swung open and we stepped inside. *Heke* glanced up at the bell swinging overhead, raised her hand toward it, and smiled as she recognized it as a miniature of the larger, highly-polished bell at the station and the one which had governed all the men aboard the *Sagittarius*. Then her eyes went around the shop, wide in wonderment at all the fancy fabrics, the rolls of lace, and brightly hued ribbons. At Blind Bay the only fabrics traded had been calico, duck, and wool blankets. The colors of the dresses astonished her, and she guessed from the nature of the shop that she was to get one of them. She smiled at the thought. The shopkeeper, a stoutish woman, summoned by the bell came from the back room. After scanning *Heke's* sailor outfit and spying the *moko* on her chin, the woman's greeting quickly cooled. Yet we were customers and her business sense urged a shade of her smile to return. She tugged a little at her apron to straighten it and announced, "I am Mrs. Phillips." Then she inquired, "And what will you have, madam?"

I dropped my bundle to the floor, took the baby, and nodded toward *Heke*, "She doesn't speak but a mite of English. She needs a frock."

"For Sunday meeting?" Mrs. Phillips asked, turning her head to estimate *Heke's* size.

"No, something plain and sturdy that will last. We're traveling."

"Ump. Yes. I have one in the back room that should fit her. It was bespoke and I finished it last month, but it was never called for. It will need to be hemmed, though. I will get it."

Heke slipped off her red shirt and duck trousers and stood waiting for the woman to return.

Mrs. Phillips was aghast when she arrived with the dress and caught sight of the brown, naked girl standing in the middle of her shop. "They're not exceptional modest where she comes from, ma'm," I explained.

"Oh, Heavens! Heavens! Has she no chemise?" the woman asked as she hustled *Heke* into the back room with one hand and carried the gown on her other arm.

"None whatever, ma'm," I called after Mrs. Phillips. "She has never seen one."

Mrs. Phillips' face was still flushed, but more composed several minutes later when she brought *Heke* out wearing the selected gown. The seamstress smoothed the fabric across her shoulders and picked off a stray thread. "There, will this do?" she asked.

The high-waisted garment, made of a material with a small white and brown check pattern, was very plain.

"Aye, it will do, and she'll need a bonnet too, ma'm."

"There are several there in the window. You look them over while I begin the hemming. We will be in back."

She led *Heke* away once more.

I busied myself considering bonnets, particularly one made from a soft cap and fitted with a starched brim. Fancy, large straws would catch the wind near a shore or on a ship and kite off to leeward. A small, plain one would be better, as we had more than a hundred miles yet to travel.

It was a long wait until Mrs. Phillips finally brought *Heke* out dressed in the finished garment, which reached within a few inches of the floor. The seamstress slipped my chosen bonnet onto *Heke's* head and tied the ribbon in a big bow beneath her chin. After inspecting it from the right and left, Mrs. Phillips tucked some of *Heke's* hair under the bonnet. *Heke* looked up to focus her eyes on the brim. She felt its edge with one hand and turned her head from side to side to discover how much it limited her vision. Mrs. Phillips held up a forefinger and noted, "I have fitted a chemise on her. She cannot be without one. What does sleep in?"

"Naught but her skin," I said with a wink and a smile.

Mrs. Phillipps' face reddened again, but she gathered her composure quickly and asked, "Do you want another? She should have at the least, two."

"For sure, tot it up."

Mrs. Phillips found the other chemise and added the prices. I walked around *Heke* inspecting the frock. The tattoo on *Heke's* lip and chin contrasted with the womanly attire. Between the brim of the bonnet and the ribbon of the bow, the *moko* on her chin became far more apparent as the mark of the wild savage. While wrapped in her flax skirt or wearing the ducks and the shirtwaist of a sailor, the tattoo was more acceptable, hardly noticeable after the first few glances. Now that she was in a dress and bonnet, the dark, incised lines looked odder, even fierce; and they took on a meaning which might draw many more stares as we walked the streets of the city.

Heke took *Tiro* back. I counted out the coins to Mrs. Phillips, then added *Heke's* sailor clothes and the extra chemise to our roll of blankets and mats.

Mrs. Phillips kept her eyes on us as we departed, and we had taken only a few paces outside the door when her face appeared between the bonnets and behind the half-transparent reflections on the window. Her head turned slowly side to side.

Heke ran her right hand up and down her left arm which held the baby, feeling the fabric of sleeve. Then she raised the frock to look at her shoes again. She smiled and purred, "I rikah, Toma Kina. I rikah *nui, nui.*"

Passage up to Stonington was our next pressing need. With fever in the city, I would not remain there a minute longer than needful. For sure I would not stay the night with my wife and child in any of the rooms that were there to let. The hot, foul miasmas from mudflats and the river bank carried the fever into the city. It would be far safer to take my family anywhere out on the Sound, away from the smelly city with its dangerous fevers. We went back toward the waterfront along the same street taken to the dress shop. At the Bowsprit tavern I asked one of the three men still seated there, "Where can I get passage up the Sound to Mystick or Stonington?"

The older man of the trio, wearing a shabby hat, drew his pipe from his mouth. Shouts erupted from interior of the Bowsprit. He tilted his head back slightly, squinted up at the building across the street, and urged his fogged mind to recall where the coasters were tied up. "Well now … up the Sound … that should be no problem," he drawled. "Some goes up there most everyday … even more of them of a Saturday." He required another two draws on his pipe and blew them out before he continued, "Well now … think it best you look near them shipways." He nodded to the man sitting next to him and asked, "Right?" The man there, dulled with drink, might have heard the question, but if he had he was apparently unable to answer. At least he made no effort. The other man sitting at his other side slowly lifted his head to reply but, not waiting to remove his pipe from his mouth, hummed out a positive, "Ummph." The older man pointed with his pipe stem and continued giving directions. "You go there along the next street east … then 'bout two, three slips over and you come onto some schooners and sloops this side of the shipyards. Coasters? … yes, they're somewheres about there. Two or three'll be goin' out … maybe today … or tomorrow… north or south."

"You damned duck fucker!" A man shouted from the interior of the tavern. Thumps and the clatter of overturned tables and chairs came out with the loud, swearing voices.

"I thank you, sir," I replied and, grasping *Heke's* elbow, hurried her away. When we reached the next street there was more yelling from the tavern. We looked back and saw one man dash from the door. Four other men in the dress of sailors spilled from the tavern and surrounded him. They shouted and struck at him until he was knocked onto his hands and knees. One of the sailors stepped forward and booted him in the ribs. The victim rolled in pain on the paving stones; then another kicked at his body from the other side. The driver of a loaded market wagon coming down the street reined his team up and turned them aside to avoid them.

I guided *Heke* around the corner and said, "*Waipiro.*"

"*Waipiro,*" she repeated in an uneasy voice and hurried with me toward the slips.

After several inquiries I found a sloop readying to go north.

"New London, but I go no farther," the captain replied to my question about his destination, "and I must return as soon as I unload."

"Well enough, we will find our way from there. I wish to leave today."

"I'll put you on the Groton side of the river near the ferry landing," the captain promised. "Get your things and bring them aboard."

I lifted the roll of mats, blankets, and clothes, showing him they were the extent of our possessions.

An hour later the captain's two sons cast the vessel loose and worked it carefully through the river, around the islands, and then made good progress up the Sound.

Casks and crates cluttered the deck of the vessel. After dark we found enough space to lie down on the hatch cover. The night was warm and, covering not needed, we slept on top of our blankets and mats.

After midnight I was awakened by one of the crew calling out soundings from the starboard side. He swung the hand lead in a full circle three times and released it to fly forward beyond the bow.

"Five less a quarter," he reported.

The captain made a small change in our course. There was need for soundings, for the night air had cooled and made into a mist. It was very dark and not one light could be seen in any direction, forcing the master to feel the way north with the tide helping or hindering progress. Every few minutes the lead splashed, and then the boy called out the depth. He brought the lead to the lantern and inspected the tallow in its bottom. Whatever stuck there was the captain's guide, for he probably knew where he was by the fineness of the sand, broken shells, or color of the mud. He cunned the ship from what showed in the arming and the depth. The next call was for a full five. Each sounding after that was deeper and showed we were finding our way up the Sound. The line and plummet were guiding us to the Connecticut shore and to home.

I had been to New London many years before; thus the moment my foot touched the shore it would mark my circling of the globe. I had left with the dream of returning with hundreds of dollars, perhaps nigh five to six hundred paid out of my share of seal skins and oil. I had also expected to add two hundred or even three hundred dollars to that sum by some adventure made at Canton in jade, silk, or carved ivory. It appeared a foolish dream now that all had been lost on a lee shore.

Dawn revealed a low, gray coast to the north. Trees formed into their shapes out of a thinning mist. There was nothing in the haze which would guide us. The shore there was low and featureless compared to the great bluff coasts of *Tovy Poenamoo*.

After midday the Captain pointed out the lighthouse several miles distant. "There she be," he said, "just there, and that's Fisher's Island off the other way."

I looked at the lighthouse and turned and located the island.

Heke was there beside me holding *Tiro*. Within a day or two, I would present them to Father. There would be a look of delight in his eyes when he saw the little fellow, bright and growing well. He would embrace *Heke*, take *Tiro* in his arms, and hold him and rock him. Such might be their meeting and so bring a smile at last to Father's face.

All youngsters of the port understood they were welcome to visit his shop anytime to watch him cut leather and work at his bench. They received a smile when in winter they entered to sit and warm their hands by his fire, and he took pleasure in their laughter and sound of their voices even when they squabbled. Happiness in him needed those sounds of life. It could not exist in silence.

I knew there was an unspoken wish in him that another child had come into the family, surely part of the melancholy that had come over him in later years.

From the day of Mother's death, his words were sparse and not readily given, and once her coffin had been lowered at the burying ground he rarely went out except to church. The purchase of hides from the tanneries and the collection of debts were the only other reasons that took him from the shop, and he remained at the window most of each day fitting leather to a last or patiently sewing soles while the light held. Our old housekeeper had put meals before him which he ate as if it were a chore. Any pleasure in his life, other than the visits of children, was to pass his hands over a properly sewn shoe.

Three heavy drays were parked at the land end of the dock where we landed; their teams had been unhitched and probably led off to an empty lot to feed. The drivers, wearing worn leather aprons, were sitting on the side of one of the drays. Two hounds with scarred heads and ragged ears were asleep beside the forward wheel. Two of the men were laughing and smoking pipes. The third had just taken a swallow from a jug and was replacing the stopper as we approached. They were a tough, dirty looking lot even for draymen, but I gave them a polite nod. All three broke into oily grins when they looked at *Heke* walking beside me. We passed the dray, and the one who had taken the drink jumped off onto his feet and called out, "Hoy there, fellah! Got you a gal with a lick o' the tar brush." He turned his head to one side, spit, and then added, "Hee, hee, hee. Is she good to ya? I mean a really good punch? Hee, hee, hee."

I slowly turned about.

"Ooh, ooh, ooh," the drayman groaned and held his clenched fists out before of him. He thrust his hips forward and back several times, rolled his eyes up and blinked.

I dropped the roll of clothes and bedding, walked back to the dray, and stood a fathom before the man. "She is my wife and she suits me fine," I said. Then I asked him softly, "How does that suit you?" I held my right hand close to my hip, muscles tensed, and ready to whip out the knife from the sheath laced to my belt. It was honed keen enough to slash through his apron. I stared into his eyes. His two stout friends were sitting on the dray watching me. One move by any of them and I would instantly whip my knife out; and though they might overcome me there would be much blood on the ground. Some would certainly be their blood; and a neck or stomach might be slashed open, perhaps ribs pierced. The grin drained from the man's face. He nodded and said, "Aye, aye … it suits me … it suits me." What probably awed them more than the blade of the knife were my eyes filled with my determination to protect my family.

I backed away carefully while watching him and flicking a glance at the two others on the dray. I would not give them an opportunity to leap upon me and pin my arms. They might do that, take any advantage. If they knew there was gold and silver in the leather pouch hanging about my neck, they would certainly try it. There was the lesson I learned well on the coast of *Tovy Poenamoo*. Never show fear.

I picked up the roll, and with *Heke* beside me averting her gaze from the draymen, we headed for the main road. Before we reached it we met two young boys going toward the dock. "Good day," I greeted them and asked, "Where might we get a good meal?"

One of them pointed back and replied, "There, two streets down and to the left there's a tavern called the Bankside. It's a fair place."

The other boy nodded, adding his approval.

We followed their directions and in a few minutes turned a corner and found the tavern. The portly proprietor was sweeping the floor when we entered.

"Good day to you," the man greeted us.

"And the same to you, innkeeper. Do you know many of the seafaring folk about the river here?" It was not a needed question. If the man had been at the inn two months or even less, he would know a good number, possibly most of them on both shores.

"That I do. Are you looking for someone, for a cruise maybe?" he asked.

"No, I bring news for any who had men aboard the barque *Dove* that left from Stonington several years past in 1818. I wish to post a notice on your wall here that the vessel has foundered in the Southern Ocean. Every man of her crew was lost then or later. That is, save me. I am the only one who was spared and found my way here."

"Ah, that cannot be," the innkeeper objected. "We heard that no one was saved. That news was given out I think nine, ten months since."

"And who gave that report?"

The innkeeper thought a minute and replied, "I believe it was from a coaster from Providence or New Bedford. Then it was printed in the papers, too."

"Someone has given false news then. True the barque foundered, but one survived and stands before you now. As you can see, I am no specter."

He looked from me to *Heke* and *Tiro*, and, apparently satisfied that I was the one I claimed to be, stepped behind the counter. He placed a heavy brass inkstand with a quill before me, laid a sheet of paper out and folded it once. After creasing it several times he tore it in two and slid one half forward.

I flipped the lid open and dipped the quill into the well. It took me a minute to compose the lines before I tapped off the excess ink and slowly wrote, "NOTICE TO ALL. I, Thomas Wightman, am the sole survivor from the wreck of the barque *Dove*, Seth Tobit master. I belong to Stonington Boro. If you call at my father's shoe shop there I will give the particulars of the Tragedy."

"I will post this up here and direct people to it," the innkeeper said. He picked up the paper and waved it several times to dry the ink. Then he read the lines and murmured, "Yes, I believe I recall someone who had a man aboard." He mounted the notice on the wall with two pins among the many others, some new, some curled and yellowed, regarding lost animals or offers of boats for sale.

How had the report of the sinking arrived before me by so many months? Captain Jones met some whalers off the east coast of the Middle Island, but it was unlikely those ships would have reached home that early, for the *Sagittarius* was then nearly a full ship and the ones he spoke needed more whales. Most likely it was the *Achilles* or the *Free Settler* which had passed the news on to others, and then the report was brought to America.

We ordered and finished our meal. While paying the bill I inquired of the innkeeper, "Is there a coach going to Stonington or Mystick anytime soon?"

He shook his head and replied, "None today, but you might ask if a dray is going that way."

"A dray? Ha, I have more of a desire to walk."

I picked up our bundle, and with my free hand motioned to *Heke* that we were leaving.

The innkeeper followed us out the door and pointing with a hand said, "The Post Road is that way. Good day to you."

"And to you sir," I replied. Then I warned *Heke*, "Well, it looks as if we'll have to shank it for a while."

"Tank it?" she repeated.

"Foot it," I explained, pointing to my shoes. "We ride shank's mare, to be sure."

Heke smiled, mounted *Tiro* onto her back, and secured him there with the square of blanket. We started off in the direction the innkeeper indicated. The road became rutted and muddy after an hour of walking. *Heke*, not wishing to soil her new pumps and stockings, took them off and carried them in her hand. Another good reason to travel barefooted was that at the wading places she could simply gather up her dress and walk through.

The walk was quickly warming me and I slipped my jacket off. A fine haze created by the heat and muggy air was noticeable between us and any distant trees when we came up on a rise. It was late afternoon when we stopped to rest at the edge of the road. If I remembered rightly, it crossed the head of the Mystick.

Heke took *Tiro* from her back. "Toma Kina?" she asked, nodding to her left shoulder.

I undid the top buttons of her dress. She slipped it off her shoulder and put *Tiro* to her breast.

Sunlight angled low through the trees from the west, dappling bright patterns on the tree trunks and the ruts and weeds of the roadway. Bright specks, minute insects with their bodies and wings back-lighted by the sun, drifted in lazy, erratic paths within shadows of the trees. It was becoming familiar thereabout, a place near home. I had traveled the road many times as a boy. A little farther on we would arrive near some shipyards and a few houses. If we turned south at the crossing and walked along the crooked channel of the Mystik, there would be more houses. I had no desire to go there and hoped to reach home before the light was all gone to meet Father and give the town news of the *Dove*'s loss. It was only five or six more miles to Stonington and I was anxious to continue.

Father would be elated that I had survived and brought him a grandchild. He will smile now. The neighbors will gather and fill the shop to bursting. It will be a jolly time. After everyone left for the evening, *Heke, Tiro,* and I would sleep in my room at the back of the shop, a needed rest after our long walk. We started off again and crossed the brook that ran into the inlet. I should certainly find my way if few things had changed.

The sound of horse's hooves clomping on the road came from behind. We both turned and watched a man on horseback gallop toward us and slow to a walk on approaching. His mount was lathered with sweat from its strenuous pace. *Heke* slipped behind me and gripped my shirt.

"A good day to you," the rider greeted me and reined up. He extended a hand and said, "I am Cal Billings of Groton."

I shook his hand and replied, "Good day to you, sir, I am Thomas Wightman." I indicated my family with a wave of my hand.

The horseman was not a person I might have known. His dress was new and neat with a hat tipped to one side, hinting self-assurance. He wore fine boots and was seated in a new saddle. Not a tradesman there, no, not one of laboring habits that was quite plain. Perhaps he had shares in enterprises or owned them wholly. Might I have become such a man had I not signed on the sealer?

"And where are you bound for?" the rider inquired. His gaze quickly left my face and settled on *Heke*'s.

"The Boro," I said. "We expect to get there before dark."

"Perhaps. Getting late though," the horseman said, then added, "A sailor, I see." He didn't drop the pitch of his last word. It was not a question; yet it showed an answer would be welcome.

I held my hands out from my sides to display the white ducks and the round jacket that were the dress of seafarers.

"Ah, yes, for sure," the man said, letting his eyes return to *Heke's* face. "Have a good walk," were his last words and he gave his mount a kick to start him on his way.

Chapter Twenty-three

In the gathering dusk I missed the turn off the Post Road. We were lost. Perhaps some bit of the road had been changed, and I would hardly find it in the dark. *Heke* was weary and we stopped. I spread our mats and blankets on the ground a few yards from the road; and, with *Tiro* between us, we tried to sleep. Mosquitoes kept up their hum about our ears and landed to feed on our faces until we drew the blanket over our heads to bar the pests.

A few minutes after we were settled, a cow lowed close by. *Heke* tossed the blanket aside. "Toma Kina!" she gasped and seized my arm.

"Merely a cow," I reassured her and pulled the blanket back over us. For a comforting touch I slid my hand across and held her shoulder. With full trust in my words, she rested her head on the mat again.

One thought kept me awake. We were nearing the Port where I would face those who had relatives on the barque. My sudden appearance there as a survivor might give them hope. Then moments later I must tell them the fate of the vessel and all others aboard. They would relive their grief.

At first light the crowing of cocks sounded from several directions. I fixed in my mind where I was from the sunrise and knew in which direction to start off. We found the turning and approached some of the cows we had heard in the night.

Heke had seen some oxen on the shore in Rio, and some cows at a distance from the road the day before; but these were quite near at hand and she stared at their hooves and horns and swinging tails. "Dey no cuma heera?" she asked anxiously, pointing to the ground at her feet.

"They are like the horses you saw," I explained, "but they just eat the grass out there all day."

She accepted my answer, yet looked back several times to be sure they were not following us.

We approached some cleared planting grounds, and it all began to fit with my memory of the roads I knew. A few women and children were working in the gardens of the first outlying houses we approached. They waved and called out a good day to us. Around me I found the familiar images of home: trees, fences, styles, gardens plots. On slightly higher ground more of the Port was visible. Each house and field fit with the mental chart I had remembered in detail as I rambled about for years. Nothing much had changed. A brig and a sloop each rode by their cable in the middle of the harbor. A boat glided between one ship and the shore, rowed by two men on some errand not urgent. Farther down the Long Point there would be vessels at the docks, new boats, and perhaps a sloop or schooner a-building.

My eyes swept over the view, and I had to confess that the chance to earn a round sum from skins and oil was not the only reason I had left. The stories of the other boys returning from their cruises had made me more restive each year and sharpened an urge to see new places. They had boasted of events and sights seen on voyages taken to Copenhagen, Hamburg, and other ports in Spain and France. Their stories pointed to my work at the bench as not fit for an able man. The gentle craft some men called shoemaking, perhaps with a tinge of either envy or contempt. Working at the trade with its dullness and tameness during those years had prodded my mind; and at eighteen I was restless, anxious to sign on any vessel that was bound off soundings. Now I had returned from adventures in the past few years that more than matched theirs.

Heke handed me the baby and sat on the ground to slip on her stockings and shoes. She stood up again and we resumed our way. Afoot on the road with a roll of bedding under my arm, dressed in worn clothing, and with a wife beside me carrying our child on her back was not the return to the Boro I had imagined. Yet, it was not a return to be despised. I felt it was a victory of sorts, having threaded my way through so many dangers and trials and returned home with a fair stock of wisdom, if with little wealth.

A whiff of drying fish in the air reminded me our last meal had been at the inn the day before. *Heke* must be hungry. On our route to the shop we would pass near Allen's Inn, only a few yards out of the way, and we could eat before we went home to greet father. My meeting with him and his with his new grandson would be delayed only by a half hour.

From the doorway of the inn, I saw little inside it had changed. The tables were still set in their accustomed places. In the far corner of the room, the shelves were still provided with the usual flasks and jugs of various sizes. Opposite the bar was the fireplace, but it had no fire, though a wisp of gray smoke rose from glowing coals and rippled up the chimney. The rack of pipes hung on the wall right of the fireplace with the smoking tongs on a nail below them. Zacharia, Allen's dog, as usual snoozed under a table; but he had gray hairs well speckled over his snout and head that had once been a jet black.

Mr. Allen had altered some, having grown a little more portly and showing a face with cheeks redder and fuller. He looked up slowly from his account book as *Heke* and I crossed to a table. The innkeeper showed no sign that he recognized me and gave *Heke's* chin and our child much more attention.

I knew him well enough and asked, "Mister Allen, could Fanny favor us with a meal?"

He quickly turned to look at me again, curious that a man wholly a stranger and with a peculiar companion would know his wife's name. He eyed me carefully. Perhaps he saw something familiar in my appearance, yet doubt began to show in his face when he looked again at *Heke* and her tattoo.

Mr. Allen crossed over and inquired cautiously, "Yes, she might, what would you be wanting this morning?"

"Whatever pleases her to cook. That most likely would be some bacon and eggs, johnnycake with fresh, sweet butter … and some cheese, if I recall."

"You know my Fanny?" he asked. His eyes, carrying a mix of interest and suspicion, glanced from me to the baby and *Heke* and back again.

I seated *Heke* in a chair, turned to the tavern keeper, and explained, "That I do, Mr. Allen, having lived here all of my life. I am Wightman, Thomas Wightman. And this is my wife *Heke* and our son *Tiro*."

"Wightman? Wightman? Yes, yes, Thomas and Hannah's boy. Ah … yes, you went a-sealing."

"That I did. We had ill luck on the return voyage, and I carry the news that the *Dove* struck on a lee shore and was lost with all hands save four. Later of those four, three were lost and only I remain."

Mr. Allen stood open-mouthed for a moment, absorbing my words. His eyes went the length of my figure from hat to shoes. *Heke* drew his attention for a few seconds and then it returned to me. "We were told … the whole of the crew … all were gone," he sputtered.

"You have been misled. The report was not quite true. You see I am the last of them, now here and in good fettle."

The innkeeper looked me over again, still with some disbelief, and explained, "We did fear the ship was lost when it didn't return months after expected. I remember the very day I put up the notice there on the board when the news was brought to us. Why this is a wonder! Yes, a wonder! All you say? … all but you?" He turned about and took quick strides toward the door at the back of the room. "Fanny, Sally, come here," he called out sharply at the opening.

Fanny entered, followed by her daughter, a girl I now barely recognized.

"This is Young Wightman," he announced. "He's come back though all others were lost."

Mrs. Allen, holding a bowl in one hand and a large wooden spoon in the other, came forward, stared for a moment, and cried out, "Oh! Oh, what terrible misfortune it was, but you have been saved! Oh, thank heaven for that. You have come for your father's things?"

"Father's things? What do you mean, his things? Isn't he well?"

Mrs. Allen eyes opened wide. The spoon slipped from her grasp and bounced on the floor. She took a short gasp and asked, "Oh! … oh, you have not been to the shop yet?"

"No, where is my father? What's happened here?"

Fanny pressed her empty hand to the side of her face and cried out, "Oh, Thomas, Mr. Wightman died shortly after you left. We were all taken aback, surprised. No one expected …"

I turned to *Heke* and took her by the hand. She rose from her chair and followed me to the door.

"A Mister Cutter has the shop now," Allen called after us. "We have your father's chest here."

I hurried *Heke* along the road toward the shop and then slowed as we approached. The old sign had been replaced with a newer, larger one bearing the name: "J. Cutter." Whoever painted it hadn't laid out the letters beforehand and the J. C-U-T-T were full sized, but the E-R were slimmer and crowded in at the right edge of the board. The new sign was fixed to a bracket at a right angle to the wall and an old boot last, painted black, dangled from the bottom of it by a piece of strong cord. Heke and I stepped through the open door. There was no one in the shop. Father had always been seated at the window every morning, save Sunday, as soon the light was favorable; and if he wasn't making bespoke work he was making a pair of ready-for-sale shoes simply to keep busy. Now there was no last in the jack though it was three hours into the morning. A dozen pairs of shoes were arranged by sizes on a table, and from three paces away I could see they were made by piece work. Voices came through the door from the back of the shop, and then a man and woman entered. The woman, wearing a loose cap with the ties left dangling free, was a thick-boned thing half a head taller than the man. He stepped forward and ran his left hand over his head to smooth his thinning red hair.

"Jabez Cutter," he announced smiling and presented his other hand to be shaken.

I ignored the offered hand and sized the man up from head to foot. He had a well-freckled face, a bran face some would call it.

To cover the awkward seconds after my snub, Cutter shifted his attention quickly to *Heke's* footwear.

"Ah, you need boots, shoes, something for the lady?" he suggested. "Let's say a pair of pumps lighter than what she has there, with a nice bow. Yes, something fit for Sunday."

I remained silent and scanned completely around the interior of the shop. The woman stood near the door she had entered. Unlike Cutter, she did not smile. With a mouth that turned down at the corners and set firmly, she looked as if she were incapable of making even a slight one. Her dark, hard eyes stared back at me from either side of a bony nose. Apparently she thought there was no need or advantage in welcoming or putting customers at their ease. If Cutter claimed her as his wife, the fellow had a real Tartar on his hands.

"What I need is an accounting, Mr. Cutter!" I demanded. "Yes, an accounting of how you have come by this shop."

Cutter, with mouth half-open, nervously cast his eyes about the walls. They came back to pass over me, but only for half a second. He hoisted the waistband of his trousers higher on his belly. "Heh, heh, heh," he tittered nervously. "Well, everyone here about knows I loaned money to the previous owner." He stepped over and busied himself re-aligning the pairs of shoes on the table. When that was finished he walked to the soaking tub in the corner and stooped to pick up a few parings of leather from the floor.

"Ah, did you now. And so the owner came to be in your debt?"

"He borrowed quite a sum from me, yes."

I ignored the answer and strolled slowly around, looking at everything in the room. My presence in the shop had raised an ill-concealed tenseness in Cutter.

To ease it the man took a half step back and explained further, "I later found the shop didn't earn as much as I thought it would."

"And why would the owner borrow?"

"Well, he gave me no partic'lars. Perhaps he was in debt to someone who demanded his money." Cutter turned to the woman who had been listening intently to every word. He whispered something quickly in her ear. Though a large woman, she moved lightly on her feet and glided through the back door.

"He never owed anyone one a penny," I declared. "It was not in his nature to be in debt."

Cutter raised his open hands out to each side in a plea of ignorance and suggested, "I might then guess that he used the money to take a share in an adventure, a vessel perhaps."

"He would not. He had no need to hazard this shop. If he did, where did the money go? What ship, what business?" I knew that the loan the man claimed he had given Father was nothing but a monstrous lie.

"I was never told the least thing of it," Cutter said huffily. "Now if you have no wish to buy boots, I beg you to be on your way and leave me to my work."

"He had no need to borrow. Half the people here owed him for boots and leather work."

"Ha. What concern is it of yours, and how would you know aught of his accounts, sir?"

"I know them as much as my own. I am Thomas Wightman, his son, and I will have an accounting of this!"

Cutter's face blanched for a few seconds. To avoid my accusing look, he turned away and stepped to the window. Outside, a knot of people had gathered. Two were standing at the open door listening. He turned about and drew himself up in a stiff pose and stated, "I have this property by honest means. There are witnesses to the paper. This shop and the accounts were sold by auction to someone in Westerly and I was given my money. I wished to have a business and I then later bought it of that buyer."

The woman came back into the room, followed by large man. She neared Cutter and nudged his elbow.

He turned and saw the new arrival. "Ah, here we are," he said. "This is Mr. Sampson Glines. He witnessed the loan to your father when it was made."

Glines was a bull of a man wearing thick boots and an old, sweat-stained straw hat on his head.

"Mr. Glines," Cutter asked, "did you witness when Mr. Wightman made a loan from me years ago? In October of 1818?"

Glines took his pipe from his mouth and leaned slightly back to give his answer. "Ummp ... Aye, aye that I did," he stated with one deep, confirming nod.

His dirty smock, the cow dung on his boots, and the two week's growth of beard on his slab face were sure signs he was a farmer and not fit to be much more. He also looked to be a man who would gladly swear geese could fly upside down and backwards if offered enough money.

I could see how the cozenage was carried off. The loan was never made. When father died and they learned that he confided his business to no one, they contrived it all between them. They knew that I, the son, the only relation, would be gone for as long as two years sealing or might never return. Cutter then came forward to make his claim with the counterfeit paper. Perhaps others were a party to it, even the one who bought the shop and sold it to Cutter. Perhaps someone's fist was greased to see it all went well. Once the news was given out that the *Dove* was lost, he must have felt relief that he had the shop wholly secure and there was not a soul to ask questions.

Cutter smiled and the words fairly oozed out of his mouth. "There," he said, "that should settle your doubts, Mr. Wightman."

It was all clear. The man was cunning and had gained the shop in a way that appeared honest on the face of it.

The woman stepped forward, almost pushing Cutter aside. "You are Mr. Wightman's son, are you?" she crowed. "Well he did not watch his affairs closely. If you have any doubt, ask people here. They will tell you it was all legal. This is our shop. Now be on your way."

Who was she to put her oar in, to order me about? Even if she were the wife, this was men's business. Her words made me furious, and I was ready to turn and strike out at Cutter. But I held back. I remained as cool as I could while facing the woman. If I were to have the shop returned, I could not do it in that way ... by driving the couple off. I must fight them another way ... find and reveal their fraud. I waved *Heke* toward the door. There was no advantage staying there longer and trading sour words with the damned miserable thieves. I took *Heke's* arm and led her to the people outside, crowded together beyond the hitching rail.

"This is my wife *Heke* and my son, *Tiro,*" I said, introducing them to those standing about us. Some spoke their greetings and let their eyes linger for several seconds on *Heke's* tattooed chin. There could be no women's chatter with *Heke* and no questions asked about the baby. Though she understood a good many English words and caught the sense of what was said, responding in that language was difficult for her.

All crowded about while I told the tale of the foundering of the vessel and my capture. From the corner of my eye, I saw the citizens, young and old, were still inspecting *Heke*. She was not the first such Indian with a tattooed face to arrive there. There had been two others many years ago, but they had been men. A tattooed woman had never been seen, and that was the most remarkable oddity. Well, they might stare and become quite familiar with her tattoo, for I intended to remain and to have my shop back.

At the end of my tale I remembered we had no lodging for the night. I nodded to *Heke* and we began a return up to the inn. I replied to more questions from several boys following us up the road.

"Ooh. And cannibals," one of the boys cooed, "you lived with cannibals and there were bones and skulls all scattered about?"

"No, nothing like that, my young fellow," I replied. Then I remembered the skeletons I had uncovered when we were fleeing and added, "No, not all scattered everywhere, but there were some."

"And how far did you sail in the canoe, a thousand miles?" he asked next.

"Perhaps not rising two hundred miles, and I was most fortunate there was no ill weather, no storms."

Someone called the boy's name and he hesitated, considering if he should obey the summons. He looked to me, hoping to hear more of the shipwreck; but the call came again, more insistent, and he left with other boys following along.

I put my arm around *Heke's* shoulders as we walked.

"Notta you *whare*, Toma Kina?" she asked.

"Not my *whare*? That one. The shop … the house back there?"

Heke nodded.

"Oh, yes, my *whare*, my house, my shop. That man Cutter has taken it from me. Aye, stolen it from me."

"You keer him, Toma Kina," *Heke* advised coolly. "*Patu*," she added and mimed with her right hand striking several times with a club.

"I can't do that here."

"*Poo!*" she snapped, extending her arm with her forefinger pointing straight ahead, "You keer him wita a *poo*."

I shook my head and explained, "No, I cannot shoot him even if I had a musket. Here there is much *korero*, talk, talk. Yes, we must talk about it and look in the *pukapuka*." I meant looking at papers, but *pukapuka* would do, for she understood that it meant book. "Then more *korero* and then look in another *pukapuka*. Maybe I will get my shop back after a few years of talk and looking into more *pukapuka* … maybe not. *Heke* looked at me and repeated, "You keer him. Datah be *tika*."

Ahhh, how could I explain to her that it was not a simple matter of killing Cutter for *utu*? This enemy must be studied and the advice of a lawyer sought. Father's name on any note for a loan was certain to be a false one set there by Cutter, Glines, or someone else in the fraud, perhaps that Amazon. Father had signed his name for hides at the tanneries. There must be many of those papers still around and the signature on them will not match the one on the alleged note. I was most sure of that and must talk to those who accepted it as a true signing and show them the differences in the two hands. I was determined to move against Cutter in the courts. This injustice, this crime, would not stand good. In one way or another I meant to reclaim my shop.

We reached the inn. I stomped through the door and flumped into a chair. I nodded *Heke* to another one.

Mr. Allen approached and said, "It was quite a surprise when we learned that your father went into debt to Cutter."

"Ach! It's a damned fraud. Did you ever know my father to borrow?"

"No, we thought it very odd he would, and even more so to borrow from a stranger to the town. It didn't look right, but they were sure he had."

"I mean to have my shop. Father would never have borrowed. I can get many samples of his hand. It won't be but a short while before *Heke* and I will be in the property. In one way or another."

Mr. Allen slipped his hands against his paunch, behind the waistband of his apron. "Well, yes," he began, "I expected your father would collect all the money owing him before he borrowed. I owed him myself for Fanny's shoes and had to pay the money to Cutter. When he got hold of your father's accounts, he made everyone settle up that had any hard money; and those who didn't have any had to pay in goods and have it discounted at that."

I heard Mr. Allen speaking, but I was staring out the door planning my next action. Finally I broke out of those thoughts and asked, "We have need of a room for a while, Mr. Allen. Do you have one?"

"We will find a place for you certainly, oh yes," he replied and called to the next room, "Fanny, Fanny." When she appeared he asked, "Can you fit up one of the upper rooms for Thomas and his wife?"

"Why surely, Thomas," she said and smiled, "and you need your breakfast of course. I'll have Sally see to the room now. Oh, oh, your father's things. We brought them out for you." Fanny pointed to a chest placed against the wall.

"They did the listing of everything sooner than usual since you were gone," Allan explained. "Before the vendue they set aside some few things if it happened you ever came back and gave them to me to keep. This has been in the back room for all these years. When we heard that the *Dove* was lost, I had no idea what to do with it."

All of my life I had seen the familiar, valued, oak wood chest resting in the corner of Father and Mother's room. I remembered the brass lock, the scratches, and the bumped corners. Mr. Allen went to his tall desk and poked around in it for a minute or two. He finally found what he was looking for and returned with a small key, which he handed to me. I looked at it resting in the palm of my hand for a few seconds and then unlocked the chest. Mother's bonnets and dresses were on top. Beneath them were Father's Sunday clothes and his old, patched work shirts and trousers lying over the looking glass. Four dishes were on the bottom, each separated from the other by a doubled piece of flannel. Mother's pride. She had bought them from a peddler's wagon when charmed by the scenes on them of Chinese ladies standing in a neat garden. Each plate presented a different view. There were three bowls nested together next to them. Under the dishes and cradling them from any hard knocks were folds of new linen mother had bought but never had the chance to sew into shirts. To one side were knives, spoons, two candle sticks, and a lantern. Mother's little horn box of needles, pins, and buttons was on the Bible in one corner. I drew the Bible out and opened it to the back pages. There was the note of my birth in father's hand: "Born this day to Hannah and Thomas Samuel Wightman, a son Thomas Haley Wightman January 10, 1800." The last entry entered was: "Passed to her rest on this day Hannah Wightman, aged 42 years, 2 months, three days. September 28, 1817." Those lines put down there might be the best of all to compare to Father's alleged signature on the loan paper.

"Have you a quill and ink here close by?" I asked Fanny.

She stepped to the back of the room.

I rose to my feet, placed the Bible on the table, and sat on a chair. Fanny returned with the writing tools. With the quill in my hand, I spoke as I wrote: "Passed to his rest on …," but then I had to ask, "What was the day my father died?"

Fanny frowned, thinking for a minute.

Mr. Allen said, "Ah, the near the end of November. Yes, it was on the twenty-eighth or twenty- ninth. I remember it well … yes the twenty-eighth, a Saturday. Yes, we had no one come to the inn. It was a Saturday and a mighty cold one."

I completed the entry, reciting as I wrote: "Passed to his rest on November 28, 1818 Thomas Samuel Wightman." I calculated the numbers by touching fingers of my left hand to the table and added: "Aged 49 years, 3 months, 12 days."

I blew on the wet ink and asked Mr. Allen, "So they sold the beds, the table and chairs? And all of Father's tools, and his bench? This chest is the sum of the man's life? Everything else he had labored for was seized by these harpies?"

"A man from Westley named Swan gave the high bid," the innkeeper explained, "and after the vendue, money was allotted for the last hides your father bought, and to pay for his coffin and a marker. When Cutter got his money he bought the shop and everything from Swan. Then later we learned Cutter was married to Swan's daughter. We all thought that a mite too cozy."

I replaced all the items in the chest as I had found them and locked the lid. I held the key in my hand up before me and waved it back and forth. I would have the shop back if it took years, if it took every dollar I earned. I would have it back if I had to waylay Cutter some dark night.

Chapter Twenty-four

Sally helped her mother bring the cups and plates for our meal to the table. When I left the Port the girl had been about twelve, lathy, with hardly enough of a body to hold against a puff of wind. She was taller now; but still not grown out to a woman's form. Her blonde hair and pale skin gave her a slack-baked, unfinished look while standing next to *Heke* who, though small, had a browned and very capable appearance. Here in the Port the *moko* on her chin was considered far from genteel, suspect; but in Blind Bay it had its meaning.

Sally was taken a little aback when *Heke* ignored her fork and stuffed johnnycake and pieces of bacon into her mouth with her fingers. I frowned slightly. *Heke* paused eating, looked about the room, and picked up her fork.

Mrs. Allen called to me from the top of the stairs, "When you're finished eating, come up. I have the room ready for you."

The room was small, fitted in under the roof of the building and furnished with a simple bed, one chair, and a small table. A candle stick and a double-wicked oil lamp had been placed on the table. Fanny patted the bed and finding it not to her liking promised, "Sally and I will get some new straw for the tick."

There was a small window which faced south, down the length of the Point. I looked to the right and left to determine how much of the Port and the houses could be seen from the opening. The shoe shop was visible. At least the roof and one side wall of it were in sight. Ah, greed, I thought. Cutter's impudence galled me when I looked toward the shop. Damn! How can a man work such chicanery on another, steal from him, and yet face him? My hands gripped the sill and I imagined them around Cutter's throat.

Fanny seeing *Tiro* in *Heke's* arms quickly offered, "Oh, oh, dear me, the baby. Sally's crib. Yes. I'll get it now and you may use it while you are here."

Sally helped her mother bring the crib in and then take the bed tick out to refill it with new straw. They returned a few minutes later and rolled it out across the cords of the bed, poking and pushing to make it lie flat.

Father had arranged for his burial many years before; and remembering vaguely where it was, I led *Heke* along the road to the small cemetery.

At the entrance I said, "Here, my father lies here."

Heke halted. She looked about the ground, and then understanding what it was exclaimed, "No! No! We no go dera, Thoma Kina, arra *tapu*!"

"No, not *tapu* for us," I assured her, and then led her around while looking for Father's stone. On her island she would never have entered, moreover never touched the least thing near a burying ground. "No *tapu*. Here we all go," I said when we stood before the marker. With my wife and child beside me, I vowed to expose the trickery of Cutter and his crew in some way. I must learn what people thought, suspected, or knew of their dealings. There might be some overlooked detail that would help reveal his fraud and could be used against the man.

From the cemetery we walked along the roads toward the Sound and met with some old friends. *Heke* stepped forward on each introduction, and there was always a slight pause while they eyed and judged the tattoo on her chin. What they thought of her could not be divined through the amiable smiles and the words of welcome. It didn't matter a doit to me anyway.

Many sorts of seaman and travelers had sailed the oceans and debarked at the Long Point: West Indians, Africans, Java men, and Hindoos. None had been women, though, and that was the unusual thing at the moment.

Old friends recalled some events that had occurred while I was away, but no chance remark was made about Cutter taking the shop.

We reached the end of the Point, where many times on that finger of land I had imagined sailing to Jamaica, the Northwest Coast, and even farther on to China. My dream of returning with a small fortune had come to naught. What matter? Few men made great fortunes. For those who did it was never enough, and new ventures to gain even more wealth forever bedeviled their minds. Money seemed to raise a hunger in them; greed fed upon greed. After my trials I was alive, unhurt, and with wife and son. That was a fortune enough, so what else was needed?

We returned along the warehouses and piers. There was no great hubbub as in the New York port; yet along our way we heard the thump of a big maul, the squeal of tackle blocks, and the whinny of horses. Two drays rumbled along one dock. Halfway back to the inn we heard a loud tapping inside a small shed. I wondered if it was still old Elisha Beecher's place and led *Heke* to the open door. Mr. Beecher was there as he had always been on any day but Sunday. He was hammering a spreader inside the hull of a nearly finished boat still resting on its block and held upright by the molds braced to the joists above. Beecher wore his usual square cap of folded paper to keep the dust off his bald head.

The boat he was bending over was a very familiar one, about twenty-nine or thirty feet long and six feet in the beam. The identical shape of its bow and stern and its hull of thin cedar planking meant it was to ride on the cranes of a whale ship and be lowered for the chase. Beecher stood up and passed his calloused hand slowly along the gunwale. The stroking assured him the boat would shoot forward or aft at the pull or push of the oars and ride almost any wave. Beecher noticed us standing in the doorway when he turned about for a clamp. He tightened it in place, and then dusted his apron with sweeps of his hands.

"A good day to you, Mr. Beecher," I greeted him.

The old man peered through his glasses at me for a few seconds and then greeted me with, "Ah, Wightman. Good day to you. I heard you had come back. Sad to hear so many were lost."

"Well, I considered myself lost a few times; yet found my way here to the Port again. Brought my wife and son, too. This is *Heke* and *Tiro*."

Beecher took a step forward and said, "A good day to you Mrs. Wightman. Well, you have a fine looking child there, yes, and a fat little fellow, too."

"We thank you. I see you are still building whale boats. I've rowed some of them more miles than I care to recall."

"I have orders for four more. I don't believe I can finish them all in time. Everyone is going out after the whale. A lot of money to be made, I guess."

I looked about and asked, "You had an apprentice. Dodds, wasn't it? Isn't he a journeyman now?"

"Oh, yes, but he left after his time was up. Then I took on one more, but the fool ran off to Providence or Boston. I can't remember which. Just as well. He had not the feel for the work and wasn't a great help to me, so I decided not to pursue him."

"Will you take on another?"

Beecher held his apron aside and dug his fingers into the small pocket at his waistband. They came out holding a tortoise shell snuff box. With a tap on its lid and flick of his right thumb, he opened the box and offered its contents to me. I took a polite pinch. Beecher allowed himself more, placed on the back of his hand, and touched his nose to it.

He settled himself on a stack of lumber and groaned, "All these youngsters want is to do is sail, fish, or go to some city, Boston, New York. Five years is too long for them. The first year they're no more help to me than a sheep, a thick-headed one at that, and they eat like wolves when they live in. What I need is one good journeyman, like a partner, if I am to finish my orders when they're due. I can't hold both ends of a strake and clinch the nails by myself."

Around the walls of the shed were stacks of seasoned oak, cedar, and pine. Each wood had its place in building the boat and each one when freshly cut had its familiar, comforting scent. Together they filled the shed with a pleasant mix of odors. Patterns for the stem pieces and all the different frames hung on the wall. Near the door where the light was better, Beecher had his grindstone mounted over its water trough. Outside, just visible through the back door, were the long steam box and its kettle.

"Well, Mr. Beecher," I proposed, "I will need some employment since my father's shop has been taken from me. Landings on the sealing grounds were chancy and I spent many a day repairing these boats. Out there I had only a saw, a hatchet, sheets of lead, and a few nails. Would you accept me as an apprentice?"

Beecher thought a few seconds, then nodded and offered, "If you prove a good mechanic, yes. I'll even give you journeyman's wages."

"I think building boats would be more to my liking with not one whit of the danger of sealing and whaling."

"You have lodgings?" Beecher asked.

"At Mr. Allen's."

"Well, I have my apprentice's room. It will serve us both if you take it and live in. I never thought of having married help before, but as a journeyman the room can be part of your wage and it will cost you less than at Allen's."

"I say done to that. But first I must see a lawyer. Who would be best?"

"Ah, yes. You intend to bring suit, I expect? You will not find it easy. Cutter was said to have come by the shop honestly, but some of us here think that's not so. As for lawyers, I've had naught to do with any of them."

"Well, I cannot let that man keep my father's shop. I will have it back, I swear. I am going to Groton and will return in a day or two. For now, *Heke* will stay at Mr. Allen's."

I found some of father's signed orders at one of the tanners, carried them to Groton, and offered them to a lawyer there for his inspection. "Mr. Pitt," I began, "these are good samples of my father's hand. They are some of the last he signed. Note the dates."

Mr. Pitt cleaned his glasses with a handkerchief, reseated them, and made a few adjustments until he felt they were comfortable. Then he reached for the bills with his left hand and with his right hand lifted the top one from the others. I watched his eyes as they moved from the head to the foot of the page, searching every inch of its surface. When finished reading the front, he turned the paper over to scan the back. Each of the others received the same scrutiny. He leaned back in his chair and asked, "You assert that these are your father's signatures and that the note Mr. Cutter presented for his claim is a forgery?"

"Yes, I am quite certain of it."

"Have you ever seen the alleged forgery?"

"No, I have not. I have been gone near five years now."

The lawyer laid the bills at one side of his desk and turned back to me. His head tilted to one side in some doubt and he pointed out, "Well now, you are assuming that it is a forged name not having seen it."

"My father had no need to borrow. Half of his customers were always in his debt. He had their notes. It was not in his nature to owe other people. He had few wants … and for sure he was not over genteel in his living."

"Such would not preclude his borrowing. We know nothing of why he borrowed, but the paper presented and the witnesses who came forward have satisfied all that he did. I have heard the facts of the case, Mr. Wightman. I feel there is small chance you will succeed."

"How can you be sure when many people in the Port find it unbelievable?" I protested, pacing around as I spoke. "This Cutter is a stranger. He comes from Boston, or so he claims. He was in no trade or business when he arrived. They say had he not married the Swan woman in Westerly he would have been sleeping in a barn. She and her father are both in this fraud with Cutter and another man named Glines. When I was at sea and father died, Cutter saw his great chance. So I am left with a chest of clothes, a few dishes, and a Bible!" I was furious and pounded my fist on Pitt's desk with my last words, "Damn his rotten guts!"

"Do sit down, Mr. Wightman. You excite yourself."

I plunked down in the chair offered by the lawyer.

"Now let me lay out our problem," he resumed. "If we bring suit perhaps two or three others must admit they were much in error. No one likes to do that. What's done is done. Closed. Finished. An after clap is never welcome."

"What has that to do with justice?"

"Nothing. I merely point out the difficulties with the suit."

I snapped back, "My father was at his bench every day of his life. He earned every penny that was ever put into his purse by hard work, thus he would never buy into ships or any enterprise. He was not given to risk. He could afford no loss. I know this is arrant fraud. If I do not get my shop back by law, I know other ways. Yes, I will consider other ways."

Mr. Pitt slowly shook his head and a frown gathered over his brows. "I assure you violence will never settle this matter," he advised. "I will see what I can do."

"And what will I owe you for that?"

"To start with, five dollars."

I laid out the equivalent value in shillings and said, "Well, I may have to make a choice if the law fails me, between losing what is rightfully mine or dealing out some hard knocks. I believe you would do the same, though I expect you would never confess to it. So I will be on my way and await results."

I left the office, then turned for a moment, and looked back at the sign nailed to the wall at the right side of the door: "R. Pitt, lawyer." I wondered if that man could get the shop back for me. His look as I left was not the most hopeful one I'd seen.

Suddenly I considered a duel, but just as quickly discarded the idea. Cutter was not one to accept. No, that was not his way. Even if Cutter oddly enough accepted and I killed or wounded him, that would not put the shop back into my possession in a way that would stand good. I mulled other things I might do as I made my way toward the Groton-Mystick road.

Elisha Beecher trued a piece of wood with his plane and listened to me relate what the lawyer in Groton had advised. "Well, Thomas," Beecher said, "all such law things are slow. When there is property and much money to be decided upon, they get much slower. I believe, like you, Cutter has worked a great fraud here. It takes a man of some meanness to do that. Why, he's no more than a pirate, only he used the law in place of a gun and dirk to do his thieving. Some of us suspected him, but what's that to lawyers and judges? Proof they ask, where's your proof?"

"I'll have to study it. Somewhere there's a weak place in him like in a chain cable, a worn swivel or a pin that is loose. You know what I mean?"

"Aye, not a man alive with no fault somewhere," Beecher replied, then asked, "Are you and your wife ready to move to the house? The room is fit up for you."

"We will bring our things in the morning. Then I will be ready to work."

"Good, I want to finish this boat before the end of the month. The blacksmith is making the iron for the next two now."

At sunrise *Heke* and I arrived at Beecher's house, pushing a hand cart borrowed from the inn. On it were our only possessions: our bedding, clothes, and father's chest. Beecher's wife, white-haired and buxom, came to the door and greeted us. Her pink, chubby face bore a kindly look for *Tiro*; and she flowed with words, cooed in hopes of enticing a smile from the child. Failing in that she said, "It will be so nice to have you and your family here. Oh, with a child moving about in the house and making noises, it is so much brighter and happier. It has been years since our girls were babies and now they are gone and have little ones of their own. They don't visit us often enough. Ah! I am so foolish. Here I am talking and talking away and you want to see your room. Well, such foolishness comes with age, I expect. Come this way."

She turned about and led us to the apprentice's room containing a bed that looked to be a new one from the fresh plane marks on the wood. Mrs. Beecher pointed to it and explained, "Elisha widened the old one and strung it with new cords for you and your wife. Will it serve, Thomas?"

"Yes, Mrs. Beecher, quite well."

In the remainder of the day at the shop, Elisha and I put the pine ceiling in the bottom of the boat; the decking aft, and mounted the loggerhead. Once we had the thwarts and a few other blocks in, it was ready for paint.

Chapter Twenty-five

Each morning we were in the shed at sunrise to start our work and listen to the cocks in the nearby yards calling out their bravado to the world.

Each evening we could see the results of our labor. The eye traced the strakes of the nearly finished boat as they flowed smoothly from the canoe-like stem out to the widest point of the beam and back in to the same shape at the stern. There was a delicacy in its light frames, yet the boat would be stout enough to carry six men and all their gear while pounding through the swells at the end of a taut whale line. There was grace in the length and sheer of its hull and integrity in its breadth which fit it for the sea as much as a gull's wing was fit for the wind. Any other boat was a lump of wood. By the end of the next month we had completed the second boat, delivered it, and had a third well in hand.

I was closing the shed one evening when Beecher asked me, "Did all of the whalers at your station have Indian wives?"

"Every one. There are no others to choose from. Protection from raids is needed there and it's got by taking women from among the tribes. Fishing from their land on the coast makes it necessary. Someone of us had to be related to a nob for protection."

"When Phoebe goes out to visit, she hears some women have named your wife 'the wild Indian.' Others call her 'that savage with the ink marks on her chin.' So it goes."

"Well, what might they say if they learned two pound nine shillings worth of trade goods were given for her? Well, I don't give a damn for any of their names or opinions. They know nothing of how things are done on that island. It's two oceans away, far beyond their ideas of the world. She is very much my wife; *Tiro* is my son and they remain so. And we will remain here no matter what names the gossips invent."

We walked back to the house and after supper turned our chairs toward the fireplace and watched the last dying embers. It was growing dark. Elisha rose and held the end of a twig in the coals until it popped into a flame and with it lighted the lamp.

Mrs. Beecher came in with a pair of trousers on her arm and spread them on the table beside the lamp. The small box she had in her other hand showed her intent to spend the evening sewing patches on them.

Heke entered a few minutes later and drew a chair up next to mine. She put the palm of her right hand to the side of her face and whispered, "He sreepy."

Mrs. Beecher had questioning look and I explained, "She means he's asleep."

"Oh, dear me," she replied, "I must learn what she means so I can speak with her."

I turned to Elisha and said, "I will have to leave work one day this week and go to Groton. I have heard nothing from Mr. Pitt. Something should have happened."

"He will be asking for more money when you see him," Beecher cautioned. "I do believe they all wait for a good time before they do anything."

"I will see him and wait for a month more, but no longer. If there is no action I will find some other means to get my property back."

"Oh, Thomas," Mrs. Beecher said. She rose from her seat at the end of the table and stepped over to my chair. She held her work in one hand and a threaded needle poised in the other. "Mrs. Pound has told me something strange about Mr. Cutter."

I turned to her with my chin raised in question.

"You know Mrs. Pound? She lives there on an angle across from the shop on the east side."

"Yes, I see her about the Port."

"There have been times when she has seen Mr. Cutter leave the shop at night. Well now, it's not that she keeps a watch on people, you know."

Elisha sputtered his lips. I turned to him just as his eyes rolled upward.

"Now, Elisha, don't you make that noise," Mrs. Beecher chided. "She's a very nice woman. She has the good of us all at heart."

Elisha held one hand in front of his eyes and peeked at me through the gap between the first and second fingers. Then with his lips pressed together he chuckled to noiselessly himself.

I turned back to Mrs. Beecher to hear what more she had to report.

"Mrs. Pound said however dark it is, he never carries a lantern. It's the most odd thing. Well, you might stumble or step into anything at night, mud or droppings. He can't be out looking for an animal. Even if just wandering about, he would need a lantern, surely."

"Does he have any animals?" I asked.

"Oh, none at all. No chickens or geese. The sty behind the house has been empty since he moved in. He keeps no garden and has no dog. I tell you this because it is all so strange … and of course …" Her words trailed off and she leaned her head to one side, a hint that she, like some others, questioned Cutter's right to have the shop.

With my interest sparked, I agreed, "Yes, Mrs. Beecher, it is most peculiar."

Yes, a peculiar thing indeed. What was Cutter doing? What would send him out at night? Had he a cache some place where he kept his money … a mass of sovereigns and silver he did not want Glines or his wife to learn about? Perhaps there was some scheme he was setting afoot to cheat even them. They were all thieves and what thief trusted another thief? Thieving in them flowed with the very blood in their veins. The craving to get something of great value with little or no effort possessed them far more than any religious zeal. I looked up and said, "Well, Mrs. Beecher, I find it most curious too. If Mrs. Pound has the good of us all at heart, it would be well for her take note of what passes around her house and perhaps discover what Mr. Cutter is up to at night."

"Oh, indeed I will. I will talk about it with Mrs. Pound," she promised and went back to her chair to continue her mending.

That little item might prove useful to me. Something suspicious was in it. I must find out what times Cutter goes out and in what direction he goes. Then, how long does he stay out? How often? Was it once a week? Would Cutter go out at night more than that if it was simply to hide money? Where would he get sums so large and so often that he must keep them from the others? Could he have found some specie taken from a prize and concealed during the war … a great treasure? Did he go somewhere to gamble? Yes. Yes, that might draw him out and he would not want his wife to know of it.

"Mrs. Beecher," I said, "when you see Mrs. Pound again, ask how often she has seen Cutter leave at night. I am curious about this, but never mention that anyone asked you."

She looked up from her stitching and replied, "Oh, yes, I will ask but say nothing of you."

The next evening before we sat down to eat, Mrs. Beecher reported to me, "I called by Mrs. Pound today. She says it's almost every other Saturday Mr. Cutter goes out at night. Mrs. Pound is sure of it. Mrs. Cutter goes on Saturdays to visit her mother over toward Westerly and stays over to take her to church Sunday."

Ah, for sure. For certain it is some secret he wishes to keep from his wife and Glines. It could be a wedge, some discontent I might use to set one against the other. If they fell out … oh, yes, if they all fell out. Ha!

"Does Mrs. Pound visit much with Mrs. Cutter?" I asked. "I mean, do they speak more than their 'good-day-to-you' greetings?"

"Oh, yes, they visit. When Mr. Pound is out fishing as he is now, they visit every day."

"Ummp, and has she revealed Mr. Cutter's wandering at night to Mrs. Cutter?"

"I believe not. Mrs. Pound is still unsure of what it means."

My next move began to form in my mind.

After the evening meal the next Saturday, I went outside and watched the last twilight in the sky fade away. Candles and lamps, at first only weak points of light, became more noticeable at windows at full darkness. When it was obscure enough to suit me, I stepped back into the house. "I'm going for a walk," I announced and left. I made my way up towards the shoe shop along the road that was empty except for a wandering sow with piglets and one man on a horse who trotted past into the darkness before I had gone twenty yards. A dog behind one house gave a few cursory barks, and with a resigned growl settled into silence again. The only light in town not from a window was the one hanging in front of the tavern, and it gave only enough illumination to reveal the entrance to customers and make the sign readable at twenty yards. It was farther up and gave no useable light for me. I arrived across the road from the shoe shop, and stepped around one corner of a shed on the side road opposite Mrs. Pound's house. There was a good view of the front of the shop, and if someone approached along the road I could step back out of sight. For an hour I waited, ready to follow if Cutter appeared and took his nightly stroll. The curtains drawn across the shop window were lighted by a lamp inside. Nothing moved around the building. Frogs croaked near me. A cow lowed in the distance. I waved my hands at mosquitoes humming about my head without discomforting them the least. I gave my watch on the shop another few minutes and then left.

When I returned to the Beecher house, I found everyone had gone to bed. The fire had been banked and the lamp on the table was still burning, but with a small flame.

At breakfast the next morning neither Elisha nor his wife mentioned my night excursion. They dressed for church and left me and *Heke* sitting at the table. After I declined their first invitation to attend church with them, the Beechers never mentioned it again. I suspected there were others in the Port who shook their heads and spoke of me as one enticed by the "island woman" to abandon Christianity. Well, let them believe I will be damned in hell. I would spend any of my Sundays as I pleased: work, fish, even go to a cockfight.

It was a puzzle that Cutter did not go out the night before, but then Mrs. Pound had said he went out every other week. Then the next Saturday night should be the one on which he would slip from the shop. I would try again, and if the man appeared I would find where he went and for what purpose.

Once it became dark the following Saturday evening, I slipped along the road to my lookout behind the corner of the shed. I stood there peering at the shop and noted that there was no light behind the drawn curtains as before. If one burned in either of the two back rooms, I could not see it from where I stood.

Most of an hour passed. My vigil that far had been tiring, fruitless; and the pestering mosquitoes around my head again made it miserable. The bolder stars and a little moonlight bore through a thin mist overhead. By that dim light I searched the road north to south; and as far as I could see, everyone was keeping to their houses. No one was abroad. I debated if I should continue the watch or return home. Perhaps Mrs. Pound was in error and it was every third or even forth Saturday night on which Cutter made his foray into the dark. Then I caught the movement of a dark shape edging along the side wall of the shop. It stopped for a few seconds where the wall met the fence. It might have been an animal, but it proved to be a man when he threw a leg up and stepped over the fence. A figure moving so furtively had to be Cutter. He went north and then at the next corner turned east. I followed, keeping close to the fences. Cutter stopped only once in his walk. At that instant I quickly sank into the weeds at the edge of the road. I hoped I had not been seen. The shadowy form ahead continued on to the higher ground until it neared the single, one room house which overlooked the marsh.

Old Tabby Jane had lived there for years and still did. In the first years after her husband had drowned at sea, no widowers came calling, which was not surprising since she squinted like a bag of nails and the moustache on her upper lip was growing ever more noticeable. As a boy I had been inside the little house several times when sent for some of Tabby's butter and eggs. She managed to keep off any meager charity by selling the product of her cows and chickens. Another source of trade which yielded a few pennies, and even shillings some claimed, was one in teas and charms made from herbs, leaves, roots, and evil-looking dried mushrooms. Baskets of the ingredients were lined along one wall of the single room. Tabby wandered the cleared fields and woods, gathering them on nights of a full moon and vowed to her customers that its beams made the items more powerful, whether they were intended to entice a lover or to remove a wart. When I grew older, some of the young bucks of the Port told me of an item very useful for a man that could be purchased from her.

Cutter passed under a tree at the edge of the road and went up to the door of the house. He was apparently rapping lightly on it, but being too far away, I didn't hear a sound. A few seconds later the light behind the thin curtains of the small front window was snuffed. Slowly the door opened, admitted Cutter, and closed after him.

What business could Cutter have with the old cundum peddler? Was he buying a cure for some ailment or something to give him luck at cards and dice?

I hurried the last thirty yards up the road, turned off, and dropped to crouch behind the tree trunk. Bit by bit I advanced through the weeds on my hands and knees until I was near the wall and under the side window. It was open a few inches to admit the cooler night air. The floor creaked as those inside stepped around in the ramshackle house. Muffled stirrings emanated from the chicken coop in the backyard and then ceased after a few sleepy clucks and caws. A man's voice whispered some unintelligible sentence inside the house. They were answered by a woman's voice, but it was not Tabby's raspy words I heard. They were high-pitched, girlish.

I leaned my head back and shook with soundless laughter. How could I have been so dull-witted? Why had I fixed on gambling or a cache of gold and silver as the reason for his strolls at night? Aye, I should have guessed the reason long before. Cutter's wife was not one to excite a passion, at least not of that kind. One look at that horse face of hers would put off the lustiest of men. Saturday evening was Cutter's time to slip away and dock with a good-natured wench. Ha! Yes. On the Saturday nights when Cutter's miss arrived, Tabby Jane let her house for their trysts and added another coin or two to her purse. Cutter was being most wary, knowing Mrs. Pound might spy his lover if she came to the shop. I leaned my head back to rest against the boards of the wall. The couple talked a bit at a time in constrained voices. I caught two or three of Cutter's words; but the woman's were too faint, too sibilant, to make out any meaning. More creaking of the floor and then the sound of rustling clothes came through the window. The wall of the small house began to creak slightly in time with their groans. In a few minutes I heard their urgent whisperings rising to their climax. I crawled away, got to my feet, and walked out to the road. Better to leave while Cutter was so well distracted. I had heard enough. Yes, I had found what I needed. HA!

On the road back I imagined how Cutter's wife would be bursting with wrath when she learned how her husband amused himself while she was away. She would stand like a Turk with fire in her eyes, deciding on the fate of her spouse. I expected she would have a burning want for revenge when she heard of Jabez's dalliance. How might I use it? Could I in some manner insinuate to her that the one thing which would injure Cutter most was revealing the fraud of the signature set to the paper and the false words of the witnesses? Jabez Cutter would be undone if she revealed it. What many people in the Port suspected would be proved by a half dozen of her words. Could I fix that idea in her mind? Yes. Yes. That was the split to receive the wedge.

I found Mrs. Beecher in the backyard the next morning just after she had returned from church. She was feeding her chickens, advising them with smiles and soft words to eat heartily, grow, and lay many eggs.

"Mrs. Beecher, can you call on Mrs. Pound this week?" I asked. "She must tell

Cutter's wife about what she has seen and that she may learn something about Jabez the Saturday night after next if she does not go to her mother's but returns and stays at her house across the road. When it is dark she can watch and follow him to Tabby Jane's above the marsh. But she must not be seen and must listen at Tabby's window. Say it comes from someone who knows Jabez wagers much."

She looked up at me, her smile fading to puzzlement, and asked, "Oh dear me, Tabby Jane's? … Tabby Jane's? … What is this all about? This is such a mystery."

"I do not care to say just now, but it may mean I will get the shop back. And here …" I held out a square of paper folded tightly several times and sealed with a rosette of red wax. "Mrs. Pound is to give this to Mrs. Cutter but only after … only after she returns from Tabby's house. Do not say where it came from."

Mrs. Beecher looked at it and with an uncertain move opened her hand to receive it. She murmured, "Oh dear! Oh dear me! … well, if it means you will have your property back …"

"Mrs. Pound should also tell Mrs. Cutter that it is good advice from someone who cannot give a name."

"Oh, bless me. It is all such a mystery."

I left her to her chickens, unsure if she would carry it off as I had planned it. Would Mrs. Cutter act to betray her husband when she read what was written on that bit of paper? Damn, but it was such a chancy way to do it. Shame and ire should prompt the result I wanted from her, enough to spark retaliation. From my one meeting with her she appeared capable of it. If she listened at the window as I had done, then the words on the paper would be evidence that someone else in the Boro knew of Jabez's hot business in the little house. It was worth a try, though it might not carry out as I hoped. It would be better to crack Cutter's skull with a club than do this shifty business, but that would not put the shop back into my hands. Threatening him with a *poo* or anything else would not work, as Mr. Pitt had cautioned. No, this was the only choice for now. If it did not succeed I must wait for what might result through the law, however long that might take … or devise something else.

I stepped out of Beecher's shed the Saturday I expected Cutter was to meet his woman. The wind, blowing fresh since noon, had kept me thinking of what might happen up at Tabby Jane's little house that night. Through the day clouds boiled up into great masses, their gray undersides growing ever darker over the land and the Sound. Thunder muttered alternately from one direction, then another; trees and cleared fields were in sunlight, then minutes later deeply shadowed. The hot air was soft to the skin, muggy, expectant. To the north a kinked, white filament suddenly snapped twice for the briefest part of a second between a black cloud bottom and the trees. Its bright image persisted in the eyes for an instant. A second later a sharp crack of thunder echoed around the harbor. Leaves torn from trees were swept upward in gusts and tumbled in the air. At near sunset we finished for the day, closed the door of the shop, and watched orange twilight glow within the booming, swelling stacks of clouds. They had risen to their limits, sending their tops all shelving off in the same direction. The tints faded away, leaving the remaining pale grays sharp against the darkening sky.

Cutter might have his tryst, meet his woman; and hopefully his wife will be there to listen at the open window. How she will respond could not be predicted, and it may not result in the fraud being confessed to people of the Port. The plan was made, and with luck would be carried out. There will be a wait until tomorrow or the next day or longer for a result, if there were to be any.

Chapter Twenty-six

The church bells were still an hour from being rung in the morning, and I was still abed when there was the sound of the front door opening and closing and hushed but insistent voices at the front of the house. I slipped from the covers, stepped to the door, and eased it open a mite. Through the narrow slot I could see Mrs. Beecher dressed in her Sunday frock and bonnet listening to Mrs. Pound spill out rapid words.

"I could not believe what she told me!" Mrs. Pound gushed. "Oh, naked they were! She saw them by a flash of lightning. As naked as Adam and Eve! Thrashing about on the bed! Can you imagine? I could not see how she could bear to tell me such a thing of her husband. But she was furious. Oh, the look in her eyes!"

"Did you give her the note?" Mrs. Beecher asked.

"Yes, and she read it and swore such words I have never heard a women use. I feared the neighbors would hear such a screaming."

"What did the note say? Did you read it? I must know."

"Oh, yes, it said, 'What single thing might you do to injure him most?' That was puzzling to me until she said she would injure Jabez by telling all, how he made the false note for a loan to Mr. Wightman and got the shop."

"Ah, then it is true, they have swindled young Wightman. You have told others?"

"Yes," Mrs. Pound said. "People are all at the church or the inn and are talking about it. Mrs. Cutter left last night. Alone in the middle of the night with all her things on a cart!"

"And Mr. Cutter?"

"No one has seen him. Some men have guessed he has fled to Providence."

I let out a long breath. So, it had worked. Against many odds it had worked. Cutter's wife had gone up to Tabby Jane's and had heard and even seen her husband with the other woman. My message had reached her at just the right moment and directed her fury. When Jabez found out, he had no other choice but to cut cable and run. It could have gone awry … ahh … but it did not. It would have been more satisfying to chase the swine off with my old sealing club, beating his head and back bloody all the way. *Utu* of the best kind! Cutter was brought down by his own deeds. All it took was a little nudging. Patience had brought justice, and the shop was mine without question.

I went back to our room and awakened *Heke*. We dressed, picked up *Tiro*, and went to the front of the house.

Elisha and his wife were there, standing about with several of the neighbors.

"Well, Thomas," Elisha asked, "do you want to hear some fine news? You will have your shop back. Mrs. Cutter has confessed the fraud. Jabez is gone. Some think he's on his way to Providence."

I nodded and said, "Good."

"What a to-do, oh, what a stir I have caused," Mrs. Beecher whined.

"Oh, hang it all, Phoebe," Elisha scolded, "you just delivered a message to the woman. That's not wrong. See what they did to Thomas; that was wrongdoing. You just helped set it aright. Think on that awhile."

Mrs. Beecher went toward the door muttering, "Dear me, oh dear me."

Elisha watched her, and shaking his head and snickering, said, "What a woman. It's a damn wonder she can kill a goose for supper. Well, Thomas, will you be going back to your shoe business?"

"I'm thinking about it. I like the boat building, though. Perhaps I might work the shoe trade in the cold months and build boats in the summer."

"There's plenty of work. Many more ships fitting out along the coast from Boston to New York, and they'll all need maybe five, maybe six boats apiece. Think on it. That's fifty-five dollars for every boat we finish."

"You know Cutter has left?" I asked *Heke*.

She looked puzzled as if she wasn't wholly sure of all that had been said.

"Cutter's gone," I explained, waving a hand off to the east. "Ran away. I get my shop now."

"Betta you keer him. Den he no cuma back."

I shifted *Tiro* to my left arm and slipped my right arm around *Heke*. I hugged her, kissed her cheek, and laughed, "He no coma back. No, he will never show himself within three hundred miles of this place."

That afternoon I opened the door of the shop and led *Heke* in. The stock of shoes was still on the table. The pincers, knives, hammers, and markers lay on the bench. I opened the small drawers in it and absently looked at the hobnails and tacks they contained. Blacking, sealing wax, bees wax, spools of thread were there, but not in the places father had kept them.

Cutter had been in such a panic he had not taken a thing. In one of the back rooms his clothes still hung from the pegs, but Mrs. Cutter had taken all of her possessions when she left in the early hours of the morning.

Though that pair was now gone and I had the shop, I still felt a loss; slighted, insulted, and even injured by those who accepted Cutter's word and the paper without question. I had been robbed. And where was their loyalty? The man was a stranger to the town, a stranger! If it were not for his wenching he would still be there in my shop smugly selling shoes.

Well, it was now mine firm and good. *Heke* and I would live there and raise *Tiro* and the other children yet to come.

In the backyard nothing had been planted, and it was overgrown nearly as high as the fence. The manure-charged ground in the sty had nurtured a mass of rank weeds. I could not abide the mess, and it would be my first chore to clear it. Though I would be taking produce, flesh, and fish for many of my boots and leather work, I liked to see the yield of the garden and animals. Later when there were more children they would help their mother weed the crops and pick the peas and beans. As a small child I had wandered that garden learning the nature each flower, spear of grass, and bug. It was a place of discovery, all in bright sunlight, where I had ventured along the fences and between the rows of tall corn stalks. In that time the world was far larger and limned in brighter colors.

Autumn began in earnest with the change in the trees; and such leaves that did not fall by their weight were wind-whipped from their supporting twigs. Flutters of them sailed across the Long Point as they had the day I left for the seal fishery. A sudden cold night wilted the vines and stalks out in the planting grounds and gardens. In the morning there were needles of frost on those limp and blackened remains. Breath steamed in the chill air. Winter had sent its first omens.

Heke and I sat in the shop for the warmth of the fireplace before bedtime. *Tiro,* filled with the pleasure of existence, toddled about; and wherever his whims took him he found some novel thing every minute or two. The boy's fingers explored crannies. Objects had to be felt to learn their textures and picked up and dropped to discover their heft. Bit by bit the world was being revealed to him. The frame of the man he was to become was forming within him.

I stared at the flames in the fireplace and they spread to the right and left, becoming the inferno rising to consume Monk's house. Out of them came the faces of Bryan and *Kotuku* … ah, the old lag and his kind lady. Those of Monk, Knobby, Peck, and *Ruru* arrived one after the other with a cluster of their wives and children. Then it was Scratch's and Scarhead's tattooed faces, and after them the great flukes of the whale rising over my head as I sat at my bow oar. The flukes faded and *Heke* appeared in lamplight, in that faraway *whare,* offering me the plate of food.

Now she watched the flames with me.

Glossary

Atua: A spirit, a god.

Ballocks: Testicles.

Bayside: The penal colonies in Australia. To be sent Bayside was to be transported to one of them.

Beam reach: Sailing with the wind at a right angle to the keel.

Bight: A loop in a line. A bend in a coast forming a large open bay.

Bilge: The middle portion of a cask at its largest diameter. The bottom of a boat or ship where water collects, and the water itself.

Black oil: Not oil of the color black, but oil rendered from whales other than sperm.

Boards: The distances sailed on each tack.

Boglander: An Irishman.

Bower: A large anchor kept at the bow of the ship.

Bragg: An old card game.

Brig: A vessel with two masts square-rigged.

Brister's: Bristrow's Island, now named the Auckland Islands.

Bumfiddle: The backside.

Buz-bloke: A pickpocket.

Cable length: A measurement of 100 to 120 fathoms.

Canaries: Convicts, jailbirds.

Cape South Island: South Cape Island, or Stewart Island, The last major island of the New Zealand group.

Carlings: Beams running lengthwise in a ship.

Ceiling: The inside planking or decking of a boat or vessel.

Channels: Planks set edgewise at a ship's side which spread the shrouds.

Chatter broth: Tea.

Chimes: The ends of the staves of a cask that extend beyond the heads.

Chips: The traditional name for a carpenter aboard ships.

Clanker: A great lie in convict cant.

Cloven hoof: To see the cloven hoof in any business is to detect something bad in it. An allusion to the devil.

Cock-a-hoop: To be in very high spirits.

Corn: To corn meat is to salt it. To be corned is to be very drunk.

Cove: A man, a fellow, or a rogue.

Crane: A support under whaleboats when they are raised on their davits.

Craw thumpers: Roman Catholics.

Cresset: An iron basket to hold burning fuel for heat or light.

Crutch: A forked holder for the harpoons at the starboard bow of the whaleboat.

Cubby: A snug place.

Cuddy: The short section of decking at the aft end of a whale boat, also a small room or cupboard.

Cum grano salis: Latin, with a grain of salt.

Cun or con: To direct the helmsman how to steer.

Cundum: A condom.

Dance on air: To hang from the gallows.

Daylights: The eyes, in convict cant.

Deals: Lengths of lumber sawn to two or three inch thickness and in various widths.

Deal table: A table made from planks.

Dippers: Anabaptists.

Dipsea lead: The deep sea lead for sounding, usually to a depth of one hundred fathoms.

Dog's soup: Rain in convict cant.

Doit: A small Dutch coin.

Doxy, Doxies: She beggars, whores, and wenches.

Doxy: A doctrine or creed, esp. in religion.

Dray: A heavy freight wagon.

Drugg: A drogue attached to the whale line.

Ducks: See white ducks.

Duff: A boiled pudding of flour, sometimes mixed with dried fruit.

Dumb leg: A lame leg.

Dump: A small coin punched out of a larger one and used to make change.

Dust: Black powder for guns in whaler's argot.

Fid: A tapered piece of hardwood used to open the strands of a cable.

File: A pickpocket in convict cant.

Flag: A kind of bulrush, the *raupo*.

Flax: The New Zealand flax lily, *Phormium tenax*.

Flux: A looseness of the bowels.

Frame breakers: The Luddites in Britain who smashed labor-saving machinery.

First rate: The largest class of warship in the sailing era.

Fulham: A loaded die.

Full and by: Close hauled. Sailing as close to the eye of the wind as the ship will lie, hence pushing limits.

Gally: To frighten. A whale which hears or sees a whale boat approaching and flees is said to be gallied.

Gammy: Said of a lame limb.

Gill: A liquid measure of one quarter pint.

Girt line: A line rove through a single block for hoisting light loads.

Glass: Spyglass.

Gleet: Gonorrhea.

Glimms: Eyes.

Goashore: A legged iron kettle used by sealers for cooking when ashore.

Grumbling time: Time of the year when food was scarce.

Grunter: A pig in whalers' argot.

Gut: As used in this instance, a very narrow passage for a vessel.

Haere mai: A welcoming phrase.

Half seas over: Almost drunk.

Hang an arse: To hold back in timidity or fear.

Hawse: The anchoring cable. To freshen the hawse is to let out a little cable to spread the wear along the mooring line.

Heifer: A woman in the whalers' argot.

Hempseed: A candidate for the gallows. One expected to come to no good.

Horse: The footrope mounted below the spars of square-rigged vessels.

Hulks: Old warships moored in the Thames River and used to house prisoners before they were transported to Australia.

Humbox: The pulpit of a church in convict cant.

Hundred: To receive a hundred is to be flogged with a hundred lashes.

Idlers: Those of the crew not standing a watch such as the cook, carpenter, sail maker, and steward.

Ika: A fish.

Ironbound: A rocky, turbulent coast where landing in a boat is dangerous or impossible.

Irons: The harpoons, spades, and killing lances of the whaling trade.

Joiner: A long wood plane.

Kainga: A village.

Kai: As a noun, food. As a verb, to eat.

Kake: A sea lion.

Kid: A small coopered tub.

Killick: A small anchor for a boat.

Kino: Bad.

Korero: Talk, discussion.

Kumera: A variety of potato.

Kuri: A dog.

Lag: A convict. From 'to be lagged,' to be transported as a criminal.

Lance: The killing lance. It is made like a longer harpoon and with a sharp, leaf-shaped head.

Laudanum: A preparation of opium.

Lay: A share in the profits of a whaling or a sealing cruise. A long lay is a very small share. A short lay is larger share.

League: A distance of about three nautical miles.

Live irons: The harpoons resting in the crutch on the boat, bent to the whale line, and ready to be "darted" (i. e. thrown).

Live on the cross: Support one's self by dishonest means.

Lobcock: A country clown, a clumsy fellow. A shiftless man. Also a flaccid penis.

Lobsters: British soldiers, so called because of their red coats.

Loggerhead: A short, thick post at the stern of a whaleboat around which the whale line is looped for control.

Lying rough: Sleeping on deck or out in the open.

Macquarie: An island about 800 miles south of New Zealand.

Mana: Prestige, authority, sway, sanctity, good fortune.

Marline: A small, two-stranded spun yarn to make seizings on the rigging of a ship.

Mataku: Power to bewitch, black magic, evil eye.

Matua wahine: A mother.

Mihinare: The Maori version of the word 'missionary'. To become *mihinare* is to become a Christian or to favor them.

Muka: Prepared flax fiber.

My arse on a bandbox: A phrase meaning what is offered will not suffice any more than a bandbox will make a secure seat.

Newgate: An old prison in London.

New Holland: An old name for Australia.

Nob: Someone of importance, originally a member of the nobility.

Nogging: Brick or wattle and daub fill between the timber frames of a building.

Notch: An indentation in the short decking at the bow of a whale boat where the steersman places his leg for stability when throwing the harpoon.

Nui: Large, much, many, broad.

One: Sand. Pronounced *o-neh*.

Orlop: The lowest deck in a ship.

Overhaul: To inspect, survey. To overhaul a block is to pull line through it to gain slack.

Pah: A defensible structure usually built on a high or inaccessible place.

Painter: The short rope permanently fixed to the bow of a boat. To slip the painter is to leave quickly. To cut someone's painter is to send them packing.

Parankiti: The Maori version of the word blanket.

Patu: As a noun, a club; as a verb, to kill.

Piggin: A small coopered bucket with one extended stave for a handle.

Pipe: An old term for the penis.

Poo: A Maori name for a musket.

Pox: The great pox or syphilis.

Pratique: Clearance given to an incoming ship by the health authority of a port.

Presbyters: Presbyterians.

Protection: A sailor's papers, identification.

Pukapuka: A book.

Quavers: Those of Quaker faith.

Quim: Sex in general. The vagina.

Rangatira: A chief of a clan and by extension his relatives. The upper class.

Raupo: The bulrush or flag.

Reach: A narrow arm of the sea extending into the land.

Reals: Spanish coins.

Red shirt: A man's back bloodied by much flogging.

Redemptioner: One who puts himself in debt for passage on a ship and must work it off as a bound laborer or servant.

Riders: The top rows of small oil casks in the hold a whale ship.

Rockweed: Seaweed, kelp.

Roger: The penis.

Round shot: The solid cannon ball, as opposed to grape, chain, or bar shot.

Saint Crispin: The patron saint of shoemakers.

Saleratus: A leavening powder.

Sea Ears: Haliotis shellfish. Abalone.

Serving mallet: A tool for wrapping (serving) rigging with small cord to make it sturdier and when tarred, more weatherproof.

Shakes: See shook.

Sheers: An A-frame of tall poles used to lift heavy weights.

Shingle: Deposits of pebbles in streams and on beaches.

Shook: A complete set of pieces to make up a barrel. Barrels carried on board a ship were disassembled to save space.

Shooting sticks: Muskets in whalers' argot.

Simples: Medicinal plants and the medicines made from them.

Single peeper: A person who has lost one eye.

Six Pounder: A small cannon firing a six pound ball.

Slide boards: Guides on the sides of ships for the whale boat when it is being raised or lowered by the davits.

Slops: Ships' small stores and clothes sold to sailors.

Smoking tongs: A light pair of tongs for lifting a hot coal from a fire to light a pipe.

Soundings: A vessel is on soundings when it approaches near enough to land to reach the bottom with the deep sea lead.

Southern Ocean: The part of the Pacific Ocean that reaches to the Antarctic. Named on some old maps as *Mer Du Sud, Mare Del Sud*.

Spade: A long-handled spade-like tool to cut blubber from a whale. A boat spade is a shorter one.

Spermaceti: The light wax taken from the head of the sperm whale and used to make superior candles.

Sperm oil: The oil rendered from sperm whale blubber, more valuable than that from other whales.

Spoke, or to speak: When vessels meet at sea they "speak" and exchange information, check positions, visit, etc.

Spreader: A blanket in whalers' argot.

Squeaker: A baby in whalers' argot.

Staves: See shook.

Steamers: Smoking pipes in whalers' argot.

Steerage: Part of the hold just forward of the captain's cabin.

Steersman: The steersman, also called the harpooneer, pulled an oar at the bow of the whaleboat and stood up to "dart" the harpoon at the whale. When it was time to lance a weakened whale, he exchanged places with the headsman aft. The steersman then at the steering oar was directed by the headsman where to place the boat so that he might be at the proper place to kill the whale with the lance.

Stone: A measure of weight, about 14 pounds.

Stones: A man's testicles.

Strakes: Planks that form the sides of a ship or boat.

Stunsail: Fully, a studingsail. A sail set on a boom extended beyond the end of a yard.

Tack: Hard tack, hard bread as distinguished from soft tack or soft bread. To tack a vessel is to sail it on alternate courses to windward.

Tafferal: The rail around a ship's stern.

Taihoa: In good time, later on.

Tangi: Mourning or lamenting accompanied with much self-laceration and crying.

Taniwha: An evil spirit, monster.

Tapu: A restriction setting off some person, place, or a thing from use, trespass, touch, etc. A prohibition.

Tar: A sailor.

Tarpaulin: A waterproofed material. A sailor's hat sewn of canvas and painted several times to make it stiff. Also another name for a sailor.

Taua: A war party.

Taunt: Tall, said of masts and sails.

Tika: Correct, proper, right.

T'galant: The sail set above the topsail. Fully spelled, the topgalant.

T"galant royal: The sail set above the t'galant sail.

Thief: A slim, cylindrical container lowered into a barrel through the bung to sample its contents.

Three side: See two side.

Thrummy: Fuzzy or fringed.

Ticket: Fully: a ticket of leave. A parole given transported prisoners in New South Wales and Van Diemen's Land after serving a portion of their sentences.

Tip us your daddle: In convict cant, "Give me your hand to shake."

Toa: A successful and experienced warrior.

Touchwood: Decayed wood used as tinder.

Toetoe: Thatch, building material for houses.

Tohunga: A seer, priestly expert. Craftsman.

Tovy Poenamoo: The Middle of island New Zealand. Sometimes spelled *Te Wai Pounamu* or in various other spellings.

Train: A fuse or line of powder to set off a charge.

The Triangle: The constellation *Triangulum Australe.*

Tricorne: The three cornered hat of the Eighteenth Century.

Trunnels: Long wooden pins used to fasten ship's planks to its timbers. Also used for rungs of ladders.

Tun: The old measure of liquid used for whale oil. A tun cask holds 252 old wine gallons and the approximate weight is one ton.

Tungane: A male cousin.

Two side: Whaleboats used five propelling oars, three on the starboard side and two the larboard or port. Rowers sat on the opposite end of their thwart from their tholepins. Orders were given thus: 'pull three, stern two' (or the reverse) to turn the boat quickly.

Uru: Hair.

Utu: Payment. Avenging wrongs committed by another person or group. Squaring accounts with opponents.

Van Diemen's: Van Diemen's Land, the original name of Tasmania.

'Vast: Short for avast. Stop the action being done, viz: stop rowing, pulling, talking, etc.

Vendue: An auction.

Wai: Water.

Waif: To mark a dead whale with a flag and anchor it or let it drift when it cannot be towed to the ship or the try works ashore.

Waipiro: Any form of spirituous liquors, literally stinking water in Maori.

Waka: A canoe.

Wales: Planks on the side of a vessel running for and aft.

Warp: To warp a ship is to move it with a windlass or capstan and a line attached to an anchor, dock, or some other secure point.

Wahine: A Polynesian woman.

Watch glass: The sand glass used aboard ship for timing.

Whare: A building.

Whiff: A small flag on a staff to mark a waifed whale.

White ducks: Sailors' trousers made of cotton duck.

Wigs: Mature male fur seals.

Spelling

Translating Maori names and words poses a great problem. The Maori language does not use all the sounds employed in English; but the early explorers, sealers, and whalers had no problem with that for they simply spoke and recorded what words they heard in any fashion they liked. There was no lexicon they could refer too. Even on early maps spellings varied widely from one publication to the next. The names of the North Island, *Eeka-na-Mowee*, and the South or The Middle Island, *Tovy Poenamoo*, are some versions of their names seen on old maps. The remainder of the Maori words are those that have been settled by general usage. One or two words were taken from *"The World of John Boultbee,"* a study of John Boultbee's *"Journal of a Rambler"* by A. Charles Begg and Neil C. Begg. Chirstchurch: Whitcoulls Publishers, 1979.

Acknowledgements

Being a dinosaur excuses one for doubting the great wonders and usefulness of high tech. Fortunately, my daughters Susan Hamrick, Judie Swartz, and granddaughter Kirsten Clapp convinced me that my computer was not inhabited by a jinni with fell intent and showed me, after numerous examples, where to click and double click. In addition they and Maggie Van Ess pointed out errors and many items that might be improved.

Full editing was done by Joyce Krieg.